PRAISE FOR

ANIMAL MAGNETISM

"I'm a big animal lover, and this series is centered on animals. Animals and hot heroes. How can you not love a romance like that?"
—Jaci Burton, *New York Times* bestselling author

"A captivating story that will have you laughing out loud, rooting for a happy ending . . . and hoping that this won't be your last visit to Sunshine."
—*Romance Reviews Today*

"Jill Shalvis's signature light tone and terrific sense of humor are alive and well."
—*All About Romance*

"That rare find—an excellent, straight-up contemporary romance. From the small-town setting to the fun (and intriguing) supporting cast, to a fabulous hero and heroine—everything works. This book is an entertaining and romantic story you won't want to put down!"
—*The Good, The Bad and The Unread*

"Anyone remember those funny fluttering butterfly feelings you get when you're in love for the first time? That is what I felt while I was reading *Animal Magnetism* . . . If you love a true romance with amazing characters that leave you wanting more, go out and grab a copy of *Animal Magnetism*. It is so worth it!"
—*Joyfully Reviewed*

"*Animal Magnetism* ramps up the pet-friendly book trend . . . {A} steamy, romantic, barn burner."
—*Library Journal*

"There's plenty of sizzle . . . An entertaining read and a good choice for readers who like cooing over cute animals as well as a cute romance."
—*Publishers Weekly*

ANIMAL ATTRACTION

"Definitely a good way to spend a few hours with some sexy characters."

—*USA Today*

"A delightful read full of cuddly animals, hot men, and confident women . . . This book is definitely a must-read for fans of contemporary romance."

—*Fresh Fiction*

"Funny and hot as hell . . . Moving, empowering, and engaging."

—*All About Romance*

"Fast-paced, filled with great dialogue, a strong story line, and most of all some really sexy scenes . . . I can't wait for the next book in this series."

—*Fiction Vixen Book Reviews*

"Beautifully written . . . Jill Shalvis has become one of my 'go-to' authors for contemporary romance. Her stories are fun, sexy, moving, and always put a smile on my face."

—*The Romance Dish*

MORE PRAISE FOR JILL SHALVIS

"Fall in love with Jill Shalvis! She's my go-to read for humor and heart."

—Susan Mallery, *New York Times* bestselling author

"Shalvis writes with humor, heart, and sizzling heat!"

—Carly Phillips, *New York Times* bestselling author

"A fun, sexy story of the redemptive powers of love . . . Red-hot!"

—JoAnn Ross, *New York Times* bestselling author

"Clever, steamy, fun. Jill Shalvis will make you laugh and fall in love."

—Rachel Gibson, *New York Times* bestselling author

"Jill Shalvis has a knack for creating characters that are lovable, witty, and [that] make you wish they were real so you could befriend them."

—*Night Owl Reviews*

"Exactly what a romance story should be." —*Dear Author*

"Light, funny, sexy, and just plain enjoyable to read."

—*All About Romance*

"Any book by Jill Shalvis is guaranteed to be a hit!"

—*The Romance Studio*

"Sexy fun with heartfelt excitement. A very pleasurable read!"

—*Fresh Fiction*

"Jill Shalvis excels at writing charming characters that leap right off the pages and into your heart." —*Book Binge*

"A Jill Shalvis hero is the stuff naughty dreams are made of."

—Vicki Lewis Thompson, *New York Times* bestselling author

"Witty, fun, and sexy—the perfect romance!"

—Lori Foster, *New York Times* bestselling author

"Riveting suspense laced with humor and heart is her hallmark, and Jill Shalvis always delivers."

—Donna Kauffman, *USA Today* bestselling author

Berkley titles by Jill Shalvis

THE TROUBLE WITH PARADISE
DOUBLE PLAY
SLOW HEAT

The Animal Magnetism Novels

ANIMAL MAGNETISM
ANIMAL ATTRACTION
RESCUE MY HEART
RUMOR HAS IT
THEN CAME YOU
STILL THE ONE
ALL I WANT

Omnibus

STRAY HEARTS

Stray HEARTS

Jill Shalvis

BERKLEY
NEW YORK

BERKLEY
An imprint of Penguin Random House LLC
penguinrandomhouse.com

Second Berkley trade paperback omnibus ISBN: 9780593437186

The Library of Congress has catalogued the first Berkley trade edition of this book as follows:

Shalvis, Jill.
[Novels. Selections]
Stray hearts / Jill Shalvis.—Trade paperback omnibus edition.
pages cm
ISBN 978-0-425-27403-3
1. Man-woman relationships—Fiction. I. Shalvis, Jill.
Animal magetism. II. Shalvis, Jill.
Animal attraction. III. Title.
PS3619.H3534S635 2014
813'.6—dc23
2013042335

Animal Magnetism first Berkley Sensation mass-market edition / February 2011
Animal Attraction first Berkley Sensation mass-market edition / October 2011
Target trade paperback omnibus edition / January 2014
First Berkley trade paperback omnibus edition / April 2014
Second Berkley trade paperback omnibus edition / July 2021

Printed in the United States of America
1st Printing

Stray HEARTS

Contents

Animal
MAGNETISM

To Frat Boy, Ashes, and Sadie
for the animal inspiration and unconditional love.

One

Brady Miller's ideal Saturday was pretty simple—sleep in, be woken by a hot, naked woman for sex, followed by a breakfast that he didn't have to cook.

On this particularly early June Saturday, he consoled himself with one out of the three, stopping at 7-Eleven for coffee, two egg and sausage breakfast wraps, and a Snickers bar.

Breakfast of champions.

Heading to the counter to check out, he nodded to the convenience store clerk.

She had her Bluetooth in her ear, presumably connected to the cell phone glowing in her pocket as she rang him up. "He can't help it, Kim," she was saying. "He's a *guy*." At this, she sent Brady a half-apologetic, half-commiserating smile. She was twentysomething, wearing spray-painted-on skinny jeans, a white wife-beater tank top revealing black lacy bra straps, and so much mascara that Brady had no idea how she kept her eyes open.

"You know what they say," she went on as she scanned his items. "A guy thinks about sex once every eight seconds. No, it's true, I read it in *Cosmo*. Uh-huh, hang on." She glanced at Brady, pursing her glossy lips. "Hey, cutie, you're a guy."

"Last I checked."

She popped her gum and grinned at him. "Would you say you think about sex every eight seconds?"

"Nah." Every ten, tops. He fished through his pocket for cash.

"My customer says no," she said into her phone, sounding disappointed. "But *Cosmo* said a man might deny it out of self-preservation. And in any case, how can you trust a guy who has sex on the brain 24/7?"

Brady nodded to the truth of that statement and accepted his change. Gathering his breakfast, he stepped outside where he was hit by the morning fresh air of the rugged, majestic Idaho Bitterroot mountain range. Quite a change from the stifling airlessness of the Middle East or the bitter desolation and frigid temps of Afghanistan. But being back on friendly soil was new enough that his eyes still automatically swept his immediate surroundings.

Always a soldier, his last girlfriend had complained.

And that was probably true. It was who he was, the discipline and carefulness deeply engrained, and he didn't see that changing anytime soon. Noting nothing that required his immediate attention, he went back to mainlining his caffeine. Sighing in sheer pleasure, he took a big bite of the first breakfast wrap, then hissed out a sharp breath because damn. *Hot.* This didn't slow him down much. He was so hungry his legs felt hollow. In spite of the threat of scalding his tongue to the roof of his mouth, he sucked down nearly the entire thing before he began to relax.

Traffic was nonexistent, but Sunshine, Idaho, wasn't exactly hopping. It had been a damn long time since he'd been here, *years* in fact. And longer still since he'd wanted to be here. He took another drag of fresh air. Hard to believe, but he'd actually missed the good old US of A. He'd missed the sports. He'd missed the women. He'd missed the price of gas. He'd missed free will.

But mostly he'd missed the food. He tossed the wrapper from the first breakfast wrap into a trash bin and started in on his second, feeling almost . . . content. Yeah, damn it was good to be back, even if he was only here temporarily, as a favor. Hell, anything without third-world starvation, terrorists, or snipers and bombs would be a five-star vacation.

"Look out, incoming!"

At the warning, Brady deftly stepped out of the path of the bike barreling down at him.

"Sorry!" the kid yelled back.

Up until yesterday, a shout like that would have meant dropping to the ground, covering his head, and hoping for the best. Since there were no enemy insurgents, Brady merely raised the hand still gripping his coffee in a friendly salute. "No problem."

But the kid was already long gone, and Brady shook his head. The quiet was amazing, and he took in the oak tree–lined sidewalks, the clean and neat little shops, galleries, and cafés—all designed to bring in some tourist money to subsidize the mining and ranching community. For someone who'd spent so much time in places where grime and suffering trumped hope and joy, it felt a little bit like landing in the Twilight Zone.

"Easy now, Duchess."

At the soft, feminine voice, Brady turned and looked into the eyes of a woman walking a . . . hell, he had no idea. The thing pranced around like it had a stick up its ass.

Okay, a dog. He was pretty sure.

The woman smiled at Brady. "Hello, how are you?"

"Fine, thanks," he responded automatically, but she hadn't slowed her pace.

Just being polite, he thought, and tried to remember the concept. Culture shock, he decided. He was suffering from a hell of a culture shock. Probably he should have given himself some time to adjust before doing this, before coming here of all places, but it was too late now.

Besides, he'd put it off long enough. He'd been asked to come, multiple times over the years. He'd employed every tactic at his disposal: avoiding, evading, ignoring, but nothing worked with the two people on the planet more stubborn than him.

His brothers.

Not blood brothers, but that didn't appear to matter to Dell or Adam. The three of them had been in the same foster home for two years about a million years ago. Twenty-four months. A blink of an eye really. But to Dell and Adam, it had been enough to bond the three of them for life.

Brady stuffed in another bite of his second breakfast wrap, added coffee, and squinted in the bright June sunshine. Jerking his chin down, the sunglasses on top of his head obligingly slipped to his nose.

Better.

He headed to his truck parked at the corner but stopped short just in time to watch a woman in an old Jeep rear-end it.

"Crap. Crap." Lilah Young stared at the truck she'd just rear-ended and gave herself exactly two seconds to have a pity party. This is what her life had come to. She had to work in increments of seconds.

A wet, warm tongue laved her hand and she looked over at the three wriggling little bodies in the box on the passenger's seat of her Jeep.

Two puppies and a potbellied pig.

As the co-owner of the sole kennel in town, she was babysitting Mrs. Swanson's "babies" again today, which included pickup and drop-off services. This was in part because Mrs. Swanson was married to the doctor who'd delivered Lilah twenty-eight years ago, but also because Mrs. Swanson was the mother of Lilah's favorite ex-boyfriend.

Not that Lilah had a lot of exes. Only two.

Okay, three. But one of them didn't count, the one who after four years she *still* hoped all of his good parts shriveled up and fell off. And he'd had good parts, too, damn him. She'd read somewhere that every woman got a freebie stupid mistake when it came to men. She liked that. She only wished it applied to everything in life.

Because driving with Mrs. Swanson's babies and—

"Quack-quack!" said the mallard duck loose in the backseat.

—A mallard duck loose in the backseat had been a doozy of a mistake.

Resisting the urge to thunk her head against the steering wheel, Lilah hopped out of the Jeep to check the damage she'd caused to the truck, eyes squinted because everyone knew that helped.

The truck's bumper sported a sizable dent and crack, but thanks to the tow hitch, there was no real obvious frame damage. The realization brought a rush of relief so great her knees wobbled.

That is until she caught sight of the front of her Jeep. It was so ancient that it was hard to tell if it had ever really been red once upon a time or if it was just one big friggin' rust bucket, but that no longer seemed important given that her front end was mashed up.

"Quack-quack." In the backseat, Abigail was flapping her wings, getting enough lift to stick her head out the window.

Lilah put her hand on the duck's face and gently pressed her back inside. "Stay."

"Quack—"

"Stay." Wanting to make sure the Jeep would start before she began the task of either looking for the truck's owner or leaving a note, Lilah hopped behind the wheel. She never should have turned off the engine because her starter had been trying to die for several weeks now. She'd

be lucky to get it running again. Beside her, the puppies and piglet were wriggling like crazy, whimpering and panting as they scrambled to stand on each other, trying to escape their box. She took a minute to pat them all, soothing them, and then with her sole thought being *Please start*, she turned the ignition key.

And got only an ominous click.

"Come on, baby," she coaxed, trying again. "There's no New Transportation budget, so *please* come on . . ."

Nothing.

"Pretty sure you killed it."

With a gasp, she turned her head. A man stood there. Tall, broad-shouldered, with dark brown hair that was cut short and slightly spiky, like maybe he hadn't bothered to do much with it after his last shower except run his fingers through it. His clothes were simple: cargoes and a plain shirt, both emphasizing a leanly muscled body so completely devoid of body fat that it would have made any woman sigh—if she hadn't just rear-ended a truck.

Probably *his truck*.

Having clearly just come out of the convenience store, he held a large coffee and what smelled deliriously, deliciously like an egg and sausage and cheese breakfast wrap.

Be still, her hungry heart . . .

"Quack-quack."

"Hush, Abigail," Lilah murmured, flicking the duck a glance in the rearview mirror before turning back to the man.

His eyes were hidden behind reflective sunglasses, but she had no doubt they were on her. She could feel them, sharp and assessing. Everything about his carriage said military or cop. She wasn't sure if that was good or bad. He was a stranger to her, and there weren't that many of them in Sunshine. Or anywhere in Idaho for that matter. "Your truck?" she asked, fingers crossed that he'd say no.

"Yep." He popped the last of the breakfast wrap in his mouth and calmly tossed the wrapper into the trash can a good ten feet away. Chewing thoughtfully, he swallowed and then sucked down some coffee.

Just the scent of it had her sighing in jealousy. Probably, she shouldn't have skipped breakfast. And just as probably, she'd give a body part up for that coffee. Hell, she'd give up *two* for the candy bar sticking out of his shirt pocket. Just thinking about it had her stomach rumbling loud as thunder. She looked upward to see if she could blame the sound on an impending storm, but for the first time in two weeks there wasn't a cloud in the sky. "I'm sorry," she said. "About this."

He pushed the sunglasses to the top of his head, further disheveling his hair—not that he appeared to care.

"Luckily the damage seems to be mostly to my Jeep," she went on.

Sharp blue eyes held hers. "Karma?"

"Actually, I don't believe in karma." Nope, she believed in making one's own fate—which she'd done by once again studying too late into the night, not getting enough sleep, and . . . crashing into his truck.

"Hmm." He sipped some more coffee, and she told herself that leaping out of the Jeep to snatch it from his hands would be bad form.

"How about felony hit-and-run?" he asked conversationally. "You believe in that?"

"I wasn't running off."

"Because you can't," he ever so helpfully pointed out. "The Jeep's dead."

"Yes, but . . ." She broke off, realizing how it must look to him. He'd found her behind her own wheel, cursing her vehicle for not starting. He couldn't know that she'd never just leave the scene of an accident. Most likely he'd taken one look at the panic surely all over her face and assumed the worst about her.

The panic doubled. And also, her pity party was back, and for a beat, she let the despair rise from her gut and block her throat, where it threatened to choke her. With a bone-deep weary sigh, she dropped her head to the steering wheel.

"Hey. *Hey.*" Suddenly he was at her side. "Did you hit your head?"

"No, I—"

But before she could finish that sentence, he opened the Jeep door and crouched at her side, looking her over.

"I'm fine. Really," she promised when he cupped and lifted her face to his, staring into her eyes, making her squirm like the babies in the box next to her.

"How many fingers am I holding up?" A quiet demand. His hand was big, the two fingers he held up long. His eyes were calmly intense, his mouth grim. He hadn't shaved that morning she noted inanely, maybe not the day before either, but the scruff only made him seem all the more . . . male.

"Two," she whispered.

Nodding, he dropped his gaze to run over her body. She had dressed for work this morning, which included cleaning out the kennels, so she wore a denim jacket over a T-shirt, baggy Carhartts, boots, and a knit cap to cover her hair.

To say she wasn't looking ready for her close-up was the understatement of the year. "Do you think you can close the door before—"

Too late.

Sensing a means of escape, Abigail started flapping her wings, attempting to fly out past Lilah's face.

She nearly made it, too, but the man, still hunkered at Lilah's side, caught the duck.

By the neck.

"Gak," said a strangled Abigail.

"Don't hurt her!" Lilah cried.

With what might have been a very small smile playing at the corners of his mouth, the man leaned past Lilah and settled the duck on the passenger floorboard.

"Stay," he said in a low-pitched, authoritative voice that brooked no argument.

Lilah opened her mouth to tell him that ducks didn't follow directions, but Abigail totally did. She not only stayed, she shut up. Probably afraid she'd be roasted duck if she didn't. Staring at the brown-headed, orange-footed duck in shock, she said, "I really am sorry about your truck. I'll give you my number so I can pay for damages."

"You could just give me your insurance info."

Her insurance. *Damn.* The rates would go up this time, for sure. Hell, they'd gone up last quarter when she'd had that little run-in with her own mailbox.

But that one hadn't been her fault. The snake she'd been transporting had gotten loose and startled her, and she'd accidentally aligned her front bumper with the mailbox.

But today, this one—definitely her fault.

"Let me guess," he said dryly when she sat there nibbling on her lip. "You don't have insurance."

"No, I do." To prove it, she reached for her wallet, which she kept between the two front seats. Except, of course, it wasn't there. "Hang on, I know I have it . . ." Twisting, she searched the floor, beneath the box of puppies and piglet, in the backseat . . .

And then she remembered.

In her hurry to pick up Mrs. Swanson's animals on time, she'd left it in her office at the kennels. "Okay, this looks bad but I left my wallet at home."

His expression was dialed into Resignation.

"I swear," she said. "I really do have insurance. I just got the new certificate and I put it in my wallet to stick in my glove box, but I hadn't gotten to that yet. I'll give you my number and you can call me for the information."

He gazed at her steadily. "You have a name?"

"Lilah." She scrounged around for a piece of paper. Nothing, of course. But she did find five bucks and the earring she'd thought that Abigail had eaten, and a pen.

Still crouched at her side, the man held out his cell phone. Impossibly aware of how big he was, how very good looking, not to mention how he surrounded her still crouched at her side balanced easily on the balls of his feet, she entered her number into his phone. When it came to keying in her name, she nearly titled herself Dumbass of the Day.

"You fake-numbering me, Lilah?" he asked softly, still close, so very close.

"No." This came out as a squeak so she cleared her throat. And, when he just looked at her, she added truthfully, "I only fake-number the jerk tourists inside Crystal's, the ones who won't take no for an answer."

"Crystal's?"

"The bar down the street. Listen, you might want to wait awhile before you call me. It's going to take me at least an hour to get home." *Carrying the mewling, wriggling babies* and *walking a duck.*

He paused, utterly motionless in a way that she admired, since she'd never managed to sit still for longer than two minutes. Okay, thirty seconds, but who was counting. "What?" she asked.

"I'm just trying to figure out if you're for real or if you're a master bullshit specialist."

That surprised a laugh out of her. "Well, I *can* be a master bullshit specialist," she admitted. "But I'm not bullshitting you right now."

He studied her face for another long moment, then nodded. "Fine, I'll wait to call you. You going to ask my name?"

Her gaze ran over his very masculine features, then dropped traitorously to linger over his very fine body for a single beat. "I was really sort of hoping that I wasn't going to need it."

He laughed, the sound washing over her and making something low in her belly quiver again.

"Okay, yes," she said. "I want to know your name."

"Brady Miller."

A flicker of something went through her, like the name should mean something to her, but discombobulated as she was, she couldn't concentrate. "Well, Brady Miller, thanks for being patient with me." She reached for Abigail's leash, attaching it to the collar around the duck's neck.

"Quack."

"Shh." Then she grabbed the box of babies. It was damn heavy, but she had her dignity to consider so she soldiered on, turning to get out of the Jeep, bumping right into Brady's broad chest. "Excuse me."

He straightened to his full height and backed up enough to let her out, helping her support the box with an ease that had her envying his muscles now instead of drooling over them.

Actually, that was a lie. She managed both the envying and the drooling. She was an excellent multitasker.

"You're really going to walk?" he asked, rubbing his chin as he considered the box.

"Well, when I skip or run, Abigail's leash gets tangled in my legs."

"Smart-ass." Brady peered at the two puppies and potbellied piglet. To his credit, he didn't so much as blink. "They potty trained?"

"No."

He grimaced. "How about the duck?"

"She'd say yes, but she'd be lying."

He exhaled. "That's what I was afraid of." He took the box from her, the underside of his arms brushing the outside of hers.

He was warm. And smelled delicious. Like sexy man and something even better—breakfast wraps and coffee.

"What are you doing?"

"Giving you a ride." He narrowed his eyes at the duck on the leash. "You," he said, "behave."

"Quack."

Without another word, Brady strode to his truck and put the box inside.

Lilah looked down at Abigail. "You heard him," she whispered, having no choice but to follow. "Behave."

Two

Brady wasn't an impulsive guy. Years on the streets as an untethered, unwanted kid had taught him a certain innate caution—which had saved his life on more than one occasion. A stint flying for the army and then Special Forces had only hammered it home.

But it hadn't been until he'd left the military and became a pilot for hire in places that weren't safe for so much as a cockroach that he'd really learned to appreciate his instincts.

And yet those instincts abandoned him in a blink as he offered his Danica Patrick wannabe a ride.

Luckily, she was smarter than him.

She was still standing by her Jeep, watching him carefully, clearly unwilling to just hop into his truck.

"I don't bite."

She laughed a little. Nervous, he realized. He made her nervous. She walked to his truck and peered cautiously inside. He wasn't sure what she was looking for; signs that he was a murderer or rapist maybe, and he looked into the truck as well. She straightened, gasped at how close he now was, and stumbled back a step.

Reaching out, he steadied her with a hand to her hip—which, he couldn't help but notice, was nice and curvy and warm beneath his palm. Her eyes were a clear, deep mossy green. She had a few freckles across her pert nose and the hint of a sunburn. Beneath her blue knit cap, her straight brown hair hit her shoulders, with long bangs shoved off to the side as if in afterthought. Her mouth was full but naked. No makeup for this pretty little felon. She wasn't model beautiful, but there was something undeniably arresting about her features, something that drew him right in . . .

Probably it was the blatant mistrust she had all over her face. "I'm not a kidnapper. Or a woman-napper."

"And yet you do have candy in your pocket."

"If I promise not to offer it to you, or say 'Hey, little girl' in a really creepy voice, will you get in?"

Her gaze was locked onto the Snickers sticking out of his pocket, and into the silence her stomach once again rumbled with shocking vehemence.

He actually felt a smile curve his mouth. "Or maybe I *should* offer it to you. Are you hungry?" He hadn't considered the fact that maybe she was homeless, but he took in her clothes and rust bucket Jeep and wondered. He held out the Snickers bar.

Looking away, a faint tinge colored her cheeks, she shook her head. "I couldn't possibly—"

"I have another," he lied.

Shielding her eyes from the bright sun, she gave him a long, serious once-over. Not playing fair, he tore open the candy bar and wafted the chocolate beneath her nose.

"You're evil," she said, and snatched it out of his hand. She broke it in half and then slid his part back into his pocket. Sinking her teeth into her portion with a big bite, she went still, then moaned in pleasure.

"Do you need a moment alone with that?" he asked, amused. And also a little turned on.

"Oh my God." Her voice was thick and throaty. *"Good."*

"So it's true," he murmured, watching her mouth avidly. It was a really great mouth, soft, with a plump lower lip. "Everyone has their price."

"Yes, and mine is chocolate. Offer me some and probably I'd follow you anywhere," she admitted.

"Probably?"

"Well, you're still a stranger."

"I told you my name."

"I'd need more than that."

He just looked at her, smiling. They both knew he'd had her at chocolate.

Laughing at herself, she took another bite of the Snickers, licking that lower lip of hers to get a stray strand of caramel. "Seriously, I was raised better than this. Make me feel okay about getting into a stranger's truck."

What could he possibly tell her that wouldn't scare her off or deepen the mistrust? And why did he even care? "I'm a pilot," he said.

"Okay." She nodded. "That's good. I've never heard of a pilot who murders people. Who do you fly for?"

"An international organization who hires me out to places like Doctors Without Borders, the government, whoever's paying. So see? You're safe enough from me. Get in."

She looked into the back again. "What's with the camera case?"

An *observant*, junk-food-loving felon. "I'm also a photographer." Sometimes even a paid one. His photos had been in both *Outsider* and *National Geographic* this last year. Given his adrenaline-fueled life, taking pictures grounded him in a way nothing else could.

Well, except sex. Sex was always his first choice, of course. Not that *that* would be happening while here in Sunshine.

Lilah was watching him closely again. Mistrustful little thing, which for some reason, made him like her all the more. "It's just a ride," he said quietly.

"Yeah. Um, so do you ever lure women into your truck with candy bars in order to get them to pose naked for you?"

"Nah. My editor frowns on the exploitation of women. It'd have to be a side job and only if you say please."

She rolled her eyes at him but took a step closer to the passenger door. "So does being a photographer ever get you laid?"

There was no good answer to that question, but yeah, sometimes it got him laid.

Clearly reading his face, she shook her head. "Don't tell me. You trade on your good looks and that whole sort of badass vibe you've got going on, right? And women fall for it hook, line, and sinker."

"Yes, but you're on to me, so no falling for you. Plus you've got protection." He jerked his chin toward the mallard at her feet. "A guard duck."

They both looked at Abigail, who was busy preening and fussing with her feathers to get them just right. "Is it legal to own a duck?" he asked.

"I'm duck-sitting. Are you sure you're not also a cop?" Lilah wanted to know.

"Why, do I look like one?" He felt the weight of her scrutiny. He knew what she saw when she looked at him. Dark hair cut short enough to be maintenance-free—when he remembered to have it cut at all. Tanned skin and a rangy, tough build from long months at a time in places where three squares a day were pure fantasy. The nondescript clothes he'd gotten used to wearing so as not to be marked as an American in places where being an American meant certain death or far worse.

"Actually," she finally said, "you look like trouble." Her gaze touched over his features. "The sort of trouble that women actively seek out against their better judgment. It's sort of a fatal genetic flaw of my entire gender."

She was right about the trouble part, but he'd never met a woman who liked it for long. "So now that we've established that I'm probably not a murderer, what's it going to be? A long walk home with . . ." He gestured to the box on the front passenger's-side floorboards. "Two puppies and whatever that thing is, or—"

"A potbellied pig."

He looked closer. "Are you sure?"

She laughed. "Yes!"

"Okay, I'll take your word for it. You getting in or what?"

She took another bite of his Snickers and studied him from those remarkable eyes. "The road out to my place needs some work," she finally said. "It got washed out in the floods last week and hasn't been repaired yet."

At least she had a place. "I can handle it."

"I don't know . . ." Her eyes sized him up as if she were six feet tall instead of *maybe* five foot four in her steel-toe work boots. "In my experience, guys are rarely the drivers that they think they are."

In the army, he'd driven in and out of hot spots that made Iraq and Afghanistan look like Disneyland. Hell, for his more recent work, piloting for hire, he'd driven on roads that didn't officially exist. He had no doubt he could take on anything the serene mining town of Sunshine dished up.

Having apparently made a decision, Lilah slapped a hand to his chest to push him out of her way. Because it amused him that she thought she could move him at all, he let her. As she shifted past him, the scent of her hair filled his nostrils with something like . . . honey, maybe? Whatever it was, it was better than anything he'd smelled in a long time.

She climbed up into his truck, her baggy Carhartts tightening across her back end as she stretched farther to check on her box of babies. *Yeah,* he thought, *there really is nothing on God's green earth nicer than a woman's ass*, and he took a minute to soak in the sweet view before walking around and angling behind the wheel. "Where to?"

"North straight through town."

Town was relatively quiet, and so was his passenger. The human one. Not the animal ones. The duck in the backseat hadn't shut up for more than two seconds since he'd turned on the engine.

"Quack, quack, quack . . ."

Brady finally cut his eyes to it via the rearview mirror. "Hey."

Abigail looked at him.

"I know this great duck soup recipe," he told her.

Lilah gasped.

Abigail shut up.

Not the animals in the box at her feet, though. The two puppies and little piglet were wrestling and rolling around each other, having a party for three.

At the end of town, the road went from smooth concrete to torn-up, pitted asphalt, and as Lilah had promised, it was a mess. He hit a pothole and got a little air.

"Uh-oh," Lilah said.

"What?" He couldn't look, because she'd been right—the road was bad. If he took his eyes off of it, they were going to go flying. "And Jesus, you weren't kidding about—" He broke off when Lilah clicked out of her seat belt and dropped to her knees on the floorboard.

"It's okay," she cooed softly, and crawled toward Brady, touching his calf.

He went very, very still as she leaned down even farther, reaching between his legs . . .

"I've got you." Her voice pure sex, and still in that erotic position, began to make kissy kissy noises that went straight to his . . .

"There," she murmured, lifting the potbellied piglet to cuddle against her chest.

Brady let out a very long breath and realized he was jealous of a fucking pig.

Lilah flashed an apologetic smile and climbed back into her seat, rebuckling her seat belt. "Runaway."

It took him a full sixty seconds to find his voice. "You seem to have your hands full."

"Little bit." She turned in her seat to face him. "And I really am sorry about all this. Not that it's an excuse, but I stayed up too late last night studying, and I wasn't paying close enough attention to what I was doing."

"What are you studying?"

"Animal science. I'm trying to finish up my degree online at night. I'd like to go on to vet school after that."

"Makes for a long day."

"Yeah. Keep going straight here."

On the outside of Sunshine now, the road was lined by forest, thick and unforgiving. Classic northern Idaho. After the glaciers of the last great Ice Age had melted away, they'd left meandering rivers and lakes of all sizes, most pristine, some more remote and intimate than any of the places in the far corners of the planet in which he'd been. Once upon a time, the vastness of those Bitterroot Mountains and the waters of the Coeur d'Alene had changed his life, given him a sense of self when he'd desperately needed it. He didn't need it now. He knew who he was.

A man not quite ready to face the past that was about to be shoved in his face.

"So what brings you to Sunshine?" she asked, smiling when he glanced at her. "Maybe I just want to know more about the guy I'm going to buy a new rear bumper for. Thanks for sharing."

"No problem." He watched as she licked the last of the chocolate off her lips. "Still hungry?" he asked, amused.

"Yeah." She licked her finger, scooping up a fleck of chocolate. He was certain she didn't mean for it to be sexual, but watching her tongue run over her lips, hearing the sweet sounds of suction as she worked those fingers, was giving him a zing nevertheless. It was hard to tell what the rest of her body was like in those baggy clothes, but apparently it didn't matter in the least.

He was attracted to her, and he handed her the other half of his candy bar.

She stared at it like it was a brick of gold. "I'm on a diet." But she took it. "A see-food diet, apparently. I see food and I eat it." She took another big bite. "I mean, I *try* to eat healthy, but I have a little thing for junk food. Uh–oh . . ."

"What now?"

"Abigail, no." She reached back and pulled the strap of Brady's duffel bag from the duck's beak. "She also likes to eat." She laughed easily, and he found himself smiling at the sound with rusty facial muscles. His shoulders loosened and he realized he was feeling relaxed.

And even more odd—at ease.

"Are you here on vacation?" Lilah asked, petting the creatures in the box at her feet.

"Not exactly."

She let that go, leaning back to watch the scenery, which was admittedly worthy of the fascination. Lush and green, the mountains loomed high thirty miles off in the distance, the exotic rock formation forming mouth-gaping canyons he'd once explored as an angry teen looking for a place to belong.

His passenger let the silence linger, which he suspected was unusual for her. When he felt her watching him instead of the landscape, he turned his head and briefly met her gaze. Yep, she was waiting patiently for him to crack the silence. A good tactic, but it wouldn't work on him.

"Huh," she finally said, slightly disgruntled.

He felt the corners of his mouth turn up. "Used to people caving?"

"*And* spilling their guts." She eyed him again, thoughtfully. "You're a tough one to crack, Brady Miller, pilot and photographer. Really tough."

Not anything he hadn't heard before. "I was thinking the same could be said of you," he said.

That got him a two-hundred-watt smile, along with a sweet, musical laugh. "True," she agreed.

The road ended, and he had two choices—the highway straight ahead, or left to head away from the towering peaks and out to ranching land, where as far as the eye could see was nothing but gently rolling hills and hidden lakes and rivers.

"Left," she said, pointing to a dirt road. "And then left again."

The road here was narrow, rutted, and far rougher. "Ah. You're bringing me to the boondocks to off me so you don't have to pay for the damages to my truck."

She laughed. She really did have a great laugh, and something went through him, a long-forgotten surge of emotion. "Not going to deny it?" he asked, sliding her a look meant to intimidate.

She wasn't. Intimidated. Not in the least. In fact, she was smiling. "Worried?" she asked, brow raised, face lit with humor.

Giving her another long look—which she simply steadily returned—he shook his head and kept driving. "I never worry."

"No? Maybe you could teach me the trick of *that* sometime."

Yeah, except he didn't plan on being around long enough to teach anyone anything.

His enigmatic passenger shifted in her seat and crossed her legs. The hem of her Carhartts rose up, giving him a good look at her scuffed work boots and the cute little black and pink polka-dotted socks peeking over the top of them. Which of course made him wonder what else she was hiding beneath those work clothes.

The growth thickened on either side of the road, which narrowed, commanding his attention. He caught glimpses of a sprawling ranch, and then a glistening body of water, flashes of brilliance in a color that changed the definition of blue. The road narrowed again, and at the hairpin turn, two of his four tires caught air.

"Not bad," she said in admiration. "So how does a pilot get such mad driving skills, anyway? Because you're not just a pilot and photographer."

"No?"

"No. You've got a quiet intensity about you, an edge. It's why I thought cop or military."

She was good. "Army."

"Ah," she murmured, saying nothing more, which both surprised him and left him grateful at the same time. People were naturally curious, and his life choices and experiences tended to bring that curiosity out, but he didn't like talking about himself.

"Here we are," Lilah said a minute later. "Home sweet home."

The road ended in a small clearing, at the top of which sat a tiny cabin next to what looked like a large barn. The sign on the barn read SUNSHINE KENNELS.

Peeking behind the property was a small lake, shining brightly, surrounded by a meadow radiant with flowers, and lined by the not-so-distant jagged ridges stabbing into the sky.

Actually, Brady knew this land fairly well, though it'd been a long time. Emotions tangled with the need to reach for the beauty wherever he could find it, and he soaked it all in, letting it bring him something that had been sorely lacking in his life.

Pleasure.

Lilah unhooked her seat belt. "It's special."

"Yeah."

"The Coeur d'Alene Indians found it," she said. "They lived here." She paused. "The myth goes that the water has healing powers."

He slid his gaze her way, wondering if she believed it.

"They based their lives around the legend." She paused and bit her lower lip, like she knew damn well he didn't buy it. "Don't laugh when I tell you the rest."

He wasn't feeling much like laughing. Not while watching her abuse that lush lower lip that he suddenly wanted to soothe. With his tongue. No, laughing was the last thing on his mind.

"Legend says that if you take a moonlight dip, you'll supposedly find your one true love."

"Of course." He nodded. "It's always midnight. So, do you swim often?"

"Never at midnight."

He couldn't help it, he laughed.

With a slow shake of her head and a smile curving her mouth, she reached out and touched a finger to his curved lips. "You're a cynic," she chided.

It'd been a long time since someone had touched him, unexpected or otherwise. A very long time, and he wrapped his finger around her wrist to hold her to him, letting his eyes drift closed.

"For how big and tough you are," she said very softly, "you have a kind mouth."

He opened his eyes and met her gaze. "You should know it's not kindness I'm feeling at the moment."

"No?" A brow arched, and the light in her eyes spoke of amusement, along with a flash of heat. "What *do* you feel?"

Dangerous territory there. Nothing new for him. He did some of his best work in dangerous territory. "Guess."

Still smiling, she leaned in so that their lips were nothing but a whisper apart. Even surrounded by a duck, two puppies, and a potbellied piglet, she still smelled amazing. He wanted to yank her in and smell her some more, but he held very still, absorbing her closeness, letting her take the lead.

When she spoke, every word had her lips ghosting against his, her breath all warm, chocolately goodness. "I'm more of a doer," she whispered, and kissed him.

She tasted as good as she smelled. Then almost before it'd even begun, she pulled back. "Thank you."

He had no idea what exactly she was thanking him for now but he was all for more of it. Their connection, light as it had been, had still carried enough spark to jump-start his engines. "For . . . ?"

"For driving me all the way out here." Again she was letting her lips brush his with every word. "And for not being a serial killer." She was staring at his mouth. "And for . . . everything."

Not wholly in charge of his faculties, he took over the lead, pulling her in until she was straining over the console before covering her mouth with his.

With a low murmur of acquiescence, she wrapped her arms around his neck, angling her head for the best fit, deepening the kiss.

Which worked for him.

He lost track of time, but when she pulled back, breathless and panting for air, she licked her bottom lip as if she needed that last little taste of him.

He knew the feeling. He was more than a little flummoxed by the loss of blood to his brain. She'd felt good. Good and soft and willing. He had one hand low at her back, the tips of his fingers tucked into the waistband of her pants, against warm, satiny skin while his other hand cupped her jaw.

"Gotta go," she whispered, and pulled free. Twice she tried to grab the door and missed. Leaning past her, he pushed it open for her.

"And we're still at least a hundred yards from the water," she muttered. "Imagine if we got *in* it."

He heard himself laugh. "It's not the water." He wasn't sure what it was, but he was positive it wasn't the water.

"Cynic," she repeated without heat, looking both flustered, and aroused.

An incredibly appealing combination that made him want to haul her onto his lap and show her *cynic.* "True enough," he agreed. "But it takes one to know one."

She snorted and it was the craziest thing, but hell if he didn't feel the tug of attraction for her all the way to his toes.

Yeah. Definitely dangerous territory.

"Wait here." She slipped out of the truck and vanished inside the kennels. Twenty seconds later she was back with her insurance card. "Keep it, I have another." She wrapped Abigail's leash around her wrist and grabbed the box. "Thanks for the ride, stranger." Then, with a flash of a smile, she sauntered off in those baggy Carhartts toward the kennels, looking for all the world like a princess going into her palace.

Three

Lilah Young forced herself to cross the yard and get all the way to the front door of the kennels before allowing herself to glance back at the truck.

He was still there: Brady Miller, pilot, photographer, kisser extraordinaire, slouched behind the wheel, hair still messed up from her fingers, watching her.

Letting out a low breath, she pressed a hand low to her abdomen. "Sweet baby Jesus," she whispered.

"Quack," Abigail said.

With a low laugh, Lilah opened the door and managed a smile at her business partner, Cruz Delgado. "I'm back. Again."

Cruz's perfectly toned hard body was still where it had been two minutes ago when she'd come running in—sprawled flat on his back in the center of their greeting room, with Lulu on top of him.

Lulu was a lamb that thought she was a puppy. She belonged to one of their clients who was out of town for a few days, and she sometimes needed a little extra TLC in the middle of her day. Okay, all of the time she needed a little extra TLC. Lulu was a 'ho for TLC. "How many times do I have to tell you," Lilah said to the lamb. "Cruz is mine."

From the floor, Cruz grinned, then pushed Lulu off of him and sat up. His silky dark hair fell into his face, but he shoved it back, flashing laughing melted-chocolate eyes Lilah's way. "She was feeling lonely. We were playing tag. She won." He rose to his feet, scooped Abigail up, and disappeared into the back. When he returned without the duck, he took the box from Lilah's arms next and smiled down at the three sleeping babies. "They were good for you?"

"Not even close, the little heathens. Don't get me started."

Cruz looked out the window at the truck turning around in the front yard. "So where's your Jeep?"

She didn't really want to talk about it, not when she could still hear Brady's truck's motor, just the sound making her nipples hard. "The Jeep's on Main. Don't ask. Today's crazy enough. We have a full house, and I have a message that there's a new rescue at Belle Haven."

She and Cruz had rotating shifts that allowed the kennel to be open for enough hours in the day to be effective. They traded off between two shifts—six A.M. to two P.M., and noon to eight P.M.—with part-time help from high school kids on the weekends and as needed.

Lilah typically took the early shift because Cruz didn't do early. But he had a gig tonight in Coeur d'Alene, where he moonlighted as a bass guitarist in a cover rock band, so he'd come in at six o'clock.

Along with the kennels, Lilah was the go-to person in town when there was an abandoned animal. There was no official humane society in the area, so if an animal needed temporary shelter, she was it. This came mostly from her inability to bear seeing anything suffer and the fact that she got far too attached to every animal she met. The rescue part of the business was extremely nonprofit and depended on grants and donations, so Lilah—along with Cruz—worked hard to keep the kennels afloat.

Their only source of income. A typical workday began at the crack of dawn with the day's client files spread out in front of her. She reviewed all the pets coming in or going out and decided where they would be kept. The facility had several sections: the outside pens, the inside pens, and the inside playroom, where the friendly, well-adjusted animals could hang out together under careful supervision. The not-so-friendly and grumpy older clients were separated out from the pack and dealt with individually. It was usually those animals that claimed Lilah's heart the fastest.

Part of the morning's record-keeping process always involved reviewing any other important events such as vet appointments, client visits, and employee notes. In today's case, there'd been an abandoned dog dumped off at Belle Haven, the veterinary center a half mile down the road.

Belle Haven was run by her two closest friends, Adam and Dell. They were holding the dog for her. She'd pick him up and care for him until she placed him in a foster home. But first she looked herself over. "I got up too late to grab a shower. I'm going to go take a quick one now before I head to Belle Haven."

"Need me to soap your back?"

She slid Cruz a long look. "Been there, done that, remember?"

"I remember it was good."

"Uh-huh." They'd dated for approximately two weeks several years back, until they'd realized they were far more suited for this, for a friendship. "Except for the part where we drove each other crazy," she reminded him.

"Yeah." He blew out a sigh. "Maybe you could work on not driving me crazy."

She laughed. Living in a small town had made it hard for her to find a guy she meshed with. There weren't all that many to choose from in the first place, and the few that there were, she'd known a long time. Forever.

She loved Cruz, but they were day and night when it came right down to it. And the biggie: she wasn't in love with him, and she never would be.

Ditto for him. He liked to be the center of a woman's universe, and she had too many things in her orbit to give herself wholly. Luckily, they'd both survived the attempt, and so had their business. "Let me guess—Marie dumped your sorry ass again?"

He shrugged. "Little bit, yeah."

Lulu bumped her head into Lilah's thighs until Lilah bent and stroked the lamb's ears. "What did you do this time?"

He sighed. "I forgot our anniversary."

"What anniversary? You've only been dating a few months."

"Not that kind of anniversary." When he waggled a brow, she rolled her eyes.

"TMI. And just make it up to her. I'm sure you can figure out how."

He was thinking about that when Lilah headed out. She lived in a small cabin next door, and when she slipped inside the small cozy place, she sighed. It was neat and clean and warm, and unlike just about everything else in her life, all hers.

But.

But even with the three years that had gone by, it was still too quiet without her grandma's cheerful voice.

"Mew."

Lilah looked down at the three-legged black cat winding her way around her ankles. There were rescues coming in and out of her life, waiting patiently for the right home, but Sadie was her favorite. Lilah knew that wasn't fair, but tell that to her heart. Twice she could have placed Sadie with a foster home, but she hadn't been able to do it.

Whenever there was even a hint of an animal being fragile, she had a hard time letting it go to an adoptive family. And though Sadie wasn't fragile, she was special.

Okay, so the truth was, they were all special to her. She couldn't help it, she just couldn't make herself abandon anything, ever. After all, she knew what that felt like.

"Mew," Sadie said, bumping her little head to Lilah's calf.

Lilah scooped her up and nuzzled her close.

Sadie was deceptively small, and it made her look like a kitten even though she was full grown. The mistake was in thinking that she had a kitten's temperament. She didn't. She was ornery as hell.

"Miss me today?"

Sadie blinked up at her sleepily, the rumble of a purr thick in her throat as she leaned in—and bit Lilah's chin.

"Gee, hungry?"

"Mew."

Rubbing her chin, Lilah moved to the window. Brady's truck might be gone, but the memory of his mouth on hers was not. "He was a bit more attitude-ridden than I usually go for, but trust me, it worked for him." She met Sadie's narrowed gaze. "Hey, don't judge me. It's been a long time for me."

And she'd been lonely.

The truth was, she needed . . . something.

Actually, someone. She needed someone. But Sunshine was small, and the problem wasn't helped by the fact that Adam and Dell tended to watch over her like they were her big brothers, making it clear that anyone with less-than-honorable intentions was risking life and limb.

Which had left her with slim pickings and a secret yearning for a guy with some not-so-honorable intentions.

Like Brady . . .

She knew why Adam and Dell did it. They'd been the ones to help her pick up the pieces when she'd come back to Sunshine during her second year of college to quietly and completely fall apart. The reasons had been complicated, but in short, her grandma had died and she'd let a guy devastate her. It had taken a while, but eventually she'd picked up the pieces and moved on. Gotten stronger. Adam and Dell knew this, but old habits were hard to break. "Is it so wrong to want a guy in my bed?" she asked Sadie.

Sadie just stared at her with those pale green eyes, and Lilah sighed. Much to her annoyance, she'd been fairly unsuccessful at getting any man she knew to cross Adam or Dell. *Fairly*, because certain guys were just good at being sneaky and getting around the watchdogs.

Cruz, for one.

But she didn't count Cruz because she didn't ache for him.

She wanted to ache, dammit.

Her thoughts drifted to Brady and she shivered. "He kissed me," she told Sadie.

Actually, she'd kissed him first, and then he'd taken over. And oh boy how he'd taken over, with that bone-melting aggression that had seriously rocked her world. It'd taken her right off her axis, in a good way, a way she'd been unconsciously needing quite badly.

And she'd hit his truck. "God," she moaned, and covered her face. "I am such an idiot."

"Mew."

"Okay, no opinions from the peanut gallery, thank you very much." She pulled out her cell phone and speed-dialed Dell. The three of them had gotten tight a few years back, when the guys had bought the property down the road from hers and built the animal center. They had no family to speak of and she'd just lost her grandma so they'd created a tight-knit family of their own.

Dell's phone went right to voice mail, so she tried Adam. Same thing. "I had an *I Love Lucy* moment," she admitted in her message. "A doozy. I'm going to shower, then head over to get the rescue dog and I'll tell you guys about it then. Oh, and I'm sort of going to need a little help with the Jeep."

The Belle Haven center was close enough to Coeur d'Alene and neighboring smaller towns like Sunshine to serve domesticated animals but it was also ideally located in ranching country to specialize in bigger animals, both wild and ranching-based as well. Dell ran the place with a growing staff and a reputation that had spread to the entire northern state area. Adam was in search and rescue. He trained and bred dogs for S&R teams across the country and was also extremely well known—much to his discomfort.

Lilah set her phone down and stripped on her way to the bathroom, passing her kitchen table in the process, which was still strewn with her laptop and books. She'd fallen asleep there sometime past midnight and had woken with a page from her biochem book stuck to her face.

She still hadn't finished studying and had a paper due and a midterm coming up in both physics and animal biology, but that would have to wait. She let the baggy, grungy work clothes fall where they might. They'd suited their purpose this morning cleaning out stalls, but they sure hadn't suited her purpose to meet an enigmatic stranger. She wondered what he'd thought of her, then told herself it didn't matter.

Besides, he'd kissed her—so how put off by her appearance could he have been?

She let the water pound over her body and then turned to her shelf, filled with her guilty pleasure—soaps and scrubs of all scents. Coconut, she decided. She felt like being a coconut today.

As the warm scent permeated the bathroom around her, she relaxed, standing there under the spray for long moments, dragging it out as long as she could, in no hurry to get on with the rest of her day.

"Ack!" she screeched when the water went suddenly icy, as it did every day thanks to her ancient water heater. Shivering, she stepped out of the shower and onto the mat of her teeny bathroom, banging her knee on the toilet, which was the last straw. "Shit!"

Sadie, sitting in the sink prissy as could be, smirked.

"*Shit* doesn't really count as a bad word," Lilah said in her own defense as she grabbed a towel. "It's practically a legitimate adjective."

Sadie lifted her back leg to wash her Lady Town.

"Yeah, yeah." Lilah bent for her clothes and shoved her hand into the front pocket to pull out a dollar. She walked it to the kitchen and dropped it into her swear jar on the counter. The jar had been Mrs. Morrison's idea, the owner of a parrot who'd stayed with Lilah for a week last month when Mrs. Morrison had gone on a Mexican cruise. When she'd come home, her parrot had a new vocabulary made up of "crap," "shit," and "Dammit, Cruz!"

The jar had at least fifty bucks in it.

When it reached two hundred, Lilah was going to splurge on a spa day. At this rate, she'd have it by next week.

She pulled on fresh jeans and a scoop-necked T-shirt, then dropped two pieces of bread into her toaster, one of them being the heel because she needed to go grocery shopping, a chore she put up there with cleaning out the crates at the kennels. When the toast popped up, the lights in the kitchen flickered and went out. She'd blown the fuse again. She swallowed the very bad four-letter word on the tip of her tongue because she was broke and grabbed a new fuse from the stack in the drawer.

The cabin needed work more than she needed her next breath of air, but for now, with business loans hanging over her head and school debt looming, Lilah was like a drowning victim going down for the last count. She replaced the fuses as they blew—which was all the time—because it was still cheaper than trying to redo the entire electrical in the place, something that needed to be done sooner than later. Just thinking about it had her chest tightening.

Save the stress, she told herself, *for when you have a spare pint of double-fudge ice cream to go with it.* Sighing, she looked at the toast. She had to skip the butter because it was healthier that way—and also because then she could justify the ice cream later. But she did add strawberry jelly, because hey, that was a fruit.

Stepping outside, she started walking to Belle Haven. The trail was drenched from the heavy rains of the night before, and the rough terrain gave beneath her boots like live sponges. She loved being outside after any rain, and she inhaled deeply the scent of wet nature. Her very favorite scent of all.

The lake was backed by rolling hill after rolling hill, and beyond those, the towering peaks of the Coeur d'Alene's, the colors so deep and mesmerizing the whole setting looked like a painting.

The trail ended at the center. The building itself was a two-story sprawling place, with several pens and a large barn alongside, with several more smaller buildings for equipment. Lilah walked through the parking lot and saw Adam's and Dell's trucks. Adam's was freshly washed and shiny as always, and Dell's was covered in a fine layer of dust and filled with work equipment, sporting gear, and whatever other stuff he'd put in there and forgotten. She might have smiled. After all, just being here filled her with a warm peace. Except that right next to their trucks sat a third.

This truck's back bumper was cracked and dented, as if someone in a Jeep—a very tired, overworked someone—had rear-ended it.

Oh God. Brady was parked in the lot next to her best friends as if he belonged in their world right alongside them.

And that's when it hit her. Where she'd heard his name before. An odd mixture of dread and anticipation mingled in her gut along with something else that she couldn't quite put her finger on, something that she didn't know what to do with. She walked through the front entrance and waved at Jade, the receptionist on the phone behind the big welcome desk. There was a wide-open space that greeted both two- and four-footed clients alike, and a comfortable seating area spread out strategically to encourage people to hang out in front of the huge wall of windows overlooking the land and the animals on it.

Three horses were out in one of the paddocks, a sheep in another, and on the outskirts stood a flock of geese who'd waddled over from the lake to watch the goings-on.

Inside, several people sat in the waiting room along with their dogs and cats and, in one case, a caged bunny.

Lilah walked through, heading to the offices, stopping to take a quick look out into the glorious day, the first without rain in two weeks. What she would give to be sitting on a blanket in front of the lake, the water lapping at her feet, a good book in her hand—and not her animal biology book. But it'd been a long time since she'd had enough wriggling room to just hang out and be.

"Never gets old, does it?"

She turned at the masculine voice that was as familiar to her as her own.

Dell slung a friendly arm over her shoulder. He was an outrageous but harmless flirt and could make ninety-year-old women preen and get infant girls to bat their eyelashes. One reason was his easy good looks. He was six foot two and still built like the football quarterback that he'd once been. He had the warm mocha skin that spoke of Native heritage and the sharp eyes to match. His black hair framed a striking face. He wore his sleeves rolled up, his shirt unbuttoned at the collar and untucked over a pair of well-worn jeans, and he would have looked like a college kid except for his eyes. His eyes said he'd seen too much for his barely three decades.

But his smile was pure devil. It never failed to crack her up that he broke hearts right and left and had no clue to his own power. He was the heart and soul of Sunshine, and the rock of all of them.

"I tried calling you," she murmured, turning into him for a hug.

"I was in surgery. I called you back—you didn't get my message?"

"No." She pulled out her cell, which now showed one missed call. "Must have been in the shower."

"It's okay." They were out of view from the people that were waiting on him, and he smiled into her eyes. "We have news."

"About . . . ?"

Dell turned her toward the hallway, where Adam was coming out of his office. Leaner than Dell, Adam was built more like one of those cage fighters, tough and edgy and hard—except for that face.

An angel's face. Her angel. Dark disheveled hair, strong features, and like Dell, a devastating smile when he chose to use it.

The man with Adam had the same badass smile—as she already knew all too well. She watched Brady walk toward them and had to acknowledge their odd attraction as something low in her belly quivered. She kept herself cool on the outside, but on the inside she was thinking that a half hour ago he'd kissed her till she purred.

"Remember when Adam and I lived in that foster home on Outback Road?" Dell asked her quietly.

"Yes. With the man who eventually left you the money to buy this land."

"Sol Anders," Dell said. "He took on Adam and me, but he had another kid first."

Lilah hadn't known them then, but Dell had told her about the other boy. He'd been a few years older than Adam and he'd graduated early and gone off to the military.

Brady. Of course. She'd heard his name before, but she'd just not connected it to her gorgeous stranger. And it wasn't as if Brady had visited—he hadn't, not once in the past few years since she'd been close friends with Dell and Adam. "The missing foster brother."

"Not missing," Dell said. "He was Special Forces, then working out of the country. We've been trying to get him to come see our operation for a long time. Now he's finally here."

Brady hadn't yet spoken; he was just now getting close enough to them to do so, but she felt the weight of his assessing gaze. And in fact, all three men were looking at her. There was so much freaking testosterone in the room that she could scarcely breathe. Brady had the same tough, sharp always-aware-of-his-surroundings demeanor as Adam and Dell, and the three of them together—good Lord.

Three magnificent peas in a pod.

She'd never really understood what had kept Brady away all this time. Neither Dell nor Adam had ever said. Guys, she'd long ago discovered, weren't exactly forthcoming with emotions and details.

As she stood there absorbing that shock, Adam shifted close to greet her with his usual—a tug on her hair. "Hey, Trouble."

"Hey." She couldn't object to the nickname. She'd earned it. Hell, she'd earned it this morning alone.

Adam ran his hand down her arm to her hand, which he squeezed, then gestured to the man whose truck she'd hit, the man who was so yummy he'd reminded her hormones that they could still indeed do a heck of a tap dance. "Lilah," Adam said. "This is—"

"Brady Miller," she murmured.

Brady's mouth curved in a slight ironic smile, his eyes lit with the same. He bowed his head slightly in her direction. "Lilah."

Dell divided a surprised look between them. "You two know each other?"

Brady lifted a brow in Lilah's direction, clearly giving her the floor.

Great. She hated having the floor. "Well, it's a funny story, actually." She managed a weak smile. "We, um"—she lifted a shoulder—"had a little run-in this morning."

Brady was hands in pockets, rolled back on his heels. He was obviously enjoying himself, the bastard, and damn if something deep within her didn't react to all that annoying charisma and male confidence.

"You had a little run-in," Dell repeated, and shook his head. "What does that mean exactly?"

"It means . . ." *Crap.* "Okay, so it's more like I ran into him."

"Explain," Adam said. No words were ever wasted when Adam spoke.

"Literally," she said. "I ran into him. As in, I hit his truck with my Jeep."

Brady's mouth twitched, though his eyes remained sharp.

But not as sharp as those on the two men that Lilah thought of as her brothers as they took in both Lilah and Brady, more specifically Brady and the way he was looking at her.

Which was a little bit how a tiger might eye his prey after a long, cold, hungry winter.

Oh good Lord. She definitely hadn't put on enough deodorant for this. And even more unsettling? Just this morning she'd have sworn she was completely happy and settled with her life. Sure she was overworked and stressed and about an inch from financial disaster at all times, and yeah, she'd been battling that vague sense of loneliness, but compared to lots of people she had things good.

So she couldn't explain this new restlessness.

But then her gaze locked with Brady and she had to revise. She could explain.

It was all his fault.

Four

Brady had been to every continent. He could speak three languages enough to get by and could understand a handful more. Over the years he'd amassed a whole host of skills—some he was proud of, some not so much. He'd seen a lot of shit. Hell, he'd done a lot of shit.

So he knew when to back off and let a situation take its course.

This was one of those times.

The reason he was here was complicated, and went back years, to old ties he hadn't even realized he still had. He'd been given up by his too-young, drug-dependent mother when he'd been five to a distant uncle not all that keen on kids. By the time he'd gotten to his teens, he'd been downgraded to group foster homes. He'd been a puny, scrawny runt, and an easy mark.

Until he'd landed at Sol Anders's.

Sol had been a badass cowboy and a large-animal vet. With him, Brady had been given two things he'd never had before—acceptance and an outlet for his anger. There'd been a gym in Sol's basement, specifically a punching bag, and Sol had encouraged Brady to make good use of it.

Later, two more "lost boys" had come along to be under Sol's care. They'd all lived together for two years before Brady graduated high school a year early and went into the army.

Adam and Dell.

By the time Sol died in a freak riding accident a few years later—on a wild mustang in Montana while gathering a herd for the government—Brady had been a pro at survival and winning his fights. He went on to serve multiple tours with the army, which is where he'd learned to fly anything with an engine, working in some college in between.

All with Sol's solid memory guiding him.

He'd been well aware that Sol had left some money, that he'd divided it among the three lost boys; himself, Adam, and Dell. But Brady had refused to take his share. He hadn't needed it. So he'd signed it over to Dell and Adam and had continued with his wanderlust lifestyle while they'd bought this land and built the animal center. Made a life for themselves.

They'd put Brady's name on the deed to the land, which he hadn't known. And now they were in the black this year and wanted Brady to be a part of it.

Brady didn't have the same wants. He didn't have a need for either a place to call home or the money Dell and Adam felt they owed him.

They'd known that and had come at him with a dangling carrot, something he'd found he couldn't quite resist—a helicopter that needed restoring and the chance to, for however briefly, fly in the good old safe USA.

It was nice what they'd done to honor their brief history together from a million years ago, one that had involved stolen candy, pilfered porn, and many late nights sneaking out on their bikes . . . But there was no doubt in Brady's mind that Lilah's history with them went far deeper.

So he let the drama unfold, fascinated in spite of himself.

"Is that why you walked over here instead of driving?" Adam asked Lilah, voice low so that the patients and their owners, just around the corner waiting to see Dell, couldn't hear. "Because you had an accident?"

Adam's voice was curt and gruff. And though not as obviously dark-skinned and dark-eyed as Dell, he was dark in persona and could be as intimidating as hell.

Except Lilah didn't seem intimidated.

At all.

"It's a half mile," she said. "Good exercise."

"Uh-huh. Except you hate exercise."

"Maybe my jeans are tight and I needed to burn the calories," she said. "And to be honest, it wasn't an accident so much as a little oops. It could have happened to anyone."

Brady choked out a cough, and she sent him a dark look before turning back to Adam. "And maybe we can review my stupidity later because I'm really busy today."

One corner of Adam's mouth turned up. "Really? We can discuss your stupidity later? Do you promise? Because normally you hate discussing your stupidity."

Lilah shoved him with the ease of two people extremely comfortable with each other, and extremely familiar.

Brady studied them both for hints of sexual tension, wondering if they were lovers as well as friends.

Lilah shoved Adam again. Adam didn't budge. Instead he caught her up, wrapped an arm around her neck and hauled her in close, rubbing his knuckles against her head until she swore at him and slugged him in the gut.

Nope, Brady decided. Definitely not lovers. This was definitely a brother-sister relationship.

"Pendejo," Lilah muttered, attempting to fix the hair Adam had ruffled.

Dumbass. She'd just called Adam, six feet of solid muscle, a dumbass.

"It's the only bad word she knows," Adam said, sidestepping another shove. "Probably time to learn something new, Trouble."

Lilah straightened her shoulders and gave a little toss of her head, like she couldn't be bothered with details. "Listen, while this is ever so much fun, I have two puppies, a piglet, two cats, a lamb, and a duck boarding today. I need to get back to it. Where's the rescue dog?"

"Pen three," Dell said. "Male, grown, neutered, mutt. Heads up—he was abandoned in a warehouse and, as far as we can tell, hit by a car."

Brady watched the undisguised emotions chase each other across Lilah's face. Horror, sorrow, determination. "Injuries?" she asked.

"Herniated diaphragm," Dell said. "And yes, I operated. Fixed him right up."

All the worry drained from her and she smiled sweetly at Dell, heart in her eyes. "How bad's the monetary damage?"

"Pro bono for you as always, sweetness. He's already feeling much better and is ready to go when you are. His meds are with him. Oh, and be careful, he's a little skittish and anxious, especially with men. You should probably warn Cruz."

Adam reruffled the hair she'd just fixed. "Meet me out front with him in five and I'll give you a ride back. We'll go look at your Jeep."

Sighing, she gave up on her hair and strode past both Dell and Adam. As she came up even with Brady, her eyes went a little guarded.

She'd showered and changed. Her long brown hair was wet and wavy past her shoulders, held off her face by the sunglasses she'd pushed to the top of her head. The work clothes were gone, and the body he'd only caught a hint of before was much more visible now in snug, hip-hugging jeans and a knit T-shirt that revealed a set of curves hot enough to sizzle.

Lilah Young cleaned up good.

Without a word, she walked by him as well, giving him a quick hint of the scent of her hair.

Coconut. She smelled like a piña colada, and it was making him thirsty.

And hungry.

Or maybe that was just her. Maybe she was making him hungry.

Hips swaying, she moved past the receptionist desk, exchanged a smile with the mid-twentysomething woman behind the counter, and then disappeared into the back without another glance. Which was okay, because Brady was probably doing enough looking for the both of them. But hell, she had a very fine ass. He met Adam's dark gaze—a fairly clear tell-me-you-are-not-looking-at-her-ass kind of gaze.

"She get hurt today?" Adam asked. His voice was low, casual even, but Brady wasn't fooled.

Adam wasn't happy.

It didn't take a genius to figure out who he was unhappy with, and it wasn't the Easter Bunny. "No," Brady said. "And I'm fine—thanks for asking. Look, it was just as she said, a fender bender. I wasn't even in the truck at the time. It was out front of 7-Eleven."

Dell shook his head at Adam. "She's pushing it too hard again."

Pushing it too hard? What did that mean?

"Adam," the woman at the receptionist desk called out. "There's a woman on line one who saw your picture in the *Coeur d'Alene Chronicle*."

"So?" Adam asked.

"So she says you're hot and wants to know if you're single. She says she's like one of your golden retrievers, cute and trainable."

Dell grinned.

Adam's left eye twitched.

"That's Jade at the desk," Dell told Brady. "She's in charge of things, and when I say in charge, I mean In Charge."

From behind her desk, the coolly beautiful Jade raised a brow, not amused.

Dell, looking amused enough for the both of them, went on. "You want to stay on her good side. She's the sharpest of all of us, but she never learned how to chill."

"Sitting right here, you know," Jade said.

Dell grinned outright. "So I should just come right out and say you're anal and uptight then?"

Jade turned her back on him, nose in the air. It went with the runway clothes and crazy-ass heels she had on.

Adam shook his head. "Man, you're going to pay for that. You know you are. She'll double-book you from now until hell freezes over, or switch the sugar and salt again, or something equally evil."

Dell wasn't looking too concerned as he turned to Brady. "So, what do you think of the place?"

"It's a pretty sweet setup," Brady said. "Between the animal care and the breeding and training, you're meeting a lot of needs here."

"And the helicopter," Dell said. "Adam showed you the helicopter."

"Yeah." Adam had also told him that up until six months ago, there'd been a pet groomer here as well. The company had leased one of the smaller buildings, but they'd gone belly-up, breaking the lease without paying out. Apparently a month ago Dell and Adam had finally received back payment in the form of a Bell Soloy 47 helicopter. It had been delivered from Smitty's, the small-craft airport directly across the meadow from the center, and was sitting in the yard like an eyesore.

Brady had taken a good long look at it, feeling a stir of interest he hadn't wanted to acknowledge. The Bell 47 was a legendary and pioneer flying adventure. The thing needed some serious work before it would be fly-worthy, but Adam and Dell had been looking for a way to further expand their business. They were fairly isolated out here in Sunshine, and Dell was sometimes spending entire days on the road to get to some of the patients that couldn't come to him, so they'd thought that maybe the helicopter could actually be of use.

If it ran.

And if they had a pilot.

Which was where Brady came in. The Bell 47 was the bait, of course. Dell had used it ruthlessly, knowing damn well Brady wouldn't be able to resist, that he'd want the challenge of fixing it up until it sang, that he'd want to fly it.

He'd been right. "It's a beauty," he admitted.

"Can you fix it?" Dell asked.

"Yes." He could fix pretty much anything, but the Bell he could do in his sleep.

"Can you fly it?"

"Yes." He could also fly anything and started to say so when a tingle of awareness raced down the back of his neck. He turned as Lilah came back through, holding a dark brown shaggy dog in her arms.

The dog was scrawny to the point of being painfully lean, with dull eyes and an expression that said he no longer cared what happened to him.

"How long do you think to get it running?" Dell asked, still talking about the helicopter.

Brady pretended to think about that while watching Lilah hug her rescue dog.

"Good boy," she was murmuring softly, rubbing her jaw to the top of his head.

The dog hesitated, then gave her a hesitant little lick on the chin.

"Aw, that's a really good boy," she said again, nuzzling him close.

And once again Brady found himself jealous of a four-legged creature.

"I was hoping you'd stay a month," Dell said.

"A month? Why?"

"I figured that would be enough time to decide if having a pilot and the helicopter on staff is worth the expense."

Lilah lifted her face from the dog and leveled those mossy green eyes on Brady.

A month . . . He had several assignments within the next couple of weeks.

"Come on," Dell said. "It'd be great to have you."

A fucking month. In one place. He glanced at Lilah and felt something within him ache. Don't do it . . . But the truth was he was due a break, and no one, least of all the company he flew for, would begrudge him taking one.

And he sure as hell could do worse than the Coeur d'Alene mountains in summer.

He made the mistake of looking at Lilah again. If he let the sexual tension shimmering between them choose, he knew exactly what his answer would be—but he never let his dick rule. He put what he needed ahead of what he wanted.

Always. "Look, thanks for the offer. But I'm going to get a room for the night. I have some calls to make before I can commit to anything."

"Take the upstairs loft," Dell said. "It's Adam's, but he's not staying there right now." He swiveled a look in his brother's direction and smirked. "Not since he was stalked by one of his crazy-ass exes."

Adam's expression didn't change, but he slid his eyes to Dell in a go-there-and-die look.

"Cameron," Dell said. "Pretty little thing, too. Only there was a . . . misunderstanding. She thought they were exclusive, except Adam here doesn't really know the meaning of the word. So Cameron broke in one night and tried to convince him she was his one and only. With handcuffs. Adam walked away from her after that. Actually, he ran away like a little girl, but he doesn't like to talk about it."

"She had a fucking taser," Adam said tightly. "You always leave that part out."

"No, we understand," Dell said, nodding. "She's terrifying. All five feet two inches of her. It's been six months," he said. "And he still twitches at the sight of a stacked blonde. It's probably plenty safe enough for you to stay there. Plus you can handle yourself."

"Hey, I could have handled myself just fine without the taser," Adam said. "And you're an asshole. Come on, Lilah, let's look at your Jeep."

With one last indecipherable look at Brady, Lilah and her dog left with Adam.

Five minutes later when Dell had finished fielding a phone call from a worried pet owner, he accompanied Brady outside to get his duffel bag from his truck before showing him the loft. It ran the entire length of the upper floor of the center. The slanted ceiling gave the wide open space a warm feel, certainly warmer than anywhere Brady had stayed in recent memory. Hell, any place that didn't have dirt floors would be a step up from where he'd stayed in recent memory.

"The heater doesn't work for shit up here," Dell said, nodding to the stack of wood beside a large fireplace. "Takes that in the winter to heat the place."

Which wouldn't be Brady's problem. By winter, he'd be in some third-world country dreaming about being cold enough to need a fireplace. He walked to the far wall, which was nearly all windows. He looked out into the meadow behind the center, rich and lush with growth.

"This was my favorite part of the place when I lived here," Dell said.

"Did you get chased out of here by a crazy ex, too?"

"No." Dell grinned. "I bought a house in town last year. Probably I shouldn't bait Adam like that but Christ, he's so easy."

"What happened to him? I don't remember him being so . . ."

"Surly? Rude? Pissy? He forgot to take his Midol." But Dell's smile faded and he lifted a shoulder. "He had a rescue go bad."

"Bad?"

"Shit intel, lost half his crew, and he blames himself. Which is stupid because it wasn't his fault, but you try telling him that. He likes guilt. Anyway, after he got out of the Guards, he started working with the rescue dogs, training and breeding. He's still not quite back on the people train."

"PTSD?"

"Oh yeah," Dell said. "But don't let him hear you say that."

"And you help by, what, poking at him?"

"It's my brotherly duty."

Brady opened one of the windowpanes, and seeing there was no screen, he gave in and pulled his camera from his bag, snapping a few shots right then and there. His usual subject of choice was faces, but this land drew him.

It always had.

Off to the side, Adam and Lilah came into view. Adam had an arm slung around Lilah's shoulders, and though he wasn't smiling, she was. And laughing, too, her smile open and easy and unguarded as she set the rescue dog down, probably for a pit stop.

Brady snapped a few shots of them before turning away for reasons he didn't understand, or care to.

Dell was watching him. "You and Adam are a lot alike these days."

"I'm not suffering from anything."

"Except an inability to connect."

Brady snorted. "Look at you, not letting your psych degree go to waste."

Dell smiled. "It was only my minor."

Brady turned back to the window.

"We're updating the center's website, which has really taken off. Appointments, self-help with animals, training—it's all going on there. Adam took pictures of our clients, both the owners and the animals. People love to see themselves on the site. Or they would, except Adam has this tendency to cut heads off. Think you could do better?"

Brady sighed. "Dell—"

"I just thought while you're here . . ."

Fuck. "Yeah. I can take pictures that include heads."

"I was hoping you'd say that."

There were framed pictures on the windowsill. Adam in full search-and-rescue gear surrounded by four beautiful golden retrievers, all wearing red rescue totes. Lilah and a guy he didn't recognize, both seated on a tailgate of a truck mugging for the camera. Dell on a horse. "You're happy here," Brady said.

"Very. Maybe you'll feel the same."

Brady shook his head. "Why does it matter so much to you?"

"Sol gave us this land. All of us. But Adam and I have gotten all the benefits."

"You guys built this place. It's yours."

"You know, once we meant something to each other."

Surprised by the vehemence in Dell's voice, Brady looked at him. "Yes."

At that, Del seemed to relax marginally. "We came from nothing—less than nothing—the three of us. And we forged a family. Your family, you stubborn ass, whether you like it or not."

Brady's eyes locked on the last picture. A lone man, head shaved, built like a tree trunk, staring into the camera with fierce intensity, and just looking at him made Brady's chest ache like hell. Sol. "I know," he said very quietly.

Beside him, Dell let out a breath. "I was beginning to wonder if I was going to have to kick your ass to remind you."

Brady let out a rare smile. Because it was true that Dell had kicked Brady's ass, exactly once. Of course Brady had been drunk as a skunk at the time and already down for the count. They'd been teenagers, and once Sol had gotten hold of them, they'd all been down for the count because

Sol had made them drink the rest of the stolen vodka, watching in stoic silence as each of them had puked up their guts. Probably not a condoned method of parenting, but it had worked.

Brady had never overindulged again.

"I could have taken you even without the vodka," Dell said, reading Brady's mind.

"Hey, whatever helps you sleep at night."

They both laughed softly, the tension gone. "When the Bell came into our possession," Dell said, "I knew we had you."

Brady blew out a breath. What the hell. No use denying that. He was here in the States with nowhere else pressing to be, and it was a sweet old chopper. "Yeah."

"You going to stick, then?"

Chances were he'd stick all right. He'd stick out like a sore thumb. But he was used to that. And what the hell. He watched as below Lilah carefully picked back up her precious bundle, loving him up as she did so.

He wouldn't mind being loved up by those arms, that was for damn sure. "For a month," he heard himself say. "Just a month."

Five

Lilah took Toby back to the kennels. Actually, she had no idea what the dog's name was since he hadn't come with a collar, but he was an adorable mass of tangled fluff and looked like a Toby to her. He was also in desperate need of a bath, but getting him cleaned up turned out to be tricky since he told her he was deathly afraid of water.

Loudly.

She sweet-talked him into calming down and carefully soaped him up, working around the stitches from his surgery, and ended up wearing more of the soap than he did. Keeping up a steady stream of soft cooing and baby talk seemed to soothe his concerns quite a bit.

"There," she murmured. "Doesn't that feel better, to be clean?" Giving him a final rinse, she wrapped him in a towel.

He watched her solemnly from the most adorable, soul-searching eyes she'd ever seen, then very carefully licked her face.

"My second kiss of the day," she said.

"And the first?" Cruz asked, coming into the back, leading Lulu the lamb to her pen.

"Not telling," Lilah said.

Lulu stretched her neck and tried to take a nip out of Cruz's tush, and Lilah burst out laughing.

"That's okay," Cruz told the lamb. "All the ladies want to bite my ass. You can't help yourself."

Lilah rolled her eyes. "You leaving for your gig?"

"Yes. Unless you want to take a bite out of my ass. No?" he asked, grinning when Lilah just gave him a shove to the door. "Okay, but you're missing out. I taste better than the jelly filling you have on your right boob."

Lilah looked down. Strawberry jelly, from her toast. "Balls!"

"Balls?"

She sighed. "I can't afford to say 'Goddammit.' I'm out of cash for the swear jar. And stop looking at my boob!"

He fished a five out of his pocket and slapped it into her hand for her swear jar. "Even though I don't like to hear a woman talk disparagingly about my second favorite body part," he said on a laugh as he left.

Alone, Lilah began the afternoon routine of cleaning out cages, changing blankets, changing water bowls, and starting laundry. She fed everyone and administered any medicines required. Then she cleaned and disinfected the entire kennel.

After that, she dealt with all the animal pickups and drop-offs for the day, which they had scheduled for certain hours only to make the running of the place go a little smoother. Then she took their overnight guests—all dogs today, plus Abigail—for one last walk before tucking everyone in for the night.

With that done, she faced her desk. She was behind in the paperwork and needed to type up their monthly newsletter and file, not to mention a little thing called study.

It used to stress her out how much endless work there always seemed to be, but it piled up in the best of times and she'd learned to let some of the little stuff go.

She gave Toby an extra treat, and while he wolfed it down, she went to her computer and pulled up the database of people in town who were willing to foster animals and had already been thoroughly checked out and approved. She ran through the list, calling potential candidates and hitting bingo on the third try. A woman named Shelly who worked at the rec center had lost her dog to a coyote earlier in the year. Lilah didn't know Shelly personally, just in passing, but she was relieved to find her so ecstatic about Toby. Shelly said she could get him first thing in the morning if Lilah wouldn't mind meeting her in town since the roads out to the kennels were still bad from the rains and Shelly only had a VW Beetle. They arranged to meet at the bakery, which worked for Lilah. Two birds with one stone and all that.

She'd have to eat a bag of carrots tonight to make up for the donuts she'd consume in the morning but it would be worth it.

With that accomplished, Lilah broke her own rules by taking Toby home with her, letting him sleep on a soft blanket next to her bed.

Sadie hopped up onto the mattress to look disdainfully down at the rumpled, tired dog.

"You were a stray, too," Lilah reminded her.

Sadie gave her a banal stare.

"Stop. It's just for the night. And you will not smack him around."

Sadie lifted her nose in the air, turned in a circle, and daintily sat with her back to Toby, as if to drive the point home that he wasn't even worth watching.

Sighing, Lilah pulled open her books to study, but she had trouble concentrating. Her mind was on the new strays. Toby, of course, but also the six foot, blue-eyed, badass stray who'd kissed like heaven on earth.

The next morning started at the usual crack of dawn. Sadie mewled a protest at the blare of the alarm. Not Toby. He was much perkier than he'd been the night before, even seeming to smile at Lilah as he padded with her into the small bathroom. He lay quietly on the rug while she showered—cherry blossom soap today—and yelped along with her as the hot water gave way to cold.

Lilah dressed and headed outside, the dog so close on her heels that he ran into her when she stopped short.

Early as it was, someone had been up earlier than her because her Jeep was in her yard waiting for her, a note taped to the windshield:

Hey Trouble—Note that the brake is not the skinny one on the right but the fat pedal on the left.

Adam humor. Lilah sighed and looked the Jeep over. The front end was still dented in pretty good, but it had been hammered out a bit, and best of all, the engine started.

She and Toby turned away from the Jeep and headed inside the kennels, where Lilah made her way through her morning routine: feeding, watering, walking, cleaning . . . From seven to nine was drop-off/pickup time. This was when clients could drop off their animals for the day or pick up from the night before. They had another two-hour stretch at the end of the day for the same thing. At nine thirty, she put a sign on the door saying she'd be back at ten and told all the animals she'd return. Time to bring Toby to Shelly.

Lilah bribed Toby into the Jeep with his antibiotics wrapped in a piece of cheese, which he took with a sweet lick, and then they took off. Ten minutes later they stood outside the town bakery. "We can't go in," she told Toby. "I didn't eat any carrots last night."

Toby looked sad. She couldn't blame him. But she'd promised herself to eat healthier and she meant it. "Of course, we could buy, say, a bran muffin. Or . . . carrot cake." Yeah, that was brilliant. Cake and veggies, all in one. "Let's do it," she said, and Toby's ears perked up. Clearly, he agreed wholeheartedly.

"Plus," Lilah said, "it's cold, right? It'll be much warmer inside. And Dee allows dogs—she even has a canister where she has doggie treats. You'll see."

Toby nodded. He was on board. So Lilah opened the door. They were immediately blasted by the heated oven air and the scent of fresh sugary goodness and coffee. Her stomach growled. "Let's get in line," she said. "For carrot cake."

The bakery was set up buffet style, meaning customers grabbed a tray for themselves and then had to walk by the open displays of all the goods in order to get to the cash register.

Cruel, cruel setup.

Lilah grabbed a tray, and oh look at that, two old-fashioned chocolate-glazed donuts somehow landed on it. "I don't know, must be fate," she told Toby, who followed closely on her heels, the leash slack and unnecessary.

The guy in front of her turned around and smiled. "Thought you didn't believe in fate."

Nick McFarlan, who ran the hardware store down the street. Lilah and Nick had gone together on and off through high school and had gone to prom together. He'd been her first kiss, her first boyfriend, her first everything.

Until they'd gone their separate ways for college, breaking up to experience new things. Lilah had done that all right, only it hadn't exactly been as positive as she'd hoped for. When Nick had returned home after college, he had wanted to pick up right where they'd left off. But Lilah had been too raw and devastated over two unexpected things—her grandma's death and a bad relationship experience while she'd been away.

So they'd fallen into a sort of friendship zone instead. Nick, buying two dozen donuts for his customers, smiled. "You're looking good," he said softly.

She laughed. "I'm wearing Carhartts."

"I have fantasies about those Carhartts."

"Really?"

"Okay, I have fantasies about what you might be wearing beneath them." He leaned in playfully as if to peek for himself.

"Stop it."

He grinned. "Admit it, one of these days I'm going to wear you down."

She smiled, but the truth was he probably could. Like Cruz, he was good-looking, kind, and familiar.

But she was tired, oh so very tired of familiar.

Dee smiled as she rang him up. "You can look beneath my Carhartts, Nick. Anytime."

Game, he looked her over. She was ten years older than them but still trim and pretty. And wore a man-eater smile. "You're not wearing Carhartts," Nick said.

Dee leaned over the counter, eyes sultry and laughing. "For you, I'd buy some."

While Lilah waited for them to stop flirting, a jelly-filled donut fell onto her tray, all by itself, joining the two old-fashioned glazes. "Oh, look at that," she murmured to Toby. "Fruit." She started in on that one first and moaned in sheer bliss. "God, so much better than carrots."

"You're going to start a riot."

At the low, familiar voice in her ear, she went still, then slowly turned to face Brady.

He was halfway through his own donut—a chocolate-frosted by the looks of it. And good Lord, talk about starting a riot. He was wearing army flight cargoes today and a soft-washed long-sleeved polo that was form-fitted to his toned body.

"Hey," she said.

"Hey back, Crash."

"Okay," she said. "I object to that—" But she was talking to air because he'd crouched in front of Toby, elbows braced on his thighs as he offered a hand for the dog to sniff. "How's he doing today?"

"Good." She kneeled down as well. "But he's really skittish, so you need to—"

Toby licked Brady's hand, then arched up to lick his chin as well.

"Go slow," Lilah finished on a sigh.

Toby was rewarded by Brady with a behind-the-ear scratching that had the little guy sliding to the floor in a boneless heap of pleasure.

"Ah, good boy," Brady praised, giving him an allover body rub that left Lilah yearning for the same.

Brady rose fluidly on his feet, and for a beat, she found herself eye to eye with his flat, zero-fat stomach. That he could even have a flat, zero-fat stomach with the way he ate really irritated the hell out of her.

And/or turned her on. She couldn't decide which. It was early yet.

A small smile curved his sexy mouth as he offered her a hand, telling her that he knew of her battle, and hell if that didn't settle it. Irritation.

He gestured to the choice on her tray. "Nice."

She winced, then realized he wasn't judging her but truly complimenting her choice of breakfast. "I almost got one of those," she admitted, gesturing to his chocolate-frosted. "But I didn't eat carrots last night."

Nodding as if this made perfect sense, he sank strong white teeth into his donut, licking chocolate frosting off his upper lip. "Mmm . . ."

Her mouth watered. "I'll give you a piece of mine for a piece of yours."

His eyes darkened and he immediately broke off a large part of his donut and offered it to her. She did the same and felt his warm breath brush over her fingers before he sank his teeth into her jelly-filled.

Eyes on hers, he smiled as he chewed and swallowed. "Yeah, that's good, too. Hey!" He pulled his tray back and looked at the second chunk she'd quickly snagged from his donut.

"Sorry," she said with an easy grin. She wasn't sorry. At all. And she might have laughed at the look on his face as he studied what was left, but she was up next at the cash register. She gently nudged Toby forward, as just ahead, Nick picked up his bag and turned to her.

"Hey, I saw your Jeep. I meant to ask what happened."

"A little fender bender," she said, extremely aware of Brady behind her.

Brady coughed and said, "Bullshit," softly in her ear at the same time.

Lilah gave him a little nudge with her hip, knocking him out of her personal space bubble. He might kiss like heaven, and maybe he had great taste in food, but he was far too cocky.

Nick divided a look between them, then settled on Lilah. "I'm sensing a story here."

"No. No stories, good or otherwise, and it wasn't my fault." She paused and sighed. "Okay, it was totally my fault."

"She has a parking problem," Brady said.

Nick laughed. "She has a lot of 'parking' problems."

Great. Lilah loved Nick, but he had a big mouth. "My foot slipped," she said. "No big deal."

"Uh-huh. Remember our senior year when your foot 'slipped' and you drove off the bridge in your granny's SUV?" Nick asked.

Both men were smiling now, and Lilah took a moment for a deep breath. "We're not discussing this." Digging through her purse for her wallet, she turned to Dee.

From over her shoulder a ten appeared. "For both of us," Brady said.

Dee shot Lilah a brows-up look.

Lilah ignored the unspoken question. "Thanks," she said to Brady. "I'll owe you."

"Donuts," he clarified. "Not carrots."

Dee smiled. "So, who's the cutie?"

Lilah very carefully didn't look at Brady. "Brady Miller. He's come to visit Adam and Dell."

Dee cackled. In fact she laughed so hard, she ended up doubled over. "Honey, I meant the dog."

"Oh." Lilah grimaced as her face heated and tried to pretend that Brady wasn't right behind her, looking far too amused.

"You're right, though," Dee said, sizing up Brady. "He's a real cutie, too."

Lilah sighed. "The dog," she said firmly, "is a rescue. He's going to a good home." And finally, as she said this, she saw Shelly pull up out front. Which made her realize she had only a few minutes left with Toby.

She was well aware that the whole point to running the humane society was to place animals in loving homes. She knew this, but her gut didn't always get it, and both it and her heart squeezed hard as she looked down at Toby waiting patiently at her feet, so quiet and accepting of whatever fate came his way. Dammit. Every one. She mourned every single one. "I have to go."

Dee cocked her head, then looked to the door as Shelly entered the bakery. "Aw, honey," she murmured, covering Lilah's hand with her own, her voice holding so much sympathy that Lilah's throat closed. "Never gets easier for you, does it?"

"What?" Brady asked, looking into Lilah's eyes with a frown. "What doesn't get easier? You stay up all night studying again?"

"Studying?" Dee asked in surprise. "Studying what?"

Lilah sighed. Her studies weren't classified information, but neither had she told anyone other than Dell and Adam. And Brady—by accident. Literally. It was just that she'd quit college and come home with her tail between her legs. This time if something happened, she'd rather be a two-time failure in private. "Nothing," she said, grabbing a bottle of water to offset the donut calories. She fumbled through the bottom of her purse for loose change.

"Oh, don't worry about it." Dee patted her hand. "It's on the house since I know you're about to get your heart broken." She smiled sweetly over Lilah's head at Brady. "I adopted my own sweet Lexie from her last year. She cried for a week. Lilah, not Lexie."

"I did not," Lilah said. She'd cried for two weeks. She knew exactly how ridiculous that was, just as she knew how silly she was being over dreading handing Toby off. She'd only had him one night, and he was going to a woman who really wanted him.

"She still comes and visits," Dee told Brady.

Lilah felt the weight of Brady's gaze as he studied her thoughtfully, but she couldn't concentrate on that with Shelly waving at her. She was midforties, with wavy brown hair piled on top of her head and a friendly, kind face. She wore jeans and a rec center sweatshirt, perfect for a day with kids at the rec center and for being a new doggy mama.

Lilah grabbed the donuts Dee had bagged, murmured "Let's go" to Toby, and walked blindly toward Shelly. The two of them moved outside for some privacy. Lilah gave Shelly both her bag of donuts—she'd lost her appetite—and an introduction to Toby. In five minutes Shelly and Toby were fast friends, walking off together into the sunset.

Okay, it was morning, and the sun was nowhere close to setting, but to Lilah it felt like an ending nevertheless. She swiped at her eyes. "Suck it up," she whispered fiercely to herself. "It's all good, no matter how hard it is."

"I'm going to refrain from saying 'That's what she said' since you seem to be having a moment."

Whirling around, she glared at Brady, who was leaning against the front wall of the building. "Why do you keep sneaking up on me?"

Instead of answering, he handed her a bag.

Opening it, she found two additional old-fashioned chocolate glazes. "Since you handed yours off. Thought you could use them," he said with a shrug.

"I gave them away so I wouldn't eat all three. I was saving myself."

"Okay." He tried to take the bag back, but she slapped his hand and hugged the bag to her chest.

He appeared to fight a smile, but his voice was serious. "Are you okay?"

"Yes. Though I'd be a hell of a lot better if you hadn't told the whole world that I have a parking problem."

"I didn't tell the whole world. Just what's-his-name. Your friendly ex."

She blew out a sigh. "Nick. And how do you know he's an ex?"

"It's either that, or he's a prospect. Which would explain the hungry look on his face."

"Ex," she admitted. "And he looked hungry because he was. For donuts."

"And for you as well." Stepping into her personal space bubble as he had a habit of doing, Brady cupped her face and tilted it up to his, running his thumb under her eye, catching a tear she'd missed. "You don't look like you're okay," he said quietly.

She sent him another glare just for the heck of it and tried to turn away, but he held her still.

And close.

And Lord, he was deadly up close. "What?" she asked, sounding testy. Because she was.

He backed her closer to the building, under the eaves and away from the window, giving them a little bit of privacy. "You look like you need . . ." His eyes darkened a little and his thumb brushed over her bottom lip now, making it tingle and tremble open.

"What? I need what?"

"This." Holding her gaze for as long as possible, he leaned in and lightly brushed her mouth with his warm, firm one.

She heard a sound, a whimper really, and realized it was her. He was right. She needed this. Bad. Fisting his shirt to hold him close, she heard the sound again, horrifyingly, embarrassingly needy.

"Shh," he whispered soothingly, and then kissed her once more, not lightly this time.

She promptly forgot everything, including the fact that they were standing on the sidewalk in broad daylight, with cars going by and people moving in and out of the bakery. It all faded away behind the wild pounding of her heart.

With a hand on the nape of her neck, Brady deepened the kiss, his other hand gliding down to the small of her back to hold her against him.

On board with that, she loosened her hands from his shirt and slid them up his chest and around his neck, pressing as close as she could to his hard, warm body.

When they were both breathless, he pressed his lips to her throat and murmured something she couldn't quite catch because her blood was still roaring through her veins. "What?" she murmured.

He rocked her against him. "No idea what I'm going to do with you."

She didn't know what he was going to do with her either, but she hoped it was good. She might have asked him to speak slowly and in great detail but she became aware that her hands had migrated and were now perched precariously low on what felt like perfect eight-pack abs.

Two inches south and she'd have hit the jackpot.

She glanced down and revised. One inch. He hadn't moved so she tipped her head back up and found his eyes on hers, dark and scorching. "We seem to have a little chemistry," she whispered.

His lips curved slightly in acknowledgment.

"I should go," she said slowly, but her mind wasn't on the words. Instead it was thinking, *One more inch!* "Really. You're going to need to back off a little, because I need to—"

He lifted his hands, indicating that he wasn't holding her in any way and she felt the blush on her face. Gathering her dignity, she forced herself to back away and turned to the Jeep.

"Lilah."

She kept her back to him and closed her eyes. "Yeah?"

When he didn't say anything, she glanced back.

"Why do you give the animals away if you want to keep them?"

"Because that's what I do," she said, surprised. "It's my job."

He came up behind her, putting his hand on hers on the Jeep handle, preventing her from opening the door. "And what's up with the studying all night and not telling anyone?"

"That's . . . private."

"A secret?"

"Sort of." She paused. "Okay, yes, I told you a secret. I was frazzled and had just hit your truck, and you were holding the babies in the box for me, and . . ."

And she'd been thinking he looked so cute holding them, too, looking all helpful and tough at the same time.

Oh, and that he had a nice ass, and that she hadn't been with a man in a long time. Too long.

And that he wasn't a fixture in this town, which made him both dangerous and safe . . . "I was momentarily distracted," she admitted. "And it slipped out. But now that you've reminded me of it, you do owe me a secret in return. Make it a good one. I could use a distraction."

"I don't do secrets."

Okay, then. Good to know. Drawing a deep breath, she pushed his hand out of her way and he let her. She opened the Jeep's driver door and climbed in, taking just one more last quick glance. But only one because more than that with him tended to render her incapable of reason. "Thanks for the donuts," she said. "Twice."

He nodded but didn't otherwise move. She blew out a sigh and eyed the truck parked in front of her. "You should probably go first. I'm even more distracted today than yesterday. And as you know, I tend to do stupid things when distracted."

"Something to remember," he said lightly.

Six

The next evening, after Dell had seen all his patients, he closed up shop and set Brady up for a website photo shoot. He showed Brady into one of the exam rooms and patted the exam table. "I was thinking we could have a series of pictures of 'patients' in various rooms, as if maybe animals led this place, you know?"

"That's good," Brady said, nodding. "Funny. Warm. Makes the place seem welcome and readily inviting. None of you?"

"Nah," Dell said. "I like the idea of just the animals. You can put one in Jade's reading glasses behind her desk. One with my stethoscope sitting on this table, maybe."

Brady had spent the day cataloging all that was wrong with the Bell 47, in a hurry to get that renovation on track. He'd spent the hours alone with his own thoughts, and they hadn't always been good ones. At least ten times he'd started to go in search of Adam and Dell to tell them he didn't want to stay for another twenty-nine days. He couldn't handle the thinking.

But he hadn't.

Now all he wanted to do was grab a shower and hit the sack, but he'd promised to take these pictures. He'd been dreading this, knowing the only time he liked being behind the camera was on his own terms. It was, after all, a creative release for him, not a chore. But he found himself liking Dell's ideas for the pictures and felt an energetic creative surge. "Yeah," he said. "We can do that. But are you going to materialize your patients? Because you sent them all home."

"I've got that handled," Dell said, just as the sounds of a wild stampede sounded from down the hall.

Brady poked his head out of the examination room in time to see

Lilah appear, both hands occupied with myriad leashes. In one hand she had one, two, three dogs. No. Two dogs and a lamb. In her other hand she held Abigail's leash. And Brady couldn't help it—he felt the smile crack his face.

"I've got two cats and a bunny available as well," she called out, blowing a few strands of hair from her eyes. "Where do you want us?"

Brady didn't give a shit about where the animals went, but he knew exactly where he wanted her.

Beneath him, panting his name.

A little unsettled at that thought, he shoved a hand through his hair and shrugged at Dell. "You're the director."

"Um," Dell said, looking guilty as he pulled his keys out of his pocket. "Actually, you are. I've got a date."

"What?"

"Now don't let the lamb scare you. Lulu's really very sweet. Just don't let her get her nose in the family jewels, man. She's been known to take an unexpected bite."

It wasn't Lulu he was afraid of, and something of that must have shown on his face.

Dell studied him a moment, brow drawn. "I can trust you with her, right?"

"The lamb? Sure."

When Dell only looked at him, Brady glanced at Lilah as she moved toward them and slowly shook his head. "Definitely not."

"Christ," Dell muttered, and swiped a hand down his face. "I'm going to hope to God you're kidding." And with that, he met Lilah halfway, kissed her cheek, shot one last long warning glance in Brady's direction, and was gone.

Lilah came to a stop before Brady. "What was that?"

"Nothing."

"You told him you couldn't be trusted with me."

Brady arched a brow. "So if you overheard, why did you ask?"

"Because I wanted to see what you would say. What kind of an answer was that?"

"What did you want me to say?" Brady asked her.

"Not that."

He shrugged. "It was the truth."

She stared up at him, looking a little flummoxed at that. "Oh," she breathed.

Yeah, oh. Just being near her like this—she smelled like mangoes tonight—drained some of the tension in him, in spite of himself. No matter what she thought, she was a sight for sore eyes, that was for damn sure. She wore snug, hip-hugging jeans and a lacy white T-shirt that was sheer enough to reveal the white cami beneath it and a faint hint of an equally white bra.

Which he found ridiculously, inexplicably hot. The past few nights he'd fantasized about Lilah. He'd told himself that he was an ass, but his self seemed completely unconcerned.

The lamb—Lulu, he presumed—stepped forward and tried to shove her face into his crotch, but duly warned by Dell, Brady backed up.

"Don't be afraid. She's sweet."

At Lilah's words, Lulu appeared to smile, pulling back her lips to show her teeth, which didn't look sweet to Brady.

"She just wants to catch your scent," Lilah assured him.

Pushing aside images of dropping to his knees and pressing his face to Lilah's crotch to catch her scent, he grabbed the dogs' leashes from Lilah. Given the unstableness of his brain tonight, it was best to get this over with.

Two hours later, he got the last shot of the night, a cat sitting on Jade's desk daintily washing her face with the computer opened on the schedule behind her.

Lilah gathered up all the animals while Brady slipped his camera back into its case. "Think you have everything you need?"

He knew he didn't. Not even close. She looked up from wrapping a leash around her wrist, caught his expression, and went still. "Are you going to kiss me again?"

"Yeah," he said, surprising himself as he moved in. With two dogs, a duck, a lamb, and a cat between them, he cupped her face and kissed her. A brush of his lips to hers, once, twice. Unable to pull away without more, he settled in against her mouth, their lips the only points of their body touching. He'd meant it to be short and sweet, but she made a sound that went straight through him and the kiss deepened, a hot, intense tangle of tongues that ended abruptly when one of the dogs at their feet barked.

She let out a shaky breath and backed to the door. "I don't know what that means."

He did. It meant he was fucked. "It means good night."

She nodded and turned away but not before he caught the quick flash of disappointment and hurt.

"Lilah—"

But she was gone.

For two days Lilah worked and avoided going to Belle Haven, and for two days all she thought about was Brady. She knew from Adam that Brady had started uploading pics for their website and brochures. She knew from Jade that he was also working on the Bell, and apparently upping foot traffic to the center because he was looking good while doing it.

A part of Lilah had wanted to go see but she'd been busy. Busy thinking about her growing restlessness and what she needed. She was pretty sure that what she needed was Brady, but she wasn't sure he was on board with the program.

"You okay?" Cruz asked after they worked the midday shift together.

"Yeah. Why?"

"We've had three customers mention the new guy"—Cruz put air quotes around *new guy*—"and you've gotten a look on your face each and every time." He gave her an exaggerated look of dazed lust, complete with dopey eyes and tongue hanging out.

"I never look like that," she said, and shoved him. They were in the back, organizing outside playtime. They had two of the dogs separated from the others because they were elderly and liked sedate, quiet playtime, which they'd just had. They were now lying happily on the floor at Lilah's feet, cooling down, and she took a moment to hug each of them.

"You do so get that look. When it's been a while since you got laid."

"Bite me, Cruz."

"I'd love to bite you," he said as they escorted the older dogs back to their area and took out their three other guests; Lulu and two rambunctious dogs. "But been there, done that. And you bit back, remember?"

She laughed and, not for the first time, felt grateful that they'd realized that they were so much better together like this, bicker-buddies. It would have been awful if they couldn't make this work because she cared about him so very much and knew the feeling was mutual. "Kissing and telling, Cruz?"

"Biting and telling."

They took the rest of the animals outside for supervised playtime in the sunshine and fresh air. Later, when they were back inside, Cruz administered meds and Lilah moved to the kitchen to do the dishes and general cleaning. Afterward, she worked on paperwork until it was pickup and drop-off time.

Celia came in for Lulu. Celia Ayala had been Lilah's grandma Estelle's frenemy and bridge partner for fifty years—until Estelle had committed the ultimate faux pas and gone to the Big Bridge Game in the sky. Alone.

Lilah accepted Celia's check and wrote up a receipt.

Celia was the approximate size and shape of an Oompa-Loompa, and thanks to the new tanning salon in town, she had the same skin tone as one, too. "Can you book me for next Thursday, dear? Oh, and also tell me about the new sexy hunk working at Belle Haven. What's his name?"

"Brady," Lilah said without thinking, making Celia grin. "What?"

"I hear you're seeing him."

"What? No. No. I'm not, I only—" *Kiss him every chance I get . . .* "No," she said again weakly.

"Someone told me you'd been seen in his truck."

Lilah sighed. "I hit it. I was tired and—"

"You work too hard. Listen, dear. Your grandmother—bless her ornery soul—agreed with me on one thing."

"Are you sure? Because I never knew you two to agree on anything."

Celia waggled a finger. "We agreed on this. You only get one life. So you need to find the right man. Do you understand what I'm saying?"

"Do you?"

"Listen to you," Celia chided. "You have a mouth on you, just like Estelle did."

Lilah thought about her beloved grandma, who for all intents and purposes had been her mom, her dad, her everything, and smiled even though her chest felt too tight. "You miss her."

"She drove me crazy." Celia sighed. "But yes, I miss her. She was my last friend. The rest are all dead. Since I'm planning on living forever, it's going to be lonely. Now stop changing the subject. I'm old, not stupid. We all know how much you gave up to care for her in the end, but she's gone, Lilah. It's your turn to live."

"I am."

"Then stop wasting time talking to old ladies. Go back to kissing the hunk."

Lilah stared at her. "How did you know?"

"Well, honey, if you want to keep a man a secret, you don't kiss him out in front of the bakery on Main."

Later, Lilah was in the middle of an online lecture for her animal biology class when she got a call from Dell.

"Got a check for you," he said. "For last week when you boarded those two beagles for us."

Belle Haven didn't keep overnight guests; they paid the kennels to do that for them. "My favorite kind of call," she said.

"And here I thought just hearing my voice was your favorite kind of call."

"That, too."

"Oh no, it's too late. You've given yourself away. You only want the money."

"Yes, it's ridiculous how fond of eating I've become."

Dell was silent for a beat. "You were supposed to tell me if you need help."

And wasn't that just the problem. She hated needing help. Always had. "I'm fine, I was kidding."

Mostly.

"I'll bring the check over with dinner," he said. "We'll talk."

Oh great. A talk. Where he'd try to butt in and she'd dance around her money problems. "No, I'll come to you. I have some files for you, anyway. And I'm busy for dinner."

She had a date with a very healthy, very green salad, followed by a little ice cream—or the whole pint, depending on how her studying went.

A few minutes later, Lilah walked to the center, eyeing the dark clouds drifting down from the peaks, turning into shreds of mist that gave substance to the raw wind. She zipped up her sweatshirt and picked up the pace. Either Mother Nature had forgotten it was summer, or she needed some Midol.

At Belle Haven, she went straight to the reception desk. Jade sat behind the counter working the phone and the computer at the same time with her usual calm, implacable efficiency, with a kitten sleeping in her lap. Behind her chair on the floor lay a 150-pound St. Bernard dog, snoring with shocking volume.

Jade had glorious strawberry blond hair that she kept perfectly twisted on top of her head and sharp green eyes that didn't take shit from anyone. Her clothes looked straight out of a magazine, some sort of belted shirtdress, bangles up one arm, and shoes to die for. She'd moved to Sunshine a few years ago from Chicago so she could ski her way through the winters. She and Lilah had since become good friends, so Lilah knew the real story, that Jade's move hadn't so much been a desire to ski as it'd been a need for some space from a tough situation.

"Check it out," Jade whispered, nudging her chin in the direction of the windows.

Lilah's attention was first caught by the very full waiting room and the women whose noses were practically glued to the windows leading to the side yard. "What's going on?"

"That's what I'm trying to show you. It's our newest attraction." Jade pointed outside, off to the right where the Bell had been parked for weeks now, ever since it had been delivered from Smitty's airport across the meadow. From the hood the lower half of a male body stuck out. Scuffed work boots and long legs that led to—

"The best ass I've ever seen," Jade whispered.

It was true. Brady absolutely had the best ass ever seen. Lilah took a minute to admire it.

"Don't you think?" Jade asked.

"Well . . . he sure looks good in cargo pants," she said carefully. "All those pockets for his stuff."

"And you just know that not all of his . . . stuff is in his pockets." Jade slid her a look. "You kiss him again?"

"What?" Lilah started guiltily. How the hell did everyone know this? "I don't . . . I haven't . . ."

"Main Street, Lilah," Jade said patiently. "You might as well have sent a clip to YouTube yourself."

Oh, good grief. "Dell said there was a check . . . ?"

Jade laughed, but took mercy on her. "In his office."

Lilah made her way through the crowded reception area to the offices. Dell wasn't behind his big desk, but there was an envelope leaning up against his computer with her name on it. In it was the check for services rendered, plus three hundred bucks in cash. "Oh, hell no."

"Not enough?" he asked, coming into the room. He was wearing scrubs and a white lab coat, both emphasizing his tall, lean form in a favorable way. His charming smile only added to his appeal. It was the smile of a man who knew it rendered most females stupid.

"Don't you smile at me." She pulled out the three hundred-dollar bills and slapped them down on his desk. "I don't take pity cash."

"Noted, but that's not what that is. It's a loan." Clearly seeing the ready denial on her face, he added softly, "We just want to help, Lilah."

Damn if that didn't melt her. "You can. By believing in me."

"I do."

She sighed and hugged him hard. "The kennels are doing better this year, really. I'm going to be fine."

Hopefully.

He held her a minute, cheek pressed to the top of her head as he let out a long breath, a good indicator that she was being a pain in his ass. With a sigh of her own, she patted his chest, took the check, and left him. She was back at the main counter saying good-bye to Jade when the front door opened.

Brady strode inside, moving with that easy economical grace that spoke of a lifetime of discipline and military training. His T-shirt was snug around his broad chest and biceps, loose over his flat abs. He was streaked with grease and looking hot enough to be on the cover of *Aviation* as he stopped in front of Jade's desk with a bundle in his hands. "Either of you know what the hell this is?"

Lilah took a look at the small brown dog, though its color might have been due more to the dirt and mud that was stuck to its tangled and matted fur. His floppy ears nearly covered his sweet soulful eyes. He sneezed once, hard, and then the ears did cover his eyes. With a violent shake of his head, they fell back into place.

"It was sitting in front of my truck," Brady said, frowning.

"It's a dog," Jade said.

Brady lifted the scrawny, clearly neglected dog up a little higher and inspected it. It licked his chin.

"Aw," Jade said. "He likes you."

Brady looked so horrified, Lilah laughed.

Brady turned his head and narrowed his razor-sharp blue eyes on her. Probably he wasn't used to being a source of amusement. Probably, mostly women just lay down at his feet and begged him to take them.

Not that she was even close to doing that. No siree. She had some pride. She did all of her begging in private.

"It looks hungry and thirsty," Brady said. "And maybe he has a cold, I don't know. I thought I'd bring him inside, out of the sun."

Oh. Oh, damn. He cared.

Either she made a sound or he sensed her softening because he thrust the dog at her. "Here. I think it needs to be checked out by Dell."

The dog wore a midnight blue rhinestone encrusted collar, though most of the rhinestones were missing: TWINKLES.

"Cute," she said, but didn't take the dog. She couldn't have said why. She automatically gravitated to all animals, especially lost, hurting ones, but there was something so innately sweet about seeing the little thing in Brady's big, capable hands.

"Twinkles," Brady said with disgust. "It should be illegal to name a dog that."

"Twinkles is a perfectly fine name for a little girl dog."

Brady shifted the dog, rolling it easily over in his big hands, revealing his distinct boy parts.

"Oh," Lilah said. "Huh. Well, maybe he's named after someone."

"Not my problem. You're the humane society." He was still holding out the thing as if maybe the dog was a ticking time bomb. "So it's your job to take him, right?" He looked to Jade for confirmation of this.

"Yes," Jade said. "We do get abandoned animals dropped off here all the time. Since we're the biggest animal center in this part of the state, we get a lot of business from the outlying areas, so who knows where he could have come from. If there's no owner to call, we get them to Lilah here."

"Hopefully he has an owner nearby." But Lilah could tell by the look of the little guy that he'd been on his own for a while, and in her experience that meant there'd probably be no owner forthcoming. "I'll put up flyers and get it on the website."

Brady nodded, looking a little impatient that neither she nor Jade had relieved him of his burden. "Here," he said again.

She couldn't explain even to herself why she did it. Temporary insanity owing to a severe lack of sugar. That, or a case of severe unfulfilled and overworked hormones, she decided as she turned the sign-in sheet toward him. Because how many times had he kissed her now? Three.

Three.

She felt like she was going to self-combust. And she'd even self-combusted in the shower that morning. "Dell's pretty busy today, but I'm sure Jade can squeeze you in to see him at some point. Does your dog need any vaccines?"

Brady scowled. "My dog? Is that supposed to be funny?"

Lilah smiled and stepped on Jade's foot when the receptionist opened her mouth to speak. "As I said, I'm sure Jade can work Twinkles in, but there's a bit of a wait at the moment."

Brady stared at her for a long moment. She'd bet that there'd been many who'd cowered beneath that look. And she might have, except that the pathetic little creature quaking in his big hands, the one her heart was dying to grab and snuggle, was looking up at him like he was salvation.

She recently felt the same way.

"You're the humane society," Brady said a little tightly.

"I am. And you know where my kennel is, if you decide to abandon the animal."

Brady glanced down at the dog's miserable face and his own took on a pained expression. "I didn't abandon it. Someone else did. Christ," he muttered when she just looked at him serenely. "Is this about me telling your ex you rear-ended my truck?"

"Cruz?" Jade asked, surprised.

"Cruz?" Brady slid a look at Lilah. "I was talking about Nick. How many exes do you have?"

"None of your business."

"Two," Jade told him. "She doesn't get out much since her grandma passed on."

"Really?" Lilah said to her, heavy on the disbelief. "You're going to go there?"

Jade lifted a shoulder. "Sorry. It's been a long day."

Brady gave Lilah a long look she couldn't begin to interpret to save her own life before turning to Jade. "Book me for the last appointment of the day. I'll be back." He glanced down at the dog. "He looks like he's healthy enough to make it until then." Clearly frustrated with the lot of them, he made his way back toward the door to leave, the dog tucked against his chest.

The sexy cuteness, Lilah thought. *Oh good Lord, the sexy cuteness . . .*

Jade was brows up. "What was that?" she whispered.

"Don't start. And why did you bring my grandma into it?"

"It slipped out. I'm telling you. I need a nap. But seriously, what was that, making him keep the stray? What are you up to?"

Lilah watched Brady stop just outside the door and stare down at the dog in his arms. "I don't know what you're talking about."

"Really? Because forgive me if I'm wrong," the receptionist said dryly, "but I was under the impression that you take in all the neglected, forgotten animals around here."

Lilah shrugged.

Jade's smile came slow and proud. "You wanted him to suffer. Nice. So what did he do to you exactly—besides kiss you into apparent insanity?"

Exactly? Lilah had no idea.

Except she did. She was horribly, devastatingly attracted to him, like moth-to-the-flame attracted. Which technically wasn't his fault, but she felt that if she had to suffer, then so did he. "Does there have to be a reason?"

"To make a guy suffer? Absolutely not," Jade said with certainty.

That night Lilah was sitting at her table doing a balancing act with her bills when the knock came at her door.

"Mew," Sadie said, all soft and warm and cozy in Lilah's lap. The watchdog on the job.

"Have to get up," Lilah told her.

The cat dug her claws in just enough to have Lilah hissing in a breath, but before she could dislodge the cat, Adam let himself in. His big body filled up her kitchen as he dropped a large pizza box, a six-pack, and a bag on the table.

"Dinner," he said. "A meat supreme special and, in case you're feeling girlie, a salad."

She stared at the food, torn by the rumbling in her belly and the sick feeling that he was babysitting her. "I told Dell I was busy."

"Yeah, but I'm not the sucker he is."

This was true. Nothing got by Adam. Which is what worried her. "He told you that I didn't take the money."

Not answering, he handed her a bottle of Corona before getting another for himself. Then he opened the pizza box.

They ate in silence for a while, silence being Adam's favorite state of being. She tried going with that, but in the end she was just not in the mood. "So . . . you're worried about me," she said flatly.

Adam grabbed another slice of pizza.

"Let me guess—you lost the coin toss with Dell, which left you stuck with me. Only you don't know how to tell me this because you're a penis-carrying human and can't figure out how to communicate with a mere vagina."

He choked on a bite and reached for his beer.

She clapped him on his broad-as-a-mountain back, then ruffled his short, silky dark hair. "I'm okay, you know. Really." She looked at the last piece of pizza. She didn't need it. Problem was, it was calling her name.

"It's got the same amount of calories if you eat it now or after agonizing over it for another two minutes," Adam said.

Blowing out a breath, she snatched it before he could.

"And I didn't lose the coin toss," he said. "I won it. Loser had to talk to Brady."

That caught her interest. She licked cheese off her thumb. "About?"

His silence was answer enough.

"Oh, for God's sake!" she burst out. "Are you kidding me? Haven't you done enough to my sex life?"

He choked again and spilled beer down the front of him. "Fuck," he muttered, rising, then tripping over Sadie.

"Mew!"

He scooped up the three-legged cat and held her to his wide chest in apology as he grabbed the paper towels. "Want to run that by me again?"

"Sure. You're ruining my sex life!"

He carefully set Sadie back down. "I didn't realize you had a sex life."

"Exactly!" She rose, too, giving him, for good measure, a shove to the chest that didn't budge him one single inch. "You hover like an overprotective mama bear, scaring all the guys away except for the ones I don't want anymore. And I'm . . . Argh!" Turning away from him, she went to the sink and stared out into the night, gripping the edge of the tile so she didn't smack him again.

"You're lonely," he said, sounding surprised.

"What, you think only guys need regular orgasms? And before you get all sanctimonious, I wanted Brady well before I knew he was your foster brother."

"Jesus."

In the reflection of the glass in front of her, she watched as he pressed his fingers to his eyes and grimaced. He drew a deep breath and pointed to the table. "Sit."

"Why, because you asked so nicely?"

"Sit your ass down and I'll tell you about Brady."

She fought with her curiosity and lost. She sat.

Adam strode to the freezer, grabbed her always present ice cream, retrieved two spoons from a drawer, and sat next to her. "He was fifteen when we showed up at Sol's. I was thirteen, Dell was twelve. None of us had ever had a steady home."

She already knew this, about Dell and Adam at least. They were blood brothers. Their mother was Native American and lived on a reservation somewhere. She'd left only to give birth and had gone back to that world. Their father had taken the boys but then had died when they'd been young. Their mother, already moved on to another husband and family, had not wanted them back.

"Dell kept getting beat up at school," Adam said, staring at the beer in his fingers. "I kept getting suspended for fighting—badly, by the way. I had no idea what I was doing. Brady scared the shit out of us. He was silent. And tough as nails."

Lilah could imagine that without too much difficulty.

"Sol had a gym in his basement," Adam went on. He ran a finger over the bottle. "One day Brady took us down there. We were pretty sure that he was going to kill us and no one would ever find the bodies, but instead he taught us how to protect ourselves."

"He taught you how to fight?"

"Yeah. It took a good long while, too—we were pretty pathetic. About a month into this, we were out past curfew. I can't remember why. And a group of, I don't know, maybe five or six kids tried to jump us." He laughed softly but without much mirth. "Dell was feeling brave and swung the first punch. The guy ducked and Dell hit Brady by accident."

Lilah gasped. "Oh no."

"Brady had to fight the guys trying to jump us and keep Dell from hindering the process."

"Well?" she demanded when he didn't go on. "What happened?"

"We managed to come out on top but only because of Brady's skill at hand to hand."

"Did any of you get hurt?"

"Some. Not too badly." He rubbed his jaw as if remembering the old aches.

"So that's how you got so tough," she said, going with a teasing tone to lighten the mood.

But Adam didn't smile. Instead he hesitated. He never hesitated.

"Uh-oh," she said. "Is this where you tell me the three of you launched into a life of crime?"

"No, I was already well into my criminal career by then, all on my own." He rubbed a hand over his eyes, looking weary. "I already had two arrests for underage drinking and then I got caught trying to steal a car."

"Oh, Adam."

He shook the sympathy off. I was young and stupid and angry. Brady helped steer me through the aftermath of that disaster on the condition that I straighten my shit out or he'd straighten me out himself. Painfully."

Lilah felt her heart turn over in her chest. "He cared about you, like a brother."

"At the time it felt more like a prison warden, but yeah. The point is, he always came through for us when we needed him."

"And you want to come through for him now?"

"Yeah. This land is one-third his. And it's good to have him here."

"Where he's safe," she guessed. "For those few years he kept you safe, and you'd like to return the favor. Look at you trying to save us all."

He grimaced. "Jesus, don't make me out like a saint."

"No, a saint would have brought something good to top off my ice cream with." She smiled at him. "And I think it's sweet. Even if Brady, and me for that matter, don't like to accept help."

"No," he said quietly. "But you want him."

"Yes," she admitted, unwilling to lie. "Is that going to be a problem?"

He shrugged, his eyes dark and troubled. "Just . . . be careful. He's not the white-picket-fence type."

"I don't want a white picket fence." Yet. Because the truth was, she did want to meet the One and get married. Someday. But she'd waited this long, she could wait a little longer.

And in the meantime, there could be Brady. The pros far outweighed the cons. He wouldn't let Adam and Dell scare him off, and she didn't have anything to lose because they both knew the score up front. He was leaving. So there were no expectations and she could be free to enjoy herself.

A lot.

A corner of Adam's mouth quirked as he read her thought like a book. "Brady was tossed around more than we were. Something like four or five foster homes before Sol got him."

"Which makes it all the better that he has you guys and this place." And me . . .

Adam nodded. "Yes. He's had a lot of people in his life who didn't stick. So you should know . . . he doesn't tend to stick either."

"That's actually pretty funny coming from you." She hugged him. "Listen to me, okay? I'm not looking to make him stick. I'm just looking for some company."

"So you're okay being his one-night stand?"

"Not a one-night stand, no," she said. "I'll take a couple of nights. Or as long as it lasts. On our terms, his and mine. Not yours." She kissed his tense jaw. "Love you, though. Always will."

Adam just sighed and reached for the ice cream.

Seven

Brady stood by the unlit fireplace and stared at the rug in front of it. Or more accurately, the thing on the rug.

It was staring back at him. It was now midnight. An hour ago Brady had gone to sleep. Or tried to. The loft, being one room, allowed noise to carry, so when the dog had started crying and howling almost immediately, it was a shocking decibel level considering the pup was maybe seven pounds.

He'd tried everything. A blanket. A ticking clock from the mantel. Soft music from his own iPod. Okay, not soft, he didn't have soft, but hell, it was hard rock, the good stuff.

Every single time, the dog would appear to settle and Brady would crawl cautiously off to bed. He'd get comfortable and start to drift off.

And then the hell would begin all over again.

"They tell me that you're one hundred percent canine," Brady said, hands on hips. "But I'm thinking you're one hundred percent pussy."

The dog—Brady refused to think of it as Twinkles—let out a low whimper and rolled over, exposing its belly.

"Jesus." Brady sank to the couch in nothing but his knit boxers. "Come here, then."

Its sorrow apparently forgotten, the dog leapt up with enthusiasm and bounded over. He tried to jump up onto the couch, making it only about six inches off the ground before falling to his back on the floor.

Brady shook his head. "Failing is not an option, soldier. Try again."

Gamefully, the dog did just that, getting even less height this time before he once more hit the floor. With another sad whimper, he sat at Brady's feet, tail tentatively sweeping the floor.

Brady sighed and scooped a hand beneath his little concave belly, lifting him up so that they were eye to eye. "Out of all the trucks in all the land, why mine?"

The dog wriggled joyfully. "Arf."

Brady blinked, then found himself grinning at the unexpected bark. It had been high-pitched and soprano, but hell it was better than a meow. "So you are a dog. You've got to work on the pitch, man. Can't have all the chick dogs thinking your boys never dropped." No need in telling him he probably wouldn't get to keep his boys.

"Arf!"

He'd created a monster. Brady laughed, then started to set the dog down, but he clung to his hand. Shaking his head, Brady set the thing on the couch next to him, where he immediately crawled into his lap.

Brady stared down at him and realized he was shivering. "You're nothing but a bag of bones." Pulling the dog against his chest, they had a little moment, and finally the dog stopped shivering. He licked Brady's chin.

"Listen," Brady said. "This is just temporary. Tomorrow we figure out what the hell Lilah's game is and she'll find you a home. She's good at it."

The dog didn't even blink, but in its chocolately eyes, Brady saw a hint of sadness. "Don't even try the puppy eyes, they don't work on me."

The dog blinked slowly.

Brady pointed at him. "Knock that off."

His answer was a soft whine.

"Look, I'm just passing through, that's it."

Not getting it, the dog set his head against Brady's chest and let out a shuddery sigh.

And Brady did the same. In his life, he'd taken responsibility for more people than he could count, but he'd steered clear of animals, never keeping one for himself. He'd not needed the extra burden. "If I were going to keep a dog," he said, "it would be a big one. Or at least one that could get up on the couch by himself."

He would have sworn censure filled the dog's dark gaze. "Hey, I'm just being honest here. You little things are yappers."

The little guy put his ears down, the picture of innocence.

And Brady had to laugh. "Right. Save it for someone you can manipulate, okay? Maybe the ladies." He thought of Jade and Lilah, both of whom had manipulated the hell out of him. "I deserve this," he muttered.

The dog cocked its head.

"Never mind. I'm so tired I'm talking to a dog." He got up, set the dog on the blanket, and then dropped like a stone onto the bed. He remained tense a moment, waiting, but he heard nothing and slowly relaxed.

Ahhh, sleep. He was halfway to paradise, lying on a warm beach with a beer in one hand and the silky coconut-scented skin of a woman under the other. And yeah, okay, maybe the woman looked a little like Lilah, right down to the mossy green eyes and deliciously curvy body, which was at the moment wearing nothing but the smallest of string bikinis . . .

And that's when he heard it, the one sound that could bring him back from the beach and the sexy woman on it: "Arf!"

Fuck.

"Arf, arf, arf . . ."

The next morning, Brady came awake to a noise he didn't recognize and rolled off the bed, automatically reaching for his weapon.

When he realized he wasn't in combat, was in fact a million miles from any combat zone, he lay back down and scrubbed a hand over his face.

Then the sound came again.

What the hell?

He sat up and found the dog sitting in front of the kitchen sink, head deep in the trash he'd clearly hauled out from its place in the cupboard beneath. He was surrounded by a pizza box, an orange juice container, and two bottles of beer.

All empty.

"You are a menace to society," Brady said, and scrubbed a hand over his face. What had he gotten, maybe half an hour of sleep? Well used to sleep deprivation, he staggered out of bed thinking he might as well get on with what he'd agreed to do here.

Work on the Bell. "No more trash," he told the dog after he'd showered and dressed. "It'll make you sick." And with the little guy happy at his side, clearly not sick at all, they headed downstairs, stopping at Jade's desk. "Anyone come looking for him yet?"

Jade was one of those women who looked like she belonged in *Vogue*. Gorgeous but . . . different. Today she was wearing a sunshine yellow sundress that required sunglasses to look at her straight on. Her hair was piled on top of her head in a haphazard knot, held there by wooden tongue depressors. Her makeup was photo-ready. He nearly looked around to see if he'd stepped onto a movie set. "His name is Twinkles," she said.

He just looked at her.

Not particularly intimidated, her mouth twitched suspiciously.

He narrowed his eyes, and she let a very small smile free. "Lilah did her thing, putting out notices and flyers. We'll let you know."

"It's been two days."

"It has. Dell told me he examined him. He's about a year old, and other than slightly malnourished, he's healthy. Great news."

"Uh-huh. And you're certain Lilah's trying to find the owner," he said.

Jade smiled and patted his hand. "Lilah would never put a dog's well-being at risk for her own amusement."

"But she is amused."

"Oh, honey. There's no doubt."

It took Brady three days just to clean out the Bell 47. Not surprising, considering the chopper had suffered nearly three decades of neglect and abuse. It also needed airframe repairs, battery servicing, and a whole long list of engine and parts maintenance.

He enjoyed the work. In the army, he'd started out as a nobody, but well used to that he'd worked his ass off and through performance had earned a warrant officer slot, which had qualified him for flight training.

He'd never looked back. He loved being in the air, but when he couldn't be, his second love was this, taking apart and reassembling a chopper. As he worked, his new shadow stuck close, alternately snoozing in the sun or watching him with hero worship.

Belle Haven continued to do business around them. Del and Adam ran a tight ship, and it was a busy one. Adam, apparently the resident dog whisperer, was currently in the yard with three golden retrievers and their owners, teaching a class. Even from twenty-five yards away, Brady could tell it was more about training the wayward owners than the dogs.

When class ended, Adam ambled over.

"The dogs are pretty good listeners," Brady said, wiping his hands on a rag.

"It's not the dogs that need to listen."

"This one does." Brady nodded to the dog sleeping his day away in the sole sunspot as close to Brady as he could possibly get.

"What's his problem?" Adam asked.

"He won't sleep."

There was a moment of silence while Adam took in the dog doing just that. Well, not complete silence, since the mutt was snoring like a buzz saw.

"I mean at night," Brady said with a disbelieving shake of his head.

"What does he do instead of sleep?"

"Cries. Barks. Drives me up the fucking wall."

Adam's mouth hinted at a smile. "I'm going to tell you what I tell all of my clients. You're the one in need of training, not him."

"What are you talking about? I'd sleep all night just fine if he'd shut the hell up."

Adam let the smile escape. "Okay, man. Let me know when you're interested in being trained." He crouched and ruffled the dog's fur, and the little guy immediately rolled over on his back, exposing his belly for more.

Brady slid the dog a dark look, at least glad to see that his little belly was rounder now, no longer concave. "Traitor."

With a smirk, Adam rose. "So what's going on with you and Lilah?"

Dell had tried asking him this question days ago. Brady hadn't answered. Not because he wanted to be an ass, but because he honestly hadn't known. "Other than she saddled me with this thing?"

"Yeah. Other than that."

"Not sure."

"But something," Adam said.

Brady nodded. Yeah. There was definitely . . . something. And holy Christ, that something was explosive whenever they got too close.

"She's important to Dell and me."

"I know." He wondered if Adam was telling him to back the fuck off, and if it mattered. Could he back off? He honestly didn't know.

Adam was quiet a moment, just studying the Bell. "You're important to us, too," he finally said.

Brady let out a breath and nodded, feeling an unexpected tightening in his chest at that. There sure as hell weren't that many people who felt that way about him. He started to say something, he had no idea what really, when a truck pulled into the lot, interrupting him.

A leggy blonde hopped out of the truck wearing a business suit, the skirt as narrow as a pencil, emphasizing mile-long, perfectly toned legs. The high heels added an I'm Sophisticated and Expensive tone.

Turning to her truck, she reached back in and the red suit tightened across a world-class ass, wrenching a sound from Adam.

Brady looked at him but his face was carefully blank. Too blank. "Know her?"

"Yes," Adam said tightly.

The woman straightened and Brady saw that she was carrying a golden retriever puppy. She glanced over, drew herself up at the sight of Adam, then strode toward them, face cool and impassive.

Actually, Adam's expression was impassive. A battle-ready soldier.

The woman's face was set in stone. Angry, cold stone.

Brady figured she was one of those snooty bitches who was wound too tight. And going off the steam coming out of her ears, her hair was also wound too tight.

"Holly," Adam said with no inflection in his voice.

"Adam." There was plenty of inflection in her voice. Mostly temper. "Here." She thrust the puppy into Adam's arms. "She's defective."

Adam looked down at the puppy, who wriggled and licked his nose. A genuine light of affection came into his eyes. "Defective?"

"She's up all night crying."

At that, Brady was forced to rethink his opinion of her. She wasn't bitchy. She was exhausted.

He knew the feeling.

Adam gave Brady a brief look. "He's in a new place, Holly. He's scared." He thrust the puppy back into her arms, where it wriggled some more and licked her, too.

"I suppose you think this is funny," Holly said, attempting to stay lick-free.

"A little bit," Adam said evenly, not showing the smile that was in his voice.

Her mouth tightened. "My father's a domineering, annoying, meddling ass. And you. You're . . ." Breaking off, she shook her head. Turning on her heels, she strode off, long gorgeous legs churning up the distance while her puppy looked back over her shoulder at Adam, head bouncing.

"Big fan of yours?" Brady asked.

Adam didn't rise to the bait. He merely looked at the helicopter and then back into Brady's eyes. "You in for the month or not? I need to know whether to make plans."

"I said I'd do it. Make your plans."

With a nod, Adam was gone.

Brady went back to work for the rest of the day and then spent the night hours once again attempting to get the mutt to sleep.

But the damn dog was not interested in anything but driving Brady to the edge of sanity. At two in the morning, he was over it and reached for his cell phone to call Adam. "Fine," Brady grated to Adam's voice mail. "I'm waving the white flag. I need training."

At three A.M., Adam hadn't called back, and desperate, Brady tried Lilah, feeling completely justified at the late hour since she was the one who'd foisted the damn mutt on him in the first place. If he had to be up, she should, too.

He got her voice mail as well. "Come get him or I'm shipping him to Afghanistan," he said, and tossed his cell phone aside to flop to his back on the bed, listening to the damn dog cry.

Thing was, Brady was used to going on little sleep. He'd been trained for sleep deprivation in the military. But this wasn't an enemy thing. Hell, this wasn't even a logical thing.

It was one damn little dog getting the best of him. He'd tried everything short of strangling him, and finally somewhere near dawn, the mutt finally crashed. A grateful Brady fell into one of those dead slumbers that nothing short of a worldwide catastrophe could rise him from.

And yet he came suddenly awake what felt like a minute later to the sun poking him in the eyeballs. Sprawled facedown and spread-eagle on the bed, he cracked open one eye and blinked blearily at the clock.

Seven thirty.

Since the last time the dog had woken him up had been seven, he'd had exactly thirty minutes of sleep. "Fucking mutt."

"Aw. Is that any way to talk about your bedmate?"

"Jesus!" He pushed up on his arms and turned his head, his gaze landing on Lilah's. She stood at the foot of his bed in a pair of hip-hugging, ass-snugging jeans, a knit top, and a smile he couldn't quite read but was pretty sure was smug.

Then he realized there was a weight on his lower back, and that it was the dog.

Sleeping.

Brady dislodged it and rolled to his back. Grabbing his pillow, he shoved it behind him to lean back against the headboard.

The dog simply rolled onto its back and kept sleeping. The fucker.

Lilah's eyes were on Brady's bare chest. "Um."

Brady raised a brow and waited for her gaze to meet his.

When it did, she had two spots of color high on her cheeks. "Sorry, my phone was off last night, but I came over as soon as I got your message. Wanted to see if you were still alive."

Which he most definitely was. Alive. Very . . . alive. Some parts more than others.

Her gaze jerked back up to his eyes. "I thought you'd be . . . up."

They both knew just how *up* he was. "It was a rough night." He jabbed a finger in the direction of the dog, who was slowly coming awake and blinking innocently. "That thing kept me awake all night."

"What did you do to get him to go to sleep?"

"I told him to shut up."

She looked at him like he was an idiot. "Twinkles is a rescue. He needs love and affection."

"Sorry, fresh out of both." He sighed at her look of disappointment. He'd gone years and years, and to his recollection, he'd never once sighed. And yet he'd sighed more in the week he'd known her than he had in his entire life. "I gave him my blanket," he said. "I put a loud clock in that blanket to simulate the sound of a mother's heartbeat. But I'm starting to think he never had a mother, that he came from the devil himself."

"Did you try cuddling with him?"

"Huh?"

"Cuddle," she repeated. "You know, hold him close, snuggle, nestle . . . Like what you'd do if someone was with you in there . . ."

"The only someone allowed in my bed is a woman."

"Pretend he's a woman, then!"

Fascinated by her, he plumped his pillow some more and gave her a go-on gesture with his hand. "No, I don't know. Tell me what I'd do. In great detail."

She blew out a breath. "You're sick."

"Depends on your definition of sick."

"Just hug your dog!"

"Not my dog. The dog you foisted on me. Which begs the question: why?"

"Twinkles. His name is Twinkles," she grated, hands on hips now. "Not 'the dog' or 'it' or whatever else you've been calling the poor thing."

Probably best she didn't want to know what he'd called it earlier this morning around three thirty A.M.

And again at four thirty.

And five thirty.

"Haven't you ever had a dog?" she asked in exasperation.

"No. And I don't want this one. Fun's over, Lilah. You're taking him back."

She was just studying him speculatively. "Really? You've never had a dog?"

"Never."

She looked surprised for a beat, and then her expression softened. "So you don't know."

"Don't know what?"

"What having a pet can add to your life."

"Pain and suffering?"

She slanted him a pitying look and crossed her arms, which plumped up her breasts. "Unconditional love."

"Lilah, I travel all the time. I don't have time for unconditional love that comes with the responsibility of pet care."

"Or . . . you don't like attachments."

"Attachments are messy," he agreed. *She's chilly*, he thought, watching her nipples press against her white shirt. *Or maybe turned on.*

That made two of them . . .

"And messy can make you feel too much," she said. "Right?"

"Actually, at the moment I'm feeling plenty," he said softly.

Again her gaze flickered downward, past his chest to his lap, where the sheet was pooled. Two high spots of color appeared on her cheeks. I should . . ."

"Go?"

"Yes." She lifted her chin. "Good-bye, Mr. No-Strings."

"Nice."

"Just calling it like I see it."

"Are you casting stones, Ms. Safety?"

Her brow furrowed. "What does that mean?"

"You let all your animals into your heart the same way you do the people."

"I don't—"

"And," he went on. "You do it for keeps. As far as I can tell, your friends have been your friends forever."

"So? That's a good thing."

"You also have two exes, both apparently still in your life."

"It's a small town. And actually, I have three exes, if you must know."

"Fine. Three. My point is that it's a comfort for you, having familiar people around you, and I get that. But I see it as a barrier to trying new things or stretching yourself. You live your life safe, Lilah."

He could tell he was back to pissing her off again. It was a specialty of his.

"Safe," she repeated in disbelief.

"Yeah. When was the last time you left this podunk town and saw the world?"

Something crossed her face at that, but she recovered quickly and narrowed her eyes. "I came to help, not be analyzed. Now do you want my help or not?"

"Yes."

"Okay, then." She scooped the dog off the bed. "This would be a lot better if we moved this to the kitchen. Or outside."

"Fine," he said. "I'll have to get dressed."

Her gaze once again slid to the sheet. "Don't tell me you're naked under there."

"Okay, I won't tell you."

She bit her lower lip as she hugged the dog close. The smart little shit licked her cheek and gave her the big, ol' puppy-dog eyes. "Aw," she murmured, and nuzzled him. "You're so sweet."

The dog craned his neck and sent Brady a knowing grin, the little shit. Brady must have made some sound of annoyance because Lilah turned back to him. “Look, it’s a simple thing to make him feel safe and secure. It’s a simple hug or a kind word. A quick cuddle. I mean, honestly, how hard is that?”

Currently hard enough to pound nails, he thought grimly.

She thrust the dog at him. “Practice while I’m here so I can see your technique.”

“I’d rather practice with you.”

She just looked at him, a tactic she’d learned from him, Goddammit. He snatched the dog then and, dangling him from his hands, brought them nose to nose.

“Not like that!” His sexy-as-hell teacher put a knee on his bed and leaned over him to press the dog to his chest. “Like that.”

Her hair fell forward, dragging like fine silk over his shoulder and arm. Her breath was warm against his jaw as she held his hands on the dog. “Hug him.”

He’d never been one to easily follow a command, even after all those years in the military, but he held the damn dog instead of doing what he wanted, which was to roll Lilah beneath him to show her cuddling. “Maybe we can call it something other than cuddling,” he said.

“What, that threatens your manhood?”

Brady was wearing just a cotton sheet and a boner for the record books, so he was pretty fucking sure he was secure “in his manhood,” but he decided to keep that to himself. More disconcerting, the dog had settled quietly on his chest, looking at him adoringly as his big puppy-dog eyes slowly . . . fluttered . . . shut.

The little shit was going to sleep. “You have got to be kidding me.”

“See?” Lilah said. “It works.”

“Yeah, now that I have to get up. I’m supposed to go running with Adam.”

Their eyes connected, and as if she suddenly realized she’d gotten on his bed and was leaning over him, she hopped up and nearly fell to her ass.

“You okay?”

“I have to go,” she said, whirling toward the door.

“Now who’s chicken,” he murmured.

“I have a lot to do.”

Yeah, he was getting that. Maybe he should have opted for plan B which would have been pulling her down on the bed and cuddling her. They could both be naked by now. Yeah, he liked plan B. A lot.

"You're giving me mixed signals, Lilah."

She dropped her forehead to his door with an audible thunk. "I know! I'm sorry."

"When you settle on a decision, you'll let me know."

"My decision's made. It's courage I'm waiting on."

He didn't like the way that sat in his gut. "I scare you?"

Forehead still to the door, she let out a short laugh. "No. I scare me. And I should be scaring the hell out of you." She turned to him. "I'll tell Adam that you're coming—" She broke off and grimaced. "I mean that you're getting up—" She closed her eyes, her cheeks going pink.

Grinning, he set the sleeping dog next to him. When he made to toss back the covers to get out of bed, she squeaked and left, slamming his door.

He laughed—until he realized she hadn't taken the damn dog. By the time he got downstairs she was gone, and stayed gone. Which, he told himself several times throughout the following hours, was probably a good thing. A month was plenty of time for him, but he thought he knew her now, or at least he was starting to know her. And she gathered people in and kept them, not walking away after four weeks. Ever.

Yeah, she was the exact opposite from him in that respect, but he was drawn to her all the same, just as he was drawn to this small town. A novelty. A diversion. It would wear off, all of it.

Any minute now.

That night Brady stood in front of his bed staring down at the dog.

In return, the dog looked at the ceiling. At the floor. Anywhere but at Brady.

Finally Brady picked him up and dangled him nose to nose. "Here we are again. Bedtime."

The dog tried to lick him, but he wasn't holding it close enough. "And don't start with the eyes. We're going to sleep. Do you really need to"—*Jesus*—"cuddle?"

"Arf."

With a long-suffering sigh, Brady held him close and let himself be licked half to death. "There," he said, and carefully set the dog down on the blanket between the fireplace and the bed. "Stay. Sleep." Brady paused to inhale the delicious silence before getting into bed with a heartfelt groan. He was exhausted.

Three minutes later the whining started. "Christ on a stick!" He sat up, shoved his fingers through his hair and dropped his head to his knees. "I'm begging you. Shut up."

That didn't work either.

Throwing back the sheet, Brady dropped to the floor and the very nice pad of blankets he'd carefully folded, littered with stolen treasures. A shoe, a watch, a shirt—all Brady's.

The dog was a thief.

"We cuddled already. Don't tell me you need more. Come on, man, where's your self-respect?"

"Arf."

Shit. Brady crouched low and pulled the dog into his chest. The bundle wriggled with pleasure. Brady sighed, and beyond exhausted now, slowly lowered himself to the blankets.

Not bad.

"Arf!"

In the darkness, on the floor, Brady squeezed his eyes shut and tried to pretend he was back in Afghanistan, in the middle of a war zone, which was starting to seem like it might be easier.

"Arf!"

"I've been to places that look at you as a free meal," he warned softly in the dark. "Not my thing personally, but I'm willing to make an exception."

There wasn't another sound.

With a blissful, exhausted sigh, Brady began to drift off.

Only to come awake some time later. He lay there utterly still in the dark night, aware of the fact that something had woken him but not sure what. He was still on the floor, but there was no warm lump on his chest. Sitting up without a sound, he found the dog—in the middle of the fucking bed. How he'd gotten up there was a mystery, possibly by using the chest at the foot of the bed as a stepping stool.

But that's not what had woken him. Pulling on his jeans, Brady grabbed the gun he'd stowed in the nightstand, moving soundlessly through the loft.

Then he heard it again, a crash from downstairs in the center that was completely closed up for the night. Thinking of the drugs that were kept there, he headed grimly toward the door, intending to protect what was Dell and Adam's with whatever force was necessary. He turned to tell the dog to stay, but he hadn't so much as taken a break in his snoring. Shaking his head, Brady moved out.

Downstairs, the open reception area was dark and empty, but the first examination room was lit, and sounds of a struggle were coming from within. Moving quietly along the shadows of the wall, Brady stepped into the open doorway, gun drawn.

"Don't move," he said.

But he was the one to go still.

In the room, arms full with an injured dog on the examination table, was Lilah.

The dog was snarling and trying to bite her, and as she wrestled with him, she spared Brady a quick glance.

"How's this for too safe?" she asked.

Eight

Lilah took in the sight of Brady, gun in his right hand, the safety flipped off, and his hands braced in a shooter's stance and thought, *Holy shit*. That was her sole thought. *Holy shit*. She might have even murmured it in shock, in sheer appreciation for the magnificent male form standing there so utterly completely, fantastically . . . dangerous. She couldn't help it. In the overhead light, his nearly naked body gleamed muscular, lethal, and entirely too sexy. "You going to shoot me or help me?" she asked, as if her heart wasn't lodged in her throat, thundering so fast there were no pauses in between the beats.

"Fuck," he whispered under his breath and lowered the gun, thumbing the safety back on. The sound of it clicked loudly in the very still, very tense air as he tucked the gun into the back of his jeans before stepping close to lend her a hand.

Lilah let out a breath and shook it off. He seemed impossibly large and unyielding as he reached up and adjusted the overhead light so she could better see what she was doing, which she appreciated. "Thanks."

He nodded, looking a little worn, a little weary, and a whole lot rough around the edges.

When he was tired, as he clearly was now, his features were wary, as if he knew he was on autopilot and simply trusting his instincts. It did something to her, looking at him like this, almost . . . no. Vulnerable was not the right word.

Accessible.

"I'm sorry," she said quietly. "I should have let you know I was here."

He said nothing. Probably still working through his adrenaline rush.

She sure as hell was. And it was to her shame that she hadn't thought of this. Of him. She should have thought about the fact that he'd be upstairs sleeping, but the truth was that she broke in all the time with Dell's and Adam's blessing, and it hadn't occurred to her to wonder what his mental condition might be at being stirred in the middle of the night. He was ex-military but clearly not so ex. He certainly hadn't lost any of his skills.

Startling him had been bad.

He recovered far faster than she, but then again, she had her hands full. And still, all she could think was that she surely looked like crap in her baggy sweats, and he looked . . .

Hot.

God, so very very hot.

Tearing her gaze off him, she put her mind to the task at hand. She had Lucky's head tucked beneath her arm and was struggling with holding the rest of the seventy-pound animal still. She hadn't wanted to muzzle her and didn't, but now, it seemed, that might have been a mistake.

Lucky was in Lilah's care for two days while her owner was on a business trip. As had happened twice before, a porcupine had broken into the kennels through the cellar, come up the stairs to the main level, and ended up in the room where Lucky had been crated for the night. Lucky had played Houdini and gotten out, and dog and porcupine had done the tango.

Now Lucky was sporting ten quills, Lilah was up in the middle of the night playing doctor, and she'd nearly gotten shot by the sexiest, most gorgeous night prowler she'd ever seen.

Those loose Levi's of his were threatening to slip down his lean hips, and the lack of shirt was deeply distracting. Smooth tanned skin sliding over muscle, perfectly flat, ridged abs building up to a powerful triangle of chest, shoulders, and arms. His eyes, so sharp when he'd first appeared, were going back to a sleepy look. His hair was mussed as if he'd been tossing and turning. Then he made it worse by shoving his fingers through the silky strands, and when he was done with that, he came close and took over the task of holding Lucky down for her with strong, firm hands and arms.

And sweet baby Jesus, those arms. That whole body. It was completely functional, nothing wasted, no excess, and she couldn't look away from it. It was enough to make her walk into a wall if she'd been stupid enough to attempt walking and looking at him at the same time. "You going to say anything?" she finally asked.

He slid her a long look. "I was finally sleeping."

She laughed and he brooded. "It's not funny. You have me living with the devil's spawn. So nothing personal, but what can I do to help you here so you'll get the hell out?"

"Just holding her like that is great. I'm having a tough time here."

"You would have managed. You're good with animals."

"Yes," she agreed, thinking she'd rather be good with men right about now. In particular, a big, badass, silent, edgy, dangerous man who carried a gun in the waistband of his jeans and had a body so cut it made her want to run her tongue over every indention and then some. "And you're good with . . . well, just about everything," she said. "Well, except cuddling."

He flashed her a look that was so innately male, as if she'd just questioned his Guy Card or something. It should have been annoying, but instead it made her nipples contract in greedy anticipation. She busied herself with parting Lucky's fur to get a better look at the first quill.

Brady grabbed the spotlight above the table and better aimed it for her as she poured vinegar over Lucky's punctured skin. Lucky whined and Lilah did her best to soothe her before glancing at Brady. "Thanks," she said gratefully.

He leaned close to see what she was doing, and that's when she realized he smelled amazing.

Warm and sexy and . . . amazing.

Lucky was growling low in her throat, showing her teeth, worrying Lilah. The dog was older, around nine, and usually sweeter than molasses, which is where Lilah's decision not to muzzle her had come in. A mistake.

Brady came in from behind Lucky's sharp teeth and clasped the dog's head in his big hands, holding her still. "Why the vinegar?"

"It loosens up the quills. It's why I broke in to do this here. I couldn't find any white vinegar at home." Leaning over Lucky, Lilah snipped the first quill at about the halfway mark.

The dog whined and Brady stroked her face in sympathy. "You're cutting them to let out some of the air," he guessed.

"Yes." She forced her attention back to Lucky, using pliers to get a good grip on the quill as close to the dog's flesh as possible, and pulled.

The quill slid out.

Lucky cried.

Still stroking the trembling dog, Brady bent low to murmur to her softly.

"Another talent of yours?" she asked. "Soothing the scared female?"

He smiled, and she had the most ridiculous urge to pretend to be terrified so he'd hold her and murmur in that voice and hold her close, too. And maybe do other things . . . "You do this a lot on your travels?"

Brady's eyes were still amused, suggesting maybe he knew where her thoughts had gone. "Assist a sexy woman in the middle of the night with a dog? Almost never." He shifted, turning so he could more comfortably hold Lucky for her, and Lilah went very still.

Brady's back was broad and smooth and gorgeous . . . except for his side, where a long, jagged scar ran from his armpit down to his ribs. It was a few shades lighter than his normal skin tone, signaling that it was at least a few years old. There were other scars as well, but nothing as major as that one long imperfection.

Lifting his head, his gaze met hers without hesitation or resignation.

Her fingers itched to touch it, to soothe him, which would be a little bit like trying to soothe a wild, untamed mountain cat. "What happened?" she asked as casually as she could, pouring vinegar over the next quill, then snipping it with scissors as she had the first.

He remained quiet and she figured he had no intention of answering. "I suppose," she finally said, "it's one of those you-could-tell-me-but-you'd-have-to-kill-me things, right?"

His mouth quirked but he held his silence. He was good at that.

"I heard you spent some time in Afghanistan," she said softly, working out the next quill.

"I flew medical choppers."

"And in Iraq?"

"Same thing. I was good at the hot spots."

She poured the vinegar and then snipped the quill halfway as she thought about Brady out there on the front line, right in the thick of things, bringing people in and out on a daily basis, constantly in more danger than she could possibly imagine. "Does it still hurt?" she asked as she pulled out the quill.

"No."

"How—"

"A machete." His voice was easy enough, but she heard the steel undertone—he was done talking about this.

She could understand that. "I'm guessing you've seen parts of the world that would seem like another planet to me compared to this place," she said softly after yet another quiet moment.

He let out a low sound of agreement.

"You must think I'm pretty naïve and sheltered."

"No."

"But you do think I live safe."

He didn't answer, and lifting her gaze, she met his, which was sharp yet warm. It seemed impossible that he could be both, but he was.

Just outside the exam room door, the rest of the center was dark, filled with shadows. Not in the exam room, which felt . . . close. Intimate.

"You're right," she said. "I do live safe. I grew up in this one-horse town with my grandma and good friends, and it's always been a comfortable fit for me. And very safe."

"It suits you."

"It didn't always," she said wryly. "By the time I graduated high school, I was chomping at the bit to get out of town and find the real world."

He smiled, interested. "So did you?"

"I went to UNLV. University of Las Vegas."

He choked out a laugh. "About as different from here as you could get."

"You could say so," she agreed, and yet again wielded the pliers on poor Lucky. "I was a little out of my element." Like a babe in the woods. Which had been the whole point.

"Is this the part where you tell me you made your tuition by becoming a stripper?" he asked hopefully.

"No," she said on a laugh.

"A showgirl?"

"No!"

He looked her over. "I know. You became a phone sex operator."

"Stop." She rolled her shoulders, the smile fading because the truth was worse.

His expression turned serious. Reaching up, he stroked a loose strand of hair off her jaw. "Something happened to you."

There was concern in his eyes, and a protectiveness that shouldn't mean anything to her.

But it did. "No. Not like you're thinking. It's really just a very boring old story."

"You're in luck, then. I love boring old stories."

"No you don't," she said on a laugh. "You hardly talk at all unless I'm bugging the hell out of you with questions."

"True," he said stroking poor Lucky to keep her calm. "But I like to listen to you."

Her heart tumbled and she sighed, again moved by him when she shouldn't be. She supposed she could tell him a little more. "I got accepted on a scholarship into the animal science program."

"To become a vet?"

"I wasn't sure. Mostly I just wanted out to see what I was missing. Nobody wanted me to go to Vegas. They all wanted me to go to Idaho State, so of course I did the opposite."

"And hit the city of big lights."

"Yeah, I followed the scholarship, I really had no choice—I needed the money." She hadn't been able to keep it, unfortunately. Among other things, her grandma had gotten sick, and she'd ended up coming back and forth too much. Her grades had slipped and she lost her scholarship.

Okay, so it hadn't all been because of her grandma's failing health, but that part of the story wasn't in the short version, nor was it up to be shared. "Vegas was a culture shock," she allowed, and smiled a little at herself, at the good memories she could summon. "But for a time, I loved it." At least at first. "My roommate was a local girl, and she was determined to help me experience everything I'd missed by growing up in a small ranch town."

Lilah had been extremely determined to get out and live. Never look back.

Well, okay she'd planned to look back a little. After all, there were her friends here, and her grandma, but in those years, she'd been an idealist, thinking her grandma—and everything else here—would remain the same, locked in time, safe in the capsule that was Sunshine.

Which hadn't happened.

"I was going to make something of myself," she said, adjusting the overhead light to the other side of Lucky's nose and continued to work.

"I was going to be the first Young in my entire family to get a college degree and do something with my life."

Which she'd pretty much blown on all counts.

"So what happened?" he asked quietly when she stopped talking.

She shrugged.

Cocking his head, he studied her for a long moment. "You're leaving out the juicy stuff."

Yes. Yes, she was. On purpose, because she was pretty sure she couldn't tell the story without losing it and she wasn't ready for that. There were quills to remove. "Maybe it's your turn to tell me juicy stuff. Why did you come to Sunshine?"

He didn't say anything to that. Shock.

"Oh come on, that's easy enough."

"You already know why I came," he said.

"Because Dell badgered you. Yeah, yeah. But you don't seem like the kind of guy to be . . . badger-able."

His eyes slid her way. "You think there's some deep, dark reason?"

She didn't know what she thought—he was an enigma. And also, sin on a stick. "You owe me a secret," she reminded him.

That got her nothing but a little smile.

"Come on," she said. "There's got to be something you can tell me."

Apparently not.

"You and the guys grew up rough," she said. "I know that much. Then you went in the army, which was obviously a different kind of rough altogether, and now you roam at will because you never learned to settle down in one spot."

Annoyance flickered across his features. "Adam and Dell can't keep their mouths shut."

"I think it's more that they don't see us as a good fit."

"They're right," he said.

"They have no idea. And I'm not looking for a damn ring, Brady. Any more than you're looking to give one."

He studied her. "What are you looking for?"

She shrugged. "A fun and easy relationship with someone who gets me," she said without hesitation.

He took the vinegar and poured it over the last quill.

She cut the quill close to the skin and pulled it out while he soothed

Lucky, calming her with his quiet voice, assuring her that her trial was over and she'd been very brave. When the dog settled, Brady lifted his head. "I'm a short-term bet at best."

"Maybe I wasn't considering you for my fun, easy relationship. I mean, let's face it, you're not exactly easy."

He laughed softly, wryly. "Yeah." He met her gaze. "But we both know that there's no one else here in town right for you."

Her breath caught. He did want her. "No?"

"No." He put Lucky down, where she immediately twisted into a pretzel to try to inspect the damage.

Lilah was resisting the urge to check for damage as well, within herself. That he'd so accurately read her was startling. "I am content," she told him. "At least for the most part. I like my life, quiet and simple as it is. I like being anchored." She met his gaze. "Maybe you can't understand that because you've never done the anchor thing."

"Sunshine is really your anchor?"

"The people in it, yes. My grandma. She raised me. She died two years ago after a cancer battle, but until then we were a unit." Her voice had gone a little husky. That whole awful time in her life—losing her grandma, her college funding, and then Tyler—was still very hard to talk about. "Dell and Adam are my unit," she said. "My friend and business partner, Cruz, is in that unit."

"Everyone you know is in your unit." He flashed a small smile. "It's who you are. What happened to your parents?"

"My mom lives in France with her boyfriend." Squatting low, she rubbed Lucky. "She didn't take much to motherhood."

"And your dad?"

"Not around." She knew her voice was flat when it came to her father, but he deserved no less. He'd walked away before her mother had.

"So let me see if I get this right," he said. "For the most part, people stay in your life until they leave or die?"

She stared up at him, not sure she liked the fact that he'd analyzed her so accurately. "Yes." Was there any other way? And why did he make it sound like it was so unfathomable? "What about you?"

"Until coming here, I was the only one in my life." He shrugged. "Easier that way."

"Talk about safe."

He choked out a laugh. "You think my life is safe?"

"Maybe not physically, no. But emotionally? Yes. Yes, I do." She paused, watching him touch a finger to his own palm and wince. Rising, she took his hand between hers. "You got poked by a quill."

"It's okay."

"No, but it will be." With no idea what was coming over her, she pressed her lips to the rough calluses of his palm. *Take that, too safe life.*

He went very still. "What was that for?"

"To make it better." She lifted her head, closed the space between them and kissed one corner of his mouth.

"And that?" he asked, his voice lower now, and husky.

"Same." She kissed the other side of his mouth. "Is it working?"

"Getting there." He slid his arms around her, hauled her in tight against him and took over, kissing her long and wet and deep, and by the time he lifted his head, she was shaken to the core.

"And now?" she managed.

"Much better." He was reaching for her again just as a thump sounded above them.

"What was that?" she asked.

He was already moving up the stairs. "Stay here."

She and Lucky followed him, so close on his heels that she nearly plowed into the back of him when he stopped short in the center of the loft. Her hands slid up his back for balance, encountering warm skin, smooth, sleek muscle.

"Shit," Brady said.

"I'm sorry, I—" She yanked her fingers back, but he shook his head. "The damn dog."

Peering around his broad shoulder, she caught sight of Twinkles devouring the trash and having a good old time while he was at it.

At Lilah's feet, Lucky whined. She wanted some trash, too.

"He's already eaten more than his own weight today," Brady said in disgust. "Nice job on the staying put thing, by the way."

"Me or him?" she asked.

"Both."

Lilah ignored the bad temper in his voice and went to her knees to hug Twinkles close. "Oh, you are one very bad little boy."

"Yes, and you can spank me later," Brady grumbled. "When are you going to admit you've had your fun and take him to the kennels?"

"Aw. A big, tough guy like you, afraid of one teeny tiny dog." She set Twinkles on the blanket on the floor, which he'd clearly been using as a bed. Lucky joined him. They sniffed each other's hind ends and settled together.

"That's not one teeny-tiny dog," Brady said, staring at Twinkles. "That's the devil in disguise. And besides, I'm way more afraid of you."

She smiled. "You are not."

"Terrified. You'd better hold me."

She burst out laughing at that, and gave him a shove instead, her hands against his hard chest.

Damn, he felt good.

He shook his head when she continued to grin at him. She couldn't help it, she couldn't stop.

"What?" he asked.

"Nothing."

He shook his head. "With you, Lilah, it's always something."

Yeah, actually. It was. "You were right before. I'm restless and no one else in town is able to help me."

"No?"

"No." Stepping into him, she kissed him. She kissed him like she meant business, and by the time she pulled back, neither of them were breathing so steadily. "I hope you're ready for this," she said, because she'd consulted with the part of her brain in charge of making rash and stupid decisions, and it had been unanimous.

"Lilah—"

"Shh," she said. "Don't be afraid. I'll be gentle."

Nine

Brady didn't say anything, but his eyes were aroused and darkened with something else as well. He took Twinkles from Lilah's arms and set him on his blanket in front of the fireplace. He snapped his fingers and Lucky joined Twinkles, the two of them sitting perfectly still and at rest, ready for their next order.

"You're good," she said, and turned to the bed, where if the tossed bedding was any indication, Brady had been restlessly sleeping, if at all.

"And you're drowning in these sweats," he said, coming up behind her. "You must be hot."

Yes. Yes, she was.

Hot.

God, so hot.

She'd been sleeping in just a lacy tank and matching panties, but when Lucky had gotten hurt, she'd thrown on an old pair of sweats, both the top and bottoms several sizes too big. Obviously she hadn't planned on a seduction, but that's exactly what she wanted. A seduction. A night filled with passion and desire.

Brady was the man for the job, she knew it. He made her yearn and burn, he made her want. And then there was the added bonus of each of them knowing exactly what this was, and what it wasn't. When the expiration date was up and he left Sunshine, she'd watch him walk away with a smile on her face.

"I want you," he said, and stroked a finger over her shoulder, evoking a shiver. "I usually put what I need ahead of what I want, but with you the line blurs." He slipped an arm around her waist, dipping his head to press his mouth against her jaw.

She had to clear her throat to speak. "I want you, too." And needed him. Lord, how she needed him.

He ran his talented mouth up the side of her neck. His hand was low on her belly, the very tips of his fingers playing just beneath the elastic of the sweats, gliding lightly back and forth on her bare skin. "Be sure. This is unlike you, and a bad idea to boot."

"It feels like a great idea," she managed.

A low laugh escaped him, disturbing the hair at her temple.

"Christ, Lilah." His other hand pushed her hair out of his way and then his mouth was on the nape of her neck, his teeth scraping over her, making her shiver. "Tell me no."

"Yes." She clutched the arm bracing her against him, already halfway to the "great" part of "great idea." She could feel the heat of him, the strength, and it aroused her, making her shiver.

"Are you cold?" he asked against her skin.

"No. Hot." She wanted—needed—his hand to move, either north or south.

Preferably south.

"Please," she finally whispered, only to break off with a moan when his fingers trailed up her belly, along the zipper of the sweatshirt and then back, the rasp of metal on metal filling the room as he slid the zipper down. "This needs to go," he said, and urged it off her shoulders.

The camisole beneath was white silk, a little sheer, and barely contained her breasts, which were spilling out over the top.

From over her shoulder, Brady took in the sight and groaned. His hand skimmed up her belly again, his thumb tracing the heavy underside of a breast for a moment before he nudged the spaghetti straps to her elbows, pressing his mouth to her shoulder. "Pretty," he said in a voice gone so low in timbre as to be almost inaudible.

"My underwear matches."

With a rough growl, he nipped at her shoulder and palmed her breast, grinding his erection into her bottom.

Lost in pleasure, her eyes drifted shut and she let her head fall back to his chest. "I've pictured this with you. Hope you live up to the fantasy," she teased, then practically purred when his thumb rasped over her hardened nipple.

"You let me know." He turned her to face him and she slid her hands up his chest and over his scruffy jaw, feeling the roughness beneath her fingertips. It was arousing and intimate.

His eyes were dark and heated and on her. Unwavering. Fierce. Protective.

He was beautiful. Everything about him was beautiful. "It's been a long time for me," she admitted. "But I'm pretty sure I remember what comes next." She played with the top button on his Levi's, the backs of her fingers brushing against the smooth, taut skin of his abs, which were washboard ridged and hard.

"Lilah." His fingers speared into her hair, holding her head in his big palms as he searched her gaze for God knew what. "How long is a long time?"

"Long. But I hear it's just like getting on a bike."

"Yeah," he said, his words hot along her skin as his lips grazed her earlobe. "It's just like getting on a bike." He untied her sweat bottoms, causing a rush of heat to slide south.

As did her sweats.

They slid south right off her hips and onto the floor.

He took in the white boy-cut panties that indeed matched the cami and palmed her ass, which increased her heart rate and made her already hardened nipples tighten even further. "What comes next, Lilah?"

That slowed her down a second. "You mean . . . you don't know?"

His soft chuckle raised goose bumps on her skin. "This is your show. You call the shots."

The thought of doing just that, in effect bossing this big, tough edgy man around in bed gave her a rush only a millimeter below an orgasm. She pulled back enough to look into his eyes to make sure he wasn't just teasing. "Really? I'm in charge?"

His smile was slow and sure, and so hot she'd have sworn it singed the hair right off her skin. Yeah. She was in charge if that's what she wanted. "You shouldn't give someone that much power," she whispered. "What if I take advantage?"

He slid a muscled thigh between hers. "You going to take advantage of me, Lilah?"

His tone suggested that would be okay with him, very okay. His hands were on the wall on either side of her head, his body pressed tight to hers.

And he was hard. Everywhere. "Yes," she decided. "I'm going to take advantage of you."

"Just remember," he said hotly against her ear. "It's my turn next, and turnabout is fair play."

Oh boy. "M-maybe we should start easy."

He laughed softly and kissed her with such gentleness that her heart quivered. "Easy works. Tell me what you want."

"I'd rather show than tell." She let her cami slip to her hips.

"Mmm." Dipping his head, he ran his tongue across her nipple. "Show is nice. But I really like tell. Tell me what's next, Lilah."

"Fewer clothes—God," she burst out when he sucked her into his mouth, "don't stop."

His hand pushed her cami down, and her panties with it, then slid between her legs. "Don't stop what?"

She fisted her hands in his hair and pulled his mouth back to hers. "Don't stop kissing me."

"Where? Where do you want me to kiss you, Lilah?"

She shivered at the thought of where she wanted his mouth, but he pulled free to look at her, waiting for her answer. "Everywhere," she managed.

"Should I use my tongue?"

"Yes." Her eyes closed as his fingers stroked her wet flesh. Tipping her head back, she cried out and arched into him when he slid a finger into her. It was all she could do to remain standing. "I'm—"

"Hot," he said, his thumb softly outlining her wet folds. "Hot, and very, very wet." His lips were moving against her breast, and when he sucked on her nipple, holding it between his tongue and the roof of his mouth, her hips ground helplessly against him.

"Easy," he reminded her, pulling back to blow on her nipple.

A shiver wracked her. And she couldn't catch her breath. It felt like her blood had turned to liquid fire in her veins, and all she could think about was touching him, wrapping her fingers around him and making him as crazy as he was making her. She reached for the remaining buttons on his Levi's, feeling his abs clench as she ripped open the jeans.

He was commando, and . . . big.

Lifting her head, she looked into his eyes, which were dilated and darkened, burning with desire.

"Are we stopping?" he asked.

"No." She bit her lower lip. "But it's not exactly like getting back on a bike."

"It's better."

She let out a breath. "I was really hoping you'd say that." She shoved the jeans down his legs.

Hauling her back upright, he kissed her hard and deep. They kicked their fallen clothes away while his mouth continued to claim her, rough and wild and erotic.

"Inside me," she whispered. "Oh please. Please, get inside me." She backed him to the bed and shoved him onto it. He arched his brow, but stretched out on his back.

Gloriously naked.

Gloriously aroused.

"Come here," he said, and gave her a finger crook.

Forgetting that she was supposed to be the one with the orders, she crawled up the bed and straddled him, moaning in delight at the feel of him beneath her, at the way his hands slid over her hips, cupping her ass, grinding her against him.

"Do I need a condom?" he asked, and she went still, her mouth falling open.

How could she have so thoughtfully lost herself as to forget birth control?

A wry smile touched his mouth. "You don't have one?"

"No! Don't you?"

"No."

With a half laugh, half sob, she collapsed over him and dropped her head to his shoulder. "I can't believe it."

"I know where there are some stashed, does that count?"

She lifted her head. "What?"

"In the nightstand drawer," he said with a jerk of his head, not taking his hands off her.

Leaning over him, she opened the drawer and found a stack of condoms. Probably Adam's. "That was mean," she told him, sucking in a breath when, hands tightening on her hips, he surged up and ran his tongue over a nipple. When he sucked her into his hot mouth with a strong pull, she decided to forgive him.

He reached for the condom in her fingers and tore it open. She took it back and rolled it slowly down his length, so slowly that he went from cocky and teasing, to swearing roughly, to begging for her to get to it.

She was still smiling smugly about that when she lifted up and slowly let just the tip of him inside her.

But it all backfired on her when the feel of him stretching her was enough to render her a panting idiot. She arched in an attempt to draw him in deeper but he held her firmly in place, his fingers digging into her hips.

"More," she demanded.

"Thought you'd never ask." He rolled her beneath him and pinned her to the mattress beneath his welcome weight, sliding all the way home.

"I thought I was in charge," she managed to say, her hands gliding up the hard muscles of his biceps.

"My turn."

The timbre of his voice when he was aroused was like a caress as he began to move in exactly the right rhythm to drive her out of her mind. Combined with his talented mouth on hers, and a clever callused thumb oh so unerringly stroking her at ground zero, she was a goner, and she burst into orgasm with a startled cry.

"Again," he demanded while she was still trying to put herself back together.

"I know it's your turn and all," she panted. "But you should know . . . I don't take direction as well as you do." He thrust deeper now, harder, pulling back each time until he was just barely inside of her, making her clutch at him. It was torment, it was ecstasy, the feel of his hard body taking her on a ride like she'd never experienced before. "Brady . . ."

"I know." Pushing up to his knees, he dragged her up with him so that she was straddling his lap. The new angle had him touching a spot that she hadn't even known she had, and she arched back, crying out, lost in the sensations, lost in him.

Sliding his hand into her hair, he lifted her to him, staring deeply into her eyes. His mouth came down on hers, hot and demanding, pretty much just like the man himself. His hands were still holding her, completely controlling their movements, which should have been annoying. Instead, it turned her on, big-time. Her breasts were crushed to his chest, her nipples hard and aching, sending bolts of pleasure to her core every time he moved against her. His breath was hot on her neck, his teeth scraping along her throat, his muscles flexing as his hips rolled into hers.

"Open your eyes." His voice caressed her as surely as his work-roughened hands did. "Open your eyes and come with me."

And as he moved within her, she did just that. She opened her eyes, locked them on his, and her world exploded. Gripping her hips, he thrust hard inside her, finding his own long, silent release.

They kissed through the aftermath, rough and deep as they both came down from the high. Then he gentled the connection, softly touching his mouth to hers, moving it along her jaw to her forehead, where he lingered.

They collapsed together into the mattress, Lilah's bones were . . . gone. Just gone. "Okay, that was so much better than getting on a bike," she told him, still trembling.

He pulled her in tighter, holding her close, sharing his body heat, which he had plenty of. His mouth curved into a faint smile as he reached for the quilt as well, pulling it over them.

"I mean holy smokes . . ." she began, her breathing still irregular.

"I wasn't going for holy smokes, I was going for what felt good."

"Well, you nailed both. Can you imagine if there hadn't been a condom?"

"You'd have seen a grown man cry."

She laughed and he kissed her again, then rolled off the bed and vanished into the bathroom.

"So," she said when he came back out, watching his very fine ass as he strode to the pile of their discarded clothing, "you weren't kidding about the cuddle thing."

He pulled on his jeans even though he was still semihard. He managed two buttons and gave up, leaving the pants riding indecently low on his hips. It gave him a dangerous, edgy look to go with the fact that he was clearly ready for another round.

So was she.

She patted the mattress.

His gaze slid slowly over her, and her body reacted like his hands touched her everywhere his eyes traveled.

He walked back to the bed until his knees bumped the mattress. "Again?" he asked, voice thrillingly rough.

"Yes, please." She cupped him gently through the jeans. "Who gets to be in charge this time?"

With a slight smile curving his lips, he shucked the pants and got in bed, his body relaxing into hers. Sprawling over the top of her, he entwined their fingers and lifted their joined hands to either side of her face, kissing her softly. "What am I going to do with you?"

"You've asked that question before."

"Still don't have the answer."

"Neither do I, but I have several ideas."

His soft laugh disturbed the hair at her temple as he pressed his lips there. "I was thinking you might."

Ten

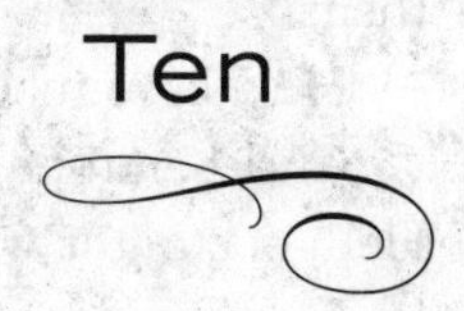

He woke up alone. Lilah had rocked his world once, twice . . . he leaned over the bed to count empty condom wrappers . . . three times, and then she'd . . .

Walked off before dawn.

That was usually his role. "My own fault," he told the mutt, who was sitting on his chest. "I was easy."

"Arf," the dog said in complete agreement, and licked Brady's chin.

"You're one to judge," Brady said in disgust. "If someone even thinks about petting you, you drop and expose your kibble and bits. No soldier worth his salt does that. You're like a damn dog."

"Arf."

"Okay, good point," he said, shaking his head. "You are a dog. And so, apparently, am I." He lay there staring at the ceiling for a moment more, replaying the night before. He'd loved watching Lilah's animated face. As someone who'd forced himself to keep every emotion in check for the better part of his entire life, he found it endlessly fascinating.

He found her endlessly fascinating. He'd not been able to get enough of her, not of her body writhing beneath his, not of her soft sighs, her scent, her taste . . . And then there'd been the way she'd begged him for release when he'd had his mouth between her thighs—

Great. And now he was hard.

Again.

Still.

It was becoming a perpetual problem.

"Arf."

"You're a pain in my ass, you know that?" Brady rolled out of bed, showered, pulled on some clothes, and prowled around in the kitchen.

He'd bought the bare minimum from the grocery store, which included the required frozen breakfast wraps. He tossed three on a plate and nuked them.

He'd have made a few for Lilah, too, except, oh yeah, she'd left.

Christ and she'd been right to do so. One night, that's all she'd wanted. Hell, one night was all he wanted as well.

So why wasn't he still grinning like a guy who'd gotten his rocks off three times?

Because he was brooding about her doing to him what he'd done to women his whole life. Which settled it. He really needed to have his head examined. A beautiful, passionate woman had had her merry way with him—and vice versa—and she'd left before dawn rather than face the awkward morning after, and he was bitching about it. "I need mental help."

"Arf."

"No comments from the peanut gallery."

The dog eyed Brady's plate and licked his chops, making Brady laugh. In the military, there'd been two kinds of people—the quick and the hungry. Brady had been the quick. "No. It's bad for you."

Although the thing did appear to have a stomach of iron. Brady ate for a minute while the dog watched him, tail thumping hopefully on the floor every time Brady looked at him. "What is it with all of you here in Sunshine anyway? You're all eternal optimists."

Another whine, and with a shake of his head, Brady shared half a Hot Pocket. "Fucking softie," he muttered to himself. "Let's go."

Grabbing his camera and the leash, they walked. The meadow between Belle Haven and Lilah's place was lined with stands of cedar, tamarack, and fir and had been calling to him for days. The dog darted around the tree trunks, eyes bright, barking happily at absolutely everything as Brady took pictures.

It was one of those glorious mornings that made him grateful to be alive, the sky such a pure blue it almost hurt to look at it, a single cotton puff of a cloud floating lazily by. The night had been chilly, but the sun made its lazy appearance, and steam rose off the rocks and treetops. The bear grass was in bloom, each plant producing a cluster of creamy white tufts atop a stalk. The stalks were as tall as five feet, but even at that impressive height they were not sturdy enough to stand tall to the breeze.

And certainly not sturdy enough to stand up to the dog, who bounded with sheer exuberance through them to get to the lake. The water was a sheet of glass, a shade of blue beyond description. It was spring fed and loaded with native trout. Yesterday morning he'd seen a bighorn sheep and a mountain lamb grazing at the edge, but all was quiet this morning—no doubt in thanks to the mutt sniffing and pouncing on anything that moved, including his own tail.

"You're going to be bear bait if you don't cool it," Brady warned him.

But the dog's joy of the morning couldn't be contained, and Brady found himself smiling when the mutt accidentally roused a pissed-off possum and came hightailing it back, eyes wide with terror as he hid behind Brady's legs.

Pulling the camera away from his face, Brady eyed the silly dog and shook his head. "That was all you, soldier. Don't write checks your ass can't cash."

After recovering, the dog headed back to the lake's edge and drank.

"That water's tainted," Brady said. "Now you're going to fall in love with the first girl to give you a sweet smile and some tail."

Totally unconcerned, the dog panted happily.

"It's true. She's going to crook her little paw at you and you're going to roll over and expose that belly."

When he said roll over, the dog plopped to the ground and rolled over.

Brady stared at him. "Let me get this straight. You can't stop barking to save your own life, but you can roll over?"

"Who'd believe that I've found Brady Miller, ex–army ranger and all around badass, talking to a dog . . ."

Brady had already heard the footsteps coming up behind him and placed them as Adam's, so he hadn't turned. Rule number one in survival—always know who's coming up behind you.

"It's the first sign that you're becoming human, you know," Adam said, coming up alongside him. "Talking to your dog."

Brady lowered the camera and squatted to rub said dog's belly. "You think I'm not human?"

"I think you think you're not." Adam hunkered down too and looked at the dog with a smirk. "He's got you trained, I see."

Brady shrugged. Useless to try to deny the truth.

"Lilah told me she broke into the center last night."

Brady was used to the quick subject change when it came to Adam. Adam didn't waste words. "She did."

"You see her?"

Actually, Brady had seen a whole hell of a lot of her, but he kept that little tidbit to himself. He could hold his own against Adam and had, but he was feeling mellow and didn't want to go there. "Yeah, I saw her."

Adam looked at him for a long moment. He couldn't have any idea that Brady had slept with Lilah, not unless Lilah had told him, which Brady highly doubted. They were tight, united by this place that was home to them like no other. They'd grown roots.

Brady wouldn't know a damn root if it wrapped itself around his ankle and tugged, and they all knew it. He waited for Adam to warn him off Lilah, but he didn't.

"How's the Bell coming?" Adam asked instead.

"It's nearly there. You ready to be rid of me?"

"You said you'd stick around for a month. You've got more than half of that left. I'm looking to book some air time."

"Give me another week. You'll have your helicopter." As for his promise to stick for a month, he'd already said he would and he never broke his word. He turned to look into the woods, because someone was coming. Maybe a mob of someones given the noise.

Both he and Adam watched as Lilah came into view a minute later with about ten leashes and a dog on each of them. She was wearing short shorts, a snug T-shirt, those hard-on-inducing work boots, and a look on her face that rendered Brady stupid as she came to a stop right before him.

"You look amazing," he murmured before his mouth could reconnect to his brain.

She smiled the smile of a woman who'd had more than a few orgasms the night before. "So do you."

"Hello," Adam said, irritated. "I'm standing right here."

"You look amazing, too," Brady said, not taking his eyes off Lilah.

"Fuck." Adam shoved his hands in his pockets. "This is just fucking awkward."

"Then maybe we could have a minute?" Lilah asked him.

Adam looked pained. "Christ. Okay."

Her low laugh filled the morning air. "I meant with Brady."

"Fuck," Adam said again, clearly not liking Lilah's response, and with a long, level look at Brady, he strode off.

Brady watched his dog sniff at the asses of all the other dogs. And Jesus, when the hell had he started to think of the dog as his? "Last night," he started, and then ended up trailing off because he didn't know what to say.

She was just looking at him, smiling sweetly. Glowing.

He took that in and thought that she was the most beautiful thing he'd ever seen. "Should we talk about it?"

"Why?"

He scratched his head, and she laughed. "Aw, look at you," she said very gently. "Fine. If you need to talk about it, by all means go ahead."

"I—" He shook his head, baffled. "But you asked Adam to leave."

"Maybe I wanted to kiss you hello in private." She went up on tiptoe and did just that, with all the dogs entangled around their legs, kissing him until they were both breathless. Brady felt dizzy from the lack of blood in his head, combined with the unusual emotion called concern. He hoped to God she remembered he was temporary. "Lilah—"

"It's okay, Brady." She secured all the leashes in one hand and patted him on the arm like he was one of the dogs at her feet. "Don't worry. I'm not going to ask you to go steady." She kissed his jaw this time. "I meant what I said," she whispered against him. "I always do. This is light and easy, remember? You're in the clear, so you can breathe now."

Shit. She was right, he wasn't breathing. He drew in some air. "You really are different, you know that?"

"Uh-huh." She flashed a smile so contagious that he found himself giving her one of his own. "You seemed to like those differences last night," she said, still grinning.

He had. Christ, he so had.

"And besides, we're not really all that different. Although I think I'm a little more . . ."

"What?"

"Optimistic." She nudged him with her shoulder. "You're Eeyore."

He blinked. "You think I'm Eeyore?"

"You tell me. I take my empty glass and try to fill it up with what happiness I can find. Friends, family, my work . . . And then there's you."

He raised a brow. "Me."

She nudged him again, looking playful and damn sexy while she was at it. It was the short shorts with the boots, he decided. Or everything. It was everything.

"You take that empty glass," she said, happily analyzing him. "And you wonder what the heck to do with it. You don't need the glass, you don't have time for the glass. Hell, you'll just drink from a spigot if you get thirsty. And in any case, there's probably another one up the road if that one runs out, so—"

"Are we still speaking English?" he asked.

Laughing, she kissed him again, blowing brain cells left and right when she touched her tongue to his. Before he could gather her close, she'd danced back with the dogs and gone on her merry way, leaving him staring after her wondering why he felt like he'd just been run over by a Mack truck.

Because you got laid by a woman who wants nothing more than sex from you, and you want . . .

Jesus.

He didn't even know how to put words to what he wanted.

Eleven

I can tell that you think you know what you're doing," Dell told Lilah a few days later. "But you don't."

They were in her office at the kennels, where she'd just come in from the drugstore, having bought herself a present.

Condoms.

Dell, who'd looked into the brown bag thinking she had something to eat, had gotten an unhappy surprise.

"I know what I'm doing," she said, and hoped that was true.

"It's just a crush," Dell said.

"Yeah. So? You crush on anything with two legs."

He winced. "Not anything."

"Brady's a good guy," she said. "Or you wouldn't have invited him here."

"He's a great guy." Dell snagged her last candy bar from her not-so-secret stash in her bottom drawer. "But—"

"No. Nothing good ever comes after a but, Dell. I hate all buts." Except for Brady's. He had one really great butt.

"But," Dell repeated patiently, ignoring her annoyed snort, "he has one foot out the door."

"I know. It's the very definition of a crush, Dell. It's got an expiration date. At least we both know it." Coming around her desk, she hugged him tight and ushered him to the door. "I'm going to be okay, and so is Brady."

When he was gone, Lilah opened a different drawer with her real junk-food stash and dove into some cookies, and then a bag of chocolate kisses, promising herself that tonight she'd eat broccoli. Maybe.

She hadn't been kidding—she was crushing on Brady. In fact, if she closed her eyes, she could still feel him deep inside of her. She could see the fiercely intense pleasure on his face when he'd climaxed.

She got aroused just thinking about it.

She'd worn him out, which had been a source of pride. He'd fallen asleep in her arms and she'd listened to the beat of his heart meshing with hers. She'd watched him sleep, his long, thick lashes resting on his cheekbones, loving how for once he was completely relaxed, completely unaware of his surroundings.

He was beautiful, and in that moment, he'd been hers. And perhaps because she liked that thought a little too much, she'd slipped out of his arms and out of his bed.

They'd seen each other over the past few days; him working on the Bell, her going back and forth between the center and the kennels, but they'd been too busy to talk.

She eyed her overcrowded desk and sighed. She and Cruz switched off months being in charge of the paperwork that they both hated: the receivables, the payables, the calendar, the promotion and publicity work that had to be done to keep new business flowing. Switching off kept them sane, but more important, it kept them from killing each other. But she wished it were Cruz's turn now.

Or that her life was light and carefree enough that she could say screw it to the work and go seek her pleasure. Her phone rang, interrupting the thought.

"I'm starving," Jade said. "And I need to get out of here before I kill any penis-carrying humans. Lunch?"

"Yes, if it has broccoli in it."

"You eat something bad again? You need some self-control, Lilah. What did you get into?"

Lilah sighed. "Everything."

"Be there in ten."

Brady surfaced after two hours inside the engine compartment of the Bell 47 and realized Twinkles wasn't in his usual sunspot. He walked around the Bell, the building, searching the entire area, but couldn't find him. Gut tight, he entered Belle Haven and found Dell behind the receptionist's desk looking hassled.

"Can't figure out her stupid system," Dell complained. "The woman runs this place tighter than a frigging ship, but no one else knows a damn thing—"

"The dog," Brady said. "You see him?"

Dell lifted his head, eyes dazed. "Man, I've seen fifty today alone. Maybe a hundred million and fifty."

Brady shook his head. "My dog. Twinkles," he corrected, saying the name out loud for the first time with a grimace. "He was outside with me while I was working and now he's gone. Have you seen him?"

Dell had gone brows up when Brady said "my dog," but without another word, he came out from behind Jade's desk. "Let's look outside."

"I did."

But Dell went outside anyway and started walking the areas that Brady already had, calling for the dog.

Brady did the same, moving around the building. He was at the horse pens, half afraid to look inside in case he found a squished dog, when he heard Dell yelling for him. He ran toward Dell's voice and ended up once again in front of the Bell 47.

"In here," Dell called out from inside the chopper.

Twinkles was on the pilot seat.

Which he'd chewed to shreds.

When he saw Brady, he thumped his tail happily and gave one loud "arf!"

"Are you kidding me?" Brady asked him, not wanting to analyze the relief making his legs weak. "You can't jump up onto the couch or get up on the bed without using the chest as a ladder, but you can get onto that chair and chew the hell out of it?"

Twinkles hopped down and sat on his left boot, gazing up at him adoringly.

"Cute," Dell said.

"Not cute. He just ate five hundred bucks' worth of leather."

"Shouldn't have let him be alone in here," Dell pointed out.

"Let him? I don't 'let' him do anything. He's utterly untrainable."

Dell grinned. "You know what Adam would say, right? He'd say it's you, that you're untrainable. And why are you always so on edge about the little guy, anyway? He's a dog. A damn good one, too." He ruffled Twinkles's head fondly. "You just have to be the boss of him, that's all. Be firm." He put a finger in Twinkles's face. "No more chewing."

Twinkles slid to the floor and exposed his belly to be scratched.

Brady shook his head.

"Oh, like you wouldn't do the same if you could." Dell crouched down and obligingly scratched Twinkles's belly.

"And why hasn't Lilah found him a home yet?" Brady wanted to know, staring grimly at the destroyed seat.

"Probably because she's having fun messing with you." Dell let out a laugh at the look on Brady's face. "Guess you don't find this as funny as I do."

"Not so much, no. Though why I care when it's your dime, I have no idea."

Still chuckling, Dell pulled out his cell phone, speed-dialed a number, and put the phone on speaker. A woman answered with a professionally irritated tone: "What do you need now?"

"Jade," Dell said.

"Nope, it's the Easter Bunny. And your keys are on your desk."

Dell shook his head. "Now darlin', I don't always call you just because I've lost my keys."

"I'm sorry, you're right. Your wallet's on your desk, too. As for your little black book, you're on your own with that one, Dr. Flirt. I'm at lunch."

Dell sighed. "What did we say about you and the whole power-play thing?"

"That it's good for your ego to have at least one woman in your life that you can't flash a smile at and have them drop their panties?"

Dell grinned. "I really like it when you say 'panties.' And for the record, I knew where my keys and wallet were."

"No you didn't."

"Okay, I didn't, but that's not why I'm calling. Can you bring burgers and fries for me and Brady? Oh, and Adam, too, or he'll bitch like a little girl."

"You mean 'Jade, will you pretty please bring us burgers and fries?'"

"Yes," Dell said, nodding. "That. And Cokes." He looked at Brady, who nodded. "And don't forget the ketchup."

"You forgot the nice words."

"Oh, I'm sorry," Dell said. "You look fantastic today, I especially love the attitude and sarcasm you're wearing."

Jade's voice went saccharine sweet. "So some low-fat chicken salads, no dressing, and ice water to go, then?"

"Fine," Dell said, and sighed. "Can we please have burgers and fries?"

"You forgot the 'Thank you, Goddess Jade,' but we'll work on that. Later, boss."

Brady looked at him. "How is food going to help with the dumbass dog and the shredded pilot seat?"

"I can't think on an empty stomach."

As promised, a week later, Brady had worked his ass off and had the Bell 47 ready to fly. He'd had it towed over to Smitty's, where it now sat on the tarmac. He'd just filed his virgin flight plan when Lilah appeared, a soft just-for-him smile on her mouth. If he'd been Twinkles, he'd have rolled over and exposed his belly. Instead, he brushed his hands off on his jeans and watched her walk toward him.

Just sex . . .

That's what she'd been looking for. Fun and easy. So he had no idea what the fuck was wrong with him that it had been bugging him for days.

Maybe because it felt like more. Which meant he was screwed.

"How's your baby today?" she asked.

"My baby?"

She ran a hand over the helicopter. "You think I don't see that even a big tough guy like you could have a weakness?"

"More than one," he murmured.

That seemed to fluster her, and liking that he could do that, he reached for her hand, intertwining his fingers with hers, bringing her hand to his mouth to kiss the palm. "You are my weakness, Lilah. The prettiest one I've ever had."

She bit her lower lip and stared up at him, definitely dazed. Call him sick, but he liked that, too. He'd been watching her twist the men in her life around her little pinkie for two weeks now—Dell, Adam, hell half the guys in Sunshine—and not a single one of them flustered her.

But he did.

He knew she thought he was tough, but the truth was, he thought the same about her. She handled her world and all it threw at her, no complaints, no whining.

And yet she didn't know how to take a compliment. It was adorable and charming, a devastating combination he discovered.

"I'm surprised you tolerate any weakness in yourself," she said.

"I usually don't."

She stared up at him, eyes sparkling with a heat and something more, something he couldn't even begin to pretend to read.

He ran a finger over her jaw and then slid his hand into her hair, which felt like silk over his skin. Tightening his grip, he drew her in a little closer.

She came willingly, her mouth opening a little in anticipation of a kiss.

Keeping eye contact, he gave her what she wanted, what he wanted, and brushed his lips over hers. "I've thought about leaving here in spite of my promise to stay the month," he said quietly. "Every day, I've thought about it."

"Hmm. Maybe you don't want to walk away from me," she teased, and nipped his bottom lip.

Holding eye contact, he nipped hers back. "I could leave. Don't ever doubt that, Lilah. Discipline runs deep."

Her smile faded and she tried to pull away from him, but he held tight. "But," he said, hating the quick flash of pain his words had put in her eyes, "I'm not going anywhere. Not yet."

She looked at him for a long beat. "You're a hard man, Brady Miller."

"In more ways than one."

Her gaze flickered to his button fly, and she let out a shaky laugh and dropped her forehead to his chest. "Why do I like you again?"

"Because I'm about to give you the ride of your life. Get in." He hitched his head toward the chopper. "We're going out."

For a week Lilah had hoped to hear those words. Or at least the out part. Not the up part. She didn't love the up part.

Brady scooped Twinkles into his arms. "I'm going to run him over to Dell, be right back."

She was just stunned enough to still be standing there in the same spot three minutes later when he came back. "Let him drive Jade and Dell crazy for the afternoon." He moved to the door of the Bell. Turning back, he realized she hadn't come any closer and stopped. "Come on, get in."

Nope, not coming on or getting in. "Yeah. No, thanks."

"Is there a problem?"

Uh-huh. A big one. She didn't like to fly. In fact, it was safe to say she hated to fly. "You want me to go up with you."

"Yes."

Her stomach quivered, and she shook her head.

He looked at her carefully. "You're not on shift now, right? Cruz is there?"

"Yes. Look, did you mean out as in . . . a date? You're taking me out on a date in a helicopter?" Just saying it made her want to curl in a ball of both terror and excitement.

"Yeah. I want to test things out. We'll fly into Boise, have a nice dinner, and come back—" He broke off and cocked his head. "You're afraid."

"Don't be ridiculous." She wasn't afraid of anything. Well, except maybe admitting she was afraid. "It's that I can't just take off. I have stuff I have to do. Thanks for asking, though," she added politely, and turned away. She wondered how fast she could run back to the kennels . . .

"Lilah."

Damn. "Yes?"

"It's just dinner."

And a flight to get there. "Boise is hours away, Brady."

"Not by chopper."

Holding her breath, she turned back. "Another time, okay?" With a smile that hopefully didn't give her away, she started moving, forcing herself to walk not run.

"Which terrifies you more," he called to her. "Going up in the Bell or going out on a date with me?"

Ah, hell. She pivoted to face him. He looked good, so damn good. She wanted to lick him from head to toe. "Look at me," she said, gesturing to her work clothes of Carhartts pants, a long-sleeved tee layered with a short-sleeved one, both covered in animal hair. "I can't go out like this, there's no way."

"Why not?"

"Why not?" She spread her arms. "Because I'm a mess."

"So go home, grab some girlie clothes or whatever you need, and let's go."

"Girlie clothes?" she asked with a choked laugh. "Where am I supposed to get them, the feed store?"

"Hell, Lilah." He rubbed his jaw, looking sorry he asked. "Wear a potato sack for all I care—it's just dinner. And anyway, I like you how you look."

Crap. Crap that shouldn't melt her right down to a puddle of goo. "Fine. I need ten minutes."

"No problem."

She stared at him for a beat, then whirled and ran home to stare at her closet. In spite of complaining that she had no girlie clothes, she had plenty. He'd just knocked her off her axis is all. She wriggled into a denim skirt and knit top. She shoved her feet into cute boots and thought she looked a little bit like a country bumkin trying to play dress up. If he laughed at her, she'd slug him, she decided and ran back, half hoping he'd left. But nope, he was there, waiting.

He smiled at the boots.

"If you laugh at me, I—"

"I'm not laughing at you," he said, rising to his full height with easy grace, and he was right. That was definitely not laughter in his eyes, but something that nearly singed her skin.

"You look beautiful," he said with such simplistic candor that it rendered her speechless.

"You shouldn't do that," she finally managed. "You shouldn't use sweet words like that. Act like my company means something to you. Like you want—" She cut herself off from saying "more." "Not if you want me to remember what this is between us." And what it isn't.

He looked at her for a long moment. "Nothing was set in stone," he said softly, and boarded the chopper.

Twelve

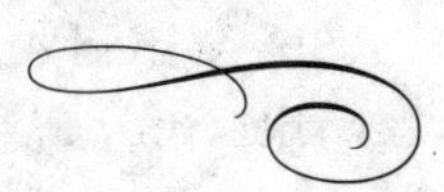

Left standing alone, Lilah looked upward. Blue sky, not a single cloud. Of all the times not to have a summer storm on the horizon.

There was a very slight breeze but definitely not the monsoon she could use right about now.

Do it, she told herself. *Get on, or you'll regret it.* So with that little pep talk out of the way, she took a deep breath and boarded. *Oh God.* She white-knuckled herself into the seat next to Brady, ignoring him watching her. "Let's get this over with," she said.

"You do realize it's supposed to be fun," he said, handing her a headset so that they could communicate over the noise while in the air.

She decided there wasn't a polite response to that so she went the route of Thumper's mother and said nothing at all.

He laughed, the sound soft and sexy, and reached over to squeeze her hand with his. "Don't worry," he said, flipping switches on the instrument panel in front of him. "I've seen a guy do this once or twice."

"Oh God." She closed her eyes.

"Are you going to look at all?"

It was weird, hearing him both in her headset and also outside of it. Brady, in stereo. "I don't know yet."

She felt more than saw him shake his head. "Here we go," he warned a minute later.

The roar of the engine, the rotation of the blades, the sheer terror of the sensation of going straight up into the air had her gripping the arms of her seat so tight her fingers went numb. She forced herself to breathe, but nothing could make her look as her stomach landed in her toes at that weightless feeling as they got air.

"You breathing over there?" he asked.

"Yes." *Barely.* "And don't talk to me. Fly the helicopter!"

"I can do both. Open your eyes."

"You're awfully demanding."

"Yes, and as I recall, you like that. Now, Lilah."

She sighed and opened her eyes, finding that they were very high off the ground. She'd had no idea how it would feel, but it looked as though there were nothing directly below her. All she could see was straight through the glass, which meant everything in front and around her. She gulped at the mix of vulnerability and excitement and studied her pilot.

His sunglasses were silver mirrored frames and gave nothing of his thoughts away. Though piloting a helicopter appeared to take all his limbs—both his hands and his feet were occupied—he was completely in control, aware of everything going on around them: the sky, the instruments, the ground, her. Her eyes were drawn time and time again to those hands, those long fingers moving precisely and surely, in perfect control, just like when they'd been in his bed and he'd handled her much in the same way he was handling instruments . . .

Turning his head, he met her gaze, the very corners of his mouth barely tilting up. "You okay?"

No. "Yes." He was far too sexy. She needed a distraction for herself. "If you don't have a home base anywhere," she said, "where do you keep all your stuff?"

He went brows up. "Where did that question come from?"

"It was either that or 'Are we there yet?'"

That got her an almost smile. "I don't tend to keep much stuff."

"Why not?"

"Is that your favorite question, 'why'?"

"Yes. Right after 'Are the donuts two for one today?'"

He laughed. "The why is simple. My life hasn't really been my own for years now. When and if that changes, I'll figure out where 'home base' is."

"But why isn't your life your own?"

The chopper dipped and she gasped and grabbed the armrests on either side of her hips. "What was that?"

"A pocket of air." Utterly unconcerned, he made an adjustment to the instruments. "I'll take us up a bit higher for a smoother ride."

Oh God. They were going even higher. *Be Amelia Earhart*, she told herself, but it didn't work. Maybe because things hadn't ended so well for Amelia. Choosing not to think on that too deeply, she pulled out her cell phone.

"You won't have reception up here," he said. "Nor would anyone be able to hear you."

"I need to text everyone my good-byes."

A big hand settled over hers. "In the seat behind you, grab my bag."

When she'd done that, he reached over and pulled out his camera. He flicked off the lens cover and turned it on. Then he set it to auto mode.

The moron-proof button.

"Go for it," he said.

She stared at him. "You want me to take your picture?"

"I want you to take pictures of whatever you want."

The Canon was digital and obviously expensive. She brought it carefully up to her face and looked through the lens at the admittedly amazing view. "Is this a distraction technique?"

"Yes."

She laughed and let it work. After a few minutes, she turned the camera on him.

He was dressed in his usual cargo pants, the pockets filled with his essentials. Probably all sorts of tools, and a variety of weapons, and maybe the secrets of his world.

Last week, when she'd been at the loft and gotten him out of those pants, she'd seen the pile of things from his pockets on the dresser. Money, a credit card, his driver's license, and a wicked-looking pocketknife was as far as she'd gotten before she'd realized he'd been watching her.

She'd braced for his annoyance at her snooping, but it turned out that her curiosity about him had amused him.

"Just ask," he'd said in that low, easy voice of his. "Ask whatever you want to know."

"And you'll answer?"

He'd just smiled at her.

At the time, she'd blown out a breath and chickened out. Now she looked at his perfectly fitted cargo pants and wondered if one of today's essentials included a condom.

She had three in her purse now. Her new emergency stash, in the same pocket as her gummy bears—also an emergency stash. Just ask . . . "Do you ever get lonely? Up here in the air?"

"Lonely for what?"

"Friends. Family."

"I'm not always in the air," he pointed out. "And anyway, there are cell phones. E-mail. Visiting . . ."

"But you don't. Visit."

"I haven't made a habit of it, no."

"So you're saying that you're a creature of habit? You stick with routine?"

That got a bark of laughter from him. "That's new," he murmured to himself, or so it seemed. "Creature of habit. Routine. Never been accused of either before."

"What about women?"

He glanced over at her. "What about them?"

"Haven't you ever wanted to change your life for a woman?"

"No."

A little shiver of disappointment went through her. "You've never been in love?"

"I've been in lust," he said with a small, private smile. "More than once."

She rolled her eyes as beside her he let out a breath. "The truthful answer is no," he said quietly. "I've never been in love."

They fell silent, and Lilah thought that was that.

"But you," he finally said. "You, Lilah, scare the hell out of me."

"Why?" she whispered.

He met her gaze and held it. "Because I could fall for you, Lilah. Hard and deep and never want to come back up."

She could scarcely breathe. "What's wrong with that?"

"We'd drown." And with that, he went back to his quiet flying zone.

Brady found himself smiling in sheer pleasure at the gorgeous day sprawled out in front of them, hundreds of miles in every direction, a maze of mountains and valleys that included a national forest.

Not a town or a paved road was visible. There was something about the high-pitched whine and whistle of a chopper, coupled with that sweet aroma of burning jet fuel that was more intoxicating than anything he'd ever experienced.

The wild northern Idaho wilderness was as untamed as it had been in the early 1800s when Lewis and Clark came through. He could see the crests of the ridges of the Bitterroots and beyond. The countless lakes and rivers and a glacier-scoured basin more formidable and rockier than just about anywhere on earth caught his breath in a way he hadn't expected.

If he ever wished to claim a home base, it would be here, the first place to make him feel wanted. He glanced over at his passenger.

And the most recent place to make him feel wanted . . .

Unlike him, Lilah wasn't smiling in sheer pleasure. They'd hit some turbulence and she was gripping the arms of the seat like she was expecting to go down any second and the armrests would save her. He'd asked her several times if she was okay, and he started to ask again. "Lilah? Are you—"

"Don't," she said through her teeth. "Don't ask me if I'm okay because I don't know. And we need to land soon, or I swear I'll stick you with the three kittens that were found at the river yesterday."

He landed soon.

She handled that with only a quietly repeated mantra that went something like "We're okay, we're okay." He was both proud and amused by her attempt at bravery. She was still sitting there, muscles clenched tight, eyes closed, when he opened her seat belt for her. "Good news," he said. "We're in one piece."

She cracked open an eye, took a peek, and then a deep breath. "We made it."

He felt his heart squeeze even as he laughed. "Lilah. Lilah, look at me."

She turned her head and met his gaze, face still pale.

He shoved his sunglasses to the top of his head so she could get a good look at him. "Two things. One, if there'd been even a sliver of a doubt about this thing being anything less than one hundred percent air-worthy, I'd never have brought you with me."

She stared at him, then nodded, even giving him a small, trusting smile. "You're right. I knew that. What's the second thing?"

He paused. "There's a problem with one of the gauges."

"Oh God. Okay." She nodded. "We'll just rent a car and drive home."

Leaning close, he ran a thumb over her pale cheek. "We can fly without it. I just don't want to. I'll get a replacement from this airport's maintenance department and have it fixed in no time."

"In no time," she repeated, clearly realizing that that meant she was indeed still taking the chopper back. "That's . . . great."

Because she was still shaking like a leaf, he leaned in and kissed her softly. "Come on, Amelia. You look like you need your feet firmly on the ground. Let's go eat."

She nodded but didn't move.

"Want me to fly us to the restaurant?"

"Ha. And no." She rose, wobbled, and pointed at him. "Not a word."

He was good at not saying a word and, with an arm slung around her shoulders, led them across the tarmac and inside the airport.

The maintenance department informed them that they were backed up and needed an hour to locate the part Brady needed. Instead of waiting, Brady got them a cab and they headed to town. At an outdoor café, they ate fresh salmon and drank beer delivered in a metal bucket, all while being serenaded by a trio of birds sitting on a branch of a tree. Afterward they window-shopped as the sun set, walking down the main drag past a few galleries and artsy shops with the other tourists. Actually, Lilah shopped, and Brady just watched her. It was quickly becoming a favorite pastime.

"None of this interests you," she said after a block.

"Not much of a shopper," he admitted.

"Me neither. It's hard to be a shopper when you're perpetually broke—Oh," she exclaimed with a gasp, and stopped in front of a shop called the Pharmacy. Only it was unlike any pharmacy Brady had ever been in. Instead of medicine and various sundries, there was lace and silk. It was a lingerie shop, and there was tons of it, all displayed and surrounded by . . . fluff. That was the only word he could think of. There were boas and feathers, lotions and soaps. Lilah was standing there taking it all in when his cell phone rang. It was work. "I'm sorry. I need to take this," he told her.

"No worries," she murmured, still enthralled by the window display. "Take your time."

Brady stepped a few feet away to talk. "Miller."

"Got a job," came the familiar voice of Tony, his boss. "How soon can you be in Somalia?" he boomed.

Tony always boomed. Probably because he'd lost fifty percent of his hearing in the Gulf War, not that he'd ever admit the handicap.

Brady's gaze tracked to Lilah, still nose up to the glass. "Not anytime soon."

"What does that mean? You said you needed a couple of weeks and it's been a couple of weeks."

"It means I'm skipping this one," Brady said. "Assign someone else."

"But you've never skipped a job."

No. No, he hadn't. He'd never had a reason to. And he didn't now, except . . .

Lilah was looking at a silk teddy set. Spaghetti-strapped cami and a tiny thong, both in a pale blue that would make her gorgeous skin shimmer. She turned her head, found him watching her, and blushed gorgeously.

He didn't want to go.

"What the hell's up?" Tony asked loudly enough that Brady winced and pulled the phone from his ear. "You said you needed personal leave," Tony said. "Nothing special, you said."

"Yes. And I'm taking a full month off." That had been his promise to Dell and Adam, and he'd honor it. "I let the office know."

"Yeah, you said you were in Idaho. What the fuck's in Idaho?"

Brady let out a breath. "It's personal—"

"Ah, Christ. You're not going off the deep end and buying a ranch out in the middle of nowhere to raise cattle, are you? You belong in the air, man."

"Two more weeks," Brady said through his teeth. "I'll be back in two weeks."

"But not now?"

"No. Not now."

"It's a woman. No, what am I saying, not even a woman keeps you grounded. It's two women, right?"

Brady shut his phone and slid it in his pocket, giving Lilah a knowing shake of his head. "You can stop pretending not to eavesdrop now."

"You turned down a job."

"I just postponed it, that's all."

"Why?"

Well, wasn't that just the million-dollar question. His cell phone rang again. The Boise airport maintenance department. When he was done with that call, he shut his phone and rubbed a hand over his jaw. "I've got good news and bad news."

"Good news first," she decided, not looking sure she wanted either.

"Yeah, there isn't really good news."

Her eyes narrowed. "Then why did you ask?"

"Because normal people always want the bad news first."

"Just tell me!"

"The part I need for the Bell 47 won't be in until the morning."

Her mouth fell open. "How were you possibly going to make that good news?"

Brady pulled out his rarely used Visa. "With a nice hotel, including a hot tub for all those sore muscles?"

"How do you know I have sore muscles?"

"Because you had them clenched tight the entire flight. You're sore."

She looked him over speculatively, and he wished he knew what the hell she was thinking. But for all that she usually wore her heart on her sleeve for the whole world to see, she was keeping this one close to the vest. Finally she pulled out her cell phone. "Cruz," she said into it. "Remember that time I covered for you when you took Marie to Vegas for the weekend on the spot? Yeah, well, I'm calling in the marker. I'll be back sometime tomorrow . . . No, you don't get to ask why. Use your imagination. Feed Sadie." She slid the phone into her pocket and looked at Brady. "What kind of a reputation do you have that this guy seriously thinks you'd sleep with two women at the same time?"

"Heard that, did you?"

"It wasn't hard, he talks pretty darn loud."

"He just couldn't imagine what would possibly be keeping me, that's all."

"Uh-huh. So tell me the truth," she said. "Was this all a plan to get lucky tonight?"

"If I'd been trying to get lucky, I wouldn't have terrified you first with the flight."

She thought about that. "Good point," she decided, and looked at the phone when it rang again, letting out a moan. "Why, Adam, what a shock," she said when she answered. "Tell Cruz he's a tattletale. We're just stuck waiting for a part, not running off to get married. Talk to you tomorrow." She shoved her phone back into her pocket and blew out a breath. "About this hotel . . ."

"Yeah?"

"I don't want you to spend a lot of money."

He knew the only thing she hated more than flying was being a burden to someone. "I don't care about the money."

"Hmm. Brady?"

"Yeah?"

"Two women?"

He sighed, and gently squeezed her fingers. "Let it go."

Half an hour later, Brady had reserved a two-bedroom suite in a boutique hotel that the restaurant had recommended. It had a lush lobby, done up in luxurious Old West–style with leather and dark, rich woods. They managed to buy some toiletries for the night in one of the shops before going upstairs.

When Brady escorted Lilah to their floor, she narrowed her eyes at him. "Penthouse? How's the penthouse being thrifty?"

He shrugged, then took her to the wide windows, where she gaped at the skyline view of Boise.

"Oh my God," she said for the tenth time as they walked through the opulent place. "What did you do?"

"My money," he reminded her.

"But it must have cost a fortune."

He opened the door to her room, nudged her inside, and then when she whirled to face him, mouth open—no doubt to bitch him out some more—he gently shut the door in her face.

And went to his bedroom. He had to, or he'd have taken her right there, and he couldn't do that. If they were going to sleep together again, it had to be her choice, not circumstance, but a real choice. He was flipping through one hundred and fifty channels on the TV when there was a quiet knock at his door. He opened it to Lilah.

"Hi," she said softly.

"Hi."

Putting her hands on his stomach to push him out of the way, she walked in.

Okaaaay. He leaned back against the door to study her. It was that or grab her and toss her to the bed. Since his fingers were itching to do just that, he jammed them into his pockets.

"Hi," she said.

He smiled. "You already said that."

She nodded. "Right. Listen, I forgot to mention one more thing that I'm afraid of besides flying."

"What's that?"

"I'm afraid to sleep alone in a hotel room. Suite. Mausoleum. Whatever." She looked around the big fancy room. "Although yours doesn't look as scary as mine."

He arched a brow. They had the exact same rooms.

She returned his look with a guileless little smile. "So I was hoping you wouldn't mind letting me in," she said.

He was beginning to think he would let her in anywhere, at any time, and in any place she wanted. His chopper, his hotel room, his life.

His fucking heart . . .

Thirteen

Lilah would have laid money down on Brady having her naked by now, but he was still standing all the way across the room, leaning back against the hotel room door just looking at her.

Silent.

He could be endlessly silent, she'd discovered. Miserly with words until she wanted to tear her hair out. Luckily she'd also learned that he was the opposite with his actions, instead being generous and infinitely giving, and it was those things she was interested in at the moment.

She wanted his hands on her. His mouth.

Everything.

"Is there a problem?" she finally asked him, unable to hold the silence.

"I don't know yet."

That had her raising a brow.

"You came here to jump my bones," he said.

That startled a laugh out of her. "Yes. Yes, I believe I did." He still didn't move, and she cocked her head. "And look at you standing over there like a virgin on her wedding night."

He didn't react. He was good at that, too, at making her come right out and say exactly what was on her mind. No games, not for Brady. "We had dinner first," she said, teasing. "Do you need more romancing?"

"Shit, Lilah." He shoved his fingers through his short hair, making it stand straight up in spikes. He should have looked ridiculous, but he didn't.

He looked hot and frustrated.

And hot.

He was staring her down, his dark blue eyes unreadable in the ambient hotel room lighting. She held his gaze, trying to outlast him, trying to convince him that she was totally cool and one hundred percent in charge of this situation, which of course she wasn't.

Not even close.

"We need to talk," he finally said.

Oh crap. The most dreaded four words in the English language. "Don't tell me. You're married."

"What? No."

"Engaged?"

"Jesus. No."

Hmm. She was starting to feel a little better about this talking thing. "Are you in a relationship?"

He shot her a look of pure alpha male annoyance, and she felt her nipples go hard. Goodness, he was a force.

"You know I'm not," he said. "Nor do I want to be."

"Great." She shrugged out of her top, leaving her in a tiger-striped demi-bra. She'd ordered it online from Victoria's Secret with a coupon, and it made her boobs look perky.

He took one look at her and groaned. "You're not listening to me."

"Oh, I'm listening." She unzipped her skirt. "You don't want to be in a relationship. Which is perfect because what I want doesn't involve much other than a condom, and I'm packing this time."

He was staring at the condom she'd pulled out of her pocket. "You just happened to have a condom in your pocket?"

"Three. You are welcome."

"You going to come any closer? Because I have to tell you, that whole smoldering, brooding thing you have going on is actually doing it for me." She grinned. "You could just watch if you'd rather."

He choked out a laugh.

"Or sit on your hands if you're absolutely determined not to be a part of this."

That did it. He shoved away from the door and slowly stalked her with the confidence of a big wildcat at the top of his food chain, crowding into her space, pushing her back until her legs hit the big, fluffy, elegant, fancy bed behind her.

"Sit on my hands?" he repeated in a voice so gruff she felt herself go damp. Suddenly the room was feeling waaay too small and she wondered if maybe she'd poked the tiger a little too hard. "If you must," she whispered.

"Do your panties match your bra?" he asked, dipping his head to breathe the words in her ear, his hands going to her hips as if he intended to look for himself.

At the quick subject change, she blinked. "Yes."

"Are they wet?"

Before she could answer, he pushed her skirt down. As she'd already learned, once he was in control, he showed no mercy, and now was no different. He dropped to his knees, his hands sliding down the backs of her thighs to open them wider. "Yeah," he said when he had her legs the way he wanted them, his voice holding more than a hint of naughty accusation. "Wet."

"I . . ."

His hands skimmed up her inner thighs, meeting in the middle, where his thumbs brushed over her center, making her gasp.

At the sound, he surged to his feet, sliding his big hands up her now quivering body. She rocked into his touch as his mouth trailed along her jawline, nuzzling into her ear. "Look at me."

With effort, she lifted her head.

"I love your eyes," he said. "They glow when you're turned on. They're glowing like emeralds now."

No man had ever said anything like that to her before, ever. And that was the thing with Brady. He was cool and distant. Tough and edgy. Smart as hell and braver than any man she'd ever known. Testosterone and danger oozed from his every pore.

Even in bed, as she had good reason to know.

But he didn't hold back. Not in life, and certainly not in bed, where if he felt like it, he could linger until she lost her mind as he touched and kissed and nibbled and licked . . .

And sometimes, when it counted, he had words, too.

She slid her fingers into his hair and pulled until his mouth was on hers. He immediately opened for her, the kiss hard and fierce, and when they broke apart, they were both breathing hard.

"More," he demanded, and then stroked a hand across the curve of her belly. His fingers were roughened from hard physical labor, bringing delicious shivers to her body as he tugged the straps of her bra off her shoulders. He kissed the plump of each breast before unhooking the bra and tossing it over his shoulder. Leaning in, he flicked his tongue over a nipple and slid a hand into her panties, unerringly finding her happy spot.

When she cried out, he dragged the silk down her legs, leaving her exposed to his hot gaze. It was dark outside, but he had the lamps on and she knew he could see everything he wanted.

"You're overdressed," she whispered.

Muscles flexed as he reached behind him and tore his shirt off over his head. It went flying in the same direction as her bra and panties had, and she moaned at the mouthwatering view of him, all those perfect sinewy lines . . .

The metallic slide of his zipper sounded shockingly loud in the room and then his pants were gone, but before she could get a good look he'd dropped to his knees again, his hands back on her inner thighs. She felt his breath stir against her.

"I've been hungry for this all week, Lilah," he said, and separated her folds with his thumbs to put his mouth on her.

A sound escaped her, a wordless cry that she couldn't have held in to save her life as he worked her over with a delicate precision that spoke of how much her pleasure meant to him. Her hands were still in his hair—she couldn't help but hold on when he found her rhythm as if he knew her body better than she did.

She'd wanted the heat, she'd needed the escape, but she found more, so much more, and her orgasm hit hard and unexpected. When her legs gave out he wrapped his arms around her, effortlessly holding her up. Even after she stopped shuddering, he lingered, bringing her down gently before he rose to his feet. He tugged the bedspread off the bed, then tossed her on the mattress, crawling up her body, eyes glittering, muscles tense, his skin gleaming. He threaded his hands into her hair and tipped up her face, staring into her eyes as if he was trying to memorize her. She did the same, loving the way his gaze lit when he looked at her, the way his mouth twitched when she was amusing him in some way, how his voice sounded when he murmured her name. And then there was how his body felt against her own, how he made her feel.

Wanted.

Craved.

Safe.

She'd never experienced anything like how she felt surrounded by his arms. And still she needed more. She pushed, and he let her roll him beneath her, where she took her mouth on a tour over his pecs, across his abs, heading downward—

He reversed their positions again.

"Hey," she said.

He showed her the condom in his fingers, the one he'd snagged from her.

"Oh," she breathed. "I like how you think."

"Yeah?" He kneeled between her legs and rolled on the condom. "Then you're going to really like what comes next." He kissed her mouth, gliding up to graze his teeth along her jaw, then the sweet spot beneath her ear, the swirl of his tongue making her squirm with the memory of where else he was good with that tongue. As if he'd followed the train of her thoughts, he laughed softly and threaded his fingers in her hair, tilting her head so that he could hold her gaze as he slid inside her.

There was no space between them, nothing but pleasure. His hands slid down her back and over the cheeks of her ass, lifting her, changing the angle, making her moan helplessly at the sensation of him filling her so completely with nothing more than one sure push of his hips. She gasped and cried out at the same time, arching against him, rocking up as he started to move inside her.

"Lilah."

His eyes were fixed and unwavering on her. She lost her breath just looking at him, and she ground her hips to his, unable to control herself.

For once his own control seemed completely absent. Breathing heavy, face tight, he brought his mouth back to hers as he thrust deep, nipping her lip, sucking it into his mouth. "God, you feel good wrapped around me. So fucking good, Lilah."

Melting, she wrapped her arms closer around his broad shoulders and stroked down his back, her hips rising to pull his body even tighter to hers.

The motion wrenched a very sexy, very male sound from him.

"You like?" she whispered.

"Love. I love."

She tried not to focus on his words, spoken in passion, about his physical pleasure. She tried not to hope that he was letting her in, letting himself fall.

But it didn't matter, her heart had its own agenda and his words made it ache. So she ground her hips into him once again, wrenching another groan from him. She throbbed in response, and the wave began to build within her as he kept moving, stroking hard, harder still, until she came with shuddering impact, crying out his name, arching up into him. He pressed himself even deeper, then stilled as he came with her, holding tight, keeping them connected.

They stayed that way, locked together, for a long time, each of them gasping for air, unable to say a word or move a muscle, shaking with the exertion and the aftershocks. Finally Brady rolled them to their sides. He had his arms around her, apparently just as content as she to prolong their connection. And as she drifted off, she realized that had been the most intimate experience she'd ever shared with a man.

Lilah came awake in slow degrees, aware only of being deliciously warm. Opening her eyes, she realized she was face-first in Brady's throat.

Mmm. A damn fine place to be.

She was also practically on top of him, a leg and an arm thrown over his body like he was her very own personal pillow.

And that wasn't all.

He had a grip on her, too, one hand cupping the back of her head, the other firmly on her ass.

His breathing was slow and deep and steady.

Unable to help herself, she pressed her lips to his throat and gently rubbed back and forth, knowing exactly when he came awake because his breathing changed. "Hey," she whispered. "Don't look now, but we're cuddling."

The hand on her ass tightened possessively, making her smile. "So whatcha doing?"

"Sleeping." His voice was morning rough and gravelly and sexy as hell. "But that's going to change quickly."

"I was hoping you'd feel that way." She gently bit the tendon where his neck met his shoulder, and in one smooth motion he rolled her beneath him.

"Let me guess." He lifted his head, his eyes and mouth soft in a way she hadn't seen from him before. "You don't want to waste our last condom."

"Well, that'd be a crime, right?" she whispered.

"Wrap your legs around me." Another command, uttered in that quiet but utterly authoritative voice of his, but since following his directives always brought her mind-blowing pleasure, she wrapped her legs around his waist and hummed her gratification. It was all she could manage because he was hard, deliciously hard and teasing them both. "Are we going to—"

"Oh yeah."

"And then again?" she murmured hopefully, sucking in a breath because his mouth was at her jaw working its way to that sweet spot beneath her ear, the one that, when he kissed it, made her want to offer him anything, anything he wanted . . .

"Greedy little thing," he accused.

He was right. When it came to him, to this, she was greedy. She was greedy as hell.

"Only one condom," he reminded her. "We used the other a few hours ago. We'll have to get creative."

Thank God. He was good at creative. Really, really good. They kissed and rocked up against each other for a few moments, the room quiet around them with the exception of her own heavy breathing and low moans, until she couldn't take the teasing any longer. "Brady."

He lifted his head and looked at her with lidded eyes. "Tell me."

"More," she said, making her own demands now. His big hands gripped her hips and tilted her in a way that pleased him, tugging a groan from deep in his throat. "Yes," she said. "More of that."

"Anything you want."

Fourteen

It was midday by the time Brady replaced the gauge on the Bell and got them back in the air. For the return flight, he plied Lilah with a glass of wine first.

She denied that it helped, but he could tell by how relaxed she looked that it did—though that might have been from all the orgasms. Hard to tell.

She was quiet this time. Not so unusual for him, but absolutely unusual for her. Halfway home, she turned to him, nibbling on her lower lip.

He braced for the worst.

"About whatever it was that you wanted to talk to me about in your hotel room last night before I—before we . . ." She grimaced. "I didn't mean to interrupt you with wild sex."

That made him smile. "Yes, you did."

"Okay, true, I did. But I'll listen now to whatever you wanted to say."

He slid her a look.

She smiled at him, completely unrepentant, and he blew out a breath. "I wanted to warn you off of me," he told her.

"I like being on you."

He let out a low laugh. "Lilah."

"You like it, too."

"I love it," he admitted. "And you know what I mean."

"I appreciate the sentiment, but I'm a big girl, Brady. You're leaving soon. I haven't forgotten. I wanted this."

This won him another heart-stopping smile, which he told himself was the wine.

It was early evening when they landed. Lilah had checked in with

Cruz several times, but she still headed right off to the kennels to make sure everything was okay. Brady went through his postflight maintenance, then walked across the meadow to Belle Haven.

Twinkles was lying beneath a tree out front looking glum, but he went bat-shit crazy when he saw Brady, wriggling, waggling, rolling in ecstasy when Brady stooped low to rub the dog down. He tried to remember the last time he'd come back from a trip and had this sort of reception but couldn't.

It was after closing time, and Dell and Adam were in the parking lot playing basketball like it was a war zone. Having clearly finished up at the kennels for the day, Cruz was playing, too, the three of them taking their game very seriously.

"Thank Christ," Adam muttered when he saw Brady. "It's these two idiots against me, and they don't know a foul from their own ass. We're skins."

Brady peeled off his shirt and joined the game.

In less than two minutes both Dell and Cruz were pissed. "You can play," Dell said to Brady in disgust. "When did you learn to play, because you were shit in high school."

It was true. He'd been shit at basketball in high school. "I played in the army every night with the guys in my unit. They were street players, hard core."

Adam grinned and passed the ball to him. Brady caught it, pivoted, and shot, making a very sweet three.

Dell swore viciously.

When the game ended, they were all sweating like hookers in a confessional, and Adam and Brady had won by two. He turned to grab his shirt and found Lilah standing there, his camera around her neck.

"I'm back," she said, and handed him his camera. "Nice game."

"Thanks." Brady watched her head off into the center. He took Twinkles and headed to the loft to shower, then checked in with work via e-mail to see if Tony was still pissed.

He was.

Brady closed the e-mail program and downloaded the pictures from his digital and realized he was in many of them.

Lilah had seen to that.

There was a photo of him flying the Bell, a look of concentration on his face as he spoke on his headset. Another of him glancing over at Lilah, eyes still serious, and then yet one more taken in the next instant, when he'd softened for her, a warm, caring smile in his eyes and on his mouth.

He would have sworn on his own life that he never looked at anyone like that, and yet here he sat staring at the proof.

Lilah had taken several pictures of the view, and they weren't half bad. There were also his shots from the restaurant, of Lilah. She was laughing in all of them, a silly, sweet little smile on her face, her eyes lit up with pure joy.

There was one of him at the table, clearly absorbed in watching Lilah. He had yet another small smile on his face, but that wasn't what caught him about that picture.

It was his eyes and the heat in them. The hunger.

The need.

A little shocked at the naked longing he'd displayed, he turned to the next group of pictures, which were of the basketball game, including a close-up of him sweaty and grinning from ear to ear as he came down from a layup.

The very last picture was him turning his head toward the camera—the exact moment he'd realized that Lilah was standing there watching. He was smiling with triumph right into the lens, looking more carefree than he could remember feeling.

He shut his computer just as Adam came up the stairs, suited up for a rescue, two of his dogs at his side. "Need a lift," he said.

"To?"

"There's a big search for a lost kid up in the Kaniksu National Forest. They need all the help they can get. You in?"

Yeah, he was in. An excuse to fly? Check. An adrenaline rush of a search and rescue? Check and check.

A reason to keep his brain from fixating on one Lilah Young? Check, check, and check.

They spent the next six hours straight in the mountains, providing assistance to the search. The kid was located, not by them personally but by a group of rescuers using dogs that Adam had trained last season, which was just as satisfying.

On the flight back, Adam looked over at Brady. "About Lilah."

"Christ. Again?"

"Just one thing. Don't play her, man. She . . . she's been hurt."

If the subject matter hadn't been so serious, Brady might have laughed. Because he was just beginning to realize the truth: for once he wasn't the one doing the playing.

Lilah woke up the next morning to Sadie bumping her little kitty nose into hers.

"Mew."

"It's not time," Lilah murmured. "The alarm hasn't gone off yet."

"Mew-mew-mew."

This was from the eight-week-old kitten trying to get around Sadie, the sole leftover from a rescue the week before. Lilah had placed both of the little guy's sisters but hadn't yet found him a home. He was black, with a white spot on top of his head that looked like a little cotton ball, and he liked to be the boss of his world, which is why Cruz had named him Boss.

Lilah pushed them both away and snuggled down into her covers. She was warm and comfy but not nearly as warm and comfy as she'd been in Brady's hotel bed, with his big, hot body as her personal furnace.

Just remembering the wild hotel sex heated her up pretty good. Sure, she had a small sneaky little feeling that maybe it hadn't been just wild sex, but that was hopefully the endorphins messing with her brain.

"*Mew*," Sadie insisted.

Dammit. "You have got to work on your aversion to the sandbox, missy." Staggering out of bed, Lilah pulled on a pair of sweats and opened the front door for the irritated cat, who was weaving in and out of her legs and threatening to topple them both over.

She caught Boss before he could escape with Sadie. "You're not old enough to run free, little man." She paused and stared down at her porch. "There's an army bag on my porch. Why is there an army duffel bag on my porch?"

Sadie didn't answer because she was already gone. Boss didn't answer because he was a man, after all, and didn't talk much.

Lilah sat on the top step in the early chilly morning, Boss in her lap and the bag at her feet. Adam had been National Guard, not army. She only knew one man who'd been army, and the thought of him bringing her something left a silly smile on her face.

Inside the duffel bag was yet another bag, this one a pretty frothy pink color, from the Pharmacy in Boise. It was filled with soaps and lotions and . . . the pretty blue lingerie she'd been drooling over in the window display. "He didn't," she said to Boss.

"Mew."

She laughed, even as her throat tightened. Heart melted clean away, she pulled out her phone and called Brady. "Morning, Santa."

He was silent.

"At least I hope you're my Secret Santa," she said. "I can't imagine Cruz or Nick picking out that thong—"

A growl sounded through the phone and she smiled. "Thank you," she said softly. "I love it, and the soaps and lotions, too. You shouldn't have."

"I like the way you always smell."

"That's the coconut and vanilla and stuff."

"It's you. You make me hungry, Lilah."

"You know," she murmured. "You don't have many words, but you seem to make the most of the ones you have."

"You going to wear that thong today?"

"You are such a guy."

"Guilty."

Their silence was comfortable, and she found herself smiling like an idiot, all alone on her porch.

"Wear it today, Lilah," he said softly, silkily.

And she knew she would do just that. "See you around, Brady."

"See you," he said, and she could hear the bad-boy smile in his voice.

She closed her phone. "I'm not falling for him," she told Boss, and pulled out a soap. She pressed her nose to it, inhaling the delicious scent. But she was.

Falling and falling hard.

That night she drove to Dell's house for their monthly poker night. Dell lived in town in a house he'd recently fixed up for himself. To Lilah's surprise, she found Brady already seated at the big round table. He was slouched in a chair, long legs stretched out in front of him, a ball cap low on his head hiding most of his gorgeous face except for his mouth.

Which had the sexiest scowl on it she'd ever seen.

Amused—and more—she plopped down beside him. "Heard about your day, Ace."

He slid her a dark look that made her nipples hard before he went back to his cards.

"I'm in," she said to Adam, who was dealing.

"Five-card draw." Adam shuffled the deck like a pro. "And he had more than a hell of a day," he said, tossing a look at Brady as he dealt, taking Lilah's ten bucks and handing her a stack of chips. "He went with Dell on rounds. They were unable to save Mr. Williams's dog after it got hit by a car, then got to the Cabreras' in time to watch their elderly cat die, and as a bonus, on the way home, they headed out to a ranch and had to euthanize a horse with a broken leg."

"It was just shit luck," Dell said, studying his cards, tapping the table to indicate he was holding. "No one's fault."

Brady tossed in some chips. "Raise you five."

"Fuck," Adam said conversationally, but put in his five.

Since she had nothing, Lilah folded.

Dell tossed in his five and shook his head. "Best part is his new nickname."

Lilah glanced at Brady, who was looking pained. "What is it?"

"Nothing," Brady said, and adjusted his hat even lower over his face.

"Dr. Death," Adam said, and flashed a rare grin.

"What?" Lilah burst out laughing. "Are you kidding me?"

The muscle in Brady's jaw bunched and Adam shook his head, still grinning. "Now no one wants him to go along on out-calls anymore, no matter how badly they need Dell."

Everyone but Brady cracked up. He just swore, with a colorful assortment of four-letter words. Lilah wanted to jump him right then and there, but she controlled herself.

Or maybe not quite.

Brady turned his head and met her gaze. He studied her a moment, and though he remained scowling, his eyes heated. He saw right through her, she realized, not knowing whether to be embarrassed or aroused.

So she settled for both.

They played two more rounds before Dell looked at the grease streaked down Lilah's jeans. "Plumbing problems again?"

Her cabin had more problems than she could count, but she loved the old place ridiculously. For one thing, it was all she had of her grandma, and it was filled with precious memories that not even bad plumbing could erase.

For another, it was her only option, given that the money she made went back into the business or toward her tuition. "Nothing I can't handle."

"Lilah, you need to—"

"Change from brass to PVC. Yeah, I know." She hadn't budgeted for it this month. Or next month, for that matter. In fact, she wasn't budgeted for anything anytime soon. "I'm babying the plumbing along for now." Well aware of Brady studying her, she smiled. "Duct tape is a girl's best friend."

Adam shook his head.

Brady was still looking at her. Slowly his gaze dropped, taking in her clothes, probably wondering if she was wearing the lingerie. She gave him a secret smile. He didn't return it, but his gaze singed her skin.

Her cell phone buzzed with a forwarded call from the office line, the one she used for the humane society, and she picked it up to hear Mrs. Sandemeyer's voice.

"Someone did it again," the elderly woman said in her eighty-year-old quavery voice. She lived on the outskirts of town right off the highway. "Dumped a dog they don't want. I'll hold her for you, dear."

"Is the dog injured?"

"Not at all. And sweet as a lamb."

Lilah closed her phone and reluctantly folded her cards. "I'm out."

"But it's just getting good," Dell complained.

"Translation," Adam said. "He thinks he's about to kick our asses."

"I don't think it," Dell said. "I know it."

"Sorry." Lilah rose. "Much as I look forward to that ass-kicking, I have to go. Someone dumped a dog off the freeway again."

"Assholes," Dell said. "Be careful, Lil."

Brady stood up. "I'll go with you."

"No worries, I'll call Cruz if I run into trouble," Lilah said. "Finish playing."

"It's late."

"She has Cruz," Adam said softly. "It's his job."

Lilah patted Brady's arm, nearly hummed in pleasure at the hard, knotted sinew of his biceps, and smiled. "Adam's right. Stay for the ass-kicking."

His eyes met hers, dark and unreadable, and more than her nipples reacted. Her heart actually skipped a beat.

Stupid heart. Because he was leaving soon, she reminded herself, ignoring the little ping in her belly at that thought. She was going to have to give him up, but then again, she was used to giving things up.

She gave her animals up all the time.

She'd given her grandma up.

She'd given certain dreams up, and knew she'd give up more before it was all said and done.

And she'd give up Brady when the time came. She would. Even if the little ache in her heart reminded her that there would be a price.

She was halfway to Mrs. Sandemeyer's house when she got her second call of the night. This one from Cruz. "Babe," he said, voice solemn. "Problem."

"Well, it'll have to get in line," she said.

"There's a tourist looking for a three-legged cat that she lost a month ago."

Lilah's heart, already aching, full-out stopped at this news. "What?" she whispered.

"She's only just now seen the lost-and-found bulletins online. Lilah . . ."

"Sadie," she whispered.

"Yeah."

Seemed she had one more thing she had to give up, after all.

Fifteen

Brady cleaned out both Dell and Adam at the poker table, which took his day from pure shit to pretty damn good, especially when Dell was reduced to whining.

By the time Brady and Twinkles got into his truck to drive back to the loft for the night, it was past midnight. Only he didn't go to the center.

Instead, he turned right. Onto Lilah's property. Twinkles got all perky as they passed the lake, but Brady kept driving. He didn't believe in the legend, but neither did he believe in tempting fate. "Don't want to risk you falling for the first dog you see."

The dog snorted because even he knew it was Brady who was afraid to take the risk. He pulled up Lilah's driveway and Twinkles looked confused. "Don't ask. I can't explain it."

Not even to himself. It wasn't as if he needed to see her—although having her naked and writhing beneath him again would be nice. "I just . . ."

Twinkles was listening, head cocked, and Brady let out a breath. "I'm talking to a dog again." And worse, he really didn't know what he was doing here. He honest to God didn't. He sure as hell didn't want to talk. In fact, the only words he wanted to hear coming out of Lilah's mouth were his name, how much she liked what he was doing to her, and whether or not she wanted it harder.

The kennels were dark. But the cabin's kitchen was lit, so he and Twinkles headed that way and knocked on the front door.

Nothing.

He glanced back at Lilah's Jeep. She was most definitely here. Was she with someone? Whoever had helped her with the rescues? Cruz . . . ?

No, she'd still have answered the door. Or at least he sure as hell hoped so. He thought of all the reasons she'd be home alone with Cruz and not answer.

Finding that he didn't much like any of those reasons, he knocked again, harder now.

Still no answer. Reaching out, he tried the handle. It turned under his hand. She'd indeed been here, working on the kitchen sink. The lower cabinet was open, tools strewn around, and the pipes were wrapped in duct tape at the seams.

But the sexy plumber was nowhere to be seen, and the cabin was empty, including the bed.

He checked.

Stepping back outside, intending to touch the hood of her Jeep to see if it was warm, he heard a soft gasp for breath that made him frown. "Lilah?"

Nothing but the dark night.

But she was out here, he could feel her. He wasn't crazy about the fact that he was so in tune to her. It made him more than a little uneasy.

And vulnerable.

He didn't do vulnerable for anyone. But he heard the sound again and followed it into the woods. Just past the first group of trees, he came to the water he'd been determined to avoid at this time of night at all costs, only to find Lilah huddled down by it. She was sitting, arms wrapped around her bent legs, forehead to her knees.

Sobbing.

Twinkles bounded forward and ran a circle around her, then sat obediently at her feet, head cocked, eyes worried. "Arf."

Brady nudged the dog aside and squatted down in front of her.

"Go away," she said through her tears. "Please, just g-go."

He'd like to, Christ he really would, but the fact was that he could no more walk away from her than he could stop himself from breathing.

Or aching for her. "Are you hurt?"

Leaving her forehead against her knees, she shook her head.

He reached out to touch her, but she shoved at him. "Don't."

Fuck that. She was dirty again, more than she had been at poker, and between that and the dark, dark night sky, he couldn't get a good look at her. So he sat next to her and dragged her into his lap.

She fought for about two seconds then gave up and slumped against him, fisting his shirt in her hands as she quietly and thoroughly went to pieces.

He'd survived roadside bombings, dickhead officers with more stripes than courage, and once, being captured and tortured for two days when his chopper had gone down in enemy territory before being dragged out half alive by the good guys.

So this, holding a small sobbing woman, should be a piece of cake.

Instead it felt like someone had put a vise on his chest and cranked it impossibly tight.

While Lilah continued to let loose with the mysterious waterworks, he ran his hands over her, making sure there was no physical injury. He was getting that it was something far deeper, but it was second nature for him to want to make sure. When he was positive she wasn't bleeding out and there were no broken bones, he just held her and let her get it all out, until she finally quieted down to the occasional hiccup. "Better?"

She tightened her grip on him, keeping her face buried in his tear-soaked shirt.

"Okay," he said. "Not quite yet."

They fell silent for a while. Which worked for him. Silence always worked for him. Around them, the night carried on. The water slapped at the rocks at the shore's edge. The crickets were going to town. Far in the distance came a howl of something, and then a beat later came a matching howl.

Lilah shivered.

Brady stroked a hand down her back and pressed his face into her hair. Coconut again, and something else, the combination both sweet and sexy. She was cold, her nose especially, which he knew because she had it pressed to the base of his throat. Her hands were tangled in the material of his shirt, her ass snug to his crotch. He was doing his damnedest not to fixate on that, but she was squirming a little.

He was aware that he shouldn't be turned on while holding an upset woman, and he gripped her hips to keep her still.

"Why are you here?" she finally whispered, voice hoarse.

The question of the day. "A friendly visit?"

"It's late for friendly. It's more like booty-call hour."

He tightened his grip on her booty and rubbed his jaw to hers. "Don't tease me."

She choked out a laugh—as he'd meant her to—and then there was more easy silence, which was his favorite kind. They continued to watch the night go by, and when her occasional shuddery inhales had dwindled away completely, he hugged her. "Tell me."

She sighed. "Sadie's mommy showed up."

"Does she have only three legs, too?"

She let out a mirthless laugh and rubbed her hands over her face. "Her human mommy. I had to give her back tonight, Brady."

Shit. He ran his hands up and down her back and neck, over her muscles which were rigid and tense. "So you reunited a family."

"Yes." She didn't say anything else, just sat there staring out at the water looking lost and sad. "Which I realize is the point. But . . ." She closed her eyes and fell quiet.

"You had this one awhile."

"Four weeks, three days."

The pain in her voice killed him. "You get attached. Emotionally."

She turned her head away from him, signifying he was an idiot. Which, of course, when it came to this stuff, he totally was. "I guess that's the brutal reality of your job, right? You care for them until you can reunite them with their family or find them a new family. I mean it sucks to let go, but doesn't it also make you feel good? A job well done?"

"Yes," she admitted. "But the letting-go thing. I have a hard time with that. Always have. I loved Sadie," she whispered. "So much."

He'd never felt so useless in his entire life. "But it's okay to let something go out of love," he said, trying logic and reason. "When you're being part of a solution, in making a situation better."

Lilah's eyes filled again, and he realized his mistake—there was no logic and reason for her right now.

"I hate letting them go," she whispered thickly.

"You'd rather keep them all?"

"Yes."

Well, if that didn't completely lay out their differences right there, he had no idea what could. "You have others still. Like that last wild kitten. Boss?" At her nod, he went on. "And you have all the others you care for, even if they're not technically yours, like the piglet. And that duck. And the lamb—"

Another tear escaped, running down her cheek. "Lilah," he said helplessly.

She choked out a laugh and dropped her head to his shoulder. Again he pulled her in, wrapping her in his arms, which by sheer luck seemed to be the right thing to do.

Letting out one shuddery sigh, she nuzzled in and he tightened his grip on the most confusing, baffling woman he'd ever met.

"Brady?" she asked, sounding waterlogged.

"Yeah?" He was still gob-smacked that logic hadn't worked but a hug had.

"About that booty call," she whispered, and it was his turn to choke out a laugh.

Lilah woke up with papers stuck to her face. She was in bed with her books and laptop.

She'd fallen asleep studying, again.

"Mew, mew, mew."

Boss, not Sadie, and her heart stuttered. Life went on . . . And Boss clearly felt that she'd slept long enough. He worked at climbing up the mountain that was her bed. It took him a while. He was tiny and new to his claws, but finally he stood triumphant on her chest.

She sighed and stroked him, and he began to rumble with his little baby purr. She'd pleased him.

She wished someone would stroke her until she purred.

Last night had been rough. Brady had brought her home, and though she'd attempted to pull him inside with her and let him distract her from her spectacularly bad night, he'd resisted. He'd tucked her into bed, kissed her long and thoroughly, then left.

Just as well, really. She'd been waaay too vulnerable, and given that being in bed with Brady tended to strip her down to a naked, raw, earthy emotional state such as she'd never felt before, she was grateful he'd been smarter than she.

Because last night? She would have fallen in love with him for sure.

So she'd forced a smile when he'd pulled free of the bone-melting kiss, playfully swatted him on his very fine ass, and watched him walk away.

And then, apparently, she'd studied until falling asleep. She dragged herself around the rest of the morning, finally stopping for a quick lunch break. Cruz had left the newspaper opened to page 2, which held a funny commentary about Dr. Death complete with a picture of Brady looking big, bad, and tough as hell standing in front of the Bell 47. Lilah grinned, tore out the picture, and taped it to the kennel's refrigerator, making Cruz shake his head.

Then she went back to work. With summer in full swing, people were in and out of town, many leaving their animals at the kennels. This was great for the bank account. Not so great for free time, not with midterms coming up, and Cruz readying to leave on vacation.

Three nights after having to give Sadie back to her owner, Lilah was in desperate need of a night's sleep that didn't include waking every hour to a ball of anxiety choking her. So she took two Tylenol PM and while waiting for them to kick in, sat at the table to study. Once again she fell asleep there and dreamed about a set of warm arms.

Brady's arms.

Mmmm . . . So nice of him to show up in her dreams. Smiling, she clung to him as he carried her off somewhere. Hopefully to an island. Maybe somewhere in the South Pacific, where it would be just the two of them, a sandy beach, warm sun, and no responsibilities. She loved her life, but sometimes she dreamed about a day that didn't begin at the crack of dawn to clean pens and stalls. No dealing with the daily grind of running two businesses. No heartache . . .

She sighed in pleasure at the thought. "Just a day . . ."

The arms holding her tightened. "Shh, I've got you . . ."

She struggled to come out of the haze, but he nuzzled her hair. "Sleep," he commanded softly.

She woke up in the morning alone in her bed. Boss was standing on her, eyeing her accusatorily for having slept for so long. Her reading glasses were on her nightstand, her clothes on the chair in the corner of her tiny bedroom—

Wait a minute. Lifting the covers, she stared down at herself. She was in a big T-shirt and her panties—and nothing else.

She'd have recognized the T-shirt by the scent of Brady alone, and she brought the material up to her face for a big, delicious sniff of him.

God, she was a sap. A sap who smelled coffee. She followed the scent to her kitchen, a wave of sadness hitting her when there was no Sadie to trip over.

On the counter sat a large coffee, and next to it—be still her heart—two breakfast burritos. And a bright red shiny apple. For the first time in a few days, she smiled. "He's good," she said to Boss.

The kitten gave her a look that said, *Of course he's good, he's a man, isn't he?*

By the time Lilah showered and dressed, she was nearly late at opening the kennels, and her day got crazy from there. It wasn't until Cruz's shift in the afternoon that she managed to walk over to Belle Haven.

Brady was gone, having flown Dell up north for a complicated foal birthing, so Lilah stopped to talk to Jade at the reception desk. She had to laugh at the Dr. Death newspaper clipping taped to Jade's computer.

"Oh, you like?" Jade asked. "He's my beefcake of the week. Plus, it drives Dell nuts. He's been working for how many years, and he's never made page two in full color."

The waiting room was packed with patients waiting for Dell's return. There were dogs and cats and a ferret. Most were well behaved, but the same couldn't be said of a young boy around five, sitting on the floor with his army men, throwing a tantrum every time any of the animals looked at him.

His mother was sitting in a chair as far from him as possible. Lorraine Talbot had been several years ahead of Lilah in school. She'd been prom queen, head cheerleader, and had never found much time for people outside her circle.

Lilah hadn't been in that circle.

Apparently neither was her own child.

Lorraine came in to Belle Haven often, mostly because she had a fat crush on Dell. It might have been the fact that he had "doctor" in front of his last name these days, as opposed to their high school days when he'd just had "dweeb."

The front door opened and in walked Brady and Dell. They were both filthy from head to toe, covered in dirt and muck and God knew what else, looking weary and worn.

Dell turned to the waiting room and Lorraine immediately leapt to her feet and gave him a finger wave and flirtatious smile.

Dell nodded. Definitely muted from his usual wattage, which had nothing to do with exhaustion but the fact that he'd learned not to encourage her. The last time he'd smiled at her she'd come by every single day for two weeks.

"Sorry for the delay, guys," he said to the room at large. "I'll go get cleaned up and be right back." He went into his office, and Lorraine sat with a huff.

Brady's gaze tracked directly to Lilah, and a little frisson of anticipation danced down her spine. At the same moment, the ferret decided he was bored and leapt out of his owner's hands to playfully bump its head to Lorraine's son's leg.

The boy went berserk, tipping his head back and screaming bloody murder.

The ferret dove beneath his owner's chair, then peeked out, eyes bright, staring at the incredibly loud little human.

Brady was the closest to the kid. "Are you hurt?"

He only screamed louder. A few of the people waiting put fingers in their ears.

Brady craned his neck and eyed the waiting room, clearly trying to figure out who the boy belonged to.

Lorraine was filing her nails.

"Hey," Brady said to the boy. "Only people who are bleeding out get to scream like that. Are you bleeding out?"

The boy stopped screaming to stare at him wide-eyed and open-mouthed.

"Are you?"

Probably having no idea what "bleeding out" even meant, the boy shook his head.

"Good." With a nod, Brady rose to his feet and headed toward the stairs but not before giving Lilah a look that had Jade fanning herself.

"Good Lord," Jade whispered. "Dr. Death is hot."

"Hot," one of the women agreed from the first chair across the desk. "He makes me sweat in interesting places."

Every other woman in the room nodded.

"Did you see the look he sent you?" Jade asked Lilah. She gulped down some of her ice water. "If he ever looked at me like that, my panties would just go whoosh, up in flames."

Lilah could understand that. Her panties did the same. It did something to her to watch Brady deal with silly women who got too attached to every animal to cross their paths with the same aplomb he handled a screaming kid, even though he clearly wasn't sure what to make of any of it. Which didn't stop him from living his life the way he wanted to.

She admired that and thought maybe she could get better at doing the same.

Ten minutes later, he came back down the stairs wearing fresh clothes, hair still damp from his shower. He headed out the door, and she followed. "You brought me breakfast."

He looked at her, eyes warm and assessing. "You looked a quart low last night. Thought maybe you could use the pick-me-up."

"I was, and did," she said. "Why didn't you sleep with me?"

They'd crossed the yard and were heading toward Smitty's, where the Bell 47 was tied down.

"Sleeping with you is . . ." He hesitated.

"What?"

At the chopper, he turned to face her. At the confused, defensive look on her face, a faint smile crossed his lips. "Amazing." Then he shocked her by leaning in to kiss her.

When she sucked in an aroused breath, he slid his tongue against hers and melted all her bones. "And," he added, "confusing."

"Confusing. What's confusing?"

"You." He ran a hand over the chopper's steel body, making Lilah remember, vividly, what it felt like to have those hands stroking her.

"Okay," she said. "Now I'm confused."

He turned to face her. "You wanted fun and easy. A light relationship, with an expiration date."

"I did."

"So this is me, trying to give you what you want."

"Sometimes," she said slowly, "what a woman wants is complicated."

"No shit." He let out a breath. "I'm just trying like hell to be a good guy here and make sure no one gets hurt."

"Who's going to get hurt?" But she already knew the answer to that, of course.

She was going to get hurt.

He stroked a strand of hair from her temple, and then ran his finger over her jaw, across her lower lip until it trembled open for him.

And then he leaned in and kissed her again, with such heat and hunger and desire that she was clinging to him, shaking, by the time he pulled back. All she could do was blink up at him, realizing just how right he was to try to hold back. Because suddenly, or maybe not so suddenly at all, she was wanting a lot more than the easy fun she'd promised him.

She struggled to get a handle on herself. Was she so obvious in her feelings for him that he had to worry about her? Yeah. Yeah, she was. She didn't have his seasoned inscrutable mask to hide her emotions. "Maybe it's going to be you who gets hurt," she finally said. "I'm pretty damn unforgettable, you know."

"You are," he agreed so softly that she had to strain to hear him, and even then, she wasn't sure if he'd really said it or if she just wanted him to.

Sixteen

Several mornings later, Brady drove into town. His plans included something hot for breakfast and caffeine, since he'd stayed up until all hours, restless.

Sleepless.

He and Twinkles had ended up going for a long drive, his mind free. No, that wasn't exactly true. His mind hadn't been free at all. He'd ended up sitting at the lake's edge, he and the dog, staring out at the supposedly magical waters. On his way home, the truck had taken him to Lilah's cabin.

Fucking truck.

Because there'd been a light on, he'd gotten out and knocked. When she hadn't answered, he'd looked into the window and seen her at her table, head down on her books, fast asleep.

Again.

He couldn't have altered what he'd done next even if he'd had to walk through an enemy camp to do it. Breaking in was no problem. Nor was being silent as he did so.

He'd been trained by the good ol' US of A.

For the second time that week, he'd carried Lilah to bed without waking her—and just how many times was she going to work herself into such exhaustion that he could even do that? Still, he savored the task and the silence of the night all around them for long moments before forcing himself to leave instead of climbing into bed with her.

He'd headed back out into the dark night from which he'd come, letting his eyes and ears search out anything that didn't belong. But this wasn't some third-world country, and he wasn't searching out some foreign operative. Unfortunately, old habits were hard to break, and at his core he was still a soldier.

But all had been as it should be, leaving him no choice but to go.

Now it was morning, and in the light of day he could only shake his head at himself. He was doing just that when a dented red Jeep pulled in behind him at 7-Eleven.

Familiar denim-clad legs and a set of scuffed boots appeared at his side.

Lilah shoved her sunglasses to the top of her head and grinned at him. "You'll notice I didn't rear-end you."

"I did notice." He looked down at the duck on the leash. "Abigail."

"Quack," Abigail said.

"Funny thing about last night," Lilah told Brady. "I fell asleep studying and woke up in bed. What do you think about that?"

"I think you need more sleep."

"I can sleep after midterms. I'm looking for breakfast. You?"

"Definitely." They walked into the convenience store together.

"Lilah Anne Young," the woman behind the register said. She was possibly a hundred years old, with an unlit cigarette hanging out of her mouth. "What did I tell you about that duck?"

Lilah smiled. "To cook her at three hundred and fifty for an hour and a half before eating?"

The woman cackled. "Yeah, and don't forget the pepper." She turned her sharp eye on Brady. "Morning, Dr. Death."

Lilah snickered and he sent her a quelling look that only made her snicker again. She had a bran muffin in her hand that he knew she would never eat and was looking over the drink choices when a guy walked up to her and slipped his arms around her waist as if she was his, whispering something in her ear.

Whatever he said made Lilah smile and lean back into him a minute before turning in his arms and giving him a hug that was warm and familiar and made Brady grind his back teeth together.

It was ten full seconds before the fucker took his hands off her, which Brady knew because he counted.

Lilah hadn't objected. Nope, she'd cupped the guy's face and grinned up into it. "When did you get back?"

"Late last night. Come on, I'll take you out for a real breakfast."

"Hey, Ian," the lady behind the counter called out. "Nice that you're back, but don't you be taking my paying customers elsewhere."

Brady decided it was a damn good time to come up behind Lilah, leaving just enough room for maybe a single sheet of paper to fit between them.

Ian took a long look at him, and from over Lilah's head, Brady looked right back.

Lilah craned her neck and gave Brady a what-the-hell-are-you-doing expression, but he ignored it.

"Ian," Lilah said with a little shake of her head, "this is Brady Miller. Brady, Ian runs an outfitter company out of Sunshine." Lilah turned back to Ian. "And sorry, no breakfast date today. I already have one." Again she looked at Brady, brows up, like yes, I'm still having breakfast with you even though you are a dumbass.

Fine. He was a dumbass. He could live with that.

"You want to explain that back there?" Lilah asked when they were outside on the sidewalk a few minutes later, with Abigail at their feet fussing with her feathers.

"Explain what?" he asked, leading her to one of the three small tables out front, where they sat to eat.

"The Neanderthal routine."

Ian came out of the store with a bag, stopping to squeeze Lilah's shoulder and give her another kiss on the cheek.

Brady considered his options. More Neanderthal-ness or play it cool. He went with cool because the poor bastard was clearly just another besotted fool. Probably another ex, which was baffling all in itself. For Brady, when things were over, they were over. He watched until Ian had walked away and shook his head.

"What," she said. "He's a friend."

"Another ex?"

She shook her head. "It never got that far."

Best thing he'd heard all morning. "And yet he's still in your orbit. You have us all just circling you, you realize that, right? Just hoping for a piece of you."

She stared at him, then laughed. "It's not like that."

"It's exactly like that. We're all pathetic." He playfully tugged a strand of her hair. "Willing to take any piece of you we can get."

"Yeah?" She cocked her head and studied him, amused. "Which piece would you want?"

Any piece you'd give me . . . "Guess."

Her smile went a little naughty. "Well, I do have a few pieces you especially like . . ."

There were more than a few actually, but he shook his head. This time he wanted something she wasn't offering. Something he wasn't even sure he wanted to admit to yearning for.

A piece of her heart.

Just a little piece so that when he left and felt the pain of the separation, he'd know someone else felt it, too. "Dell's hinting around about me staying longer," he said out of the blue, and sipped his coffee to shut himself up.

She choked on hers. "Did you tell him that you don't do 'stay'?"

"I did."

Her smile slowly faded. "Don't tell me. Just thinking about it has you rushing out of here."

He took her hand. "Oddly enough, I don't feel much like rushing."

She nodded, face solemn now. "So . . . how much longer?"

He ran his thumb over her knuckles, scraped from her latest plumbing misadventure. "Eager to get rid of me, Lilah?"

She squeezed his fingers. "Maybe I just want to make sure you get that piece of me that you want."

All of them, he thought, revising her earlier statement. *I want all of your pieces.*

Several days later a situation came up about a hundred miles north. A pack of three dogs were making pests of themselves on a small ranch owned by an older couple who couldn't, or wouldn't, take over the responsibility of placing the animals. If Lilah didn't go get the dogs, they'd be euthanized.

She was just getting into her Jeep when her passenger door opened. Twinkles leapt into the back and then Brady folded his long body into the front seat next to her. He put on his seat belt and lowered his sunglasses over his eyes before he turned and looked at her.

She stared at him while Twinkles leaned forward and licked her ear in greeting. "What's up?"

Brady shrugged. "I thought about offering to fly you, but I didn't have any wine to ply you with."

"Why?"

"Because you fly better when you're wasted."

She rolled her eyes. "I mean, why are you here? In my Jeep?"

"Now see," he said all long-limbed grace and testosterone. "That hurts. Maybe I just want to hang out with you."

She stared at him. "Dell kicked you out of Belle Haven today." She laughed. "He did, didn't he, Dr. . . . Death?"

Brady swore and slouched in the seat, six feet of dark, brooding 'tude. "He said that they had some big rancher head honcho coming by today and that he and Adam couldn't afford to have him catch wind of the Dr. Death thing."

Lilah grinned. "Well, lucky for you, I'm not nearly so selective." She hit the gas and they took off. Brady was quiet but there was no denying he was nice company and even nicer to look at. Halfway there, she had to stop for fuel. Brady pumped the gas while she headed into the convenience store, coming out arms loaded. "Got us some goodies."

He took the bags from her and the driver's spot.

"You're a control freak," she said.

"I like to drive."

"Control. Freak."

He didn't bother denying that. He searched through the bag and gave a very male sound of satisfaction as he pulled out a loaded hot dog.

Lilah tossed Twinkles a doggie bone and pulled out the nachos for herself. "I know the way to your good side," she said to Brady.

"I'll show you a better way later."

She smiled. The truth was, he could show her anything he wanted. "Uh-huh. Promises, promises."

"What does that mean?"

"That I'm thinking you're all talk and no go."

He slid her a look.

She nodded.

"You're going to be taking that back."

She smiled, like that had been her goal all along, and images of taking her right here and now in the Jeep flooded his mind.

"Take the next exit," Lilah said. "Echo Canyon."

He shook his head. "Granite Flat is faster."

She didn't protest, but she did give him a long look.

"Problem?" he asked.

"No. I don't have a problem with your control issues at all."

He rolled his eyes.

"In fact," she said, "in certain areas, your control issues are kind of hot."

Again his gaze swiveled her way. "Certain areas?"

"In bed, for instance." She sucked some melted cheese off her finger. Slowly.

"Lilah," he said, voice a little lower now.

"Yes?" She sucked on another finger.

"Stop."

She kept sucking. "Stop what?"

Without warning, and gaze still on the road, Brady reached out with quick, accurate precision and wrapped his fingers around her wrist. "What did I tell you about payback?"

"That I love it?"

He laughed softly, and sucked her last cheesy finger into his hot, wet mouth.

When her eyes drifted shut with a soft moan, he nipped her finger with his teeth, making her gasp. "And when I say later, I mean it." Smiling, he let go of her and turned his concentration back to the road.

They drove in silence for a while as Twinkles napped—and snored. Brady enjoyed the relative quiet. Lilah was wearing softly faded jeans that whenever she leaned forward to adjust the radio, sank low in the back, giving him peek-a-boo glimpses of smooth skin and the very hint of incredibly sweet twin dimples.

He wanted to dip his tongue in those dimples.

As for that ass, he wanted to cup it in his hands and—

"You're on the shoulder of the road, Brady."

Fuck. He swerved back. "Well, if you'd stop distracting me . . ."

"Distracting you?" She pulled one of her legs up and beneath her, twisting to smile at him. Her shirt gaped a little, revealing a curve of breast and another hint of baby blue silk. The lingerie from the Pharmacy. "How can I be distracting you? I'm just sitting here," she asked, the picture of innocence.

"I'll pull over," he warned her.

Damned if she didn't look intrigued, making him both groan and laugh at the same time.

"No," she finally said. "I don't think you will." She ran a hand up his thigh, found him through his jeans and outlined him with a finger.

He nearly jerked them off the road again. Luckily the narrow two-lane highway was utterly deserted. He pulled over so fast they both were rudely yanked back by their seat belts.

Twinkles scrambled for purchase on the backseat.

"Wha—" was all she got out before he'd unhooked her seat belt and hauled her over the console and into his lap.

He had his mouth on hers and his hands in her pants in one heartbeat, and in the next he had her whimpering for more. He kept that up for long minutes until she was rocking her hips and panting.

"Oh God." She arched to him. "Please . . ." She was breathless, head back, eyes closed. She was the most beautiful thing he'd ever seen. "Come for me," he whispered in her ear, stroking her in the way he knew made her crazy, making her gasp and cry out his name.

And she did. She burst and shuddered in his arms and while she made her way back to planet Earth, he held her close against his chest, face buried in her hair. She would probably call it cuddling.

He called it regaining his sanity.

Holding her was his sanity.

Before she'd stirred a muscle, her cell phone rang from somewhere in her purse on the floor. She lifted her head and stared at Brady, hair all wild, face flushed, mouth open. "My ears are ringing."

"It's your cell."

She looked so adorably, gorgeously befuddled. "Oh. I knew that." Feeling around for it, she finally got it open. "Hello? Yes, ma'am, we'll get there before dark." Craning her neck, she looked out the window.

It was already dusk. Her eyes caught on his obvious erection straining the denim, then met his, and in them was an apology but also amusement.

He pushed her back to her side of the Jeep and put it into gear before pulling back onto the road.

"I'm sorry," she said. "I owe you."

He liked the sound of that, but it didn't help his condition any. He shouldn't have touched her, but he couldn't help it—she was the hottest, sexiest thing he'd ever seen, and watching her come was his new favorite drug of choice.

"Don't you think we should fix this before we get there?" She reached out to touch, stroking him through the denim, making him groan. "Later," he said.

"You've got a lot of laters."

"Don't worry, I always collect my debts."

They got to the ranch fifteen minutes later, right at sunset. Years before, the owners had given up the actual ranching to their kids, and then their kids' kids. Mr. Leo Johnson was a big guy, but it was clear that his wife, Ellen, was completely in charge. She took one look at Brady and raised a penciled-in brow. "Dr. Death! Honey," she said to her husband, "look, it's Dr. Death! Nice article."

"Thank you," Brady said, sliding a glance at Lilah, who was grinning. He wanted to be annoyed, but the sight of her genuine amusement always derailed him.

Ellen introduced them to the three homeless dogs she'd found, each a Collie mix and probably littermates as well. They were clearly neglected but dying for affection and made immediate friends with Twinkles.

Lilah said she'd have little trouble finding them homes, but before Brady could help her load them up, Ellen had dinner on the table and refused to let them go without eating.

Leo said grace and thanked God for the food, the house, the ranch, and every single animal on the ranch, and then his children, and his children's children, and then for the past fifty years with a great woman, and just before Brady fell asleep at the table, his ears pricked up as Leo added, "and for bringing a new couple by for company tonight."

Brady turned his head to meet Lilah's wide eyes. *Couple?* she mouthed, looking so horrified he nearly laughed.

Leo smiled. "Sorry, it's just very obvious that you two are recently together."

"Yes," Ellen said. "You keep staring at each other or touching in some way."

Brady looked down and noticed that indeed he was thigh to thigh with Lilah, and even more telling, he had an arm draped over the back of her chair, his fingers tracing absent circles on her shoulder. His fingers froze midtrace.

"So, how long has it been?" Ellen asked, passing around the thick pot roast and heart-attack-in-the-making mashed potatoes that were the best mashed potatoes Brady had ever tasted. "I mean, I assume this is brand-new," she said with a secret smile at her husband. "Since there was no mention of a relationship in the Dr. Death article, and we all know how thoroughly invasive that gossip rag can be."

"Um," Lilah said, looking uncomfortable. "Well, to be honest, we're not—"

Brady reached under the table and squeezed her knee. He didn't know what came over him, probably retribution for how she'd mercilessly teased him in the Jeep, but he heard himself say, "Don't be shy, honey."

She stared at him, clearly concerned he'd lost his marbles.

And he had. The day he'd met her.

"Oh, tell us the whole story," Ellen said, clapping her hands with glee. "I love a real-life romance."

Brady smiled at Lilah. "Go ahead, darlin'. You tell it."

Lilah's eyes narrowed on Brady. Her fork was still in midair, full of potatoes that he suspected she might want to fling into his face as she contemplated him. "Well, sweetheart," she said, "it's just that I don't know where to start."

Ellen was smiling so eagerly. "At the beginning!"

Lilah looked at her and hesitated. Clearly, she was willing to go head-to-head with Brady in a battle of wills, but she wasn't so willing to be rude or cruel. But she must have gotten over that because she said, "We met at the beauty salon in town."

Brady had been smiling, feeling pretty damn pleased with himself for one-upping her—until this.

"Yeah," Lilah went on, clearly gaining steam. "Brady was at his weekly grooming session." She leaned into Ellen as if departing with a state secret and continued in a stage whisper, "He's very hairy, you see."

Brady choked on his peas.

"Wax or laser?" Ellen whispered. "My son-in-law swears by his monthly male Brazilian."

"Brady, too," Lilah said, patting a still coughing Brady on the back. "You okay, baby?" She smiled sweetly at him and began shoveling her food in as if she hadn't eaten in a week. "Oh, Mrs. Johnson, this is all so delicious!"

Brady finally recovered. "Lilah cooks, too, Ellen. Actually, she's an incredible baker. She makes the most amazing desserts."

Now it was Lilah's turn to go pale. The only thing she baked was store-bought cookie dough.

"Oh, that's lovely!" Ellen exclaimed.

"And you should see her on the fly," Brady said. "That's her specialty—improvising."

Lilah narrowed her eyes at him but before she could respond, Ellen spoke again. "Oh, that is a talent. Maybe you can demonstrate," she said hopefully. "I have just about everything you could need for any recipe."

Lilah sent Brady a look of sheer, undulated panic, followed by a look that promised her own payback.

That was okay. After the male Brazilian thing, he was pretty sure he could take whatever she dealt out. Smiling, he leaned back and shot her his best *your turn* look, which she returned with a *you-are-so-going-down* volley.

Fine by him. He'd go down with her any day. With her, on her . . . however and wherever she wanted.

Seventeen

A little while later, Lilah escaped to the Johnsons' very small, slightly fussy bathroom at the end of the hallway and stared at herself in the mirror. Her eyes were bright, and there were two spots of color on her cheeks. She looked under the influence.

And she was.

She was under the influence of lust. Damn Brady for baiting her, for making her feel . . .

Alive. The man made her feel so alive.

She was still staring at herself when the door opened. A big, warm, built body nudged her over, making room so he could squeeze in behind her.

"What are you doing?" she whispered.

Brady gave her a look that made her nipples pebble up against her shirt as he reached out and hit the lock.

Click.

It echoed over the pounding of her heart. Staring at him in the mirror, she shook her head. "Brady—"

"Lilah," he said calmly. Stepping closer, he forced her up against the sink. His hands gripped the tile at either side of her hips, trapping her in. "A male Brazilian?" His voice was that deep half growl she'd heard only when they were naked and he was whispering erotic, explicit promises in her ear, the ones that never failed to make her blush.

"Well, hey, for all I know you really do wax."

He pressed himself against her butt. He was hard.

"Oh no," she whispered on a laugh even as she rocked back against him, causing him to hiss in a breath. She stopped breathing entirely and went damp. "We can't."

Seeing right through her, he smiled into the mirror, slow and extremely badass.

Oh no. No, she wasn't going to melt just because he was giving her that look. "You have to go," she whispered, attempting to elbow him away. "Shoo."

He made a sound that might have been a snort of laughter. "Can't."

"Why not?"

He grabbed her hand and brought it behind her to cup over his crotch.

"Oh my God." But her fingers stroked him. Bad fingers.

Brushing her hair out of the way, he leaned down to nibble on her neck. "Can't help it," he murmured against her skin. "You have this effect on me."

Her eyes drifted shut, and a horrifyingly needy, hungry little whimper escaped her, loud enough that she lifted her own hands and clamped them over her mouth.

"Mmm," he barely breathed against her ear. "Love that sound." His hands slid from her hips upward, beneath her top.

"What are you doing now?"

"If you don't know, I'm doing it wrong."

Oh, she knew. And the truth was, she'd do whatever he wanted and they both knew it. Ever since he'd come to town with those sharp, assessing eyes and hard-but-oh-so-giving mouth and all that testosterone, her body had been a complete traitor. His tongue rimmed her ear and she had to lock her knees to remain upright. "Oh God."

"Give me a minute and you'll be saying 'Oh, Brady.'" He ran his fingers lightly down her arms and then encircled her wrists, setting them on the counter's edge, indicating she should keep them there. She wriggled back against him, grinding her bottom into his erection. "Hold still," he commanded softly in her ear.

She shivered and it was entirely possible she had a mini-orgasm. If he hadn't been pinning her between the hard sink and his even harder body, she'd have slithered bonelessly to the floor.

Then his hands slid beneath her shirt and ran up her rib cage, stopping just short of her breasts.

She held her breath but couldn't quite keep quiet. "Touch me!"

He pushed her shirt up and the cups of her bra down and, watching her reaction closely in the mirror, palmed her breasts. Then one of his very talented hands slid slowly down her belly and into her pants. "Oh Jesus." His breath was hot against her ear. "You're ready for me."

She'd been ready for him since she'd first laid eyes on him, and she didn't see that changing anytime soon.

His hands went to her hips and before she could draw her next breath, he'd shoved her jeans to her thighs, groaning softly in her ear at the sight of the baby blue thong he'd bought her. There was something incredibly thrilling about being so exposed while he was fully dressed behind her, watching himself touch her in the mirror.

"I—" She gasped when he gave one quick yank and ripped the underwear off her.

"I'll buy you more. Hell, I'll buy you an entire Victoria's Secret store," he promised, his voice a rough, barely there growl as he slid his hand between her thighs. "I can't get enough of you, I can't."

She met his gaze. His eyes were no longer playful but dark and filled with a dangerous emotion. Dangerous, because now it wasn't just her good parts aching. No, the nameless ache spread and hit her heart with deadly precision. Turning in his arms, she twisted her hands into his shirt, and then their mouths connected, hot and demanding. His tongue touched hers at the same moment his fingers slid home. Her toes began to curl, but he slowly withdrew, making her whimper.

"Later," he murmured, but continued to hold her close.

Panting, Lilah dropped her head to Brady's chest. "I hate later." After a minute, she pulled her clothes back into place. Without panties. God. She slumped back against Brady. Beneath her cheek, his heart was thumping steadily. Definitely faster than his usual near-hibernation beat. Lifting her head, she flashed him a tight smile. "I get to you."

"Are you kidding? You own me," he said, his voice running over her like silk.

And with that startlingly revealing statement, he unlocked the door and slipped out, leaving her leaning against the sink, heart still pounding, nipples hard enough to cut glass.

"What are you doing?" Brady demanded an hour later when they were finally back on the road heading home.

The four dogs were in the back, sleeping in a relaxed pack. Outside, the night was dark and chilly, but inside the Jeep it felt warm and toasty, and by the light of the dash, Lilah was moving around, driving him crazy as she pulled off her sweater.

"Just getting comfortable," she said. "I have a long night ahead of me. I still have hours of studying once we get back. I have a big advanced chem midterm tomorrow."

"You should have told me." He glanced over at her. "I'd have gone and gotten the dogs for you. And that's a little revealing."

She looked down at her shirt and laughed. "It's a man's cut beefy T-shirt, and I'm wearing a bra beneath it—as you already know since you had your hands on me earlier. If you're going to worry about something, worry about the fact that I'm commando."

His dick jerked inside his jeans.

"And that I'm commando at all is all your fault."

True. He had the tiny blue scrap of panties in his pocket to prove it. At the thought, he let out a frustrated groan. "And if you could stop saying commando, that might help."

She laughed again. She was laughing, and all he could think about was getting back into her pants. Where she had no panties. Nope, just warm, wet flesh. He scrubbed a hand down his face and tried to steer his mind to something else. Multiplication tables maybe. *Twelve times twelve is—*

"You're going to get a ticket," she said, glancing at the speedometer. "You in a hurry?"

He knew that she knew damn well he was in a hurry. In a hurry to get her home and naked to finish what they'd started.

Because when she was in his arms he was content, as he so rarely ever felt. He didn't want to examine that too closely, because if he did, he'd have to face that not only was he thinking about Sunshine as "home" but that he was also thinking about a future. In one spot. *Twelve times thirteen is—*

"You seem a little on edge," she said.

Yeah, he was on edge. On a very narrow one, too. Because he could get her home as fast as he wanted, but it didn't matter. She had to study and sleep. "I'm on edge, yes. Because I've been hard for hours."

She laughed. "Poor baby."

He was beginning to wonder if he was addicted to her. There'd been times in his wild, misspent youth where he'd tried just about everything under the sun—all manner of drugs and alcohol. It was amazing he'd never become addicted to anything, but how ironic that after all that he was addicted to one little woman.

Not that she had the same problem with him, of course. Nope. She was over there cool as a cucumber, looking like some kind of hot, sexy trouble.

So what the hell was bothering him? She was a dream lover, wanting nothing from him but mutual sexual bliss. No strings . . .

Perfect.

Only it wasn't. Not even close.

Lilah turned to Brady as he drove them through the dark night toward Sunshine. The mountains were nothing but black inky silhouettes, the moon a solitary half orb hanging overhead, casting Brady's face in its glow. He was in his driving zone, giving nothing of himself away.

As if sensing her interest, he glanced over, his features softening when he saw her looking at him. "That dessert you came up with was genius," he admitted.

It had been genius, if she admitted so herself. She'd seen the little pretzel twists on Ellen's kitchen counter, next to a bowl of Hershey kisses. Lilah had taken a baking sheet, spread out the pretzels, put a chocolate kiss in the center of each and then baked. When the kisses were just slightly melted, she'd pulled them out and added a single M&M on top of each, pushing down, spreading out the kiss over the pretzel.

Better than any candy bar at 7-Eleven.

"And I bet no one but me knew you made that up on the spot from the crap she had out on the counter," he said, sounding amused.

"Hey, you loved that crap. You ate like twenty of those pieces of crap."

"I did." He was leaned back, utterly relaxed as he drove, the annoyingly sexy alpha.

"You didn't do so bad yourself," she admitted. "Telling her that I could bake. We're even now, right?"

"Oh no," he said silkily, his voice like warm butter. "We're not even. Not even close."

There in the dark interior, with the darker night all around them, surrounded by the wilderness and four adorable dogs in the back, she shivered. "Don't tell me you're going to hold a grudge."

He slid her a glance. "Weekly grooming sessions? Male Brazilians?" He smiled evilly. "Yeah. I'm holding a helluva grudge. If I was you, I'd be worried. Very worried."

"I'm pretty sure they knew we were making all that up." She nibbled her lower lip. Okay, maybe she'd taken it a little far. "And I was really torn between the Brazilian and saying that we met at the dog-grooming place, where you were having your Pomeranian groomed. The one with a jeweled collar."

"Christ."

She smiled. "I've got to ask—why did you go with the whole couple thing in the first place?"

"Because they wanted it to be true."

She stared at him. "So you told a whopper to a very nice, kind middle-aged man and his wife for altruistic reasons? That's . . . sweet," she decided.

"I am sweet."

She laughed, and he smiled wryly. "Okay," he said. "Maybe sweet is a bit of a stretch."

"I don't know," she murmured, feeling herself soften inexplicably as she thought of all the little things he'd done for her. Giving the woman who'd crunched his bumper a ride home, leaving her breakfast, carrying her to bed when she'd literally fallen asleep on her face. Driving one hundred miles for a dog rescue just to keep her company . . . "You have your moments."

It was midnight when they pulled back into Sunshine. Brady walked Lilah into the kennels and waited while she got the dogs in and settled, spending a few minutes with each of them, making sure they were calm and had what they needed even though she was yawning widely every two seconds and clearly dead on her feet.

With good reason, he knew. She'd been up since before dawn. He stepped in and helped her, a physical ache in his heart, the one that he was getting used to when it came to her.

"What's the matter?" she asked when they were done.

He'd just realized what else was really bugging him. She was there for everyone and everything, and yet near as he could tell, it didn't go both ways. Not because people didn't love her and want to help her. They did. Everyone loved her. Everyone wanted to help her.

But she didn't let them. She was the most independent, feisty, sexy woman he'd ever met. "Nothing," he said, and walked her to her cabin.

"Want to come in and look beneath my bed? Or better yet, in my bed?"

He wanted her, bad. Beyond bad. But more than getting her naked and making her scream his name, he wanted her rested. She worked so damn hard, was clearly exhausted . . . "I'll tuck you in."

"I'm not going to sleep."

"You've had a long day."

"Yes, but that chem test I'm taking tomorrow counts for half of my grade. I have to burn the midnight oil." She turned in the doorway, clearly expecting him to leave.

Instead, he caught her close, lowered his head, and kissed her, and for a moment she clung to him. It was sweet and warm, and like always when he was within two inches of her, not enough. Gently he nudged her farther inside her cabin. "Get comfy."

She smiled, and he laughed. "Not that kind of comfy. I'm going to help you study."

"What? Why?"

"Because I can."

"What do you know about animal reproductive physiology?"

"I'll be holding the book," he said. "I'll know everything."

Her smile was gone, and so was the warmth in her eyes. "I can do it by myself."

He cocked his head and studied her. "What just happened, what nerve did I step on?"

"Nothing. But I can do this on my own."

That wasn't an answer to his question and they both knew it. "Of course you can do this on your own. But why should you have to if someone's willing to help? Oh," he said, nodding when she didn't respond to that either, "I get it. You don't want help."

"I don't need help."

And in her mind, he knew, there was a huge difference. "Everyone needs help sometimes, Lilah. Except for you, apparently, because that would signify some kind of weakness, right? Not accepting my help allows you to lump me in with all the other men in your life. The ones who, like everything else, are to be taken care of, not vice versa. Because no one's allowed to take care of you."

"That's . . . stupid."

"I might be temporary, Lilah, but I'm not stupid. And I'm not one of your pets, either." He nudged her to the kitchen table where her books were spread out, waiting. "Sit down. The professor is here to make sure you pass."

"Brady."

"That's Professor Brady to you," he said.

She arched a brow and gave him a level look. No longer defensive but not yet willing to concede surrender. "So is this some kind of sexual fantasy? The beleaguered student servicing her professor for an A?"

"Hmm, sounds promising." He nudged her into a chair, smiling when a trickle of good humor came into her eyes. "We'll get to that. For now, crack that book, woman. Don't make me show you what happens to naughty schoolgirls."

Eighteen

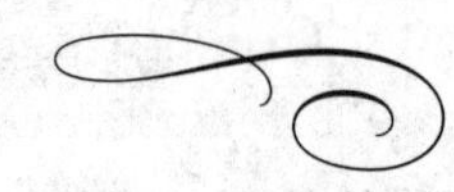

Three hours and lots of caffeine later, Lilah walked past a sleeping Twinkles and Boss and threw herself on her bed. She was frustrated and near comatose and also quite possibly close to jumping Brady's bones.

"What type of uterus is found in mares?" he asked, following her from the kitchen to stand at the foot of her bed, staring down at her in a very intense professor sort of way.

She wanted to strip him naked and lick him like a lollipop, and he wanted to know what a chemical element was.

He nudged her foot. "Lilah."

"Bipartite. Sir," she added with a little smart-aleck salute.

"I like that," he said with a firm nod as he consulted her review notes. "More of that. Now chemically, FSH is what?"

"A protein."

"A protein, sir," he corrected.

She rolled her eyes while he turned her pages. "An oocyte that is surrounded by several layers of cells but does not contain an antrum," he said.

He'd stripped out of his sweatshirt, leaving him in a loosely fitted Henley and a pair of cargo pants with more pockets than she could count. He looked edible.

"I can see you need incentive." He got on the bed and crawled up the length of her, spreading her legs with his knee. "An oocyte . . . ?"

"Secondary follicle . . ." She broke off as he rested his forearms on either side of her head, his face just inches above hers.

"And the structures on the chorion that interlock with the uterine endometrium in the ruminant?" he asked, pulling off her clothes, brushing kisses to every part of her that he exposed, making her mind go blank.

When she didn't speak, he raised his head, his eyes dark with concentration. "Lilah . . . ?"

"Um . . ." This was supposedly all review for her, but she couldn't remember. She blamed his sexiness. "I'm—" She moaned when he drew her breast into his mouth and struggled to think. "I— God, Brady."

He switched to her other breast and slid a hand between her thighs. His breath caught and he made a distinct sound of male pleasure that made her inner muscles contract.

"Brady?"

"Shh." His voice was low and delicious. "I know what will help." And he shifted, kissing her belly, her hips, a thigh . . . and then between them. "This." He rubbed his jaw to her inner thigh. "And this." He stroked her with his tongue and she promptly forgot the question.

"Oh, please," she whispered.

And he did. In a shocking short time, he had her crying out, shuddering with the surprise release. When she'd recovered she found him leaning over her, playing with her hair, face smug.

"Okay," she admitted. "I needed that." She pushed him to his back, pulled off his clothes, and climbed on top of him. "Now you, Professor Know-it-all. Your turn to beg."

"I'm not much for begging."

"Hmm." She started at his throat, working her way down, tasting every inch of him, stopping occasionally to nibble. By the time she got to his abs, he was alternately groaning her name in a plea and in warning.

But not begging. Not yet. Drunk on her own power, and also how he felt shifting restlessly beneath her, she continued southward.

"Christ, Lilah," he grounded out when she finally drew him into her mouth, his hands sliding into her hair. "Christ, don't stop."

Close enough, she thought, and didn't stop.

A long shower and another cup of coffee later, Lilah smiled softly at Brady. "Cotyledons."

"What?"

"That's the chorion that interlocks with the uterine endometrium in the ruminant. Thanks for helping me, you're my hero."

"I'm no one's hero." He pulled on his jeans by the first light of dawn slanting in the opened shades, adjusting himself with a scowl.

Either he'd slept badly after he'd put her into a pleasure coma, or her "hero" comment had gotten to him. She was betting on the latter. "In a hurry?"

"I've got to go."

Yeah. Definitely, it had been the hero comment. "Feeling claustrophobic?"

"This place isn't that small."

"That's not what I meant and you know it."

He ignored that and bent to lace up his boots. "I have a flight scheduled. I'm taking Dell to Idaho Falls for a business thing."

She nodded. "So go."

His mouth tightened, and he whistled for Twinkles, who leapt to his feet to follow blindly. As she was beginning to realize she would do as well.

At the door, Brady paused. "Shit," he muttered to himself with feeling. He turned back to her, staring at her for a long beat while she forced her expression to remain even. Then he closed his eyes. "Fucking sap," he said, and strode toward her, hauling her up to her toes to kiss her stupid. "Kick ass today," he said against her lips.

"You, too," she whispered, but he was already gone.

Brady walked through the chilly morning air, shadowed by Twinkles. It wasn't a month yet, but probably he should call Tony and at least get himself back in the queue to fly. Getting the hell out of Dodge ASAP would be a good thing.

Too bad he couldn't bring himself to do it. He wasn't ready to go.

It was as simple and terrifying as that.

"Arf."

"Yeah, yeah." He'd taken off on Lilah like a bat out of hell, and now all he could see was her face as he'd left. There hadn't been disappointment or irritation. She hadn't been offended the way any number of women in his past would have been when he did his usual vanishing routine. Lilah didn't get upset or withdraw. There'd been only those two words, her softly spoken "So go." And yet in them he'd heard all the damage, all the hurt, she felt.

She was prepared to watch him walk away.

God, he was an ass. He turned around so suddenly he tripped over Twinkles.

"Arf."

"We're going back. I don't know why, so don't ask me." Brady wasn't afraid of much. He doubted there was a boogeyman left on earth that could scare him. And yet one woman from the middle of nowhere with heartbreaking eyes and the most courageous heart he'd ever known absolutely terrified him.

As he once again entered the clearing between the cabin and the kennels, Adam was just getting out of his truck, juggling two steaming drinks and a big bag of food from New Moon, the health food store in town.

"What are you doing here at this time of morning?" Adam wanted to know.

Brady shrugged. He'd asked himself that a hundred times in as many seconds. He still didn't know. "She doesn't like health food."

"Are you just getting here?" Adam asked. "Or just leaving?"

"Both."

Adam's eyes went to slits. "I usually offer the choice of death or dismemberment to people who mess with her."

Brady sighed, and Adam stared at him for a long moment, then slowly shook his head. "You poor bastard. You're as fucked up over her as all the others, aren't you?"

"I'm not—"

Adam arched a brow, and Brady closed his eyes.

He was.

He was totally and completely fucked up over her. Which settled it. He did not need to go back inside that cabin. Nothing good would come of him going back in there except muddying up the waters with more of his crazy-ass, confused emotions. Without a word to Adam, he turned around and began walking away.

"Was it the threat of death or dismemberment?" Adam wanted to know.

The truth was, he'd welcome either.

* * *

Six hours later, Dell had finished his business and Brady had the Bell 47 aimed back at Sunshine. The trip had gone well, rendering Belle Haven a new contract handling the vet care for a 250,000-acre ranch in the Idaho Falls area.

"This trip alone was worth having the chopper," Dell said as they headed into Sunshine.

Brady shrugged. "Anyone can fly you after I'm gone. Hell, you can hire a pilot right out of Smitty's if you want."

"Rather have you."

"You might want to check with Adam on that," Brady said dryly.

"Why, because he found you coming out of the woods suspiciously near Lilah's cabin at the crack of dawn looking like you'd had a long night?" Dell shrugged. "He's always a bitch when he's not getting any."

"What are we, sixteen?"

"If we were, then he would have threatened you with death or dismemberment. Which one did you pick, by the way? I always pick death."

"And yet here you still are."

Dell grinned. "Yeah. He's all bark and no bite. Probably you should just stick around and keep us in line."

"Stick around?"

"Oh, I'm sorry. You don't know those two words in that particular order. They mean stay. Unpack. Whatever you want to call it."

"I can't."

"Why not?"

Brady stared at him. "Because."

"I realize you're allergic to permanent," Dell said. "But so's Adam, and he makes it work. He travels everywhere all over the country all the time training and delivering the search and rescue dogs, but he always comes back. That's the trick. You could do the same."

"I could train dogs?" Brady asked.

"Travel, smart-ass. Go back and forth." Dell paused. "Be a partner."

"I don't work well with others."

Dell laughed. "Well, no shit. And here I thought your sunny disposition would be such an asset."

Brady let out a breath. "I'll think about it."

"You do that. I'm thinking if you turn us down, I'll hire a female pilot instead, maybe one who wears a short, tight uniform and greets me with 'How can I serve you, sir?'"

Four days later, Lilah was near the outskirts of the county, on the edges of a ranch about to rescue a raccoon mama and her cubs. It had to be close to a hundred degrees outside and she was hot, tired, and filthy. Despite the unseasonably warm day, she was dressed for work in Carhartts and a long-sleeved T-shirt meant to protect her arms. She was tired because she hadn't slept much. Midterms were over, at least for now, but it hadn't been studying that had kept her up the past few nights.

It had been Brady.

Or the lack of Brady.

As for the filthy part . . . well, that was part of her job. She'd been sent here by Dell, who'd talked to the rancher who owned the land and was mad as hell about the raccoons who were constantly stealing the fresh eggs from the hen coops.

Lilah understood the problem. Raccoons were messy and mischievous, and they made pests of themselves on small ranches like this. Certainly it was easier to shoot them, but she hated the thought. She and Dell had a friend in Lewiston who had three thousand open acres. The woman had previously taken in various wild critters and didn't mind doing so again.

Lilah had a pile of humane cages in her Jeep ready to go, and with the hope in mind that the raccoons would be fond of the canned cat food she'd brought as bait, she got out of the Jeep and headed to the front door.

No one answered.

Knowing that she had permission via Dell from the ranch owner to try and solve his problem, she walked around to the barn, which was opened from two sides. Standing in the first opened doorway, able to see clear through to the other opened door, she caught sight of a man out on a horse in a neighboring field.

Probably the ranch owner.

Not wanting him to think she was trespassing, she waved a hand and called out to him, but the sun was in his eyes and he clearly couldn't see her. Plus, she knew he was older and couldn't hear well. She turned back to the barn and went still as she caught sight of movement in the rafters.

The resident raccoons. One big masked head appeared, and then three little matching ones perfectly lined up beside their mama.

Her cell phone rang. "How's it going out there?" Dell asked.

"Working on it," she said.

"Yeah, well be careful. Newberry's pretty determined to shoot the shit out of them. I guess they got into his kitchen yesterday and completely destroyed the place. Remind him that I sent you, that he said it was okay for you to remove the raccoons if you can. He's an older guy and can be mean as a snake. Part of the reason I called you about this in the first place is because his neighbors are threatening to call the authorities on him for using whatever moves as target practice."

"He's out in his field right now but I'll flag him down before I leave." She disconnected and went to the Jeep for two of the cages. Using a ladder she found against the far barn wall, she climbed to the top of the rafters and then precariously balanced there as she came face-to-face with the big mama herself.

Who showed her teeth.

Lilah ignored her and set the traps. This took a few minutes because she had to keep backing off to give the growling, snarling mama some space. "You'll be thanking me for this in a few days," she promised the pissed-off matriarch raccoon. "You'll—"

The crack of a shotgun ricocheted over her head and shocked the hell out of her, and she barely held on to the rafters. "What the—"

"Goddamn raccoons!" Newberry shouted, clearly frustrated that the sun was in his eyes and he was shooting into a dark barn, which didn't help his aim or his mood.

"Wait!" she cried.

But he'd already pulled the trigger and this time the bullet pinged somewhere just to her right, so close she felt it whizz through her loose hair. She flattened herself on the rafters so that she was lying belly down, and felt the contents of her pockets fall. Keys. Phone. The single buck she held in reserve for the swear jar. She gulped for air as the dollar bill slowly floated to the ground. Through the opened door she could see Mr. Newberry, still on his horse, closer now, once again sighting with his rifle through the opened doors.

He'd seen her shadowed movement, had known the raccoons were up here, and had started shooting.

Unfortunately, Lilah was a side dish on the same platter. Before she could blink, the gun went off again and this time she felt the impact jerk her body.

Fire blazed along her arm.

Barely managing to cling to her perch, she looked down the twenty-plus feet between her and the ground, which was suddenly whirling like she was on a merry-go-round. Through the spinning, she heard Mr. Newberry's horse gallop off. "Wait!" she called with a gasp, but he didn't hear her. She reached out for the ladder and then empty air as said ladder crashed to the ground. Alone, with no way down and no cell phone, she blinked past the sweat in her eyes.

Even the raccoons had deserted her. She set her forehead to the rafter she was clinging to. "Don't pass out," she told herself, knowing the fall would definitely be worse than the bullet wound. "Just keep your eyes open."

But that was hard . . .

The next thing she knew, she heard male voices raised in question, and she forced herself to lift her head. Either she was hallucinating, or the two tall, imposing figures in the doorway were Dell and Brady.

Yelling for her.

"I don't know why she wouldn't be answering her phone." This was from Dell. "Her Jeep's out there, but Mr. Newberry hasn't seen her."

"Here's why she's not answering," Brady said grimly, and crouched down to look at the pieces of her smashed phone.

Just as Lilah opened her mouth to say his name, he raised his head, his gaze landing unerringly right on her.

"Hi," she said, voice nothing but a croak.

He rose and strode toward her. "You okay?" His voice was calm. Maybe that meant everything was just fine.

"I-I think I was hit."

He was at the fallen ladder now, raising it with far more ease than she had. "Hit with what?" He broke off, focusing in on the drops of blood that had fallen from her to the ladder.

"What is it?" Dell asked, moving toward them.

"Blood. Hers, I think." He never took his eyes off her. "Hold on, Lilah," he said, climbing the ladder with agility and speed. "You hear me?"

She didn't answer because she was busy shivering. Odd to be so cold and hot at the same time, and as a bonus, someone was sticking her arm with a hot poker with every heartbeat.

"Lilah. Open your eyes right now."

Oh. Oh yeah, that was the problem. Still clinging to the beam, lying along it like she was on a balance beam, she tried to concentrate.

"Lilah, you hold on. Don't you dare let go," Brady told her.

That's when she realized that she was weaving. And the rafter was shaking, trembling beneath her. And look at that, her hands kept slipping . . .

Suddenly Brady was right there, wrapping an arm around her waist, drawing her up against his body, his free hand running over her as he balanced for the both of them. When he got to her arm, she cried out and his face went grim.

"What is it?" Dell called up.

"She's been shot and is going into shock."

"What the fuck?"

Oh, look at that, Lilah thought, eyeing her arm. There was blood dripping—everywhere. "Mr. Newberry thought he was shooting at the raccoons. It was an accident."

Brady cupped her face and forced it up so she could no longer see her arm. "Are you hit anywhere else?" Without waiting for an answer, he ran his hand over every inch of her, searching for more holes.

"Ouch," she said weakly.

"I'll kiss it later," he promised. "Let's go."

She relaxed her death grip on the rafters and wrapped her good arm around his shoulder, burying her face in his neck. Her world tilted as he descended with one hand on the ladder, the other wrapped tightly around her. As soon as their feet were on solid ground, he slid his other arm beneath her knees and carried her out of the barn to Dell's truck.

"Thought you weren't a hero," she murmured.

She thought she heard a rough, low laugh as he tore her shirt from her arm. "Christ." He ripped off his shirt and used it to staunch the bleeding.

"How bad?" Dell asked him, stroking Lilah's hair.

"Bullet's still in there."

"Fuck."

Lilah used Brady's now bare chest as a painkiller. As far as narcotics went, it was good. She smiled at the definition of muscles, the light smattering of hair that tapered to a line, vanishing into the loose waistband of his cargoes. She wanted to run a finger along it to find the hidden treasure, but then he pressed down on her arm and she cried out.

"I know." Brady gathered her back into his arms, then sat in her spot, cradling her in his lap, pulling her in so tight she couldn't breathe. "You're my hero," he murmured against her temple.

"I want to go home now."

"You're going to the hospital, sweetheart," Dell said, getting into the driver's seat.

"No," she murmured. She hated hospitals. They reminded her of losing her grandma, but as she looked down, she saw that she was bleeding right through Brady's shirt, and her world spun.

"It's okay," Brady said, holding her close. "I've got you now."

That was a good thing, because that last little pinpoint of light faded, and Lilah fell into the darkness.

Nineteen

Brady entered Lilah's bedroom balancing a tray. Nurse Nightingale, that was him. He set the tea and toast on her nightstand and eyed the white bandage on her arm, covering the spot where the bullet had penetrated her biceps.

"Lucky lady," the doctor had said, and the words rang in Brady's ears now as he sat at her side.

She was white, pasty, and out cold.

The eighteen stitches, she'd managed. Dealing with the police and their questions as she'd assured everyone that one, she hadn't been trespassing, and two, that Mr. Newberry had not in fact been trying to kill her, she'd handled as well. Sitting in a hospital room waiting to be released, though—that had been torture given how she'd hounded the hospital staff for her release papers.

The doctor had finally released her with a whispered "Good luck" to Brady beneath his breath as he left.

It had taken all three of them, Adam, Dell, and himself, to bring her home. And a silent battle of wills to see who would get to stay to take care of her. But then Adam had been called out on an S&R call.

"I'm not leaving," Dell said.

"Yes," Lilah said groggily from her bed where Brady had set her. "You are."

"Lil—"

"Don't, Dell. I'm too tired to fight with you, but if you want tears, I'll work some up."

Dell grimaced. "But—"

"I'll cry all over you," Lilah promised weakly as Brady pulled off her boots and covered her with a quilt. "Besides, you heard the doctor. I'm going to be fine. I just want to sleep off the drugs he gave me."

"Actually," Dell said, "he didn't say you were fine. He said you were a pain in his—"

"Go," Lilah said.

"You were shot because of me," he said tightly. "I sent you out there."

"I was shot because I didn't realize I looked like a raccoon from fifty yards. I want to be alone, Dell. That's all."

Dell looked pointedly at Brady.

Brady stared back at him evenly. He wasn't going anywhere. Not with the fury still churning within him.

She'd been shot.

She was the best thing to ever happen to him, even though he'd tried like hell to push her away. In fact, he'd very nearly succeeded at that, and she could have died today.

"Oh, for God's sake," Lilah burst out. "If you both don't get the hell out of here "—she looked at Dell—"I'll sic Lorraine on you."

Dell paled. "That's just mean. If he's staying, I'm staying."

"He's not." She held her ground. "Lorraine," she said again, softly, with a steel undertone.

Brady was impressed. Especially when Dell caved like a cheap suitcase, giving in with gracious defeat as he kissed her cheek and made her promise to call him if she needed anything.

He passed Jade coming in at the doorway. Jade had the latest issue of *Cosmo*. "It's what I brought my sisters when they had babies," she said to Lilah. "Wasn't sure what to bring for a gunshot wound. Which, by the way? Pretty damn cool." She eyed Brady. "Do you think if I get myself shot, I can get a bodyguard that looks like him?"

Brady decided to ignore that. "See if you can get her to agree to rest. She's not real good at that."

"No kidding. She thinks she's the Energizer Bunny." Jade looked Lilah over, still speaking to Brady. "You could try bribing her. Your woman has a love affair with crap food. You try that yet?"

"Excuse me," Lilah said. "His woman?"

Jade grinned and dropped the *Cosmo* on the nightstand. "I can see you're well taken care of here. I'll see you tomorrow, Lil."

"I'm my own woman!" Lilah yelled after Jade, who merely laughed and shut the cabin door.

Alone now, Lilah turned her glassy eyes on an admittedly smug Brady. "You heard me," she said. "Out with the others."

"No."

She arched a brow. Or she tried. But she was doped up pretty damn good. Finally she gave up with a sigh and rubbed her forehead as if it hurt. "I don't want to hear no. I want to hear the sound of the door hitting you on your very fine ass as you follow everyone out."

"Yeah, that was pretty impressive how you managed to kick them out." He sat in the chair in the corner of the room and crossed his arms.

She attempted a glare but she was drooping. "Dammit. My eyes keep closing."

He blew out a breath and leaned in to stroke her hair from her face. "Let them."

"You . . ."

She drifted off before she could finish the sentence, which undoubtedly was for the best. He waited another five full minutes to be sure, then pulled the quilt off her. Without hesitation, he stripped her out of her bloodstained clothes. He went through her dresser for something comfortable for her to sleep in.

One of his T-shirts lay neatly folded on top of her pj's. He stared down at it for a beat, discombobulated by the sight.

She had one of his shirts.

Something happened inside him at that, a warmth spread through his chest. It felt good and hurt all at the same time. "You're killing me," he murmured.

Turning back to the bed, he slipped the shirt—his shirt—over her head, taking care of her arm as he tucked her in.

"Glad you stayed," she murmured. "You're the only one who can ever make me feel better."

He stared down at her pale, beautiful face, unable to think past the surprise of that. Surprise and . . . satisfaction and pride as well, that he'd given her something, after all.

Himself.

He hadn't meant to, God knew he'd tried not to, but he had. He sat on the chair again, and with Twinkles at his feet, settled in to watch her breathe.

Lilah woke up disoriented and groggy. Her clock said four, and given the blackness at the window, it was A.M. and she'd just slept for twelve straight hours. There was a dark figure sitting near her.

"Just me," Brady said.

She let out a breath and swiped a hand over her face. "I was having a weird dream. I was shot—"

"Yes."

She let out a breath. Right. Not a dream.

He rose and offered her a pretty pink pill and two white chalky ones. "Take these and go back to sleep."

"No, I don't need them." Her arm was throbbing, but she hated the way they made her feel.

"You're taking the antibiotic, Lilah."

"Fine." She swallowed it with the water he handed her, then grabbed at him when he started for the door, ridiculously panicked over the thought of him going, when earlier she'd wanted nothing more than to be alone. "Don't." To make sure, she pulled him over her.

"Careful," he murmured, holding his weight off her by the palms he had planted on either side of her hips. "I don't want to hurt you."

She ran her good hand over him, humming in pleasure at the feel of his biceps, taut and straining. Yes, she needed more of that. She tried to pull him closer, but he held back from full contact.

Stubborn man.

She tugged again, wanting a kiss. Needing a kiss.

"Lilah—"

"Please," she whispered, her hand curling around his neck, pulling him in. "Please, Brady."

"Just one." He let their lips meet, lightly.

"Mmm," she murmured, the small brushing closed-mouthed kisses warming her from the inside out. But then it wasn't enough and she opened her mouth and touched her tongue to his lower lip.

A rough groan rumbled up from his chest, as if she were causing him physical pain. She closed her eyes and let herself live in the moment, in the delicious sensations as their tongues touched and explored with increasing pressure and hunger. His scent, his taste, the heat, everything, she loved it all, and it swirled around her like a spell, draping over her like a magical coat, suspending any ability to think.

Okay, that might have been the last of the drugs leaving her system.

But he was the best drug of all. "You take away my pain," she whispered. He also took away her ability to think straight. And she wasn't the only one affected, either. From deep in his throat came another low, masculine sound and she slid her hand down his shoulders to his chest, feeling his heart beating solidly beneath her palm. Below that, where their lower bodies were pressed together, he was hard. "You're better than pain meds, Brady."

He shifted and rested his forehead against hers, sliding his hands into her hair, his fingertips shockingly gentle against her scalp. "You're not all the way here with me."

How to tell him she was more with him than she'd ever been with anyone in her entire life? "I am. Trust me, the meds have worn off. Please, Brady, I need—"

"Rest."

"I can rest when I'm dead."

He let out a long breath, clearly fighting with his old-fashioned male moral ground. "Go back to sleep for a while." His mouth was at her ear, his breath hot against her skin.

"Can't."

Leaning over her, he rubbed his jaw to hers. "Close your eyes."

When she did, he ran his hand over her body, a light touch, caressing, teasing. She rocked up for more, but he held her down. "Just relax," he murmured, his mouth leaving hot kisses along her throat.

Her nipples were hard and pressed against the soft fabric of the shirt—his shirt, she realized. He must have removed her bloody clothes. His eyes went heavy-lidded and hot at the sight of her nipples. Then he slid his fingers beneath the cotton and desire shot through her, centering between her legs.

"Is this what you need?" he asked, strumming her like an instrument. "This?"

"Yes," she gasped, rocking into him.

His other hand went to her hips and held her still. "Don't move, you'll hurt yourself." With another long, deep kiss, he lifted the shirt up and over her head, taking great care with her arm. Then he bent to her breasts, the tip of his tongue stroking her nipple as his other hand slid between her legs.

She gasped again, writhing beneath him.

"Stay still," he reminded her sternly as his fingers worked their magic. "God, you feel like silk." He stroked her and she moaned. "Wet silk." And then he slid lower on the bed and gently pulled the material aside, out of his way. Holding her legs open with his broad shoulders, he put his mouth on her.

At the first touch of his tongue, she started to shoot straight up, but his hands caught her before she could. "No moving," he reminded her, gently holding her effortlessly immobile as he not so gently took her straight out of her mind with pleasure.

Afterward, he held her while she attempted to get herself under control. Or as under control as she could get for someone who'd been shot, drugged, and had just had the mother of all orgasms. He was sprawled on his back. She lay curled at his side, one leg and her bandaged arm over the top of him. She had no idea why having his arms tight on her calmed her more than anything she'd ever known. Maybe because she'd never let herself be vulnerable before, with anyone else.

Ever.

Even thinking it had peace settling in her heart, and she knew that she was right where she belonged. She tilted her head up to study him. His eyes were closed but she knew he wasn't sleeping. "Brady?"

"Yeah?"

She sighed dreamily. *I love you*, she thought.

He ran a hand over her, scooping her hair from her face. "Now you'll be able to sleep."

Yes. Yes she would . . . But she forced her eyes open one last time to make sure he was still there.

His arms tightened on her and he nuzzled his face in her hair. He breathed her in, his arms tightening on her. "You'd make a shitty soldier. I'll take care of you."

She knew that all his life, people had needed him in one form or another, and he'd taken care of them. He'd always come through.

But who took care of him? She wanted to be the one. "Stay," she said, knowing that if he'd only let her, she'd give him as much comfort as he always gave her.

"Yes."

"Promise?"

She held her breath when he cracked open an eye and leveled it on her. He wasn't big on promises, she knew this. But if he gave his word, it was as good as gold.

"Promise," he said, and brushed a kiss against her jaw. "Now close your damn eyes and zip it."

She closed her eyes and fell asleep smiling.

The next time she woke up, her arm felt like fire, her mouth was drier than the Sahara Desert, and . . .

And she was in Brady's T-shirt and nothing else. The sun was peeking through the blinds, casting shadows on the sheets. The other side of her bed was empty and she rolled over and took a deep breath, inhaling the scent of Brady.

He'd slept with her.

A smile broke on her face, but then it all came back to her. Being shot. Getting stitches while pretending she didn't have a needle phobia. And then . . .

Nothing.

Wait—Brady, Dell, and Adam had taken her home, then argued over who was going to stay. She remembered Adam leaving, and then Dell, and Brady covering her with a blanket. She remembered his delicious method of helping her sleep . . . That had ended well for her, very well.

She looked at the clock. It was nine. In the morning! She'd never slept past six thirty before, never, and suddenly her grogginess was gone, replaced by panic.

Cruz was on vacation, and she had the animals!

Struggling out of the covers, she staggered across the room, tripped over a startled Boss and jammed her legs into sweats. The best she could with one arm. She looked down at herself. More disconcerting than her commando status was the fact that she couldn't rein in her hair.

Glancing fondly at the painkillers sitting by her bed, she bypassed them for Motrin instead. She wouldn't be able to run the kennel if she was high as a kite, so she was going to have to suck it up, bad hair and all. Jamming her feet into boots, she bent over to tie them, got dizzy, and nearly fell on her head. Note to self: no bending. Which meant no lacing her boots.

She was going with the thug look today.

Moving as fast as she could without tripping over her own laces, she hit the bathroom and brushed her teeth—about all she could manage. She ran out the door and into the kennels, and skidded to a shocked halt.

Brady was behind the front counter. He had a cat on his lap and another at his elbow. Abigail stood guard at his feet next to Twinkles. In front of him was a short line of people and pets, waiting patiently to check in.

Actually, not quite patiently. Mrs. Lyons was in Brady's face, waggling a finger at him. "You'd best be good to my babies," she was saying. "I hear what they call you, you know. Dr. Death. Honestly, I don't know what Lilah was thinking, letting you work here."

Brady shoved his hand through his hair. "Your animals will be fine."

"My babies."

Brady looked at her, and with an utterly straight face, nodded. "Yes, ma'am."

Lilah covered her mouth and bit back her laugh as her heart slid to the floor at his feet. She couldn't help it. Watching him so completely out of his element and yet trying his best to run her world for her when he had no idea what he was doing, was it for her.

Even as she thought it, he looked up and frowned. "What are you doing out of bed?"

"No rest for the weary. Thanks for opening for me. I can take it from here."

He put his hand over hers when she tried to scoot behind the counter. "I'm also closing, Lilah."

"I'm fine."

"Yeah, maybe, but you're still going back to bed."

Everyone in the place was swiveling their heads back and forth between them like they were at a tennis match.

"Brady," she said, the voice of reason even as her legs were wobbling wildly with the need to sit down. "There's too much work to do. There's the billing, cleaning cages, feeding—"

"I'll figure it all out."

"I can't ask that of you."

"Then don't ask."

"I—"

"Stop." Dislodging the cats, he came around the counter and scooped her up into his arms.

She felt the silly little flutter deep in her belly. She had no idea what it said about her that she was enjoying his bossy, know-it-all attitude.

"You're done here," he said and turned to the room. "I'll be right back. No one move."

No one did, but the entire room gave a collective sigh, including Lilah.

One minute later, Brady set her on her bed and stood there, hands on hips, a stern look on his face. "Stay."

"Brady," she said very gently. Stupid, stupid man. "You can't tell me what to do."

"The doctor said you were to be kept quiet and still for a few days, even if I had to handcuff you to the bed myself."

Well, if that didn't cause a hot flash. "The doctor isn't trying to run his own business with his partner on vacation now, is he?"

Brady gave her a long look, then let out a breath. "Okay, I give. What'll it cost me for you to promise to stay here today, right here, all day?"

"Dinner," she said without pause.

"And?"

"Dessert."

"Goes without saying," he said, the very corners of his mouth twisting into a smile. "And?"

"And the handcuffs you just threatened me with."

The rest of his temper faded from his face, leaving something much, much better, something that nearly gave her a mini-orgasm.

"You're only teasing me," he said, eyes dark. "But I'm going to remember you said that."

Gulp.

Twenty

After being confined to the cabin, Lilah tried to keep busy while imagining the hell that Brady was going through. By the time that Adam came by to see her, she nearly pounced on him. "Oh, thank God. Would you please go help Brady at the kennels?"

Adam laughed. "Just came from there." He plopped next to her on the bed and grabbed the TV remote, flipping through the channels with male single-minded purpose. "Trust me, Dr. Death is doing better than Dell."

"What does that mean?"

"Your kennels are full up, since Brady's in the paper again—"

"Again? Why again?"

"Yeah front page this time, for being the big hero yesterday. There's some talk of featuring him weekly."

She choked out a laugh.

Adam grinned. "And Dell's all butt-hurt because he didn't make the cut. Anyway, now Brady's got chicks from three counties over dropping off their pets. You're making a mint." He tossed the remote aside. "Daytime TV is shit. You need pay-per-view."

An hour later, Jade and Dell brought Chinese for lunch. They were scowling at each other when they walked in.

"What's wrong?" Lilah asked.

"Nothing," Jade said in the tone that of course meant the exact opposite.

"I said I was sorry," Dell said to Jade, tossing up his hands. "Christ, it was just a little harmless flirting. Women generally like it."

Lilah divided a look between them. "Who was flirting?"

Jade jerked her chin in Dell's direction. "Stud man here."

"With whom now?" Lilah asked.

Jade snorted. "Exactly."

Dell looked confused. "You. I was flirting with you."

Lilah felt her brows raise at this.

Jade shook her head. "Me," she repeated, irritated.

Which clearly didn't help Dell's confusion any. "I said it was harmless!" he said, the picture of male exasperation.

"That," Jade said, poking him hard in the chest, "is the problem." She glared at him as she sat on the bed.

Lilah decided maybe they needed a moment alone and tried to get up, but Dell sat next to her and threw a leg over hers so she couldn't move, then carried on like she wasn't even there.

"You don't like when a man flirts with you?" he asked Jade over Lilah's head.

"It's the harmless part that chaps my ass." Jade grabbed the food, shoved a container and chopsticks at Lilah, and grabbed the next container for herself, closing her eyes as she chewed.

Lilah glanced at Dell and was startled to see . . . hurt and longing? But when she blinked, it was gone. "Dell—"

He grabbed the third container. "We checked on Brady."

Lilah recognized the subject change as a diversionary tactic and was just enough off her axis to let it go for now. "And? How bad is it?"

"He's running the place like boot camp. Even Lulu is behaving, though it's probably out of fear that she'll have to run laps if she doesn't." He laughed at the look on her face. "He's doing fine, Lil, stop worrying. In fact, he was telling Lorraine where to stick it," he said. He smiled. "Best moment of my day."

Shit. Lilah tried to get up, but Dell's leg was still over her. "Relax. He's got it all under control." He had the fried rice, and Lilah knew from experience if she didn't demand her share pronto, he'd eat it all in less than two minutes. "Gimme," she said.

After she'd filled her belly, she felt better and tried to get up but Dell shook his head.

"I'm getting up, Dell."

"No you're not."

"Yes I am."

"Christ, what is it with all the stubborn women today?" He spared a glance at Jade, who merely narrowed her eyes at him.

"I feel just fine," Lilah said.

"No go." Dell held firm. "If I let you up, you're going to go check on him."

"Yes."

"You're still on bed rest."

"Since when did you talk to my doctor?"

"Not your doctor, your keeper."

"Yes, well if you want to keep your pretty face, get off me."

Jade snorted and kept eating.

"Sheesh," Dell said, moving. "You're grumpy when you get shot. And I don't know what your problem is," he said to Jade.

"I'd tell you to think about it," Jade said. "But that might be a stretch for you—" She broke off, staring at him. "Are you kidding me? What, are you twelve?"

"What?" Dell said, looking around. "I didn't do a fucking thing."

Jade pointed to his Levi's, which were low slung and had sunk far enough on his hips that when he'd sat, they'd revealed the waistband of his boxers, which were pink and covered in little red lips. He looked down at himself and shrugged. "They were a gift."

"Pig," Jade said.

Later, when Lilah was alone again, she fought with discomfort and discontentment and told herself it was from being cooped up.

It wasn't from wanting things she couldn't have.

Except it was.

At eight, there was a knock at her front door, but before she could move, she heard a key in the lock.

Only three people had keys. Adam, Dell, and as of this morning, Brady. He had her set of keys, actually, so he could come and go between the kennels and the cabin. She listened as footsteps, sure and steady, came down the hall. "You're lucky I don't sleep with a gun beneath my pillow," she said to the tall, dark, built shadow who appeared in her doorway.

Brady propped up the jamb with a shoulder, and a smile flashed from him in the dark. Imperturbable as usual, the bastard.

"I think we've had enough accidental shootings for this week." He crossed his arms. "But out of curiosity, do you really think you could shoot me?"

She thought she could do a lot of things to him. Smack him for the smugness. Hug him for how hard he'd worked today.

Love him for exactly who and what he was . . .

"No," she answered honestly. "I don't think I could shoot you. But I could throw a gun at your head."

He laughed. "Now that I believe."

"Are you here with the handcuffs?" she asked hopefully.

That tugged another rough laugh out of him. "Thought I'd save that for when you're feeling better."

Heat slashed through her, pooling low in her belly. "You worked hard today."

"No harder than you do every day." There was admiration in his voice for what she did, and then there was a warmth inside her to go with the heat.

"I don't bring in women from three counties over," she said. "That's new."

Pushing off from the doorjamb, he came forward until his thighs bumped the bed. Leaning over her, a hand on either side of her head, he bent close.

It was dark, but she had enough of a glow from the moonlight outside to see his exhaustion, and concern.

For her.

"I'm okay," she told him softly. Reaching up, she cupped his face. "Really."

"Wanted to make sure." He kissed her softly, tenderly, and she kissed him back. The emotion rocked him, she could feel it in the fine tremor of his body. And suddenly it was all ferocious intensity, and she wanted to show him just how okay she was. She wanted to lessen some of the tension she felt in him, wanted to help him let go. Tugging his shirt up with her good hand, she smiled when he took over and yanked the shirt off in one fluid motion.

"Pants, too," she whispered, running her fingers down the center of his chest, past his belly button to the waistband of his cargoes.

Almost before she had the words out, he'd stripped down to skin.

And Lord, what beautiful skin.

With his careful help, she shimmied out of her pj's, then lifted the covers to make room for him. Pulling him over the top of her, she sighed in pleasure, loving the way she felt when his weight pressed her into the mattress. Arching, she wrapped her legs around him, absorbing the groan that wrenched up from deep in his chest.

"Lilah—"

"In the bedside drawer."

He pulled out a condom and put it on before he came back over her. She rocked again, shifted strategically, and then he was inside her, the sensation taking her breath away.

"Christ, you feel good . . ." He let out a long, shaky breath and kissed her jaw, her throat. "So fucking good."

She tried to rock her hips against him but he wasn't budging. Not until he was ready, and as she already knew, wasting energy on pushing him was useless, his body was like steel. "Brady . . ."

"Shh. Give me a minute. Just feel."

She let her hand roam, she couldn't help it. His body was smooth and muscular. And scarred. Her fingers traced a few of those scars, memories of long-ago battles he never spoke of, and then she pulled his face to hers to nip at his bottom lip.

Growling low in his throat, he finally began to move, setting an agonizingly slow rhythm, his hips barely grinding in a circle as he did, careful not to jar or hurt her.

She heard herself whimper but not in pain. She was dying with each and every single rock of his hips. She dug her fingers into the cheeks of his perfect ass to try to speed him up, she tried words, she even bit his shoulder, nothing rushed him.

The sensations overtook her. The rush of pleasure at the top of every thrust he made had her orgasm building from her toes. Her eyes wanted to close, but she fought the urge, not wanting to tear her gaze from the look on his face. It was beautiful.

He was beautiful.

And then she was flying over the edge, coming hard. As she gasped and cried out, lost in the pleasure, his vivid blue eyes stayed locked on hers, his expression revealing every flicker of pleasure she gave him as he quietly followed her over.

* * *

The next few days were crazy for Brady, shuffling between kennel duties and the flying he did for Adam and Dell.

It was the nights, however, that stuck with him: the long, hot, steamy, tear-up-the-sheets nights.

The best nights of his life.

Three days after Lilah had been shot, he ambled over from the kennels, dirty from head to toe. He'd had a record day, including managing to be felt up by the seventy-year-old Mrs. Lyons. At the front door of the cabin he stopped to remove his boots, going still at the wild laughter from inside.

When he walked through, he found Lilah in bed, surrounded by Jade and three other women.

His gaze soaked Lilah up, the low-cut yoga pants and snug T-shirt she wore, the color on her cheeks that said she was feeling much better, the shine in her eyes that assured him she'd finally caught up on sleep and was no longer in constant pain.

Someone had brought pizza, magazines, fingernail polish, lotions, and a bunch of other frilly shit. There was so much estrogen in the room he almost couldn't breathe. He stared at Lilah in the middle of the bed, the center of attention, wearing no bra and a bandage from getting shot—

Christ.

She smiled at him and just about melted his bones away. "Hey."

"Hey right back atcha. Everyone out," she said, not taking her eyes off him.

No one listened. The talking and laughing continued.

Lilah put her fingers to her mouth and whistled, loud and long. "Party's over," she said into the ensuing silence, snagging Brady's hand. "Except you."

"I need a shower," he said inanely.

"Yeah? Well, it just so happens that I have one."

At this, there were hoots and hollers and whistles. Brady shook his head as the women gathered their things to leave.

"Here." Jade slapped a *Cosmo* up against his chest. "You might want to keep that one. Page fifty-seven, 'Fun with Handcuffs.'"

More laughter.

He turned and met Lilah's eyes. "Telling tales?" he asked.

She lifted a shoulder. "It might have come up in conversation is all."

"Uh-huh." When everyone had left, he stripped and showered until the hot water was gone. He came out of the bathroom for the duffel bag of clean clothes he'd dropped in the bedroom.

Lilah rose to her knees on the bed and gave him the "come here" finger crook.

Raising a brow, he walked forward until his legs bumped the bed.

She wrapped her arms around his neck. "Hi," she said.

He bent his head and kissed her until they were both breathless, and then he set his forehead to hers. "Hi."

She smiled and he got hard. Just like that. "Dinner," he said. "Out. You up for it?"

"Another date?"

"If I say yes," he asked cautiously, "are you going to tell me you don't have anything to wear?"

"Hey, you're the one nearly naked." She ran her hands down his chest, over his abs, and then played with the edge of the towel low on his hips, the one barely covering him. "And you smell fantastic," she murmured, and took a bite out of his shoulder. "I could eat you up."

He was on board with that.

But she got off the bed. "I'll get dressed. I ordered something new." She stripped off the T-shirt and then the yoga pants as she walked to the closet in nothing but a teeny-tiny black pair of bikini panties.

He groaned.

She shot him a smile over her shoulder. "You've seen it all before."

Yes, up front and personal. Three nights in a row, in fact, and he couldn't imagine ever getting tired of it. "Put clothes on," he said in a voice so low and thick he barely recognized it as his own, "or you'll be dinner."

Laughing, Lilah slid a halter-style summer dress over her head and slipped her feet into sandals, then twirled for him.

"Pretty," he said, and tugged her into him so that she fell against his chest. Sliding his hands down he cupped and squeezed her ass.

"Hmmm," she hummed, face against his throat as she rocked her hips to his. "Either you're happy to see me, or"—she rocked again, grinding into him, making him groan—"you're packing again."

Giving her a light smack on her ass, he pulled away and dressed, then carried her out the door.

"I was shot in the arm, not the leg," she pointed out. "And I'm all better. I can walk."

He didn't set her down until he placed her in the passenger side of his truck.

"Where are we going?"

"State secret."

She rolled her eyes, but she didn't ask any more questions until he'd parked outside of a steak house in Coeur d'Alene.

"I needed red meat," he said to her silence.

"Yes. It's because you're a caveman."

Smiling, he came around for her, but she shoved him in the chest. "Don't even think about carrying me in there."

"Some women like to be carried."

"I'm not some women."

"True," he said.

She waited until they were seated and had ordered before she asked, "Are we celebrating something?"

"Yes. The fact that I'm not wearing duck shit today and also that for the first time in days I'm done working before bedtime."

Some of her enjoyment of the evening drained. "I know. I know and I'm so sorry. I wanted to come back to work today, but you said you'd withhold sex if I got up."

He set his hand over hers. "I'm not complaining, Lilah. You work your ass off. I know you're still hurting some, and I wanted you to have one more day off."

She studied him over the candle flickering between them. "Thanks."

"For?"

"My life, for starters. I still can't believe you and Dell got to me so fast when I needed you."

His eyes softened and he set down his glass and reached for her hand. "You'd have been fine."

"It could have gone another way." She drew a shaky breath. "I should have been more aware of my surroundings. I need to be more careful."

"More careful would be good."

She scrubbed her hands over her face. "I was just so damn tired, and then I got that call . . ."

"So next time you'll take one of us with you."

"You won't be here next time."

His eyes were steady on hers. "You know what I mean. You'll take someone."

She stared into her wineglass and nodded, trying not to think about how soon that might be. It'd already been close to a month, which meant it could conceivably be only a matter of days.

"What did you get on your test?" he asked. "Grades posted yet?"

"Got an A." She smiled. "Only two more semesters to go."

"And then what?"

And wasn't that just the scary part. She didn't know.

"You're awfully closemouthed about your hopes and dreams," he noted.

She raised a brow. "Recognize that, do you?"

Clearly not feeling playful, his eyes never wavered. "You must have ideas on what you want."

"Yes."

He waited for more, but suddenly she wasn't feeling like sharing. *Liar*, said a little voice. *You always feel like sharing. You're just afraid to give it all and then lose him. And you are going to lose him. Soon.*

He was looking at her, and when she remained silent, he said, "So you let me into your body but not into your head." He nodded but didn't look happy. "I get that."

"You don't want to be in my head," she reminded him. "And hell, Brady, half the time I don't want to be in my head."

His eyes were stormy. Filled with censure. Feeling like a jerk, she pushed around a piece of steak on her plate. She understood why she was feeling out of sorts. She'd started this whole adventure with him for fun, but then she'd gone and gotten her heart involved. Which didn't explain what his problem was. "Help me out here, Brady. I'm not sure exactly why we're doing this."

"Doing what?"

"Fighting."

"Are we fighting?"

She shrugged. "Feels like it."

"I'm just trying to get to know you better."

"But why? You're not long-term, remember?"

"Hello, pot," he said softly. "Meet kettle."

She stared into his eyes. "Not fair."

"No?" He leaned forward, intent and focused on her. "Then tell me why everyone and everything else in this town is allowed to take up residence in your fold, but you keep me out."

"You didn't want in, remember?"

"Christ." He sat back, his expression suggesting that maybe she was being an unfathomable pain in his ass.

Which was true. She was being a pain. It was called fear. Because she decided right then and there that she was absolutely not going to let herself ruin what very well might be one of the last few nights she had with him. No regrets, she reminded herself. Not ever again.

They left the restaurant in silence.

Normally that was Brady's favorite state of being but not tonight. Tonight he needed more.

And it pissed him off.

He opened the door to the truck and went to help Lilah in, but she gave him a long look and he lifted his hands in surrender, backing up to watch her struggle one-handedly.

"Goddammit," he breathed when she winced in pain from tweaking her still-healing arm, and gave her a boost.

When he walked around and angled into the driver's seat, he felt her hand settle on his arm.

"Thank you."

Turning toward her, he stroked a strand of hair from her face. "For letting you hurt yourself trying to get into the truck?"

"For letting me be as stubborn as . . . well, you. Turn left," she said when he would have turned right to take her home.

He turned left and ended up at the convenience store.

"Wait here," she demanded.

He arched a brow.

"Please," she added so sweetly that he shook his head and did what she asked. She vanished inside, only to come back five minutes later with a brown bag and a smile.

"Ian was inside," she said. "He says if you strike out tonight, I'm to call him."

"Good to know," he said, wondering if he was going to indeed strike out. He reached for the bag.

"Nope," she said, holding it out of his way. "Surprise. Go straight."

He went straight.

"Now right again."

He slid her a glance, but in the dark of the night he couldn't see her expression. "Finally decided to take me to some remote area to off me?"

Her soft laugh was a balm to the soul he hadn't realized was aching. "You afraid of me, Brady?"

More than you know. "Should I be?"

She was quiet a moment. Then she let out a soft "yes."

Twenty-one

Lilah took Brady to the lake, his earlier words echoing in her head.

You're awfully closemouthed about your hopes and dreams.

You let me into your body but not into your head.

I'm just trying to get to know you better.

The night was balmy, with a nearly full moon, and aware as she had been all week that her time with him was winding down, she took his hand, wanting to lose herself in him, wanting to feel connected.

They walked to the water's edge, sitting there, absorbing the night. The soft breeze rustling the hundred-foot pines. The distant cry of something looking for its mate. The water lapping near their feet.

He was right, she had held back. Big-time. She'd done so out of self-preservation, but that didn't make it okay. If she was going to have no regrets, she needed to be fearless. Because no way was she going to be the woman who couldn't—or wouldn't—let herself love.

She pulled the bottle of whiskey out of the bag and made him laugh softly. God, she loved making him laugh. He didn't do it often, but when he did it was a beautiful sound.

She went back into the bag for her second item—a deck of cards.

"Strip poker?" he asked hopefully.

She showed him that they weren't regular playing cards but the game Uno. "It's all they had." She shuffled and dealt, then took a swig of the whiskey and offered the bottle to Brady.

Eyes on hers, he tossed back a swallow, then smiled because she was still coughing. "So, you do this a lot," he said.

She laughed and picked up her cards. They played a round and she lost. She set down the cards.

"Strip Uno?" he asked this time, still hopeful.

* * *

When she smiled, Brady knew he wasn't going to get to see her strip.

"Something not quite as fun as stripping," she said. "But I hope you'll like it." She hesitated. "I'm going to tell you something about me."

He was surprised by this.

Lit by the glow of the moon playing off the water, she smiled at his expression. "I know, brace yourself. Are you ready?"

"Hit me," he said.

"I grew up out here."

"I already knew that." He eyed her sundress, knowing she wore only a pair of skimpy, mind-blowing panties beneath—which meant that he could have had her naked in two rounds of Strip Uno.

"Yes, but you didn't know that I grew up poor as dirt."

He stopped thinking about Strip Uno and met her gaze. "I guessed."

She nodded. "Of course at the time, I had no idea we were that bad off," she said. "My grandma never let on. She took on odds jobs like cleaning houses and sewing, taking me with her so I wouldn't be alone. She'd pretend we were going on a grand adventure, and I believed her until in second grade, when John Dayley told me I was poor white trash."

Brady's chest tightened, for her grandma, for the little girl she'd been.

Laughing a little, she shook her head. "I didn't even know what white trash meant," she said, not nearly as bothered as he. "When I got home, I asked my grandma and she said it meant that we were special. The next weekend she took me to the circus. One of her cleaning clients had left her the tickets. It was"—she closed her eyes and smiled in fond memory—"amazing. I wanted to be a circus ring leader. I wanted to grow up and have all those animals around me, and I wanted to take care of them." She paused, glancing at him to make sure he wasn't going to laugh.

But that ache in his chest had spread now, and he didn't feel much like laughing.

"It was my first personal goal for myself," she said quietly, hitting him with those mossy green depths that he could jump into and never come up for air.

He smiled past a tight throat. "I like it."

They took another shot of whiskey each and played a second round.

He lost, but only because he forgot to say Uno. Lilah looked at him expectantly.

"I'd rather strip," he said.

"Don't tempt me. Talk. Tell me something about you. Something about when you were young."

He found it far easier than he could have imagined, which was no doubt thanks to the whiskey. "I was a punk-ass teenager when I landed at Sol's, and pissed off at the world." God, so pissed off. Even now he could remember the anger burning through him at every turn. "I'd just gone through a few different foster homes, each nicer than the last, and for various reasons, I didn't get to stay at any of them."

And he'd wanted to. Stay. He'd wanted a place where he belonged to someone.

"Why couldn't you stay?" she asked.

He shrugged, able to once again feel that bone-deep helplessness at not being in charge of his own fate. He'd been through some hairy shit in his life, especially in the army rangers, where too many times to count death had been a certainty, and yet nothing had been worse than that helplessness he could still practically taste. "The first couple that took me in ended up getting pregnant, and she got too sick to care for a kid, even a nearly grown one."

"Oh, Brady," she said softly.

"The second family had four daughters of their own already. They'd requested a girl, and when one came along, they traded me in."

"What?" She straightened, eyes blazing. "You weren't a used car!" she said in outrage, making him smile and reach for her hand.

"It's okay," he said.

"No, nothing about that was okay." She took a deep breath, clearly fighting for control. "What about the third family? And if you tell me that they traded you in, too, I'm going to go hunt them down myself."

"They got transferred out of state and didn't want to go through the paperwork to keep me. So I got dumped on Sol. By then my biggest goal was to get the hell out. I was done."

"Well, no wonder!"

Because she was a little drunk and a whole lot adorable in her righteous anger for him, he pulled her close to his side and nuzzled his face into her hair. "At that point, I had no particular destination in mind. I just wanted to be free, to go."

"So what happened?"

"Sol happened. He wasn't much on patience, but he knew enough about how a teenage boy's head worked. He put me on a horse and pointed me in the direction of more than seventy-five thousand acres of wild land to explore."

"Goal accomplished?" she asked softly. "You felt free?"

"Goal accomplished."

Again they took a shot, and Brady was glad they were within walking distance of her place.

They played another round.

Lilah lost. "By the time I got to high school," she said, knocking back more whiskey, "I had a good idea of what poor white trash was and I didn't like it. I'd never left Idaho, not once in my entire life. Can you imagine?" She shook her head in amusement at herself.

The moonlight touched over her hair, her face. Brady thought he'd never seen anyone more beautiful.

"All my life," she went on, "all I wanted was to go see the world. I mean I love the people here, love my life, but I wanted to see what was out there. College was my ticket out. I got a full ride at UNLV, and off I went."

She'd been a girl from the wilds of Idaho who'd never seen a big city much less left those wilds. He could only imagine how different Vegas must have seemed to her. "What did you think of the place?"

She laughed a little. "Culture shock. But it was a free ride, at least at first." She shook her head. "And it was a goal accomplished for me as well, and I never took that lightly. Ever."

He nodded. He understood perfectly.

"My grandma was so proud," she said softly, wrapping her arms around her knees, staring out at the water reflectively, remembering. "Everyone was. And I knew I had to do it—I had to succeed. But then my second year happened. My grandma got sick and I was coming back and forth, and my grades dropped. Because of that some of my funding fell through, and I had to take a couple of jobs to make ends meet."

His heart stopped. "Is this the part where you tell me you were forced to dance or strip for tuition? Because if so, I'm going to kick Dell's and Adam's asses and enjoy it."

"No, I didn't become good friends with them until after college." She laughed. "But sweet offer, thanks. I'll shelve that for the next time either of them pisses me off. I worked at night waiting tables at a club. It was fun but hard work, and I took on more hours than I should have. I fell even more behind and needed help. So the TA of my microbiology class offered to tutor me. Tyler—" She broke off, both the words and the eye contact, and dropped her head to her knees. "I fell for him a little bit."

He couldn't quite read her tone now and for the first time felt unsure as to her feelings since her face was hidden. "Is he still in your orbit like everyone else?"

She shook her head, her entire body tense. Clearly, this had not been a lighthearted fun relationship. He slid his hands to her shoulders, which were knotted tight. He worked at them silently, tugging a low moan from her before she straightened. "I fell in love with him. With Tyler. And he . . ."

Her sudden silence had his heart stopping again, because he could read her quite clearly now. He wasn't going to like this story.

"I thought he loved me back," she said very softly. "But . . . it turned out that he had this whole other life he'd hidden from me. He was a dealer on campus. Which sounded so crazy to me when I found out—he wasn't a guy you'd ever think was dealing drugs. He didn't do them himself, he was clean cut and well liked, but . . ." She shook her head. "One day he got wind of a police search at his frat house, and he got stupid."

"How stupid?"

"He panicked and planted all his stuff in my dorm room. He had to save his stash," she said. "Screw me, right?"

Brady drew a long, slow breath. "What happened, Lilah?"

"They couldn't find what they wanted at his place, so they thought they'd check with the girlfriend. The stupid, naïve girlfriend. I was arrested." She drew a shaky breath while Brady worked through the rage churning through him for what had happened to her.

"Everything eventually got cleared up," she said. "But the damage was done. I'd missed so much class time that I couldn't make it up, and even if I could have done so, I couldn't possibly have focused while working at clearing my name."

"Tyler," Brady said past a very tight jaw. "What happened to that asshole?"

"He got off on a technicality, something to do with the way the search had been conducted. He ended up skipping town without so much as a sorry or good-bye."

Since she was facing away from him, he couldn't see her expression. Which meant she couldn't see his, and that was a good thing. He knew she was used to keeping the people in her life close, developing real, deep, lasting relationships that stuck. It was a comfort to her and made her feel like she had a full family at all times. This, he was certain, had completely devastated her on all levels. "Tell me you taught him a lesson involving your boot and his nuts before he left."

"I thought about it, but no." She paused. "I tried to shake it off, tried to go on and not think about it, but . . . well, I guess I got a little depressed."

He pulled her into his lap and hugged her. "I'm sorry."

"In the end, what happened with Tyler didn't matter. I was too busy dealing with my grandma. I came back here to take care of her."

Which is how she'd ended up not finishing school at all, he realized. "Was there no one else?" he asked. "No one to help you?"

"No one really knew how bad it was. And it didn't matter because shortly after that, I was too busy to worry about it because the doctors wanted me to put my grandma in a nursing home. I . . . couldn't. I just couldn't do it to her. She was so independent all her life, so feisty and strong . . . I just couldn't." She paused, pressing her face into his throat. He tightened his grip on her and she burrowed in like she'd been made for him.

"When she died," she said very softly, "I should have gone back to Vegas, but I couldn't even think about it. The joy of it was gone for me. I didn't want to leave Sunshine anymore. I felt like a failure."

Given how hard she worked at getting her degree at night, and how equally hard she'd hid it from everyone, she still did. "You have nothing to be ashamed of, Lilah."

"Are you kidding? I fell for the oldest trick in the book—the TA seduction. And the arrest and all that—I was so stupid."

"Not stupid," he said quietly, with rage seething through him for what had happened to her.

"Naïve then," she said. "I wasn't ready for the hurt. It surprised me and turned me off on the whole relationship thing."

"What about Nick and Cruz and Ian?"

She shrugged. "Nick's a good guy, but he's got weird feet."

Brady arched a brow. "Weird feet?"

"And he's allergic to dogs and cats."

He nodded. "And Cruz?"

"Hates junk food."

"And Ian?"

"I never got to see his feet."

Brady fought the urge to remove his boots and ask her if he had weird feet. "So you've been using excuses on why not to have a relationship. Got it. But why me?"

"Well, for starters, you're not allergic to animals." She smiled and kissed him. "That's a point for you."

"And I like junk food." Another point.

"Yeah, that was a biggie." Her smile faded as she got serious. "But mostly it's because you were a complete stranger, someone new, someone who didn't know me, someone who maybe in the end wouldn't hurt me because I'd keep it light." She smiled again but minus her usual wattage. "I was wrong about that, by the way."

She was so strong and fierce and loyal and sweet and even though she'd made it perfectly clear all along that she didn't want to keep him, that he was held in her heart but not owned, he'd let her inside him. So who was the stupid one here? Him.

Because even if she changed her mind about wanting a future, there was no future to be had. He was leaving. In a few days, as a matter of fact. Trying not to let the pain of that show, he tucked a strand of hair behind her ear and traced his finger down her soft cheek. "Lilah—"

"I don't know if you know the rules of Uno," she said, extricating herself from his lap and standing up. "But if you lose twice, there's a penalty." She looked down at him, eyes shiny but smiling.

She was trying to lighten the mood, and he was game. "What kind of penalty?"

She tugged on the halter tie of her dress and it slipped over her breasts, then her hips, and dropped to the ground, pooling at her feet, leaving her in nothing but those very tiny black panties.

"God bless the penalty," he whispered reverently.

She hooked her thumbs in the strings at her hips and let those fall as well.

Brady tried to say something but found he couldn't speak because his tongue had stuck to the roof of his mouth. He couldn't breathe either. "You are so beautiful, Lilah."

She smiled, and he felt a helpless one curve his mouth as well. "Come here," he said.

Shaking her head, she turned away, giving him a heart-stopping view from the back as she took a few running steps and then a very neat dive into the water, vanishing beneath the surface.

Twenty-two

When Lilah surfaced and shoved her sopping wet hair out of her face, she found Brady right where she'd left him, sitting on the edge of the water.

Watching her.

If she had to guess, she'd say that his expression was an intriguing mix of dark desires and warm affection. If her nipples hadn't already been hard from the shock of the cold water, they'd have tightened simply from looking at him.

When he remained still, nothing but that unfathomable stare that was alternately turning her on and making her want to stick out her tongue at him, she dunked.

When she surfaced again, farther out this time, barely able to touch her feet down, he'd gotten to his feet.

Eyes narrowed.

"What are you doing?" he asked.

He hadn't raised his voice. He knew the water carried sound with ease, as if he were standing right in front of her instead of thirty feet away. "Skinny-dipping."

"By yourself?"

"Well," she said, "I'd hoped to have company."

"Your arm—"

"Doesn't hurt." *Much.*

"You're under the influence," he said.

She smiled. "Are you worried you'd be taking advantage of me?"

"Hell, no. I'm worried you'll take advantage of me."

She laughed and he smiled, and the knot that had been tight in her chest since she'd opened up to him far more than she'd ever intended to finally loosened.

He bent and untied his boots, then kicked them off, and her pulse kicked into gear. She'd wanted this, had hoped to goad him into it, but now that the moment was here, her belly quivered and heat bounced through all her good parts like a Ping-Pong ball.

When he straightened, he pulled his shirt off and tossed it aside. "How cold is it?"

"Like bathwater."

"Liar."

She smiled. "Didn't want to scare you."

"I don't scare easily."

"Uh-huh, and now who's the liar?"

His eyes never left hers as he unbuttoned, unzipped, and shoved down his cargoes.

Her tongue was still hanging out of her mouth when he dove in. Choking back her laugh, she whirled and started swimming, hampered by her bad arm. She'd been raised out here and had swum almost as soon as she could walk, but her arm slowed her more than she'd planned on.

And sure enough, in less than five seconds Brady came up alongside of her, tempering his pace to match hers.

She flipped to her back and used her legs. And still he remained with her. She kept it up for a few more minutes, swimming as hard as she could, enjoying the exertion. After a quarter of a mile or so, she turned and headed back.

Brady beat her by a length.

Treading water about fifteen feet from where their clothes lay, she shoved her hair out of her face and breathed heavily, watching him.

He shook his head, sending water flying. His eyes were dark and hot. God, so hot. His breathing was labored, too, but not nearly as much as hers. "Cocky," she complained.

"No, I've swum in waters much colder than this, and for much farther."

"Hmm. So you're a better swimmer than me."

His smile was slow and sure as he dragged her in close against him, taking away her need to tread water as he did it for the both of them.

"Maybe we could find an area where your talents exceed mine," he said, all low and sexy.

"Hmm."

"Lilah."

His voice never failed to give her a secret little rush. She found that there were things that she desperately longed to hear from him, things she'd told herself she didn't need, but she'd lied to herself.

She needed.

So damn much.

So she pushed even closer, craving the contact, craving the connection, because when they were together like this, his body said things to her that his voice never would. She ran her hands up his chest and let her legs drift around his waist. The contrast of the cold water lapping at her with the warmth of his hard body made her shiver.

"Are you cold?" he murmured.

"No." She slid her hands into his hair and stroked his scalp with her fingernails. A sound of sheer male pleasure, nearly a purr really, escaped him, and his hands went to her ass, a cheek in each palm. He was hard against her belly. Moving them toward the shallower water, he dropped to his knees with her so that she was straddling his lap, the water at their chests. Her legs were spread by his thighs, his hands tightening on her as he stared into her face. "Every time I look at your mouth," he said huskily, "I want it on me."

With a soft smile, she pulled his head to hers and kissed him, long and deep, feeling him pulse against her. Mmm. Reaching down, she stroked him, making both his breath hitch and her inner muscles contract. "In me," she whispered against his mouth.

His face was etched in pure desire, but he shook his head. "No condom."

"Just for a minute." It was reckless, and she didn't care. Dammit, for once, she wanted to do something wild, something without thinking about the consequences. So she wrapped her fingers around him and guided him home, burying him inside her in one long fluid motion.

He choked out her name in a rough groan and then again when she lifted up until he almost came out of her. Slowly she sank back on him, the angle of their bodies pushing him even deeper. Still gripping her ass tight with one hand, his other came around and lightly stroked her where they were joined.

And then again. And again. Until she felt like she was going to burst. "Brady," she gasped. "Stop— I'm going to . . ."

"Do it," he commanded softly. "Let go for me, Lilah."

The timbre of his sexy voice alone nearly sent her over the edge. Combined with his caressing thumb as he thrust upside her with every other heartbeat was all it took, and she burst, collapsing into him.

He held her tight through the trembling. He was still rock hard inside her, and she arched her hips, eliciting another rough groan from him. "Don't." Tightening his hands on her, he pressed his forehead to hers. "Don't move. Not even an inch."

His voice was rough and strained, even lower than normal, and she wrapped her arms around his neck and pressed her mouth to his. He took control of the kiss, his fingers digging into her hips to hold her still, the muscles in his arms quaking with the effort not to move, not to take his own pleasure. She kissed his shoulder, his throat, his mouth. They were drenched from the water, but there was a heat coming from him, as if he had a fever.

Slowly he pulled out of her, closing his eyes when she made a helpless little sound of loss. Gently she kissed his jaw, then gave him a not so gentle shove toward shore. And then another. Eyes locked on hers, he let her, and when she had him in the very shallow water, he also let her kick his feet out from beneath him.

Laughing, he went down to the sand, bracing himself on his elbows, the water lapping at his thighs. She crawled between them and lapped at him, too.

With a low groan, his head fell back as she worked her way up until she came to his most impressive erection. Kissing the very tip, she absorbed the way he breathed her name. "Trust me," she whispered again.

"Already there."

When she drew him into her mouth, his fingers slid into her hair, guiding her into the rhythm he wanted, until with a deep breath, he lifted his head. "Lilah—"

"Shh."

He made a sound of frustration and closed his eyes when she resumed, his hips rocking up to meet her every move on him now. He said something completely unintelligible, gasping, his hands curling into fists in her hair. His eyes were shut tight, his teeth gritted. "Lilah—Christ! I'm going to—"

"Do it," she commanded, mirroring his words back at him. "Let go for me, Brady."

He shuddered and came hard. While he struggled to regain his breath, she kissed his thigh, his hip, the spot low on his ridged abs where his skin was so satiny smooth.

He was still lying there, eyes closed, still as a rock, as if he couldn't possibly move a muscle. She lifted her head. "You okay?"

The sound he made might have been affirmation or maybe evidence that his brain had been thoroughly scrambled. Feeling quite pleased, she sat cross-legged by his hip and waited for him to collect himself.

The water lapped at them gently. From a distance came the hoot of an owl and the song of crickets. Finally Brady turned his head and met her gaze.

She grinned.

A soft smile curved his lips as he took in her naked form by moonlight. "So who's cocky?"

She laughed, and his smile deepened as he pulled her close, pillowing her head on his shoulder. Pulling her in closer, he brushed a dazed kiss to her temple. "You undo me, Lilah. Every time."

"Do you like that?"

"You nearly rendered me unconscious with pleasure. I fucking loved it."

"Can you move yet?" she asked.

"That would be a firm negative."

Nodding, she rose and gathered all their clothes. And then started walking back to the cabin.

"Hey."

When she didn't stop, she heard him swear, heard the sounds of him staggering to his feet. "You took my clothes."

She kept going.

"We left my truck—"

"It'll keep."

"Lilah, Jesus. We can't walk through the woods naked."

"You trained for all conditions, soldier," she called back. "Keep up."

He didn't respond to that, but she could hear him right behind her, silent as they walked buck-ass naked beneath the moon.

"That was crazy," he said a moment later as they walked into her cabin. "Anyone could have seen."

"But no one did." Turning to him, she dropped their clothes onto her couch and smiled. "You swam in the magical waters, Brady. At midnight. You know what that means?"

He was very busy running his gaze over her body like a caress.

"The myth says that now you're in danger of finding your true love," she reminded him.

He snagged her by the hips and rubbed his naked body to hers. "I don't buy into myths. I buy into realism. I make my own fate."

"Yeah? And what does your fate say?"

"It says I'm about to make love to an amazing woman, right here . . ." He dragged her down the hall, grabbing a condom out of her bathroom drawer as they went. Then he wrestled her onto her bed and covered her body with his. "Right now."

When he put his mouth to her breast, she cried out in sheer pleasure. She'd barely recovered from that before he was inside her, whispering in her ear to give him everything she had, every little piece, that he wanted no less.

She had no choice but to give it to him, give him everything; her only solace was in knowing that he was doing the same.

Twenty-three

Brady woke the next morning alone in Lilah's bed with Boss on his chest and Twinkles on his feet, both of them staring at him balefully. He scrubbed a hand over his face and let out a breath. Alone again.

"Arf," Twinkles said.

"Mew," Boss said, and turned in a circle on Brady's chest, using claws.

"Jesus!" Brady pushed the kitten off of him. Bare-ass naked, with all the blankets and sheets tossed to the floor, man and kitten stared at each other. The kitten's eyes narrowed in on Brady's morning wood and crouched, butt wriggling, ready to pounce.

"Do it and die," Brady said, and rolled out of the bed. "Just once," he muttered on the way to the shower, followed by both animals like they were all in a parade. "I'd like to be the first one up."

He'd always been the first one awake in the past. Hell, he'd never spent much time sleeping with a woman, period. But Lilah seemed to throw his entire universe into a tailspin.

Setting the shower tap to scalding, he climbed in and put his hands on the tile. Head down, he let the water bead down over his shoulders and back.

The icy spray hit him without warning at the three-minute mark, and he swore the air blue. Christ, Lilah shouldn't have to live like this. He was taking a look at the hot water heater himself before he left town. He dressed and headed down the hall, tripping over Boss, who yowled his feelings on the matter and vanished under the couch. Brady sighed and dropped to his knees, bending low to peer into two pissed-off glowing eyes. "Well, you can't run in front of me, dammit."

"Arf."

"Stop it," Brady told the dog, who was trying to lick his face. "You're not helping. Boss, out now."

Nothing but daggers coming his way.

"Nice view."

Brady straightened and met the amused eyes of Lilah as she came in the front door. She was carrying two coffees and a donut bag, and right then and there, he fell in love. "If you tell me you have a chocolate-frosted," he said with great feeling, "I'll give you my life's savings and anything else you want."

"What if I brought something healthy, like a wheat-grain muffin."

"Then forget the life savings."

She laughed. "What if all I want is a repeat of last night?"

He grinned. "Then I'd say you're easy."

"When it comes to you, anyway." She set the bag and coffees on the counter. "Enjoy."

"Wait a minute," he said as she started out the door again. "Where are you going?"

"It's this little thing called work."

"You can't just show up and go."

"Sure I can. Watch me." She pulled open the door, then looked back. "But thanks for last night."

"Oh no you don't." He snagged Boss by the scruff of the neck and dragged him from beneath the couch, cradling the pissed-off kitten to his chest. Then he grabbed Lilah, too. "Thanks for last night?" he repeated, suddenly feeling a little pissed off and not sure why. "What exactly is it you're thanking me for, Lilah?"

She opened her mouth, but his cell phone rang. Ignoring it, he kept hold of her and reeled her in closer. And because he was also pretty fucking pathetic, he pressed his face into the curve of her neck and breathed her in. "You smell so damn good you're making me hungry." He licked her throat and felt her shiver.

"New lotion," she said. "Mango peach. Aren't you going to answer that?" she asked of his phone.

"No."

"It might be important."

At the moment he couldn't think of anything more important than making her respond to his question, but the moment had passed and she was looking at him as if he'd lost his marbles.

And it was entirely possible that he had. Swearing, he let go of her, yanked his cell phone out of his pocket and glanced at the screen. "It's work."

"Dell or Adam need a pilot?"

"No. Tony."

"Oh," she exhaled, taking a step back. "He's calling because—"

"Because it's been a month, which is what I said I needed. He's been calling me every day for a week telling me to get my ass back to work."

"You're leaving."

"I should have already left, Lilah."

She swallowed. "When?"

"Like I said, he wanted me yesterday."

"When, Brady?"

"Today or tomorrow maybe. Depends on what he says."

She nodded. "I see."

Yeah, except she couldn't. She couldn't possibly see, not when he couldn't. And he honestly couldn't see how the hell he was supposed to go. He answered his phone with a terse "Miller" and watched as Lilah grabbed one of the coffees and walked out of the cabin.

Lilah entered the kennels, made her way through the rooms to her office and stopped before sitting at her desk.

No.

Not where she wanted to be. She swiveled and walked out the door again and alongside the back of the building, where no one could see her. Slowly she slid down the wall, giving in to her weak knees.

Brady was leaving.

She could still see him coming out of her bedroom wearing only a pair of jeans that molded his sculpted legs to perfection and cradled her favorite part of his anatomy, a part that had never failed to deliver on its promise. His feet had been bare, his chest, too, and just looking at him laid her heart bare as well. He'd looked as if he'd belonged there in her place. Just as he'd made himself at home in her heart.

And he was leaving.

His month was up and now work was calling him. She'd known he'd already turned a few jobs down over the past few weeks, but she'd also known that he wouldn't do that forever.

Maybe he was even packing at this very moment.

She heard a car drive up and, realizing she had tears on her face, rose. Dammit. Swiping at them, she headed back inside, where she got busy fast with the usual drop-offs, feedings, walking, and general care of the animals, not to mention the dreaded paperwork.

At lunchtime Cruz showed up, tanned and rested from a week on Maui with friends. They caught up with each other, and Lilah showed off her new scar from being shot. Cruz was suitably horrified and impressed.

Later, when she was off shift, Lilah made her way to Belle Haven for a late lunch with Jade, walking in the back door before remembering that Jade had taken today off to visit an old friend. Redirecting, she turned around to leave and passed Dell's office.

He was behind his desk on the phone, looking his usual easygoing self, even though his other phone was ringing off the hook and the sounds from the waiting room and patient rooms related more to a mob scene than a veterinarian's office.

That's when she remembered that Adam was gone, too. He'd left last night for a trip back east to an S&R conference. "Need help?" she asked.

Dell nodded in relief and pointed to the waiting room.

She walked into chaos. There were dogs and cats, several birds, and a lamb. None were particularly calm, and neither were the humans that went with the pets.

Brady stood behind the reception desk, scowling darkly at the computer as if he were considering tossing it out the window. Which was undoubtedly why everyone waiting was giving the front desk—and him—a wide berth.

It didn't surprise Lilah that he'd obviously stepped in to help. Or that he'd worked as hard as he had from the moment he'd arrived in Sunshine doing whatever was needed or asked of him. Because for as big and tough as he was, he'd pretty much dedicated his entire life to others' safety and/or well-being.

What did surprise her was how well he fit in. With the town, with Adam and Dell. With her. For all that he wanted to be the lone wolf, he'd made sure to have their backs, all of them. He had a real bond here, one that she knew startled him.

And made him uncomfortable.

Well, it startled her, too. But it didn't make her uncomfortable. It made her feel good, feel connected. It made her feel happy.

That would change, very soon, when he left. And yes, she'd known this day would come, but she wasn't ready. And worse, she didn't think she ever would be.

How scary was that? The room was so noisy she had to come up very close to him to be heard. "Problem?" she asked in his ear.

He barely looked at her. "What makes you think that? The fact that my head is spinning around and around, or that there's twelve people in the waiting room here for the same appointment block and only one doctor?"

"Ah. A scheduling snafu."

"That, or someone's messing with me." He gave her a second, longer look, eyes narrowed and dark. Very dark. "It's not you, is it?"

With a low laugh, she lifted her hands and shook her head.

"Don't even try that look of innocence. I know better."

"Hey. I've never messed with you."

"I have one word for you." He gestured with his chin beneath his desk. "Twinkles."

Lilah bent low and saw Twinkles sprawled out and fast asleep on Brady's boots. "Aw. And clearly, you're both hating the situation."

The phones were still ringing.

People were still glaring at him.

That's when Brady did something Lilah knew he rarely, if ever, did. He sank to a chair, put his hands on her hips, dropped his head to her belly, and said, "Please help me."

"Sure." She'd have even done it without the please, but he didn't need to know that. Because she couldn't help herself, she stroked a hand over his hair. "Move over."

He stood and gave her the chair. She tapped her fingers on the keyboard and pulled up the schedule. "Well, damn. You're double-, triple-, and quadruple-booked."

He came up behind her, a hand on either side of her, braced on the desk as he looked over her head at the computer screen. "Tell me something I don't know."

If she turned her head, her mouth could brush the inside of either of his biceps. His skin would be warm, and just beneath, the muscles would be taut with strength. She could smell his deodorant and, beneath that, the soap he'd used.

Hers.

Unable to stop herself, she did it, she turned her head in the pretense of trying to see his face and let her mouth brush his biceps.

And maybe the very tip of her tongue.

"Lilah," he said warningly, his voice barely audible, rumbling from his chest through her back.

"It's your turn to smell like a piña colada," she whispered softly.

Bending his head, he put his mouth to her ear. "And does it make you as hungry for me as I always am for you?"

Yes. Yes, as a matter of fact, it did. "It's the soap."

"I love the scent of you," he whispered. "I love the taste of you. And it has nothing to do with the soap."

"The scheduling problem," she said unsteadily as one of his hands dropped down to squeeze her hips.

"Uh-huh." He made sure to brush his lips lightly against that spot just beneath her ear. The one he knew that melted her bones away. "I'll start pulling files," he said. "And taking the animals to an examining room. You man the desk."

"No, we should switch that," she said. "I can do the preliminaries in the exam room and speed things along for Dell."

His eyes never left hers. "Yes, but that would leave me behind this desk."

Which he was clearly hoping to avoid at all costs. "It would," she agreed, and smiled.

He arched a brow. "You'd throw me to the wolves?"

She turned and eyed the waiting room. Mostly women, looking Brady over in various degrees of interest, from hunger to outright lust. "Poor baby. Must be tough, having all these women want you."

"And how about you?" he murmured in her ear, taking a quick nip out of it. "You want me?"

Always . . .

If anyone happened to look over at them it would appear as if they were both intently studying the computer screen—which had gone into save energy mode and was running through a slide show of Belle Haven's animal patients.

Brady's pictures, actually, from the past month. They were great shots, but Lilah wasn't absorbing a single one because Brady was whispering a lurid suggestion in her ear, which made her both gasp and weak at the knees.

Forcing herself out of the chair, she avoided Brady's hot, knowing eyes. She grabbed the sign-in sheet and called the first name. "Toby?"

Shelly and Toby stood up.

Lilah turned to Brady, who wasn't saying a word, just watching her. The lion keeping its eyes on the prize. "Pull the file and bring it in to me?" she asked.

Looking both hungry and amused, he turned to the files. Her last view of him was of his fine ass when he bent to the bottom drawer.

In the exam room, Shelly fanned herself. "Damn, Dr. Death is hot."

"That's the general consensus," Lilah murmured, resisting the urge to fan herself as well.

"And your consensus?" Shelly asked slyly.

Lilah sighed. "Same as yours," she admitted, and turned to go get Dell but instead came face-to-face with Brady, who stood in the doorway, holding the file, eyes unreadable. She bit her lower lip and flashed him a quick smile.

He didn't return it, but the very corners of his mouth quirked slightly and his eyes promised retribution. Which worked for her, because she'd learned she really liked his forms of retribution.

It was two very busy hours later before there was any sort of breather. Lilah finally dropped into a chair beside Brady at the front desk. "And I thought my life was crazy."

"Your life is crazy." He got to his feet.

"Where are you going?"

He gestured to the waiting room, which was blessedly empty. "Things are under control again."

"Yes, but I have to get back to the kennels."

"No you don't. Cruz is there." He let out a breath. "I have to go."

"Seriously, you—"

"I mean I have to go, Lilah."

Oh. Oh, damn. She'd managed to work her denial up good, almost forgetting this fact. Slowly she rose to her feet, unable to sit while facing this. "You're leaving right now?"

His eyes said it all.

"But how can they expect you to just up and go at a phone call?"

"That's my job, Lilah. Pilot for hire. I go when the call comes."

Legs wobbly, she plopped back into the chair and put a hand to her aching heart. This isn't about you, Lilah. "Tell me."

"I'm needed in Africa by the end of the week. And I have to go to L.A. first."

"Oh."

"I'm sorry."

She let out a purposeful breath and tried to shake her head, but her body felt locked up tight. "Don't be. You were up front and honest with me. You weren't meant for a home base or growing roots. I've always known that." Listen to her, how mature. Even as she thought it, her eyes filled.

"Lilah," he whispered softly. "Don't."

"I'm not." She shook her head and was proud of her smile. She stood and went up on tiptoe to set her hand on his chest, brushing a kiss over his mouth.

His lips were set to grim, but she knew they could soften in a smile when he chose or drive her straight to heaven without passing Go!

What they couldn't do, however, was tell her everything was going to be okay.

Because it wasn't.

She didn't feel like she'd ever be okay again.

Twenty-four

Since packing wasn't an issue—Brady had never really unpacked—he went to Smitty's and tuned up the Bell 47 even though it was running perfectly and didn't need to be tuned up. He didn't want whomever Dell and Adam hired to have any problems. He was still sitting in the pilot's seat tinkering with the Bell's instrument panel when he heard footsteps. Something in his chest kicked hard, but as much as he'd hoped otherwise, it wasn't Lilah coming his way.

"We're not replacing you."

He turned to face Dell and Adam, who boarded looking unusually serious. Well, Adam always looked serious, but there wasn't so much as a glimmer of a smile on Dell's usually good-humored, affable face.

Brady shook his head. "You spent a lot of money for me to fix up the Bell. You've had an average of three calls a week where it's beneficial to take it up. Any of the pilots housed out of here or Coeur d'Alene would be happy to hire on and fly for you."

"Sure," Adam said. "And we'll use them as needed. But we're not hiring anyone on full-time."

"You guys want and need a third partner. You're overworked, you need—"

"You," Dell said.

Brady shoved his fingers through his hair and stared at them, frustrated at all the unexpected things he was feeling at leaving. "This was always going to be temporary." How many times had he said that in the last day?

"It could stay temporary," Dell said, "if that's what your pansy ass needs. A word. A fucking word to make it okay for you to use this place as a home base. Let's call it temporary, then."

"He's going to do what he has to do, Dell," Adam said quietly. "He's—"

Running footsteps sounded, and again Brady's heart kicked. Because this time it was Lilah.

She came rushing up to the opened door of the Bell, her cheeks flushed, out of breath. When she saw Brady, she put her hand to her chest and sagged, out of breath. "I thought—I heard the engine start—I was afraid you'd left."

"Not yet," Adam said and turned to her, brushing a kiss to her jaw, giving her a quick squeeze. With one last long look at Brady, he left.

Dell came forward and hugged Brady, slapping him on the back. "I'll miss you, you chickenshit bastard. Be safe up there." Dell looked at Lilah, and then he was gone, too, leaving the two of them alone.

The silence was heavy. Not awkward, just . . . weighted. Unable to mistake the emotion coming from her for anything other than temper, Brady let out a breath and removed her sunglasses.

She blinked up at him from eyes that were clear and . . . not full of temper, as it turned out.

But sorrow.

And somehow that was worse, far worse. "I have to go," he murmured, hating himself in that moment.

"Yes," she said, crossing her arms. "You have to go."

He hadn't expected her easy agreement and didn't believe it. "It's my job," he said carefully.

"I know that, too."

"I—"

"Shut up, Brady." She uncrossed her arms, grabbed his shirt, and yanked him in. The first brush of her lips was soft, gentle. Tender. As if she'd put her entire heart into it. Then she settled in and the kiss deepened, a hot, intense tangle of tongues that nearly brought him to his knees. Before he could recover, she gentled the connection again, retreating in slow degrees until her lips were nothing more than a barely there butterfly kiss. "Be careful with yourself," she whispered huskily against his lips.

He didn't move, his body still a breath from hers. She . . . wasn't going to devastate him with guilt? For a moment he couldn't quite wrap his head around that. Or the fact that she wasn't going to even ask him to stay.

And suddenly he remembered how he'd reasoned with her when she'd had to give up Toby and then Sadie. He'd told her that if she'd found a loving place for the animals to live where they could be happy, it was okay to let them go. That haunted the hell out of him now, because apparently she'd listened and taken his words to heart.

Only she wasn't a fraction as devastated at letting him go as she had been the animals. "I'm leaving," he said again, just in case she hadn't gotten the right idea.

"I know," she said softly.

He just stared at her, and then shook his head. "Okay, wait a minute. Why is this so easy for you, letting me go?"

"What?"

"You've made a career out of holding on to everything, pets, people . . . You gather them all to your side, in your heart, but when it's me, you give me a smile and a kiss and tell me to be careful?"

She opened her mouth, then closed it. Then stabbed him in the chest with her finger, hard. "Well, what would you have me do, fall at your feet and beg you not to go?"

Yeah. Actually. A little bit.

Maybe.

Christ, he was one pathetic asshole.

She let out a mirthless laugh. "I care about you. I want you. And neither of those two things change whether you go or not. Do you understand the helplessness of that? And even then, honestly, I wouldn't change any of it if I could." She stabbed at him again. "So don't you tell me I'm just letting you go. I hate that you're going, but I'd rather have the pain of that than not having had you in my life at all." She glared at him from brilliantly shimmering eyes, breath coming hard. "You going will leave a huge gaping hole." She pressed her open hand to her chest. "Here. You're in my heart, and there's no way around that. I consider you mine, Brady. Mine." A single, devastating tear fell and she swiped it angrily away. "But you need your happy place. If it's not here, you have to go to it. And I need to let you." She paused, let out a soft broken breath. "You taught me that."

While he was still absorbing her words, and the utter anguish in which she'd spoken them, she stood up on tiptoe and brushed another soft kiss across his lips. His hands went to her hips to hold her against him and he closed his eyes, burying his face in her hair. "Lilah." His voice was raw and matched his throat and the burning in his chest.

Her arms slid around his neck and for a moment she clung, hard. He felt a tremor go through her and then she whispered against his jaw. "It's okay to go if that's what your heart is telling you." She pulled back and cupped his face, staring into it as if to memorize his every feature. "I'll take Twinkles back when you go," she whispered. And with one last long look, she left.

Shaken to his core, he sank to the pilot seat.

He'd gotten what he wanted.

He was free to go.

Shaking his head, he hopped down out of the helicopter and whistled.

Twinkles leapt to his feet from his spot under a tree in the shade and came running. Together they walked to his truck. Brady patted the passenger's seat and Twinkles hopped up, taking the shotgun position. Brady had been left behind enough in his life to know that it sucked. No way was he doing it to the dog—his dog. He was taking Twinkles.

So why it still felt as though he were leaving his entire life behind, never mind his fucking heart, he had no idea.

This was his choice.

It was always his choice.

Nodding, he drove, refusing to look back in his rearview mirror.

Except he did.

He kept looking into his rearview mirror the entire drive to L.A. It took him all night. At LAX, just before dawn, he parked in long-term parking and started walking with Twinkles toward the terminal where the charters flew from. Tony had booked him a ride from here. "Not sure what our choices are going to be for you," he told the dog. "Or exactly where Tony has booked us a ride to. But there are rules for four-legged creatures, so you'll probably be crate-bound for this next leg of the trip."

Twinkles didn't look concerned, he was just happy to be involved. Brady shook his head and let himself run Lilah's words back through his head.

I consider you mine, Brady.

I need to let you go. You taught me that.

She'd set free what she loved. She'd done so without knowing that she was his happy. She was his everything.

Christ, he was a total and complete jackass. Leaving her wasn't going to make him happy at all. It was going to make him a very sorry sack of shit with too much pride for his own damn good.

He looked down at Twinkles, who was sniffing everything in his path. "I don't want to do this."

Well, that wasn't quite true. He still wanted his job flying to all corners of the earth. He just wanted something else to go along with it.

A life.

He no longer wanted to work 24/7, never stopping or slowing because he had no reason to.

He had a reason. A five-foot-four, messy-haired, mossy-green-eyed reason named Lilah Young. He stopped walking. "Dell was right," he said to Twinkles, who stopped, too, then sat on Brady's foot. "I am a chickenshit bastard."

"Arf."

He choked out a short laugh that was completely devoid of humor and pulled out his cell phone. "I can't make this job," he said to Tony.

"Where are you?"

"L.A., but I'm cutting out."

"Again? Christ." He gave a big sigh. "And the next job?"

"Maybe, but I'm going offline for a few days."

"You've been offline for a month."

"I need a little bit more time."

"And then?"

"I'll get back to you."

Brady and Twinkles got a hotel room to catch up on some desperately needed sleep, then got up at dusk and once more drove straight through the night. As Sunshine came into view around dawn the next morning, Brady stopped at the 7-Eleven to fortify his nerves for what he was about to do. "Breakfast?" he asked the dog.

"Arf."

"Something with sausage. Got it." He went inside and loaded up with breakfast burritos, bagels, and donuts.

"Looks like you're buying breakfast for a crowd today," the young woman said. She was the same woman who'd been manning the cash register his very first day in town, when she'd asked him if men really thought of sex 24/7.

"It's actually more of a bribe than breakfast," he said.

She popped a bubble with her gum and adjusted her purple and black polka-dotted glasses frames. "For Lilah?"

He'd almost forgotten that there were no secrets in this town.

"Honey," she said, leaning on the counter, "I'm going to help you out." She added a package of donuts and two bags of chips to the stack. "Trust me." She patted his hand and gave him his total.

"That can't be right. It's not enough," he said, looking over all the loot in front of him.

"Oh, the donuts and chips are on the house," she said, bagging it all up. "You make our Lilah happy, and that's worth more than the snack food."

He didn't know what to say. He wasn't used to people knowing his business, but the reality was that here in Sunshine, Lilah was everyone's business. "Thank you."

She nodded and handed him his bag. "But you should know, screw up with her and I'll never sell you another piece of crap food. Ever. And let me tell you, from one junk-food addict to another? Ever is a damn long time."

"Understood," he said, not telling her he'd already screwed up. Because he was going to do whatever it took to rectify the situation. As he turned to walk out, she tossed in an extra package of donuts.

"Just in case," she said.

In case of what, he wasn't sure, but he'd take all the help he could get.

Twenty-five

Lilah stood in front of her outside kennels, hose in hand. The duck and the lamb she'd been boarding had left a mess. She was literally elbow deep in things that she didn't want to think about. It was a very attractive look for her.

Not.

Adding to the stress level was the fact that today was the first Saturday of the month. She had only a few minutes before she was due to work at Belle Haven's monthly animal adoption clinic.

"My life," she said to no one in particular, "completely sucks."

Because he'd done it.

He'd left.

Brady had taken him and Twinkles and her shattered heart, and without even realizing that he had pieces of her with him, he'd gone.

She hadn't slept, she hadn't eaten, and it was all so ridiculous. She'd known he would go.

But she'd hoped . . .

The tears that she'd managed to hold at bay clogged her throat and, dammit, fogged up her sunglasses.

Stupid sunglasses.

And perfect, now her nose was running.

She tried to shove her sunglasses to the top of her head with her forearm but succeeded only in making them crooked on her face and she sighed deeply.

And maybe a tear slipped.

This was all her own fault. She hadn't told him she loved him. She hadn't told him what it would mean for him to stay. She hadn't let him know.

The thought brought a few more unwanted tears and further fogged her lens. She couldn't see a thing. So when the hose hit a corner of one of the kennels and splashed up, it thoroughly drenched her with icy water and God knew what else.

"Crap!" She dropped the hose and reached out blindly for the towel she'd set on the railing behind her. Except her feet landed in something slippery and down she went.

For a stunned beat she just sat there on the ground, absorbing how bad every inch of her felt.

A truck rumbled up the road and she went still because she knew the sound of that truck. Great, and now her mind was playing tricks on her. It had to be Adam or Dell. Or maybe a customer. She sneaked a peek and gasped out loud.

It was Brady. He'd forgotten something. Dammit. She couldn't take another good-bye. Keeping her back to the direction of the clearing where he was parking and—oh God—turning off his truck, she scrambled to her feet and grabbed the hose. *Must. Look. Busy.*

Even when covered in dirt and gunk.

No, scratch that. She hosed herself down as fast as she could because no way was she going to let the last view he had of her be like this. Because looking like she'd just been in a wet T-shirt contest was ever so much preferable. Damn, why hadn't she put on a black T-shirt instead of a white one this morning? Now she looked like she was on spring break in Florida. Or on *Girls Gone Wild.*

Eat your heart out, Brady, this is what you're leaving.

Shading her eyes from the sun, she aimed the hose at the kennels to look busy, refusing to turn and look at him as he got out of the truck.

She heard Twinkles's little paws pounding the ground as he bounded through the open gate to her, butt wriggling happily along with his tail.

"Aw," she murmured, hugging him close with her free hand, feeling her throat tighten when he licked her chin. "What did you guys forget, huh?" she murmured, cupping his face. "What are you doing here?"

"Lilah."

Her heart dropped to her toes. Keeping her back to him, she concentrated on hosing out the kennels as if it were brain surgery.

"Can I come in?" he asked very quietly, pausing at the opened gate.

He'd never asked before. He bulldozed, quietly demanded, or just did whatever the hell he wanted.

But now he was asking . . .

Oh God. She couldn't do this. She'd gotten used to the fact that he was going, and now he was standing here being sweet and gentle.

Okay, she hadn't gotten used to the fact that he was going, and him being sweet and gentle was killing her.

"Can I come in," he repeated.

She shrugged. "The gate's open."

"I don't mean into the yard, Lilah."

No, she really couldn't do this. She was miserable and she'd lost sight of any positive reasons for him to go. If she had to say good-bye again, she was going to throw herself at him and cling. She nodded, swiping her eyes with her sleeve, probably smearing the last of her mascara while she was at it.

A big hand pried the hose from her fingers. The water shut off, and then that hand was back, turning her to face him.

Fingers slid along her jaw and forced her head up. He looked . . . wary. Not something she expected. He was dressed for the job, or so she assumed, in his usual cargoes, boots, and a nondescript button-down with the usual myriad pockets. He was carrying something, but she couldn't pay attention to that at the moment.

And if he was trying to intimidate with the solemn expression, the sunglasses were a nice touch.

Reaching up, she took them off of him.

He stood still and let her look her fill, his mouth unsmiling. He had a network of fine lines around his eyes, more from the sun than age. His eyes were stark and clear.

And utterly implacable.

He reached for her sunglasses, but she needed the barrier, the wall to hide behind, so she took a step back.

"Lilah."

She closed her eyes behind the lenses. Which, oh good, were still crooked on her nose. And here she'd thought she might feel stupid.

"Look at me."

She opened her eyes and saw what he had cradled between his free hand and his chest.

A box of goodies from 7-Eleven. Be still her heart. "Breakfast?" she asked, and look at that, her voice was perfectly clear. No way to tell that she was broken.

"I was thinking more along the lines of a bribe," he said.

"For what?"

Ignoring her question, his gaze searched her face with that quiet intensity of his, the one that made her heart roll over and expose its tender underbelly. "Are you crying?" he asked.

"No. I just cut up an onion. Yes, I'm crying, you big, unfeeling, insensitive . . ."

"Chickenshit bastard?"

"I was going to say ass, but okay."

He nodded and set down the box of food on a fence post, lifting a hand to sweep his thumb beneath one of her eyes. "I'm sorry," she whispered. "I didn't mean the ass part."

Though his eyes remained very, very serious, his mouth twitched. "Just the unfeeling, insensitive part?"

Again she lifted a shoulder. "If the shoe fits."

With an exhale of air, he took her hand. "I'm in."

Confused, she lifted her face, forgetting for a moment that she was a complete disgusting wreck. "What?"

His eyes were dark and still very solemn. "I'm in this," he said.

She stared at him. "Define 'this,'" she said very carefully. "Because if you mean you're here, in the kennels, I'm going to hurt you. Badly."

"Let's start with where you are," he said. "You're here." Taking her hand, he pressed it to his chest above his heart.

Beneath her palm she could feel the reassuring heat and strength of him.

And his heart, beating steady and sure.

"I haven't had enough caffeine for this," she whispered. "And I'm easily confused. I'm going to need more words here."

"I love you, Lilah."

Her heart stopped dead in her chest. "Okay," she said shakily. "Those are some damn fine words." She swallowed. "You came back to tell me you loved me?"

He nodded.

"And . . . that's supposed to make it easier to let you go again?"

"That, and the fact that I intend to come back. Every single time. If you'll have me. And plus," he said, suddenly sounding uncharacteristically unsure of himself, "I brought junk food."

"True," she managed, nodding, throat so tight she struggled to speak. "And not that the junk food isn't perfect, but the other thing. I need you to explain the other thing to me, Brady."

"I thought the I-love-you was self-explanatory."

"Oh my God. The coming-back thing! The every-single-time thing!"

Some of the wariness drained and he tugged her close, hauling her up against him, making her gasp. "Oh, don't! I'm wet and very possibly wearing doggie puke—"

Ignoring that, he wrapped his arms around her and buried his face in her hair. He was taking comfort in her, she realized with a shock, something he'd never done before, and it touched her deep to her core. "Oh, Brady." Unable to hold back, she hugged him as tight as she could. "I love you so much."

He kissed her. It was a really great kiss, too, deep and soul searching, and by the time he lifted his head, he wasn't breathing any more steady than she. Dropping his forehead to hers, he closed his eyes. "For as long as I can remember," he told her, "from the time I was just a stupid little kid, to being in the military, to working as a pilot for hire, I've lived my life as purposely uncomplicated as possible. You changed that."

She winced. "Because I'm . . . complicated?"

"Yeah." He smiled, and it spread to a grin when she frowned. "Turns out, I like complicated," he assured her. "But I've always thought of myself as a wanderer, a guy with no roots, no home base."

Maybe even a guy who couldn't be saved.

He didn't say those words but she felt them from him, and it broke her heart.

"It changed," he said before she could speak. "It changed because Adam and Dell nag like a couple of old women. It changed because of one silly dog. It changed because of a woman with a fierce, loyal, warm heart, a woman who refuses to back down for anything."

She melted against him. "I back down for donuts. I'm a 'ho for donuts."

A smile crossed his face. "I know, I count on that."

She smacked him and he smiled and took her hand. "What's it going to be, Lilah?"

It wouldn't be easy. Despite how much she loved him, he came with flaws. He was impatient, gruff, demanding . . . but she kind of liked the demanding part.

Besides, she was no picnic herself. She was flawed, too, as flawed as they came. He was waiting for her answer, his eyes holding more emotion than she'd ever seen from him. She rested her cheek against the soft cotton of his shirt. "You were never lost," she whispered.

"I know that, too. Now. Thanks to you." He drew a long breath. "My home base is here, Lilah."

"In Sunshine."

"No. With you. It's you, you're my home base, wherever you are. In the damn magical lake, cleaning shit out of the stalls, playing Uno. It's all you. You're it for me."

"You're good at this," she murmured.

He choked out a laugh. "If I were good, I'd have done this before driving all the way to L.A. and back." Cupping her face, he caught a tear on his thumb. "I've always been on my own. I liked it that way. No one waiting on me, depending on me in any way. I thought that meant I had it all, but that's not how it works. You taught me that. You showed me what it means to belong. I need you, Lilah. I need you with me, loving me. I didn't realize how much until I tried to go."

"Sort of like home is where the heart is?"

"Yes. And mine is in the palm of your hand."

She slid her fingers into his hair as the last piece of her broken heart clicked together. "Oh, Brady."

"I mean it. Life before you . . . It wasn't the same. I wasn't the same. I can't imagine being without you."

"That's good, too," she whispered. "That's probably going to get you good and laid."

"I'm counting on it."

She laughed and he lifted his head, his eyes fierce and intense on hers. "I always thought love was a weakness," he said. "That might still be the case, but I don't want to be without you. You're it for me, Lilah. You make me a better man, you make me feel . . ."

"What?" she said breathlessly when he paused.

"Everything. You make me feel everything."

Epilogue

They showed up for the animal adoption clinic at Belle Haven together, hand in hand. They were late, because Brady had taken Lilah back to her cabin for a little review session on exactly what loving each other meant.

In the shower, of course, since she'd been such a mess.

Now she was clean but flushed, and her heart rate was still a little bit elevated as they walked into the reception area and stopped traffic.

Jade's fingers were a whirl on her keyboard. Dell stood in the doorway holding a file. They both went utterly still.

Jade took in the look on Lilah's face, the one that no doubt said *Just Fucked*, and let out a slow smile.

Dell's brow shot up.

Then the door opened behind them, hitting Lilah in the butt.

It was Adam, holding a handful of leashes, surrounded by a pack of golden retrievers, all suited up in their S&R vests. He was clearly in the middle of a training session and was followed by one of his students—the ever-uptight Holly.

Even attending a dog-training class she was wearing a business suit and heels. She was frowning, and when Adam stopped so suddenly, she plowed into the back of him.

"Adam," she started. "You can't just walk away in the middle of a class. You—"

"Shh," he said, and they all shushed.

Every single one of them in the place shushed.

Adam locked gazes with Brady.

"Dr. Death!" someone whispered from a waiting-room chair.

Beside her, Lilah felt Brady tense. She knew it was important to him that Adam and Dell accept him. And the town, too.

"You forget something?" Adam asked.

"Yes," Brady said. "A few things, actually."

When he didn't expand, Dell laughed softly from across the room. "You going to fill us in or just stand there blocking traffic?"

"I forgot to tell you that the Bell sticks at two hundred and fifty feet," Brady said. "You have to baby the throttle, ease into it. Anyone who flies it should know that."

"We told you," Adam said. "We don't have plans for anyone to fly it except you."

"Well then, I'll make a note of it," Brady said.

Dell was smiling as he came close and clapped Brady on the biceps hard enough to knock him back a step. "You didn't come back for the Bell. You came back for the girl. Our girl."

"Yes." Brady wrapped an arm around Lilah's neck and pulled her in, pressing a kiss to her temple. "I came back for the girl."

There was a collective "awwww" from the waiting room. Mrs. Sandemeyer stood up and pointed at Brady. "I'm first in line for you."

"He's taken," Lilah said.

"I meant for him to see my baby." Mrs. Sandemeyer gestured to the dog at her feet.

"You do know he's not actually licensed in anything animal related," Dell said. "Right?"

"I don't care. He helps out, I've heard he helps out. He escorts the patients into the exam rooms. I'm ready to be escorted."

"What if I live up to my nickname?" Brady asked.

"I'm more afraid this line will take too long and I'll miss bingo tonight."

Dell grinned and reached behind the desk for the sign-up clipboard. "You in?" he asked Brady, holding the clipboard out.

Brady cupped Lilah's face with one hand and held her against his body with his other as he kissed her, sending a bolt of happy right down to her toes. "I'm in."

Animal ATTRACTION

One

Come on, baby," he murmured. "Give it up for me. You know you want to."

Jade Bennett did her best to ignore the way the low, sexy voice made her shiver. Besides, it wasn't aimed at her. Dr. Dell Connelly—dog whisperer, cat whisperer, horse whisperer, and known woman whisperer—was talking to a stray kitten.

The feline in question huddled miserably beneath the bench seat in Dell's vet center waiting room, staring at him from narrowed eyes, clearly having none of the sweet talk. She was a scruffy, mangy grayish brown with sharp green eyes, and, like Jade, *not* swayed by sweet talkers.

"Huh," Jade said from behind the reception counter. "Most females leap right into your arms at the slightest encouragement."

Dell craned his neck and regarded her from eyes as dark as his secrets. "Not all."

There was a beat of silence during which she did her best not to break eye contact. He was right. Not all females—otherwise she'd have made the leap.

You're leaving in one month; it's far too late now . . .

As if suddenly realizing Dell was in the room, the huge St. Bernard snoring behind Jade's chair snorted awake and lifted her head. Seeing her beloved, Gertie lumbered up to her huge paws with a joyous bark of welcome before barreling toward Dell, skidding a little on the smooth linoleum as she scrambled around the corner of the desk and . . . launched herself into Dell's arms.

It was a good thing the guy wasn't a lightweight because Gertie moved with the velocity of a freight train. Dell braced himself, but all that delicious warm mocha skin of his—courtesy of his Native American mother—

covered an impressive amount of tough testosterone and muscle. Still, even a six-foot-two, 180-pound veterinarian extraordinaire could be leveled by the freight-train force of a chunky St. Bernard, and at impact Dell landed on his ass. He merely laughed and gathered the dog in close, not appearing to mind either the floor or the sloppy kiss on the jaw.

He was wearing dark blue scrubs that looked annoyingly good on him, the bottoms of which had slipped low in the scuffle, revealing a inch or two of forest green knit boxers and a strip of smooth, slightly paler skin, not to mention the hint of prime male ass.

Unconcerned about the display, Dell gave Gertie a full body rub, then pushed her off of him.

The stray kitten, which looked to be three to four months old, old enough to have gathered plenty of wariness, did *not* approve of Gertie's exuberance. Beneath the chair, she pressed herself closer to the wall and hissed.

"Aw, you're fine," Dell told her, rubbing his jaw as he studied her. He had a hint of stubble, like maybe he'd slept too long to spare the time to shave that morning.

It shouldn't have been so damn sexy.

Neither should the way Gertie was sidling back up to him, trying to love him from not so far.

Animals always loved Dell. Little kids, too.

And women. Let's not forget how many women loved him.

He was bending low to whisper to the kitten, using that low, undeniably authoritative but oh-so-mesmerizing voice, the one that could melt the panties off a female at five paces.

Good thing, then, that Jade was at least seven paces away.

"Gertie here's just a big hunk of love," he was assuring the kitten. "Emphasis on the big hunk. Sit, Gert," he commanded with soft demand over his shoulder.

Gertie wriggled with barely contained joy but sat. Then grinned.

"There," Dell said to the kitten. "See? We're all harmless."

Harmless? Please. Dangerously smooth, maybe. Effortlessly charming, yes. A walking orgasm . . . without a doubt.

But harmless? Hell no, and at just the thought, Jade snorted.

"Ignore her, too," Dell said to the kitten. "She's the smartest one here, but she never learned how to chill. In fact, she's a lot like you, all tough and wary and grumpy, but I'm betting you're both just big softies deep down inside."

"I can hear you, you know," Jade said.

"Way deep *deep* inside . . ."

Jade worked at ignoring his alluringly boyish smile—which she didn't buy for a second because there was *nothing* boyish about him—and went back to loading the schedule for tomorrow's patients.

You want him . . .

She worked at avoiding that little voice as well. Lots of things to avoid. But she was leaving, going back home to Chicago at month's end. Plans had been made, notice had been given. It was as good as done.

The kitten went back to being pissed off at the world.

And Dell laughed softly. "So now I've got *two* women completely ignoring me. I'm going to get a complex."

As if Dr. Dell Connelly knew the meaning of the word. He was sure and confident, always. Steady as a rock. Never second-guessed himself.

It was really annoying.

"Come on, kitty," Dell said. "Trust me."

Jade could have told her not to bother resisting, that she'd cave eventually. They always did. It was because Dell was the genuine deal, and animals could see that. Animals meant everything to him. While women flocked to him like bees to honey, she'd never seen him put his personal life ahead of his work. It was really a fascinating paradox. The gorgeous man could have anyone he wanted, and yet he didn't seem to want much more than what he had. A successful animal center, a few close friends, and speed-dial to the pizza joint.

Jade knew that she tended to shut people out and keep them at a distance. Dell did, too, but he went about it differently, making himself available to everything and everyone . . . while keeping it all shallow.

He didn't take anything too seriously, especially women.

But the kitten continued to stare at Dell with a heartbreaking defiance that Jade recognized from every time she looked into the mirror.

Gertie whined and wagged her tail, sweeping the floor with each pass, hopeful to make a new friend.

Wasn't going to happen.

"Okay, how about this," Dell said. "Come out and I'll buy you dinner."

The kitten didn't blink.

"Losing your touch," Jade murmured, sorting files.

Dell flashed her a smile that said *As if*, and her nipples hardened. Which meant he was right—he wasn't losing his touch. Not even close.

Dell eyed the unhappy kitten and wished she could talk to him. He wished the same thing about his enigmatic receptionist behind him.

Jade was working her computer with her usual slightly OCD efficiency, which was in complete opposition to her eye-popping green fuzzy angora sweater that reminded him of a lollipop. A lollipop with really great breasts. Peanut the parrot was perched on the printer at her right. Both Peanut and Gertie were part of Belle Haven, and since Belle Haven was Dell's large animal clinic, the animals and everything in the place belonged to him. Well, except Jade.

Jade belonged to no one.

"From what I can gather," she said, eyes still on her keyboard, "the kitten was deserted at some point during the mob of the free vaccine clinic this afternoon. And," she added in the same conversational tone, "if I figure out who did such a thing, I'm going to shoot them."

Nothing reached Dell's hard-shelled, softhearted receptionist faster than a neglected or abused animal.

Something they had in common.

"We'll find her a home," he assured her, looking the kitten in the eyes. "Promise. Now how about it, you, ready to come out yet?"

"Ready to come out!" Peanut chirped, doing her best imitation of Dell's low-pitched voice.

Dell didn't take his eyes from the kitten. "I know, you've had a majorly sucky day. Come tell me all your troubles."

"Does that actually ever work for you?" Jade asked.

"Shh, you," he said, and keeping his movements light and easy, he reached beneath the chair. "Come on, beautiful."

"Mew," said the kitten.

"Mew," said Peanut.

"It's all going to be okay," Dell assured the cat. "No one's going to hurt you."

When the kitten just stared at him, Dell slowly slid his hand beneath her belly, which was nearly concave. Her ribs were so prominent he could have counted them, which pissed him off, but though she growled and let out one last protesting "mew," she let him pull her from beneath the chair without slicing him raw with her claws. "Good girl," he murmured, holding her against his chest and scratching her beneath the chin.

She watched him very carefully, but it was as if she knew that he knew. Hell, maybe abandoned souls recognized abandoned souls, he wasn't sure, but she slowly relaxed until finally, unable to resist the gentle scratching, she even closed her eyes and rested her head against his chest.

"Yeah, there you go," he said quietly. Lifting his head, he flashed a grin at Jade. "If only *your* species were as easy."

"We both know that for you they are." She shook her head. "And that should be illegal."

"What?" he asked innocently. "Sweet-talking a p—"

"If you say pussy," she warned. "I'll make sure that tomorrow you'll be up to your eyeballs in vaccines and well-puppy checkups from sunup until sundown."

"I like puppies."

"Scratch the puppies. Did I say puppies? I meant anal-gland expressing. I'll find every large animal in Sunshine who needs it done and book them, just for you."

Dell laughed. She did that a lot, his stalwart, snarky, razor-tongued receptionist. Made him laugh.

As well as threaten him.

He was used to it. Hell, he even liked it, which made him all kinds of sick, he knew. Maybe it was the fact that she ran the front desk of his vet clinic in those runway clothes, never so much as blinking when she got covered in dog and kitten hair. Or worse.

Maybe it was her ability to handle his patients and their owners with equal aplomb or that she never took any of his shit. Or that she had a way of uncomplicating his life for him—a miracle considering that she'd come here with virtually no references whatsoever. Dell still had no idea what had possessed him to hire her, but he had, putting her into a position that had supposedly been only temporary while he looked for someone more qualified.

And yet he'd never looked for anyone else.

It had been eighteen months, but that ship had sailed. She was going back to her old life, whatever that was—she'd been frustratingly stingy with details—and leaving them.

Him.

He had no idea what he'd do without her sitting at the helm of his world, running it with cool, distant efficiency. Not to mention, she was a nice view. She kept her silky strawberry blond hair perfectly twisted on top of her head, except for the few errant strands that had slipped out and were brushing across her shoulders. Her eyes were green, shot through with streaks of amber, and saw everything. She had a mouth, too. Smart, cynical, and made for a man's fantasy.

And since he should absolutely not be going down that road, thinking about that mouth with the vanilla gloss that he always wanted to lick off, he shook his head to clear it. He usually had more sense, but there was something about Jade and her whole don't-touch attitude that made him want to rise to the challenge.

And he meant rise.

Her fingers were clicking on her keyboard, her screen revealing her beloved spreadsheet program, which he knew held her notes on anything and everything from which patient he was going to see tomorrow to what color her fingernails would be next.

His favorite was the bright fuck-me red.

"Adam's checked in from Boise," she said, referring to his brother. "His class went late, he's staying over." She stood. She was average height and average build, but there was nothing else average about her.

Ever.

She coaxed Peanut onto her arm, easily transferring the parrot from the printer to the bird's night cage.

"Night-night?" Peanut asked her.

"Yes, Peanut go night-night," Jade said with a sweetness that Dell never got directed at him. He watched her blow a kiss to the bird, receiving one in return, along with a soft mimicking "mew," and with a low laugh, Jade covered the cage with a blanket.

Her black trousers had pleats, Dell noted, and were snug on the best ass he'd ever seen. All business in front, party in the back . . .

That eye-straining sweater that matched her eyes and name seemed to shimmer beneath the overhead lights. He'd once asked about her name and she'd told him it was for her grandmother, who'd ruled her family with the strength and elegance of the jade gemstone.

Clearly she took the name seriously. Dell had the feeling that when it came to the family she didn't often talk about, she took everything seriously.

She wore tiny sparkling earrings up one earlobe, matching the myriad bracelets on her wrist, and heels that he wasn't sure how she managed to balance on, though he enjoyed listening to them click, click, click across his floors all day. His patients enjoyed it, too, especially their owners. The male owners. How many times had he seen a guy come through here and attempt to pick her up? Exactly the same number of times he'd seen Jade politely and firmly shut them down.

There was a little part of him that enjoyed that very much. Okay, a big part, but he'd never made a move on her. Like the government, he preferred to keep his state and church separated; never the two shall meet. Not that *that* stopped him from wondering what secrets his sexy receptionist had that kept her celibate.

Or hell, maybe she merely left Sunshine and whooped it up on the weekends somewhere else, out of the limelight of their small Idaho ranching town.

She was moving around the room, shutting down for the night. Belle Haven was a full-service clinic. Behind this main building was also a large barn housing their horses and additional equipment, both his own and his brother's. Adam was a local trainer, breeder, and search-and-rescue specialist.

Their reception area was large and airy, with wide-planked wood floors lined with comfortable benches for waiting. At one end was a long counter—Jade's—and behind it was the hub of the entire place.

Jade's jurisdiction.

She ran this front room like a drill sergeant, and half the time Dell wanted to put his hands around her neck and squeeze.

The other half of the time he wanted to put his hands on her for something else entirely. Since he was fond of living, he kept both these urges to himself.

"What are we going to do with the poor thing?" Jade asked. "Take her home? Oh, wait. You never take any of your women home."

This was true. He didn't bring women home.

He went to their place. He gave the kitten a cursory look over. Other than being far too skinny, she seemed healthy enough. "She'll need to be spayed and vaccinated."

"Want me to call Lilah for tonight?" Jade asked.

Lilah ran the kennel next to Belle Haven, and she was also the Humane Society as well as one of Dell's closest friends. Lilah would take the kitten and keep her until she could be placed in a good home. "That'd be best," he said. "Because I have a—"

"Date," she said, swiveling her chair to give him her back. "Shock." She went back to closing up.

Everything had its place with her. Files were always meticulously filed; the copier, fax, and computer were carefully covered to protect from dust. Pencils, pens, and assorted other equipment placed into their spots in drawers. Dell never got tired of watching her, and never failed to smile when the last thing she did was consult her various to-do spreadsheets to make sure everything had been done, even though she knew damn well it had been.

She never forgot a thing.

"It's not a date," he said. Or not *exactly*. "I'm heading into Coeur d'Alene for a friend of a friend's birthday party."

"Yeah, I know. I get the messages on the machine, remember?" She clicked over to another of her spreadsheets on the computer. "Your friend of a friend left a message reminding you that he wants to introduce you to—and let me give a direct quote here"—she read from her screen—"*Mandy, a stacked blonde who's hoping to play dirty doctor with a doctor.*" Jade swiveled back to arch a brow in his direction.

He shrugged. "You can't believe all of what Kenny says."

"What percentage?"

"What?"

Her expression was classic *don't mess with me*. "What percentage of what Kenny says can we believe?"

"Half." He lifted a shoulder. "Maybe forty percent."

"Okay, so by sheer odds, you're either meeting a stacked blonde, or playing dirty doctor."

Dell laughed and came around the counter. Good Christ, had she smelled that delicious all day long? He leaned over her chair and took another whiff.

"What are you doing?" she asked.

"Seeing what's left on your spreadsheet."

"Hey." She pushed him with her shoulder. "Personal space intrusion." She pushed him again as she dialed Lilah. She had to leave a message, which she did while keeping a narrowed eye on him at the same time. The same sort of narrowed eye the kitten still had on him.

Two females, both suspicious. Both wary.

Both having been hurt.

Dell would have laid money down that Jade had no idea how much of herself she gave away when she looked at him like that. And to be fair, she was good at hiding.

But he was better. The skill had been hard earned from his growing-up years, further honed by the nature of his job. There were no words when it came to animals, and out of necessity he'd become the master at reading anyone and anything. He could see past Jade's dazzling clothes and tough-girl exterior, past the uptight perfectionist to the vulnerable woman beneath.

Yeah, the woman was definitely hiding.

What he didn't know was why. He had a few ideas, none of which he liked, but whatever the reason, it made him a little heartsick for her, in the same way he felt for the kitten, sitting quiet but not compliant in the crook of his arm. Unfortunately, he knew without a shadow of a doubt that only the kitten was going to allow him to help her. He smiled down at her as he stroked her beneath the chin, which seemed to be the magic ticket because she let out a rumbling, rusty purr. "You're sweet," he murmured, rubbing his jaw along the top of her little head.

"Aw thanks," Jade said. "I try."

Dell smiled because that was a lie and they both knew it. Then she surprised him.

"I'll take the kitten," she said, and in her usual efficient way stepped back from her desk and critically eyed the clean surface as she slung her purse over her shoulder. Heels clicking, she moved to the wall of storage cabinets. Without hesitation, she opened one and pulled out a kitten carrier. Then she went to another cabinet, bending low to grab a bed liner, expertly lining the kitten carrier. "Grab me some food? And a litter box, too," she said over her shoulder.

He didn't move. "*You're* going to take the kitten overnight," he repeated dubiously.

"Yes." Her hand and arm brushed his chest as she relieved him of the kitten. "Why do you look so flummoxed?"

"Well, maybe because you've never done such a thing before. Hell, Jade, you've never even let any of us come to your place."

Ignoring that, Jade carefully slid the kitten into the carrier and turned her back on him, heading to the door.

They were the last two in the building. Keith, his animal tech, and Mike, his vet nurse, had both already left. Jade hit all the lights except one interior, casting them in a soft glow. "Look," she said. "My job is running this front reception room like a well-oiled machine, right? That includes any loose ends."

He stepped between her and the door. "And the stray is a loose end?"

"At this point, Doctor, *you're* a loose end. Everything in the back handled?"

The "back" consisted of two exam rooms, a surgical suite, an x-ray and ultrasonic suite, and his and Adam's offices. "Closed up tighter than a drum," he assured her.

"Hmm." She didn't look impressed. She liked it better when she made the last walk through. And with good reason. He'd been known to be distracted enough to forget to turn something off or to even lock himself out. He opened the front door for her, then put a hand on her arm, waiting until she met his gaze. "I owe you. Lunch tomorrow?"

"We can never agree on a place."

"Name it, then," he said. "Name your price."

This appeared to interest her given how she cocked her head. "That's a lot of power."

She had no idea how much power she already had. "Anything."

She considered this so seriously he smiled. Then she flashed him a rare one of her own and his heart actually stuttered. "You're not going to like it," she warned.

Oh, how wrong she was. "There's not much I don't like, Jade."

She poked a finger in his chest. "Okay, what did I tell you about flirting with me, about using my name in that sex-on-a-stick voice?"

Now this interested *him.* "You think my voice is sex on a stick?"

She poked him again. He liked to think it was because she had a secret thing for touching him, but then again, he was a realist. If she'd wanted him that way, she'd have let him know by now.

"I want you to let me take care of the stack of bills on your desk," she said. "The one that's threatening to fall over and hit the floor."

They both knew that the state of his desk, which looked like it had been napalmed, drove her organized, anal heart absolutely nuts. As did how he could be counted on to lose his keys, wallet, or hell, his own brain in the mess at least once a week. But though he hated paperwork with the same passion that he hated vegetables, he wasn't going to hand over the reins of his admittedly sloppy accounting. He realized that meant that he trusted the animals in his care more than he did the humans, but hell, everyone had their faults. "If you took care of the mess on my desk," he said, "that would be you doing *me* the favor."

"Not really. I *need* to organize that desk, Dell. And you hate handling the bills, I heard you swearing at them just this morning."

"I was swearing at the news. Another vet clinic was robbed last night." There'd been a series of vet robberies between here and Spokane in the past week. The threat of it happening here, at his place, the one he'd built with his own sweat and blood, pissed him off. "Just after closing time. This time a tech was still in the building, working late, and was knocked out."

"Oh my God," she said, covering her mouth. "What did they take?"

"Ketamine."

"Ketamine." She frowned. "Horse tranq?"

"Turns out it's a good human narcotic as well." Not to mention an effective date rape drug but she'd gone very still, very pale. "Hey. You okay?"

"That's why you stayed tonight," she said. "You wanted to walk me out to make sure I was safe."

"And the kitten. I wanted the kitten to be safe, too." He smiled, but Jade didn't. Instead, she looked out the window into the dark parking lot with obvious unease, making him doubly glad he'd stayed.

Belle Haven was just outside of their small town of Sunshine, five miles down a narrow, winding road. Their closest neighbor—Lilah's kennels—was a quarter mile away. They were surrounded by the rugged, majestic Idaho Bitterroot mountain range, the peaks looming high. To say that they were isolated out here was an understatement.

Since Jade was still just standing there looking out the window, Dell took the kitten carrier and litter from her and nudged her out the door.

It was early autumn and the chill on the night air cut to the bone, reminding him that winter would be here before they knew it.

At her car, Jade took the kitten back and set the carrier on the backseat, making him smile when she carefully pulled the seat belt across it. Straightening, she faced him again. "See you and your disastrous desk tomorrow."

The cell phone in his back pocket was vibrating. He was late and knew it, so he ignored the call. "Forget about my desk. It's a mess, it'll take you days."

"My greatest fantasy," she said.

"That's just sad, Jade."

"Don't distract me with your perverted mind. I was made for this."

"What, were you born with the need to organize?"

"No, I was born with a silver spoon in my mouth. The need to organize is just a freak of nature, one of life's mysteries."

Infamously private, Jade didn't talk about herself often. She'd been born and raised in Chicago, he knew that much. And that she had family there, family she'd promised that she'd come back to.

Fairly private himself, Dell had never pushed her for more, but every time she doled out a little tidbit about her past and gave him a tiny glimpse inside, he found himself all the more fascinated by her.

A silver spoon . . . If that was true, they'd grown up just about as different as two people could get.

"So, what do you say?" she asked. "You going to let me in or what?"

Actually, the question was—would she ever let *him* in . . . "You're a nut," he said. "You know that, right?"

"When I clean your office, you'll be calling me a goddess."

"I'll call you whatever you'd like, but forget about the—"

His phone was going off again. Reaching around him, Jade slid her hand into his scrubs back pocket. Through the thin cotton, her fingers stroked his ass cheek, and his brain clicked off. Just completely clicked off. This condition was not improved when her breast brushed his arm as she lifted his phone.

"Dr. Connelly's phone," she answered professionally, her face so close to his he could have turned his face and captured her lips with his.

It was her scent, he decided; it drugged him. Made him stupid. Maybe it was her skin, too, so pale compared to his, so soft and deceptively fragile-looking.

Hell. It was her. Everything about her.

The night around them was so quiet he had no problem hearing the feminine voice coming out of his phone, inquiring of his whereabouts.

"Let me check for you," Jade said, eyes back on his. "Please hold." She muted the phone and looked at him, affecting a sex kitten voice to match the one on the phone. "Are you . . . *available*?"

Having some problems accessing working brain cells, it took him a minute to answer. "Last I checked."

She pushed a button on his phone, working it better than he did. "Yes, Dr. Connelly is still here. Who's calling?" Jade listened with careful politeness, contrasted by the long look she slid his way just before she rolled her eyes.

Not at the woman.

At him.

She slapped the phone against his chest. "She says you're late." She slid behind the wheel and drove off into the night, leaving him in her dust.

Literally.

Still he watched until her taillights vanished before he lifted his phone to his ear.

Two

At her place, Jade deactivated her alarm and flipped a switch. As they'd been programmed to do, four different lights came on, one in each corner of the living area, kitchen nook, bedroom area, and entry to the bathroom.

Instant visual access.

Expensive, and worth every penny. Everything was neat as a pin and just the way she'd left it. In order.

Order meant safety, and Jade depended on both. She set the kitten carrier on the foyer floor and opened the little door. The kitten tentatively poked her nose out, definitely not quite as sure of herself without Dell's warm arms.

Jade supposed she couldn't blame her. Dell had a way of making a woman feel safe. "Get comfortable," she said as her cell rang.

Dr. Doolittle himself.

"Don't tell me," she said. "You lost your wallet and/or your car keys."

"Okay, now that hurts," Dell said, sounding anything but wounded.

"Uh-huh. Why else would you be calling after hours when you're supposed to be playing doctor?"

"If you think you know me so well, why don't you guess?"

"You've forgotten the code for the alarm," she said. "Again."

"Hey," he said. "Once."

"Yeah, once. Once a week."

"I'm calling to make sure you got home okay."

His words were a direct hit to her carefully built defenses. She'd gotten used to being on her own. But Dell was a true pack leader and took care of his own. Whether she liked it or not.

She didn't. It gave her a false sense of security. She'd been working on that, on letting people in. On trying to loosen up. She'd even put it on her to-do spreadsheets to remind herself. *Live. Open up. Have fun.*

Wasn't she driving into Coeur d'Alene every Wednesday night to take a line-dancing class? Skiing here and there on the weekends?

So she needed to not be charmed by him. She was leaving, and now was not the time to get involved, not when her time here was nearly up. "I'm home safe and sound, thanks," she said, then paused. "Good night, Dell."

"Night, Goddess Jade."

She hit the End button and looked down in surprise at the soft "Mew." She'd almost forgotten about her houseguest. "That was our boss," she said, and shook her head. "Making sure we're okay."

"Mew," the kitten said, sounding . . . lonely.

Common ground, Jade thought. Loneliness. And something she could understand that Dell could not. He wouldn't know lonely if it bit him on his very fine ass.

The kitten had stepped outside of the carrier but not a foot farther.

"It's okay," Jade told her. "It's all about baby steps."

The kitten sniffed the floor.

"Really. *Mi casa es su casa*," Jade assured her. "Well, for the night, anyway." She walked through her living room area. She'd rented this place the day she'd come to town eighteen months ago now. It was an older building, built in the 1950s, and beautifully renovated. Jade was on the top of three floors. The loft was large, the ceilings high, lined with intricately carved crown molding. It had come furnished and cost an arm and a leg.

But far more important to Jade, she could see everything in one sweeping glance.

She flipped through her mail, separating it into three piles: junk, bills, letters. The junk mail she dropped directly into the shredder under her small desk in the corner. The bills she set next to her laptop to be promptly paid. The letter she set on the mantel and then stared at for a few minutes.

It was from her mother. Everyone else in her life called, texted, or e-mailed, but her mother had never gotten the hang of modern technology.

Jade had a pretty pothos plant whose abundant leaves had worked their way in front of the few pictures she had on the mantel. Nudging them aside, she looked into the eyes of her family. Her well-meaning retired physician parents were arm in arm in front of their large successful medical center, which until eighteen months ago, Jade had overseen for them. The job had been her life, which was no wonder given that the center had five major departments to oversee; urgent care, ob-gyn, family practice, pediatrics, and orthopedics.

Then there was the picture of Jade and her cousin, Sam Bennett, a doctor as well, the two of them on skis and mugging for the camera.

Both pictures had been taken two years ago now and represented a time when Jade had known exactly who and what she was, and the path of her future.

They'd been a happy, loving, successful family.

She ran a finger over her father's face and heard his voice in her head, shaking slightly with the Parkinson's disease that was slowly killing him. *Nothing can scare you, princess. You're a natural, you were born to be strong and do anything you want.*

How often had he told her that?

Every day.

Her mother, too.

Sam had been fond of the mantra as well, and it had meant even more coming from him. Only two years older than Jade, Sam was far more a brother than a cousin. He called weekly and texted daily, checking on her, bugging her to come home.

Something she'd promised to do the day she'd left Chicago. She'd told them she'd be back within the year. But that year had come and gone and she'd had to ask for an extension because she hadn't been ready.

Now it had been eighteen months and her grace period was gone. But as it turned out, she could get her pencils and her lists and her clothes just the way she wanted, she could expect her world to fall into place just the way she wanted, but healing . . . healing couldn't be ordered.

Healing had to come from the inside.

It had to come from the "strength" her family had constantly told her she had, strength she'd blindly accepted as fact.

That had been the fatal flaw.

Because she'd never had to actually *be* strong. And as it turned out, being told you're strong and actually *being* strong were two very different things.

Which she discovered the night she'd been tested beyond endurance.

After the attack, she realized the truth—that everyone had been wrong, *very* wrong. She hadn't been strong at all. Once that had sunk in, her foundation had cracked and fallen away from beneath her feet.

And she'd run. She'd run hard and fast, from family, from well-meaning friends, from work, from everything. She'd come here to Sunshine and ordered herself to feel safe. But the attack had showed her that even ordering something to happen couldn't stop the unexpected. So even as she worked hard at creating structure to Dell's life, she wasn't facing her own weakness—dealing with the unexpected.

Her cell phone rang again, and still staring at the unopened letter, she answered without looking at the ID. "Dell, I'm going to start to think you'd rather be playing doctor with me."

There was a startled beat of silence. "You and Dell are playing doctor?"

Jade winced. "Hey, Lilah."

"Don't 'Hey, Lilah' me. You got some 'splaining to do, Lucy. You're playing doctor with Dell?"

"No! I just thought you were him again, and—"

"Again?" Jade was sounding excited now, a *big* mistake on Jade's part. Lilah had the nose of a bloodhound, and she was on the scent.

"Is there something going on that I need to be informed of pronto?" Lilah asked.

"No!" Jade drew a calming breath. Like Dell, Lilah worked with animals and could read a lie a mile away. "Okay, let's focus here. Where are you?"

"In Boise with Brady."

Damn. "Are you at least getting some action from the hottest pilot in all of Idaho?"

"In all the *land*," Lilah corrected. "Not just Idaho. And don't think I didn't spot the subject change. Nicely done. What did you do with the stray?"

"I took her."

There was a prolonged silence at this. *"You?"*

Jade sighed. "It's not that weird. You were gone and there was no one else."

"So . . . you have the stray at your place?"

"It's just for the night, Lilah."

Another pause. "Can I talk to her?" Lilah joked. "And get the secret admittance handshake?"

"Ha," Jade said at the subtle knock at the fact that she never invited any of them over. She had no idea why Lilah liked her, but she was glad. Lilah was open and welcoming and inspired trust. And she got the same feelings from Sunshine itself. "I'll bring you the kitten tomorrow."

"Sounds good. But I'm actually calling about tomorrow night. I want to get everyone together at Crystal's."

Everyone meant Lilah and her boyfriend Brady—an ex–army ranger, now a pilot for hire—and Brady's brothers, Dell and Adam. They were a tight group, and considered themselves family.

By some miracle, they'd included Jade in that group. "Sounds good."

"Tell Dell for me?"

"Okay."

"Aha!" Lilah cried triumphantly. "So there *is* something going on with you two."

"Lilah, we work together. I meant I'd tell him tomorrow at work."

"Or when you play doctor . . ."

There was no doubt Dell could show Jade a good time. But she'd seen his patterns over the past year and a half, and they didn't involve being friends with the women he slept with. And they were friends. So she could squelch the occasional yearning for more. Especially since . . . "He's on a date."

"Oh." Lilah sighed. "You got my hopes up there for a minute. I know, stupid."

Yes. Yes, Jade and Dell together would be stupid. He was her boss. He had an allergy to relationships. And she wasn't made for quickie affairs, not to mention that she was going back to Chicago soon.

All good, solid reasons to avoid said stupidity.

"Bringing this back to me," Lilah said. "Put tomorrow night at Crystal's on your fancy spreadsheet calendar thingie and send it to Dell. Wait—are you still forbidden from sending him any more spreadsheets?"

This had happened a few months back after Jade had accidentally (on purpose) mixed up his social calendar, causing him to pick up the wrong woman on the wrong night. "Nah, he got over it." Dell got over everything, it was part of his easy charm. Nothing much got to him.

"Make it seven o'clock tomorrow night," Lilah said.

"I'll be there."

"Want me to come by and get you?"

"Sure."

"I'll honk for you."

The usual routine. Jade looked around her loft. Eighteen months, and though Lilah had picked her up numerous times for a girls' night out or dinner or any of a hundred other things, Jade had never invited Lilah inside.

Or anyone.

At first it was because she'd been protective of her privacy. And then as she'd made friends, it had been a way of keeping her heart protected from becoming too attached.

Which, of course, was far too late. She drew in a breath. "Don't honk," she said.

"What?"

"Tomorrow night. When you get here, just come up."

"You mean you're finally finished painting?" Lilah asked, sounding excited.

Jade bit her lip, feeling a flush hit her cheeks at the shame of the little white lies she'd told everyone to protect herself. "Yeah. I finally finished painting."

"Well, it's about damn time, considering you're leaving next month, sheesh! Can't wait. See you tomorrow."

Jade hung up the phone and looked at the kitten sitting in the doorway of the foyer, watching her with those narrowed feline eyes. "Baby steps," she reminded the both of them.

When Lilah picked Jade up the next night, she was grinning as Jade opened the front door. "Lemme in, lemme in," she said, pressing past Jade.

Jade held her breath as Lilah walked through the place. "It's—"

"Nice," Lilah finally said, turning in a circle. "It's . . . wow nice." Lilah lived in a tiny cabin, one that was both adorable and ancient. At any given moment either the plumbing or electricity were threatening to go out and stay out. But the place had been purposely, carefully, lovingly furnished by Lilah herself, and every inch of it was . . . well, Lilah.

Jade looked around now, trying to see her loft as if for the first time to decide what these furnishings said about her. Smooth lines, glass, mostly white or pale earth tone colors.

Clean.

Neat.

They said *expensive lease.*

"So neat," Lilah said, sounding amused. "I shouldn't be surprised at that."

There was very little clutter. Jade had always been proud of that, and the clean lines. It said she was on top of things. Successful. Smart.

An illusion, and one easily shattered at that.

"It's so light and airy," Lilah said. "Fancy."

And costly. The word went unspoken, but it was true. She paid for the tight security and a good neighborhood, made all the more pricey because she was on a month-to-month, not an annual lease. The owner charged her more to give him the security he needed in case she bailed.

And she did plan on bailing.

Sooner or later . . .

Or so she'd been saying every month for over a year now.

"Mew," said the stray kitten that Jade hadn't given to Lilah this morning.

Lilah scooped the kitten up for a hug. "Aw. You're what, four months old? You're precious." She looked at Jade. "I thought you were going to bring her to the kennels for adoption."

"I am. Tomorrow."

She'd meant to do it today, but there was just something about those green eyes that said the little thing had seen too much for her few months. And the way her little ribs stuck out, it grabbed Jade by the heart and wouldn't let go. She wanted to fatten her up first, is all, give her a day off from the cruel realities of the big, bad world out there.

"You have beautiful taste," Lilah said, something new and a little different in her voice now, and Jade paused. She understood Lilah's confusion. Jade had once told her that she'd come to Sunshine for the good winter skiing and a break from her life.

Obviously the receptionist job and ski-bum premise didn't quite add up to being able to afford a place like this. "I lease it furnished."

Lilah looked at her as if she was speaking another language. "Really? Why?"

Jade hesitated. She could tell Lilah the whole sordid story. That's what friends, *real* friends, did.

But she couldn't tell. She couldn't tell anyone, not without falling apart, and falling apart was not on today's to-do spreadsheet.

But she could be honest about something, at least. "I leased it furnished, because as you know, I never intended to stay in Sunshine long."

Lilah nodded. "So the whole 'I'm painting my place' thing . . ."

"I've never painted anything in my entire life," Jade admitted. "I'm sorry. I—"

Lilah set the kitten down and squeezed Jade's hand, her eyes warm with understanding. "You don't have to explain yourself to me, Jade. Not until you're ready."

It was the first time that Lilah had ever let on that she knew that Jade hadn't been honest with her, and the knowledge made Jade's throat burn. "Thanks," she whispered.

"But you can tell me something else."

"Anything," Jade said, relieved.

Lilah watched the kitten jump up on the couch and make herself at home. "Why did you keep her?"

They both looked at the kitten now daintily licking her Lady Town.

Jade bit her lower lip. "I don't know. Anyone claim her?"

"Nope. And she's going to leave hair all over that pretty couch."

"I didn't want her to be put down," Jade said.

"I don't put animals down. Ever. And you know that."

Jade sighed. "Look, she acclimated. I can't kick her out now."

Lilah grinned. "You are so full of shit tonight. All the way around. Why can't you just admit you've fallen for her?"

"I don't fall."

At that, Lilah laughed outright. "Oh, honey. Haven't you learned yet? You can control a lot of things—work, what you watch on TV, how much ice cream you inhale—but you can't control what your heart does."

Jade brooded over that for a moment. "You can control how much ice cream you inhale?"

Lilah laughed again. "Come on, Brady's meeting us at the bar. He told me I had to be on time tonight or he wouldn't put out later." She took one last look around and sighed wistfully. "Someday," she murmured. "I'm going to have a place like this."

Jade followed Lilah out and carefully set her alarm. Maybe she had the more expensive place and bigger savings account, but out of the two of them, Lilah with her tiny cabin, kennels, and adoring boyfriend was by far the richer.

Jade accepted her small glass of wine from the bartender and lifted a brow at the *huge* margarita he placed in front of Lilah.

"I have big plans for tonight," Lilah said with a grin, licking the salt off the edge of the glass.

"Does it involve being flat on your ass?" Jade asked.

Lilah laughed and took a healthy sip of her drink. "Flat on my *back* maybe." She grinned stupidly at the man who walked into the bar and headed directly for her.

Brady Miller.

The big, badass ex–army ranger didn't look any less big and bad as he returned Lilah's goofy smile and bodily plucked her out of her chair and squeezed her tight.

Lilah sighed sweetly, cupped his face, and kissed him long and hard, like maybe she hadn't seen him in a year instead of that morning before she'd left for work.

Jade turned away to give them a moment, and herself, too. Had a man ever looked at her in the way Brady looked at Lilah? If so, she couldn't remember it.

She'd dated in Chicago, usually with men she met through her connections at work or at the charity events she'd often run for her family. Similar minded as she, these men had professional lives that took up much of their time, and for whatever reason, not a one of them had sparked a long-term interest.

They'd been wrong for her.

She was good at that, meeting men who were wrong for her.

Still, she'd managed to have relationships, some that had even hung on for a few months at a time, often longer than they should have. What hadn't happened was the magic that made her want to take the next step. Magic she would have said didn't exist.

Except it did.

She was looking at it between Brady and Lilah. Then she locked eyes on another man entirely, Dr. Dell Connelly. She felt a little quiver, which was ridiculous because out of all the men in the land, he was the most wrong for her of them all.

Three

Dell and Adam walked toward the bar, side by side, looking like the brothers they were from head to toe. Of the two, Adam was two years older but they almost could have passed for twins. Dark disheveled hair, dark eyes, features as strong and beautiful as fallen angels. Mix that with his dark skin and six feet plus of solid muscle and testosterone, and there wasn't a woman in the place not wishing they were going home with one of them.

Or both.

There were subtle differences though, if you knew them, and after working for them, Jade knew them well.

Adam was his usual unsmiling, serious self. Dell was much more open, already looking like he was having a good time, but the truth was that Dell could have a good time anywhere.

He was out of the surgical scrubs that so defined him at work, wearing a pair of jeans and a snug black T-shirt that made a woman want to drop at his knees and give him whatever he wanted.

But not her.

At least not in her waking hours. And what she fantasized about in the dark of the night was just that—fantasy.

He was smiling and would have looked younger than his thirty-two years—except for his eyes. His eyes said that he'd seen far more than his affable smile showed, and it had been those eyes to tell her eighteen months ago that she could work for him and be safe.

But safe was relative. And the fact was, she'd never seen so much male perfection grouped so closely together, and if you added Brady into the mix, it was a wonder that any woman in the place could put a thought together. These were rugged guys, built for stamina and the tough life out here that they all led. Not a single one of them were "city." They'd never had a pedicure or worried about wrinkles or the cut of their clothes. They were real, as real as they came.

These qualities had a universal appeal, proven when Dell and Adam passed a table of three women, one of whom reached out and snagged Dell's arm.

Jade recognized her as Cassie, a local rancher. Dell stopped and set a friendly hand on Cassie's shoulder and she beamed up at him. So did the others at the table. This was because Dell could make ninety-year-old women preen and get infant girls to bat their eyelashes in his sleep.

He was the heart and soul of Belle Haven, and the rock of all of them.

This morning when she'd shown back up with the kitten in her carrier and informed him she was keeping her for a few days, he'd just smiled and said, "I know." He'd known before Jade that she'd look into the strong, independent but down-on-her-luck kitten's eyes and not be able to let her go.

Yet.

Lilah finally removed her lips from Brady and waved at Adam and Dell. "Over here!"

Since Dell was currently being hugged by another woman at the table, Adam got to them first.

"'Bout time," Lilah said.

Adam looked at his watch. "We late?"

"Nope, I'm just on time for once," Lilah said. "All my pretties got picked up on time today."

These "pretties" could be anything from dogs and cats to the more exotic. Jade had seen her driving around with a duck, a pig, and a lamb, stuck on babysitting detail. The woman had more patience than anyone Jade had ever met.

Adam nudged Jade and she obliged him, moving over in the booth, making room. He looked back to where his brother was attempting to extract himself from the woman's arms and shook his head. "I told him, keep your head down and keep moving, but does he listen?" He glanced at Brady and Lilah and grimaced when he found them lip-locked again. "Ah, man, come on."

Brady lifted his head and smiled into Lilah's eyes. "Been wanting to do that all day."

"You flew me around all day," Adam said, helping himself to Jade's wine. "We've been flying S&R in Eagle Canyon searching for a lost hiker."

Brady smiled at Lilah. "I can multitask."

Adam shook his head.

Dell finally appeared, his hair looking like it'd just been tousled by a hungry female. Kicking Brady's legs out of his way, he stepped around Adam and pushed his way into the booth on Lilah's other side.

Jade knew he'd spent much of his day in surgery but you couldn't have told that by looking at him. Or smelling him. He smelled like undiluted amazingness as he bumped a broad shoulder to hers.

"Show-off," he said.

She'd organized his inventory before he'd gotten out of his second surgery. "Just trying to help," she said demurely.

His dark warm eyes held hers for a minute. "Bullshit," he said, letting the smile in his voice break through. "You couldn't help yourself, Jade."

"That's Goddess Jade to you."

He laughed, and as always, the sound did something funny low in her belly. Which was really annoying considering the fact that every other woman who came in close proximity to him felt the same way.

"So, what is it you did in your previous life again? Run the world?" he asked.

"Close enough." Running her family's medical center had been much like running a small country, complete with the politics that went with it. "I have skills. Got 'em from my grandmother Jade. I got lots of things from her."

"Such as?"

"Well, she, too, was always right."

Dell fought a smile and lost. With his warm eyes on hers and his hard thigh pressing to her own, Jade felt a silly little flutter.

No doubt this was how the women at the other table had felt when he'd focused his attention on them. At least she wasn't simpering. She refused to simper.

"Are you always right?" Adam asked. "Or do we just let you think it because it's easier?"

Jade took her wine back from him.

"Oh, and after you left," Dell told her. "I took a few phone calls and squished a few more patients in for tomorrow." He stopped to smile at someone waving to him from across the bar.

Jade poked him to get his attention back. Right in the biceps. Her finger bounced off him. "You didn't have room in your schedule. It's packed."

"Yeah, but Mrs. Kyle's cat is feeling 'peakish.'" He shrugged. "Doesn't tell me much, but Miss Kitty's like a hundred, so it could be anything. She needs to be seen."

Jade didn't bother to sigh. It wouldn't help. If there was an animal in need, Dell would work around the clock. "Tell me you did not even attempt to update the computer yourself."

"Okay, I won't tell you."

"Man," Adam muttered beneath his breath. "You never learn."

Dell's eyes were lit and Jade relaxed. "You're just messing with me."

A small smile crossed his face as he studied her. "How can you be sure?"

"Because if you'd messed anything up, you'd have brought me flowers, or you'd be kissing my ass like last time."

"I'll cop to the flowers, because you are one scary woman when you're mad at me. But I've *never* kissed your ass." He cocked his head and pretended to study said ass, even though she was sitting on it. "I'd be happy to do so, though. Anytime."

She reached out to shove him, but he had lightning reflexes and grabbed her hand in his much bigger, darker one. His was callused and work-roughed, and because that gave her an odd flutter, she pulled free. "Save it for someone that those moo-moo eyes actually work on."

The band kicked into high gear. Lilah had pulled a reluctant Brady onto the dance floor.

"Better Fly Boy than me," Adam muttered, and headed to the bar for a pitcher of beer.

Dell nudged Jade.

"In your dreams," she said.

"What, is Goddess Jade afraid of something as innocuous as a dance?"

No, what she was afraid of was getting too close and getting sucked into his Hotness Vortex. She wasn't afraid he'd ask anything of her she wasn't willing to give.

She was afraid of what she was willing to give.

But you're leaving, said the little devil on her shoulder. Her inner slut. *You're going back, you're better now, what would it hurt to have him, just once?*

Before Jade could thoroughly process this thought and take any action, Cassie appeared at their table. "Dell," she said, tugging him up. "You owe me a dance."

His smile was light. Flirty. But he shook his head. "Actually, I was just going to dance with Jade."

"Go ahead," Jade said. This was the little angel on her other shoulder. She wasn't an inner slut.

Beaming, Cassie pulled Dell out of his chair. Jade shook her head at herself and headed to the bar.

Adam was there. He eyed Dell on the dance floor and he gave her a long look.

"What?" she asked, maybe a little snappish.

He just shook his head.

When Dell finally escaped the dance floor, he turned back to their table. Jade was back from the bar, and there was a guy trying to pick her up.

Poor sucker, he thought with a good amount of sympathy, watching as Jade shook her head. As Dell moved closer, he heard the guy say, "Aw, come on, Red. I've seen you swing your sweet thang in class, let's take it to the dance floor."

"I'm with someone," Jade said.

The guy admitted defeat and moved off. Dell dropped into the coveted spot right next to her, sprawling out. "Hey, Red?"

She sipped her drink.

"Class?"

She shrugged.

"Oh come on. Tell me about swinging your sweet thang." He accepted her eat-shit-and-die look and laughed.

She rolled her eyes. "So I take a line-dancing class once a week in the city."

"Which clearly you're not doing so that you'll get picked up by guys in bars."

"It's for exercise." She blew out a breath. "And because I sort of promised myself I'd do things for me. For fun. It's the year of the fun for Jade."

"Well, I'm all for that."

At that, she cocked her head and looked at him. "You don't think it's silly?"

"Everyone deserves fun, Jade." He smiled at her and reached for his drink. "Their own brand of fun."

Jade's eyes cut to Brady and Lilah, plastered up against each other on the dance floor. "What do you think of their brand?"

Dell took in the expression on Brady's face, which held warmth and love and a whole hell of a lot of lust, and shrugged. It would be nice to know there was a woman waiting on him at the end of the day. He wouldn't mind that. It was the emotional depth and level of attachment that bothered him. The love part. Love would take trust and blind faith. It would take allowing access to parts of him that he didn't allow himself access to. "I'm not really cut out for it."

"So you've tried it, then?"

"Not so much. You? I'm betting you have a spreadsheet for this, for meeting the right guy to give you a white picket fence and two point four kids."

"Some things even my spreadsheets can't do," she said, and he laughed softly just as Brady and Lilah came back looking flushed and happy as they slid into the booth.

"Okay," Lilah said. "It's been an hour and no one has said one freaking word about the bling." She spread her hands on the table. "Seriously?"

Jade's eyes went directly to Lilah's left ring finger, and the fat diamond there. "Holy shit!"

Lilah grinned. "I know, right?" She flashed the ring in each of their faces. "Brady had it made for me. It's the most sparkly thing I've ever owned." Turning to Brady, she clapped her hands to either side of his face and kissed him on the mouth. "I've never been all that sparkly, but I am now, cuz of you."

Brady smiled up at her. "Sparkly, *and* you smell like a strawberry."

"It's the margaritas."

Adam toasted to Brady and Lilah, and Dell added his congratulations, genuinely thrilled for them. Lilah felt like as much a sibling to him as

Brady was. And though he might not quite get why two of his favorite people in the world wanted to tie themselves to each other and give up all the other possible options, it meant that Brady would be sticking around Sunshine. And Dell was all for that, so he grinned and topped off their glasses from the pitcher, giving Lilah the last of it and the most.

Brady slid him a look.

"What, you're already going to have to pour her into your truck to take her home," Dell told him. "Might as well make it a night to remember."

Lilah laughed and slapped Brady's shoulder, as if he'd been the one to say it. "It *will* be a night to remember." Indeed, two sheets to the wind, she blew a strand of her hair from her face and waggled a finger at her new fiancé. "But just so we're clear—we're still not crossing that one last thing off the taboo list. I'm not *that* far gone."

Adam looked pained.

Brady didn't look concerned. He was smiling affectionately at Lilah, looking content and confident that he could talk her into anything he wanted, wasted or not.

"You have a taboo list?" Jade asked.

"You don't?" Lilah asked.

Jade bit her lower lip and Adam laughed. "Jade has a list for *everything*."

"True," Dell said, studying her, getting nothing from her expression. She had quite the game face, his Jade. "You do, you have lists for everything."

"Not *everything*."

"Jade, you have a list for every situation, big or small, from when to brush your teeth, to how to handle every potential patient to cross my door. Hell, you've got a list on what's in your purse and my office fridge and—"

"And don't forget the list on how many different ways I could kill you," she said, sipping her drink.

"Now that's one I'd like to see," Brady said.

Adam looked intrigued. "How many ways are there really to do that?"

"You have no idea . . ." she murmured serenely.

Dell laughed. "Come on. There's no doubt in my mind, you have a list of sexual taboos. Tell us."

"Yeah," Lilah said, leaning forward. "Tell us! I might need to add to my list."

"Why are we still talking about this?" Jade wanted to know.

"The question is," Dell said, "why are you avoiding talking about this?" He smiled at her and though she blushed a little, she held his gaze evenly.

He didn't have a hard time imagining Jade as a sexual creature. She was beautiful, innately sensual, from that full bottom lip, to her glorious curves, to the way she moaned while eating her hidden stash of chocolate from her bottom desk drawer.

What he had a hard time imagining was her having a one-night stand. Which meant that she'd have to let someone in close enough to have a relationship with before she had sex. And she wasn't any better at that than . . . well, him. He got her, he really did. Because other than the people right here at this table, he never felt the overwhelming need to let anyone in, either. "Come on," he coaxed, teasing. "Give us something from your taboo list."

She smiled at him. "You should be far more concerned with what's on tomorrow's to-do list."

"Ha," Adam said to his brother. "You have a to-do list."

"So do you," Jade said, and Brady laughed.

"Nice deflection," Lilah said to Jade. "You're good at that."

It was a definite talent, Dell thought, and let her have the deflection. They all hung out for another hour before Brady stood and grabbed Lilah's hand. "We're out," he said.

Lilah smiled wickedly. "'Bout time." She looked at Jade. "Can we drop you off?"

"No, that's okay," Jade said, shaking her head. "Go home with Brady."

"You sure?"

"Very."

Lilah hugged her and then she and Brady made tracks. Adam's cell vibrated, and he excused himself out into the night as well. Dell looked at Jade, who was scrolling through her contacts. "Looks like it's you and me. Come on, I'll give you a ride."

"No, it's out of your way. I'll call . . ."

"That guy from your line-dancing class?"

She sighed. "Okay, so I could use a ride."

He walked her out to his truck and then had to clear her a spot in the passenger's seat because he had a stack of work files, his hockey gear from the weekend league he played on, and some other shit he'd shoved into the truck and forgotten about. "There," he said, tossing everything to the back.

"Thanks," she murmured, and got in. "Your truck looks like your desk."

True statement. "I have a little organizational problem."

Her gaze met his. "I could help you with that."

"Sure, if you'll let me help you with your taboos list."

"How do you know that you don't have the same taboos?"

"I don't have any."

That shocked her into silence, and the rest of the drive to her place stayed quiet, though she was thinking so loud he could almost hear her thoughts.

The minute he pulled into her lot, her hand was on the door. She was in a hurry. He wondered which of them she didn't trust.

"Thanks for the ride," she said.

"Anytime, Jade."

She glanced back at him, and in a purely feminine move, bit her lower lip, her teeth pressing into the plump curve. "So, tomorrow I thought I'd tackle your office."

There was a light in her eyes. *Lust,* he thought, dazed. He nearly groaned. But the lust wasn't for him, it was for his damn desk. She looked practically orgasmic at the thought of getting her hands on his messy office. "If only I could get you to look at *me* like that."

They both smiled because they each recognized the lie. If she looked at him like that, he'd run like hell. He didn't have anything against a good old-fashioned love affair. It was just that the love part wasn't for him. He was missing the for-keeps gene, both the ability to love that way, and to be loved that way.

"You're not a spreadsheet," Jade said. "Or I would."

"If you gave it a shot, I'd let you at my accounting system, too."

"Don't tease me," she said, her eyes dilating with even more lust.

His own reaction was far more base, making him laugh, at himself. Time to call it a night before he did something really stupid. He leaned past her to open the door for her.

Jade's eyes dropped to his mouth, lingering a moment before returning to meet his gaze.

He had the brief thought that he hadn't called it a night fast enough because then one of them moved, he wasn't sure who, but they were kissing. She made a soft sound of approval that went right through him, as did the hand she set on his chest, landing right over his heart as she pressed in closer. God, yeah. Closer. His hand slid around the back of her neck, over satiny soft skin, his thumb brushing the exquisite hollow behind her ear.

Her hands slid to his shoulders, his biceps, and dug in as if to hold him here, right here. But he wasn't going anywhere. He liked her hands on him, liked her tongue in his mouth, and when she made that noise deep in her throat, the one that said she was as lost as him, he groaned, both in pleasure and with a good amount of what-the-fuckery, because he knew.

He was in trouble.

Down-to-the-bone trouble, and he didn't give one single shit. Knowing this was crazy, that they had no place to go with this kiss, he still slanted his mouth over hers and took more, took everything she gave, and she gave her all, her soft sigh as they pulled apart turning him on almost more than the kiss had.

Still, she didn't move far, only a fraction of an inch, which meant that they sat there, still wrapped up in each other, noses touching, their exhales coming in fast pants on each other's skin. One of his hands was still in her hair, his fingers brushing the nape of her neck, the other just brushing the swell of her breast. The temperature of the night had dropped considerably but here inside his truck it was at least two hundred degrees.

Sanity was painfully slow to return. It helped to remember that she was leaving in a month. Theoretically, that took him off the hook. *She* was going to be the one to walk away.

Pressure off.

"Okay," she said shakily, finally pulling back.

Apparently the only one of them with a lick of sense.

"Not sure what that was," she said. "But for now, I'm going to ignore it."

He wasn't sure how to do that but he kept his doubts to himself and got out with her.

She narrowed her eyes.

"Just walking you to the door," he said.

"Fine." She pulled out her keys. "But I'm going to still be ignoring this tomorrow."

He'd be watching her try. "Night, Jade."

"Night." She didn't go in right away.

He didn't move, and not just because he hadn't been inside her place and was curious.

Though he was curious, very much so.

But mostly he wanted a repeat of that holy-shit kiss. He wanted that bad. Because she was leaving. Which meant that he wouldn't be the one to have to walk away, not this time.

The slight darkening of her eyes said she was considering the same line of thought. He looked at her mouth but the moment had passed and she was shifting back, away from him.

Already ignoring.

Thankfully Jade's workday was predictably crazy. Thankfully, because then she couldn't think too much about the night before.

The Kiss That Had Rocked Her World.

Dell had indeed mucked up the schedule. This demoted him from wildly sexy to downright irritating. It took her all morning and quite a bit of juggling to get it back to a manageable pace but she did it. And to be honest, nothing perked her up or kicked her brain into high gear faster than a problem that she could solve with a spreadsheet.

The phones stayed busy and the waiting room at a dull roar thanks to the patients and the owners that filled it. She knew the chaos would drive most people nuts but it was an organized chaos and she felt right at home, the noise settling over her like a security blanket.

In her not-too-distant past, her day had been filled with grumpy, sick, tired, distraught, rude people trying to get medical attention. She'd discovered that she preferred animals any day of the week. They didn't talk back, they didn't scream in your face if you were five minutes late getting them into their appointment.

Peanut the parrot sat in her opened cage, eyeballing the room with interest, occasionally squawking out a "mew" or "wuff wuff" because she liked to be a part of every conversation. Behind Jade's chair lay Gertie,

Dell's ten-year-old "baby." The St. Bernard liked the chaos as much as Jade did and had decided she liked hanging out with Jade.

Gertie was currently snoring over the din.

The stray kitten was still with her and had gotten very attached to the carrier that Jade had been using to transport her to and from the loft. Jade kept it in a position of honor on her credenza, door open.

From the carrier, the kitten loftily surveyed her kingdom, looking down her nose at the waiting patients.

Jade had named her Beans because . . . well, she wasn't exactly sure but the kitten seemed to like it.

"She still here?" Dell asked, coming through the front room holding a chart.

"Just until she gets fattened up a little."

Dell just smiled, sure and confident and smelling amazing, damn him. "I am going to give her up," she said. Tomorrow.

Okay, so maybe next week. It had to be sooner than later because Jade *was* going back to Chicago.

At some point.

"Would it be so bad to want to keep something in your life?" he asked.

She laughed. "Okay, Mr. Pot. Meet Kettle."

"I have animals."

"Just not women. At least not permanent ones." She immediately clamped her mouth shut, with no idea where that had come from. With a shake of her head, she turned back to her computer.

Dell stepped to her side, but before he could say a word, Keith, their animal tech, squished in between them, reaching for the sign-in sheet with his usual cluelessness. He brought the patients to the exam rooms for Dell and took notes and stats. He divided a look between Dell and Jade. "What?"

"Nothing," Jade said and nudged Dell out of the way.

When he was gone, Keith looked at her. "We in trouble?"

"No." They weren't in trouble. *She* was in trouble, all by herself.

Keith sighed in relief. He was a twenty-four-year-old mountain biker and mountain bum. He was great with the animals but more forgetful than anyone she'd ever met, and he moved slower than molasses. "Dude," he said—just like he did every time Jade passed him in the hallway, assisting him in bringing the animals to the back. "You in a race?"

"No, but you could pretend to be."

Keith merely grinned. "You know what you need?"

Yes. Yes, she knew exactly what she needed.

"You need yoga. Or Xanax."

"What I need is you to move it."

"Move it," Peanut repeated.

Keith grinned. "I only move it on the mountain or in my bed."

Jade sighed but kept cracking the whip. By pushing the patients along, continuing to fill and empty the exam rooms as fast as Dell worked his way through them, she made up even more lost time. This she used to help Adam as needed, who was working from the center today as well. He gave a S&R training class in the morning, and then puppy obedience classes all afternoon, and Jade helped him stay as organized as she could.

Eventually, sometime after five o'clock, the place slowed down. The last of the patients were seen. Jade was straightening up the front room when Bessie arrived from the cleaning service.

Actually, Bessie *was* the cleaning service. She came at the end of the day and sometimes at the lunch break as needed. "That's my job," she snapped at Jade, who was straightening out the waiting room.

"Move it," Peanut said.

Bessie eyeballed the parrot. "I know how to make a mean parrot soup."

Peanut ducked her head beneath her wing.

"I'm just trying to help," Jade told Bessie. The benches were heavy and she knew Bessie's back bothered her by the end of the day.

But Bessie's eyes flared with temper as if she'd been insulted. "You think I can't do my job?"

Bessie was somewhere between fifty and one hundred. Hard to tell exactly. Time hadn't been kind, and neither had gravity, but Bessie had been cleaning offices in Sunshine for decades and wasn't ready to admit defeat. "I think you do your job better than anyone I know," Jade said.

"Then leave me to it," Bessie said.

This was a nightly conversation. Jade lifted her hands in surrender and went back to her desk to close up.

Keith left, as did Mike, Dell's animal nurse. Dell, done seeing patients, was holed up in his office, hopefully catching up on returning phone calls and making final notes to the animal charts and other various but necessary paperwork.

Adam came in from the outside pens, bringing a blast of autumn air in with him. He had a golden retriever puppy tucked beneath each arm. There was a woman with him. "Thanks so much for today," she was saying as he walked her to the door. "Timmy's already in the car, but I just wanted to confirm we're on for this weekend, for the special-needs kids."

"I'll be there," Adam said.

"It'll mean so much to the kids. Your dogs just have such a way of reaching them. Having you bring your puppies, letting the kids see how you train and treat them, is such a wonderful experience for them. We can't wait."

"Looking forward to it." Adam nudged the door open with his foot for her. He walked out with her and then surprised Jade by coming back inside, still holding two pups.

"Heading out for the night," he said. "I'll walk you to your car."

One of the puppies barked happily, earning him a low, authoritative look from Adam. The puppy seemed to smile at him but obeyed and fell quiet.

"I'm not ready yet," Jade said. "I'm backing up the files right now."

Adam nudged his chin in the direction of Dell's office. "Then call him when you're ready to go."

"Believe it or not, I think I know how to find my car."

Adam didn't return her teasing smile, just shook his head. "Another animal clinic was hit last night. No one walks to their car by themselves."

"You are," she pointed out.

That did make him smile. He was over six feet, solid muscle, and intimidating as hell. "Don't worry about me," he said, lifting the puppies higher. One licked his nose, the other licked his chin. "I've got guard dogs."

Jade came around her desk, kissed each puppy, and opened the door for them. Then she went back to her desk. "Gertie," she said. "Go to Dell."

Well used to the night routine, Gertie trotted off to Dell's office, where she'd wait patiently for her master to take her home.

Jade covered up Peanut, then settled Beans in her carrier. She slung her purse over her arm, dimmed the lights, then stuck her head into Dell's office.

He'd had a long day and was still in his scrubs and white lab coat, sprawled in his big leather office chair talking on the phone. He had his feet up on his desk, his laptop in his lap, and he was hunting and pecking keys with an impressive speed for someone using only their pointer fingers. He had his cell phone open and on speaker, and at first she thought maybe he was consulting, as he often did for the other vets in the area.

That or going over the stack of paperwork she'd left for him. They had plenty of it, the most pressing tonight being the blood drawn from a jet-setting Boston terrier heading for England on a monthlong vacay with his owner. The sample needed to be sent out to a lab authorized to give a rabies-titer clearance proving the dog had an adequate level of rabies antibodies to avoid Britain's quarantine. But . . . big surprise, a soft female voice was speaking.

"I've got a steak on the barbecue with your name on it, Big Guy," that female voice said.

Big guy?

Dell's dark eyes warmed at the sight of Jade. "Sorry, Kel. I have work." His hair was even more disheveled than usual. He'd shoved his fingers through it. He did that a lot when he was tired or frustrated, and today he'd been both. He'd lost a very ill cancer-ridden cat on the table, not entirely unexpected but never easy.

I'm going, Jade mouthed, and waved to indicate she was heading out.

"Wait," he said.

"I'll wait as long as you need," the woman said.

"Sorry," Dell said, putting his feet down and setting his laptop on the desk. "I meant Jade."

"Who's Jade?"

Jade rolled her eyes at Dell and left his office. The man was gorgeous as sin, and incredible at what he did for a living, but if he couldn't see that he went through women like other men went through socks because he insisted on choosing the *wrong* women, it was really none of her business.

Not that she was one to talk. She hadn't exactly been successful in the relationship area herself, especially lately. "People in glass houses shouldn't throw stones," she murmured to Beans as they stepped outside.

It was a relatively mild night, but she could hear the rustle of the dry leaves on the trees. They were getting ready to fall. The ground crunched beneath her heels as she walked across the parking lot. She was halfway to her car when it happened.

A figure darted between her car and Dell's truck. He was tall, lean, and had a face chalk white with hollow, sightless black eyes and a black mouth, gaping wide open in a soundless scream.

Four

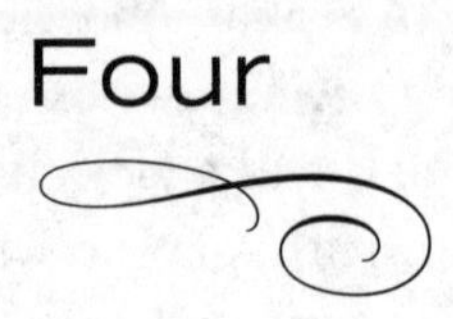

Terror gripped Jade by the throat and between one heartbeat and the next, she was transported back to another time and another place.

To the night of her attack. And this time it was worse because she knew she was weak. She was supposed to be getting better and she wasn't. She was hiding behind the same routines, different place, and she was no better than she'd been before the first attack.

Run.

She told this to her feet. *Run.* But like the last time, her feet didn't obey. And also like last time, she froze.

That long-ago night she'd been snagged up in hard, gripping hands, and dragged away at gunpoint. Knowing she couldn't survive that again, she opened her mouth to scream but only a whimper escaped.

The dark figure stopped short and tilted its head. The white face wavered in her vision, then floated disembodied as it was torn away. A mask. A zombie, she thought dimly. A cheap zombie Halloween mask.

And the figure? Just a teenager, and a young one at that. But it was too late for logic. Panic had stolen her breath, stopped her heart, and she couldn't breathe.

Couldn't move.

From a great distance she heard the second horrifyingly pathetic whimper that came from her throat. Her legs wobbled and gave, and she hit her knees, bracing herself with one hand on the rough asphalt.

The kid reached out to put a hand on her shoulder and she further embarrassed herself by cringing back.

A woman appeared, the woman who'd been talking to Adam only a few moments before, Jade realized. Michelle something. She crouched before Jade and tried to take the kitten carrier.

"No!" Jade gasped, tightening her grip on Beans.

"Your hand's bleeding, you must have scraped it when you fell," Michelle said. "I'm so sorry. Timmy didn't mean to scare you."

"He . . . he didn't say anything."

"He's deaf, he doesn't speak. I'm so sorry. I know I should take the mask from him, but he's so attached to his Halloween costume. He loves to wear it."

Only seconds ago it had been terror blocking the air in Jade's throat. Now it was humiliation. She got to her feet, still clutching Beans. "It's okay, I'm fine."

But she wasn't. With the memories she'd beaten back now pounding just behind her eyes, she was barely holding it together.

"Your hand's bleeding," Michelle said again. "Please. Let me—"

"No." Jade's jaw was clenched to keep her teeth from chattering. "I'm really fine." Whirling away, she practically ran to her car. Her hands were shaking badly, and it took three tries to find her keys in her own pocket. Glancing up, she caught sight of Dell's office window, lit from within. He was there, looking out, his phone to his ear.

It felt like five years had passed since she'd fallen, but it'd probably been less than a minute. Had he seen her mini freak-out?

Their gazes connected, and in the next beat he was gone from the window.

He was coming out.

She couldn't be here when he did, couldn't let him see her like this, shaken and trembling like a baby. Knowing she had only seconds—for a laid-back, easygoing guy Dell could really move when he wanted—she talked herself through it. *Don't lose it, not yet.*

Not.

Yet.

Shoving the key into the ignition, she mentally accessed her to-do list. One, pull the seat belt over the carrier. Two, shut the door. Three, open the driver's-side door and get in.

There. At least now she couldn't fall down again. She gripped the steering wheel with white knuckles and gulped in air. For a single heartbeat she gave in to the emotions battering at her and dropped her head to the steering wheel. "Get it together," she whispered. "Get it together." Lifting her head, she turned the key. Her engine came to life just as she saw movement from the doors.

Dell was striding through them. She caught the glint of his dark hair beneath the bright outside light hanging above the entryway of the center.

Heart in her throat, she put the car in gear and hit the gas. *Don't look back, don't look back, don't . . .*

She looked.

Dell stood there in the center of the lot, hands on hips, a grim expression on his face.

Her tires squealed a little bit leaving the lot, but she didn't slow down. From in her pocket, her cell phone vibrated. Swallowing hard, she kept driving.

She was nearly a mile down the road when her phone vibrated again. Still shaking, heart still pounding, she pried her hand from the wheel and grasped the phone.

She didn't have to look at the screen to see who it was.

Dell.

With her vision already far too blurry for safe driving thanks to the tears she refused to acknowledge, she hit Ignore and kept going.

Jade made it home and knew exactly how lucky she was to do it in one piece given her condition. Running on panic and adrenaline, she stumbled out of her car and got to her door before she remembered.

Beans.

"I'm sorry, I'm so sorry," she murmured after she'd run back to the car for the kitten. "God. I'm the worst kitten mom on the entire planet." Hugging the carrier close, she ran up the walk, up the stairs, unlocked the door, and disabled her alarm.

Inside, she hit the switch that lit up the place like Christmas and then stood stock-still, her hand on the wall for balance.

Everything was in place and she was alone. Her purse hit the floor and she slid down the wall to sit on her butt next to it, gulping in air, still hugging Beans in her carrier.

"Mew."

Beans wanted dinner. Understandable. But Jade's mind was doing a rewind and repeat.

Dark parking lot.

Dark face mask.

Dark growling voice in her ear. "Do as I say, bitch, and I won't hurt you. Yet."

Dark fear as he emphasized the words with the cold muzzle of a gun thrust under her jaw.

Frozen with fear, she tried to turn her head to get a look at him, but he stopped her cold. He ran the tip of that gun from her jaw along her throat, over her collarbone and down, skimming her breast. "Let's go," came the low, rough voice. "Unless you want to spend some time out here with me first . . ."

The only sound in her loft was her harsh breathing until Beans gave another soft, questioning "mew."

Jade opened the cage and let the kitten out. Beans wound her way around Jade's legs, giving out a rumbling purr. She accepted a scratch behind the ears and then trotted off to the kitchen nook in the obvious hope that the bowl fairy had filled hers.

Jade let out a choked laugh and thunked her head back against the door. One little thing, a silly zombie mask, a frigging kid's Halloween mask, and she was back to a complete wreck, worse than ever.

Her first instinct was to run. Hell, that's how she'd ended up here. After the attack, she'd run to get her head on straight. She'd gotten in the car and driven west.

She'd ended up in Sunshine.

And she'd never left. She'd found this sweet place to hole up and had taken a job she was way overqualified for, just so she could do something well.

A safety net.

She'd needed the confidence booster, and at the time, she'd truly believed it a very temporary move. She just needed to find herself again, that was all.

She thought she had.

Clearly she'd been wrong. Clearly she'd been living in Denial City. She'd built herself a little fantasy here, a temporary geographical cure, that was all.

Now she had to decide what to do about that. She could pack and go.

Again. Just get in the car and go. Maybe south this time. Arizona. California. Hell, she could hit Mexico and keep going if she wanted. She wrapped her arms around her knees and dropped her head.

But running meant once again leaving everyone and everything that mattered. And she'd already done that. She didn't want to do it again.

The knock at the door had her jerking upright as if shot. She stared at it, still as stone.

"Jade, it's me."

Dell, of course. Who else?

"Let me in, Jade." She covered her mouth and shook her head, like he could see her.

After a moment, the knock came again, less patient now, again accompanied by his low, unbearably familiar voice. *"Jade."*

"Mew."

Jade stared down at Beans, who was once again doing the head bump against her legs. "He's never been here," she whispered to the kitten. "Why's he here?"

Because he saw your freak-out in the parking lot, you idiot. Because he came down to check on you and you sped off into the night. Because you didn't answer your phone.

Pick one . . .

Leaning her head back on the door, Jade closed her eyes and fought with the conflicting urges to open the door and throw herself at him for the comfort she knew his very nice arms could provide or to continue to huddle in a pathetic little ball and pretend the world didn't exist.

"I can hear you breathing," he said.

Slowly she stood up. She could *feel* Dell on the other side, tall and strong, warm. Calm.

Waiting.

And he could outpatience Job, too. Once she'd seen him outwait a furious gelding who'd been out of its mind after being stung by a bee, so enraged that everyone had truly thought the poor thing would break its own leg, or worse.

Dell had stepped into the central pen while the horse ran in circles around him, and when the horse finally exhausted itself, Dell moved in, getting the thing to literally eat out of the palm of his hand.

Jade's cell phone rang, and shock, it was Dell.

Since he wasn't going to give up, she answered with, "Jade's unavailable at this time. Go away."

"Jade—"

"Leave a message at the beep," she whispered, trying for sarcastic wit, which is where she felt the most comfortable while completely coming undone.

"I want to talk to you."

"Sorry, you've been rerouted to the Office of Too Freaking Bad."

He hung up on her and she breathed a sigh of relief. Which turned out to be too soon because his voice came through the door. "Open up."

His voice was low. Calm, assertive. And she actually turned to face the door before she stopped herself. *Don't be the horse that needs taming!* "Stop woman-whispering me."

There was a pause, as if he was considering his options, weighing each against her mood. But unfortunately his silence was as compelling as his voice.

Dammit. "Go," she said, even though he hadn't spoken again. "Please, Dell. Just go away."

"I can't do that."

She began to mentally compile a new list: Dell's negative qualities. Stubborn. Single-minded. Nosy . . .

"I'm busy," she said.

"You're not."

"Yes, I am. Very, very busy."

But Dell had gone to the No Bullshitting School of Life and wasn't buying. "Jade, you're standing there right this minute, just staring at the door."

"I'm sitting." She let out a sigh, really hating it when he was right. "I have a date." The only date she'd had all year had been with her secret stash of Ben & Jerry's.

And Netflix.

And maybe once or twice with her pulsing five-speed showerhead.

"Just tell me if you're okay," he said.

No, she was most definitely not okay. In fact, she was an inch from a second meltdown and she desperately needed to be alone to have it, thank you very much.

"Jade."

Her throat burned so badly she couldn't speak so she nodded like an idiot even knowing he couldn't see her. "Yes. I'm okay."

"Open the door and prove it."

Goddammit. She tossed back her hair, lifted her chin and forced an impassive expression before pulling open the door. "What?" she asked. "What is it?"

He said nothing, but his dark eyes swept over her, doing a quick and efficient visual exam.

"I could take a picture for you, if you'd like," she offered.

Those warm brown eyes lifted to hers, the briefest flash of humor momentarily dislodging his concern. "If I thought you meant that . . ." Belying the teasing in his voice, his eyes stayed serious, and he lifted her hand to eye the scrape. He took a step forward to cross the threshold but she put her hand to his chest.

"We need to talk," he said.

"Yeah, now see, that's the *last* thing I want to do." She meant to shove him away but she'd been so shaken for the past hour, so on edge, she felt momentarily confused when she felt the warm heat of him, the easy strength radiating beneath his shirt.

And suddenly all she wanted to do was lose herself in that heat and strength. Almost against her own will, her head tilted back and she stared up into his face.

At his mouth. Because she knew now. Knew how it felt on hers. Knew the power of their connection.

As if he felt it, too, he went still as stone, then dropped his gaze to her mouth as well, and for the first time since the parking lot, she warmed—thanks to him. She didn't even realize she'd leaned in toward him until with a low groan and a curse, he put his hands on her arms. "Jade."

Galvanized into action by sheer mortification, she broke free and turned her back on him. She scooped up the kitten, pressing her red face into Beans's fur. "I told you, I'm busy."

"I'll see you tomorrow, then," he said quietly.

Tomorrow was far too many baby steps away to think about at the moment, but she nodded. When he said nothing else, she turned back to him.

A mistake. Just another one in a long line of mistakes today alone.

Because Dell had a way. For as unflappable and affable as he was, he had instincts honed as sharp as any wild animal, and he saw right through her. "You'll call me if you need anything," he said. Not a request.

A demand.

If she called, he'd be back here in an instant. She knew that. They butted heads, they teased and pushed buttons, but there was no one better than Dell in a crisis. She could count on him, she knew that. She just didn't *want* to count on him. She wanted to be able to count on herself. God, how she wanted that.

"Jade."

"I'll call," she said. "Go." *God, please, go.* "I'll see you tomorrow." She'd have promised him the full moon if it would make him leave.

With one last long look, he nodded, and then was gone.

She stared down at Beans as she let all the air out of her lungs. "What now?"

"Mew," Beans said.

"Right." Baby steps. She headed straight to the kitchen, specifically the freezer, grabbing a big wooden spoon on the way. She had a date, after all. A threesome with Ben & Jerry. Then she'd take a long shower, go to bed, and figure the rest out in the morning.

Baby steps.

Five

Dell rose before dawn. Not that he was a morning person by choice. Nope, if left to his own devices, he would stay up all night, but these days he had early morning responsibilities.

Of his own making, at least. He'd made this life for himself. He'd bled and sweated for it.

And he loved it.

But as he rolled out of bed at the asscrack of dawn and into a shower, he'd have given his left nut for a few more hours since he hadn't fallen asleep until an hour ago.

Couldn't, not when he kept reliving the look on Jade's face from the night before.

Mindless terror. That's what he'd seen when she'd torn out of his parking lot.

It had been so different from anything he'd ever seen from the coolly poised woman who sat running his world every day that it had taken a moment to compute.

It had been all he'd thought about all night, the image of her beautiful face, pale and stricken. She'd collected herself somewhat by the time he'd gotten to her loft, but when she'd opened the door he could practically feel the vibrations from the trembling she was trying so desperately to control.

Her fake bravado had broken his heart. What the fuck had happened to her? He'd stepped inside, intending to get answers, but one look at her face had told him no answers were going to be forthcoming.

And then she'd looked at his mouth. He'd read her thoughts and body language as clearly as if she'd spoken out loud. She hadn't wanted to discuss what was wrong, but for that single beat at least, she'd been amiable to losing herself in his arms.

Not much shocked him these days, but that had. All this time and she'd never expressed an interest in him that way. In fact, she'd gone out of her way to make sure he understood that she *wasn't* attracted to him.

Until two nights ago after Crystal's. In the cab of his truck, giving each other mouth to mouth, everything had changed.

And then changed again when she'd vowed to ignore their connection.

Neither of them seemed to be capable of that, but not for lack of trying. "Come on, Gert," he told the still sleeping St. Bernard. "Let's hit it."

Gertie closed her eyes. Her version of possum. She wasn't a morning creature, either.

"If you don't get up, you won't get a cookie."

Gertie scrambled to her feet. Dell drove to Belle Haven and parked next to a freshly washed, shiny truck, its interior so squeaky clean he could have eaten off the dash.

Adam's.

It had been the military to drum home that neatness in his brother, but Dell didn't have the same compulsion. His truck was covered in a fine layer of dust on the outside and Gertie hair on the inside.

The front door of the center was locked, lights off. Alarm on. The security system was being upgraded this week, a direct response to the vet clinic robberies.

It wasn't going to be his place they hit next. Or if it was, he'd be prepared. Once upon a time he might have been an easy mark but those days were long over.

It was an hour before any of his staff would show up, and as he knew Adam had, he walked around back.

He kept their horses, Reno and Kiwi, here. Dell handled most of the day-to-day care of them, but on this foggy morning as he made his way to the pens, only one equine head appeared to pop through the fog as she neighed a soft greeting.

Kiwi.

Reno and Adam were gone. "Aw, you got left behind," he said, laughing when she butted her face to his chest, knocking him back a step, letting him know what she thought of being deserted.

Kiwi always played hard-ass. "Much like another woman in my life," he said.

Kiwi snorted and searched his pockets. When she found the apple, she softened her limpid eyes and batted her lashes.

Her version of the femme fatale.

He laughed again when she ate it nearly whole and then burped in his face. "If only you were all so easy." Saddling her up, he rode into the nearby hills, where as a boy he'd gone to be invisible instead of the easy, skinny, scrawny target he'd once been.

He rode hard, grateful to not be on foot as he mostly had been in those years, trying to outrun his demons.

Halfway back, he ran into Adam and Reno.

At a wordless command, Adam halted Reno and studied Dell's face. He said nothing, just arched a brow in query.

It was rare, extremely rare, that Adam beat Dell into Belle Haven.

"Overslept," Dell said.

Or not slept at all.

Adam just looked at him and Dell sighed. "Everything's fine."

With a nod, Adam urged Reno onward.

"Good talk," Dell muttered, and followed.

They made it to the center a good half hour before any patients were due. Normally Dell cut it closer than that, but Jade always came at exactly seven thirty and he wanted to be there when she arrived.

Assuming she *would* arrive this morning.

But as he walked Kiwi onto the property, she pulled in, and he knew a moment of unrelenting relief. He hadn't realized until that very moment exactly how afraid he'd been that she might simply vanish as mysteriously as she'd arrived.

Going to happen sooner or later, he reminded himself. Because no matter what had set her off last night, she was temporary here. She'd been telling him that since the day she'd walked in with his help-wanted ad in hand.

She got out of her car and hesitated. Their gazes met for one long, charged moment.

"Well, that's new," Adam said.

Dell ignored this comment as he dismounted.

Adam slid off Reno at the same time and casually grabbed the reins from Dell's hand. He didn't say anything more, just led the horses away.

Jade reached into her backseat for Beans's carrier, then headed across the parking lot toward him. Hard to tell what she was thinking behind her big, dark Hollywood glasses.

All he'd managed to piece together about last night was that fourteen-year-old deaf and slightly mentally handicapped Timmy, had run by her, wearing a mask.

At the sight of it, Jade had completely lost it.

Clearly she'd found it again because she walked right past him now and into the office, her usual implacable self.

The phone was ringing as he followed on her heels and she answered it while unbuttoning her jacket and slipping out of it.

She left her glasses on.

"Belle Haven," she said, the phone in the crook of her neck as she gathered her hair up and held it there with two tongue depressors, the kind he had in small jars in each exam room.

She wore a black wraparound top, tied with a neat bow over her hip, and black pin-striped trousers. The sophistication was broken by the kick-ass boots with the stiletto heels and the pin above her breast in the shape of a dog cookie that said: REAL DOCTORS TREAT MORE THAN ONE SPECIES.

She looked both prim and outrageously sexy as she let Beans out, and Dell's brain stuttered and twitched. His dick also twitched, but he ignored both responses.

"He just walked in," she assured the person on the phone, not looking his way as she uncovered Peanut and booted up the computer. "We'll work you in before he heads into surgery. No problem, see you then." She hung up and nearly plowed into Gertie, who wasn't at her usual spot but standing very close to Jade staring up at her.

"Gertie," Jade admonished. "Out of my way, please."

Gertie stayed at attention, still staring up at Jade, and then let out a low whine.

With a noise of annoyance, Jade walked around the dog, avoiding Dell by turning to her computer, even though he'd stopped and leaned against the counter, also right in her way.

Dell eyed Gertie, who was watching Jade with worried eyes, clearly noticing the tension in Jade's body language. "Jade."

"Jade," Peanut squawked. "Jade, Jade. Pretty Peanut. Peanut so pretty."

"You're going to have to hustle this morning," Jade told Dell, handing him a file comprising all of the faxes that had come in.

Yes, but hustle was the usual speed around here, especially in the mornings where they always had to hit the ground running to keep up. Dell typically began his day checking on any of his patients who'd been hospitalized during the night, reading through the lab results that Jade pulled for him off the fax machine. That's what was in the file she'd just handed him.

The closest overnight animal hospital was in Coeur d'Alene, and sometimes he'd have to go there to see his patients in person and do rounds. Either he'd drive or Brady would fly him in their Bell 47 helicopter, but he flipped through the file and saw that wasn't required this morning.

Jade had turned to her printer, which was now spitting out his schedule for the day. "You've got your usual early morning rounds and four surgeries; a spay, two neuters, one dental cleaning, and then—"

"Jade."

She went still for one telling beat, then turned to face him.

Pushing away from the counter, he crossed her work space and pulled off her sunglasses. As always, her makeup was flawless. She wore lip gloss that smelled like vanilla mint and there was no sign of a sleepless night.

She'd made damn sure of it.

But as he stared at her, she drew a deep, bolstering breath and just like that, he knew. She wasn't cool, calm, or collected. Not even close. But she had a hell of a store of bravado, probably because she was braced for him to mention last night. In fact, her eyes, those mesmerizing green eyes, were daring him to.

He wouldn't. Not here, not now, when she so clearly needed to keep her shield. He handed her back her glasses.

There was a flash of surprised relief and then she slowly turned away. "I'm really swamped," she said. "So—"

"I need some help." He paused, waiting until she turned back.

"What kind of help?" she asked suspiciously.

And with good reason. He rarely, if ever, asked for help. "Work help."

He'd made it a point to never let anyone fuck around with his files. It was a lifelong habit deeply ingrained from growing up having to watch every penny, and it had carried over. His receivables and payables were as personal to him as his patients, and he handed them directly over to his accountant quarterly.

In between those times, he muddled through, sometimes messing everything up without trying, more often than not simply neglecting them. He knew the piles on his desk drove her nuts. And he'd always enjoyed driving her nuts. She looked so pretty steamed.

But today felt different. She felt different. He felt her tension, her fear every bit as much as Gertie did. Whatever it came from, he wanted to assuage it. Not that she'd let him, but she needed something to distract her, then. Something more challenging than making appointments, and he could give her this. "I'm waving the white flag," he said.

She just looked at him. He nearly smiled at having his own trick of loaded silence played against him. "If you have time," he said, "my billing needs help."

Her mouth opened, then closed. The spark that had been missing in her eyes didn't come back, but much of her wariness vanished, and she at least finally spoke to him. "Did hell freeze over?"

"Not yet."

"Did you forget your password to get into the system again?"

"Okay, one time."

"Weekly." She continued to study him, eyes narrowed. "Is this a pity offering?"

"If I were going to make a pity offering, it wouldn't be in my office."

She stared at him, then let out a low laugh. "In your dreams."

"You keep saying that. Makes me think you're the one having the dreams about me."

She bent and scooped up Beans. "Are you getting a load of this?" she murmured to the kitten, then kissed her on the nose. "He thinks I'd dream of him over Nathan Fillion."

"Mew."

Jade tapped a finger on the schedule in Dell's hands, pointing to one of his eight o'clocks. "Dixie's in heat. We're going to have to be careful that she doesn't excite every male in the place."

"What?"

"If we don't rush her through, we'll have a clinic full of boners. What's wrong with your hearing this morning?"

"Nothing," he said. "I just really like it when you say things like excite and boner."

"Boner," Peanut said.

"Oh, no," Jade said to the parrot. "No, no, no . . . you can't say—"

"Boner."

"Oh God." Jade panicked. "Peanut—"

"Pretty bird," Del broke in, smiling at the parrot and speaking low and soft. "Such a pretty girl, Peanut."

Peanut preened under his admiring tone. "Pretty Peanut."

Jade shook her head in disbelief.

"It's all about distractions." Dell eyeballed the schedule. Jade was right, it was manageable. She always made sure of that. "So are you in on the books?" he asked casually.

She stared at him for a long, interminable beat, clearly attempting to see how much of this was because of her.

All of it . . . But if she hadn't figured out that he'd do anything for her, he wasn't about to tell her. He gave her his most harmless smile.

"Dell," she said softly.

"Jade," he said just as quietly. "Or should I say Goddess Jade?"

She closed her eyes. "Is this because we . . . kissed?"

"Is that what that was? I thought it was the Fourth of July."

"Dell." She grimaced. "Tell me this isn't about last night. Because I'm not good with sympathy."

"Noted. How are you with just some good old-fashioned caring?"

"Not so good with that, either."

"Huh," he said, and crouched to rub Gertie's belly. "Maybe you should work on that."

"My family's been trying to drown me in it for a while now, but I just keep floating to the top."

He straightened. "Keeping your head above water is good, Jade. In or out?"

She blew out a breath. "You know I'm in."

"Good." He smiled. "Don't tell Adam—he'll whine like a little girl because he actually thinks he's good at the books. But he screwed up last month's billing so badly that we might have to start completely over."

Instead of looking nervous, she actually looked thrilled, and he shook his head. "You are one odd woman, you know that?"

She laughed, *laughed*, and he felt like he'd won the lotto. He turned to head into the back but she surprised him when she set her hand on his arm.

"Thanks," she said. "For not pushing."

He looked down at her fingers on his. "You're safe here, you know that, right?"

She nodded, and for a second, neither of them moved as that something new zinged between them. Smarter than him, and also faster, Jade pulled free and stared at him.

"Boner," Peanut said.

Six

As Dell walked away, Jade drew a deep breath and attempted to shrug off her tension. Only it didn't shrug off. Her shoulders were so tense they felt like pins and needles were stabbing into them, and now there was something odd going on low in her belly as well.

You could be halfway to somewhere new by now, said a little voice in her head. She told the cowardly weasel to zip it and held her chin high.

She wasn't going anywhere. So she'd had a minor setback yesterday, she could recover. She could go back to burying the past.

She could.

She would.

Her cell phone rang. Normally she'd ignore it at work, but she pounced on that sucker.

"Just looked at the calendar." It was Sam, her cousin. "And guess what, J? It's the first of October."

"Happens every month," Jade agreed, ignoring the significance. "What are you doing calling so early, is everything okay?"

"I was going to ask you the same thing."

She glanced at her watch and added an hour for Chicago time. "Wow, so you no longer sleep late?"

"Haven't slept more than five hours straight since med school. And then, to make it worse, a certain cousin of mine skipped out on her job and left us all in the lurch. I'm working my ass off."

"Poor baby. And that fat paycheck doesn't help at all?"

Sam blew out a breath and softened his voice. "Okay, truth, J. How are you doing really?"

"Fantastic." But they'd grown up together and were as close as family got. She couldn't bullshit him, she didn't even try. "I've been better."

"Goddammit," he said quietly. "Tell me you're still on track to be here by November first as promised. And if you say you need more time, I'm coming out there to drag you back here myself."

"I'm on track."

"Good," he said. "Because your town house misses you."

"My town house misses me?"

"Yeah. And the office misses you."

"Now that I believe," she said, thinking if all that missed her in Chicago was inanimate objects, why go back?

"Things are going downhill, Jade. Sandy's not on top of everything like you always were. We're suffering without you."

Guilt washed over her. "That can't be true."

"Believe it. I hate to ask anything of you, but . . ."

"But you're going to, anyway?" Jade asked dryly.

"Can you call in and talk to Sandy? She came from running just the Urgent Care, she's not used to this. She's got some computer problems and—"

"Sam, Sandy's good. She knows what to do." Jade had made sure of it.

"Yes but she's not you. The office management has gone to hell. We're losing patients, babe. People are tired of the long wait at the front desk. Phone calls are getting routed to our service in the middle of the day. We're losing out on business."

"You're not—"

Sam laughed mirthlessly. "It's a 'we,' Jade. We're a 'we,' in business and in family. In everything."

She pinched the bridge of her nose. "I'm working on it, Sam."

"I know."

The worry in his voice made her want to try to reassure him. She'd spent most of her life being the center of the family, the go-to girl. When she'd bailed from Chicago, she'd left a lot more than the city behind. "I keep thinking I'm working my way back to myself," she admitted. "But the truth is I'm not. I don't think I'm who I thought I was."

"You're still our Jade," he said firmly. "You are."

She wished she was as sure.

Sam blew out a breath. "Listen, don't worry about us right now. Tell me what's going on with you. I woke up with this need to talk to you and there's something in your voice."

"It's nothing. I just had a little setback, that's all."

"Flashbacks? Nightmares?"

"Some."

"Fuck, I hate this. I'm caught between that stupid promise I never should have made and—"

"Not a stupid promise," she interrupted. "I'm going to be okay, Sam. Really."

"You've been saying that for *eighteen* months." His voice softened. "Everyone got counseling but you."

"I wasn't hurt."

"Bullshit, you weren't. Now get your ass back here so we can take care of you. We have the best of the best, and you know it. Come home now."

There were built-in stakes to that plan, of course. Her parents. Sam. A business she'd been born to run. A town house she'd bought and loved . . . It was hard to say no.

It had always been hard to say no. She hadn't been bred for the no. She'd been a pleaser. And that deep-seated instilled need she had to make people happy had nearly killed her. She glanced around her at the animal center that she'd made her life for now.

For now . . .

A temporary haven, that's all she'd expected it to be. But Sunshine had opened its arms for her, taken her in, given her refuge. She'd made connections here, deep ones. And through those connections she'd discovered a different side of herself. A side that believed *no* was a full sentence. A side that was beginning to have her own hopes and dreams, not the ones she'd been born into.

Her eyes locked onto a pair of warm, curious brown ones.

Dell's.

"I'll be there by the first, as promised."

"Jade—"

"Bye, Sam." She closed her phone.

"Problem?" Dell asked.

"Yes, but not yours." She paused, then felt compelled by the sheer force of his personality to say more. "My old job."

He arched a brow. "You didn't list any past jobs on your app."

No, she hadn't.

"You going back to that same job when you go home?"

"Yes."

He nodded and she paused, trying to decide how best to handle this. "I didn't list the job on my résumé because I didn't have any vet experience."

"But you have office experience," he said softly. "Big office experience. You were more than a receptionist."

"Yes."

"What were you, Jade?"

The jig was up a long time ago, she reminded herself. "Chief operating officer of a medical center. It's really just a fancy title for office manager and full-charge bookkeeper." She braced herself for the questions. Like why was she a thousand miles from home working a job she was obviously *way* overqualified for? And why had she given up that job in the first place, and did it have anything to do with whatever the hell had given her a near mental breakdown in the parking lot the night before?

But Dell didn't ask her any of those questions. He didn't ask her anything. He merely nodded and slid his hands into his pockets. Totally at ease.

"I should have told you," she said.

"You didn't have to." He walked back into her work space, Gertie so close on his heels that when Dell stopped, the dog bumped into him.

Gertie slid Dell a reproachful look.

Dell ruffled the top of her head, and Gertie's expression softened with unconditional love. "Down, Gert."

"Down, Gert," Peanut said, and Gertie plopped to the floor, the ground shaking under her graceless descent.

"I like hearing about you, Jade," Dell said. "I'd like to hear more."

"Trust me, you don't."

He gave her a small smile. "Not for you to decide, is it?" He leaned over her and reached for her keyboard, logging her in with his pass code.

That was new.

At her look of surprise, he said, "For the billing." He paused. "Unless you're leaving."

"Not yet."

He held her gaze until Keith walked through the reception area and unlocked the front door. Then he came up to the counter for the first patient file. "Dudes," he said. "We ready?"

Dell didn't break eye contact with Jade. "I am. You?" he asked Jade quietly.

They weren't talking about work and she knew it. Was she ready? Hell, no. Not for anything but she'd long ago learned that to fake it was to make it. So she nodded.

Dell smiled at her in approval before turning to head to the back, stopping to greet a Newfoundland who'd just come inside with his owner. Dell laughed at something the man said, and the sound scraped at something low in Jade's belly as she let out a careful breath. One more thing she wasn't equipped to deal with at the moment.

Completely unconcerned with that fact, Dell vanished into the back, his shoulders square, that long-legged stride confident and sure.

Jade had grown up with confident men. Highly educated men. Sophisticated and elegant. Polished.

Dell was highly educated. He had to be in order to become a vet. But he wasn't sophisticated and elegant, or polished. He'd as soon be on the floor helping a dog give birth than in a boardroom.

It was one of the most attractive things about him, how much he cared about his work. He had hundreds of patients and just about every single one of them was owned by a client completely and totally devoted to providing their animal the best care available. Dell was the best, and he was beloved in these parts.

Jade hadn't had pets while growing up. Her mother was allergic, and after Jade had been out on her own she'd just never thought of it. It had been quite the learning curve when she'd first come to Belle Haven. Dell was fairly closed off emotionally with people, but he seemed to be able to access whatever an animal needed. An injured dog, a sick kitten, a horse in labor, it didn't matter . . . Dell gave his heart and soul, and in less time than it took humans to shake hands, an animal would become part of Dell's pack for life. But for as many animals in his pack, Dell's human pack was much smaller.

But he'd included Jade in that pack . . . which she'd resisted.

The room was filling up and Keith hadn't come back for the next patient to fill the other waiting room. With a sigh, Jade grabbed the file and stood. Typically, the morning brought in the clients and the animals that were the most sick or had become endangered overnight. These early appointments often began with Dell walking into the exam room to face worried and stressed-out people and animals.

He was good at assuaging fears.

He'd be good at assuaging yours . . .

"Sergio," she called, and managed a smile for Sergio's owner, Leanne Whitfield. Leanne could have been a Beverly Hills housewife, except she didn't have a husband and she lived here in Sunshine. What she did have was a short-term plan to rectify the lack of husband pronto. She wanted to marry the most eligible man in town, and she'd decided that man was Dell.

To that end, Leanne brought in her kitten every few weeks, manufacturing odd illnesses. Leanne had somehow concluded that Jade was the biggest threat to her marry-Dell goal, which could be construed as amusing given that Dell was a serial dater and Jade was a serial social hermit these days.

As for Dell's opinion on the situation, he and Jade had an understanding. Jade's job included making sure Leanne never trapped Dell alone in an exam room, where she'd "accidentally" grope him. "What's the problem with Sergio this morning?" Jade asked, pen poised over the chart.

"I'd rather go over this just once," Leanne said, and flashed a smile that said, *Bite me.* "I'll just tell the doctor myself directly."

Jade smiled a *Bite me* right back at Leanne. "Sure. I'll just go tell him so. He's running a few minutes behind."

"Oh?" Leanne didn't look happy. "He have a late night last night?"

"Here you go," Jade said, ignoring the question as she showed her into exam room two.

"When we get married," Leanne said, "your services won't be necessary."

"Married?"

"It's only a matter of time before he realizes how perfect we are together," Leanne said, eyeballing herself in the small mirror over the sink. She adjusted her boobs higher and her neckline lower. "We'll honeymoon in Cabo."

Okay, Jade wasn't in the mood for this. "Listen, it's not going to happen."

"Why?"

Yeah, Jade, why? She thought about being brutally honest and telling Leanne that she managed to do what no one else could do—she terrified the big, bad Dell Connelly, but sometimes honesty just wasn't the way to go. "Because we're engaged." The lie rolled right off her tongue so easily she couldn't even believe she'd said it.

Leanne's sharp gaze flashed immediately to Jade's ringless engagement finger.

"Getting it sized." Jade left the room, hung the chart for Dell, and practically ran down the hall, nearly plowing right into him.

He put his hands on her hips to steady her. "Oh no you don't, you're not deserting me with her. Let's go." He began to tug her back to the exam room.

"Um," she said. "She won't exactly be bothering you anymore."

"What did you do?"

She patted his chest. His hard, warm chest. "A thing."

"A thing? What thing?"

"Yeah, we don't have to talk about the thing," she said, relieved when the phone started to ring.

He caught her arm. "We'll talk about the thing later."

"Sure." *Or never.* And because just his hand on her was stirring up sensations best not stirred up, she backed away and returned to her work.

Seven

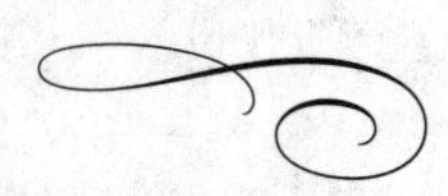

Dell was in the main surgery area cleaning up sometime later when Adam came through after a training session. "I've got the Moorelands in room two," Dell told him. "Want to come in with me?"

The Moorelands were clients of Adam's. They'd brought in their seven-week-old Labrador puppies.

"First exam?"

"And vaccinations. Eight puppies. You can help."

"Maybe you'd rather have someone else. Say, your fiancée."

"How many times do I have to tell you, crack kills brain cells."

Adam flashed a rare grin. "Didn't you wonder why Leanne didn't play grab-ass with you this morning? It was because your receptionist turned herself into your fiancée." Adam slapped him on the back. "Congrats, by the way. I didn't think you had it in you."

"Shut up. You're making this shit up."

"Are you kidding?" Adam asked. "No one could make this up. It's too good. The question is, though . . . why would Jade come up with such a story? Unless something's happened between you . . ."

Dell didn't respond to that. Didn't know *how* to respond to that.

Adam gave a shocked Dell a push down the hall and into exam room two.

Eight puppies were crawling over everything, making soft, snuffling puppy noises. Their owners, Joey and Donna Mooreland, a couple in their midfifties were sitting, supervising the best that they could with four hands against thirty-two little paws.

Adam had sold the couple their first Labrador several years ago now and had helped them through their first breeding cycle. He scooped up a black pup attempting to eat his shoelace.

"I'm nervous," Donna admitted, hand to her chest. "This is our first batch of babies."

"No worries." Adam slid Dell a look. "There's a lot of firsts going around here today."

Dell ignored him and bent over the puppies. There were four brown, two black, and two white Labs, all in various stages of mewling and climbing over each other, tails wagging, tongues out.

"It's just that we've been so frazzled with our daughter's engagement," Donna said, stopping the biggest pup from climbing on top of his siblings like a circus performer.

"A lot of that going around," Adam said.

Dell gave Adam a look that said quite clearly *Shut up or die.* But Donna smiled at Adam. "Someone you know just get engaged?"

"As a matter of fact," Adam said. "Dr. Connelly here—"

Dell stepped on Adam's foot and ground into it a little bit.

Adam drew a careful breath and stopped talking.

But it was too late. Donna had caught the scent of a possible engagement. "Doctor?" she asked Dell. "Are you engaged?"

"He is," Joe said.

Everyone looked at him in shock. Joe shrugged. "One of your clients in the waiting room was talking about it as she left."

Adam started to laugh, but Dell put more weight on his foot, and Adam turned it into a cough.

"Oh, this is so lovely!" Donna said, clapping her hands, then leaning in conspiratorially. "You probably don't know this, Dr. Connelly, but just about all the single women in the country have their hearts set on you. You're going to break them all with this news."

Adam coughed again, and Dell took his weight off Adam's foot because he felt a little woozy. And he was sweating. Christ, this was ridiculous. "The puppies," he said. "Let's concentrate on the puppies."

Adam smirked. Dell ignored him and picked up the runt, a girl. The tiny brown Lab had eyes bigger than her nose and mouth and her head bobbed as she stared at him solemnly. He smiled at her and she licked his chin.

"So when's the big day?" Donna asked.

Try never, as it would be difficult to be married to a woman who lived seventeen hundred miles away. "The reports of my"—*Christ*—"*engagement* are overexaggerated."

Adam snorted.

Dell checked the puppy's teeth to make sure they were properly aligned, then inspected her eyes, examined her skin, and palpated her hips.

"Is she okay?"

Dell set her on the scale, having to keep a hand on her because her legs were scrambling for purchase. She had places to go, things to explore. "She's slightly underweight, but she's looking strong."

Both Donna and Joe looked relieved. "That's the one my daughter wants to keep," Joe said.

"We're going to wrap her up in a white silky bow on the day of the wedding," Donna said. Her voice went sly. "Maybe you'd like us to save you one for your wedding?"

Adam grinned and looked at him. "How sweet."

Dell resisted the urge to punch him and busied himself checking for defects the Moorelands might not have recognized, like heart murmurs. He found nothing ominous, and after the longest ten minutes of his life he managed to escape. He strode toward his office, taking a quick glance out front.

Jade sat at the front desk, talking on the phone while simultaneously working on the computer, checking someone in, and checking two people out. She sat there, an oasis in the middle of a circus. As if she sensed him, she glanced up. And if he wasn't mistaken, she grimaced slightly.

He raised a brow.

She bit her lower lip but didn't look away.

Adam, hot on his heels, leaned in and whispered, "Think we should tell your fiancée that you're allergic to commitment? That you have abandonment issues? And, oh yeah, that you're never going to let your guard down enough to actually marry anyone?"

"You're an asshole."

"So are you."

Dell sighed. "Yeah," he said as Adam walked away. "But knowing it is half the battle."

By noon Jade had checked in and out a dizzying number of patients while managing to avoid being alone with Dell. He'd seen a bulldog with an ingrown tail, a duck with a mysterious throat infection that turned out to be a swallowed quarter, and a kitten with acne. He'd performed four surgeries.

Jade had grabbed the sandwich from her bagged lunch and walked outside, needing a moment of sunshine.

A soft nicker from the horse pen caught her attention.

Reno. He was close to the fencing and flirting with her. She reached out to touch him and he snapped at her fingers. It was so unexpected that she jumped back and fell to the dirt. She scrambled back to her feet as a big hand settled on the nape of her neck.

She screamed and whirled around and would have fallen again if Dell hadn't caught her. "Just me," he said calmly. "You okay?"

They both knew she wasn't but she nodded. "Reno tried to bite me."

Dell didn't say anything for a moment, just slid an arm around her, making her realize she was backing away from both the horses and the man. "What do you know about horses?" he asked quietly, his delicious warmth seeping into her.

"I know that the porcelain horse collection I had as a child wasn't made to be played with," she said, trying to lighten the tension. "But I did it, anyway, and kept breaking off their legs. My grandmother got fed up and stopped buying them."

"The grandmother you were named after?"

"Yes." She closed her eyes, concentrating on the feel of his hand on the small of her back. Comforting but something else, too. Her heart rate should have slowed by now from her fright, but it was still racing—for another reason entirely now. "They wanted me to be strong and tough like her."

"It worked. You're the strongest, toughest woman I know."

She managed to choke back her startled laugh at that.

"It's true." He paused. "Do you know anything about *real* horses?"

"I know Reno used to like me."

"He still likes you." He stroked his hand up her back, letting it settle at the nape of her neck again. "It's important with any animal, especially a spooked one, to be calm, assertive. Dominant."

"Okay."

"A horse's emotions depend on its surroundings and also on the emotions of its human counterparts."

She went still. "Are you saying that my emotions caused Reno to try to bite me?"

His silence said he was going to let her wrestle with that one. "Relax your arms," he said, making her realize she was hugging herself tight. She dropped them to her sides with effort.

"And breathe," he said.

He was right, she wasn't breathing. She sucked in some air.

"Better," he said, and leaned past her to rub Reno's neck the way he was rubbing hers.

Reno gave a snort of pleasure and shifted closer.

"It's calming," Dell said.

Yes. It was calming as hell. If he kept it up, she'd do as Reno just had and make sounds of pleasure and shift even closer, too. "You have a bond with him," she said, managing to sound like she still had bones in her legs.

"Yes, and so do you. You just have to find it, and use your touch and voice to assure the animal that you're not going to let anything harm him."

His hand was slowly moving up and down her back now. And she got the message.

He wasn't going to let anything harm her, either.

"Jade."

She closed her eyes. "I still don't want to talk about it," she said. "Ever."

The sun was warm on her face, telling her that even though it was fall, summer hadn't quite given up the fight yet. She could almost pretend that they weren't having a conversation she didn't want to have.

"Ever is a long time," Dell said.

"I mean it."

"I know." He nodded. "I felt the same."

She shook her head. This didn't compute. "What are you talking about?"

"I know what it's like to suffer a trauma. What it's like to struggle to get past it."

Deny, deny, deny. "I'm not struggling."

He just looked at her, and she blew out a breath. "Okay, so sometimes I struggle, but don't change the subject! You're six foot two and outweigh me by at least sixty pounds. How were you ever a . . ."

"Victim?" His smile was grim. "I wasn't always thirty-two and built like a linebacker, you know. Actually, I started off more like a pipe cleaner with eyes."

That surprised a laugh out of her and she sidled him a glance. No one in their right mind would confuse that well-defined, tough, rugged body with a pipe cleaner. "Come on."

"Jade, trust me when I tell you that in my freshman year I was five foot three and weighed a buck twenty soaking wet. I got my ass kicked every which way, every single day."

An ache built in her chest for the boy he'd been. "Why?"

"Because I couldn't keep my mouth closed to save my life. I was a punk-ass kid whose mother had walked away and whose dad had died. I had a chip on top of the chip on my shoulder."

His mother had been Native American. According to Lilah, when the woman had been a teenager, she'd fallen for a white kid—a big offense in her family. She'd run off with him, but after having her second baby—Dell—she'd run off again, back to the reservation. When the boys' father had died several years later, she hadn't wanted her sons back.

Jade and her own mother had some issues, basically control issues, but Jade had never once doubted that she'd been wanted, cherished, and fully, one hundred percent loved.

A luxury Dell nor Adam had been given. It made her hurt for him, for Adam, too. For the men that they'd become, not that they'd thank her for the sympathy. They were both far too proud for that. But in spite of what had happened to them, they'd become good men. For both of them, trust had to be earned, and Dell certainly didn't give it away easily. He shielded his emotions behind his intellect and his job, though he completely surrendered himself to every single patient.

"I'd been dumped into yet another foster home and was pissed off at the world," Dell said casually, letting her know it could no longer hurt him.

But she didn't believe that. He had Adam and Brady now, and Lilah. And that was about it, other than a bunch of four-legged creatures.

He wasn't all that much better than she at letting people in. The thought brought the crazy urge to . . .

Hug him.

The thought was ridiculous and almost made her laugh. Dell was the strongest, most self-reliant person she knew. Comfort wasn't anywhere on his list of needs. "What happened?"

"My first day at the new school, I picked a fight with the biggest kid there."

"Dell. *Why?*"

"Hell, I don't even remember. Because I was stupid."

"What did he do to you?"

"For starters, he had the entire football team drag me to the park after school for retaliation. They stripped me naked and told me if I begged real nice, they'd let me go. They lied."

Her heart was in her throat. "Oh, Dell."

"Yeah, it sucked."

"Who saved you?"

"Nobody."

"They just stood there?" she asked, pissed and horrified for him.

"No. They beat the shit out of me, swearing that if I ever told anyone, it'd be worse next time." He shook his head. "Later, at the hospital, I tried to tell the nurses I'd walked into a door."

She gasped. "You didn't tell the truth?"

"I still had to go to that school," he said. "And I wanted to live." He rubbed his jaw ruefully, as if soothing an old ache.

"Who was in charge of you?" she asked.

"We went back into the system. Then we were taken in by a guy named Sol Anders." He said the name with fondness. "It was the last foster home I ever had. He kept us, Adam and me. Brady was already there when we arrived and he quickly became our older brother. After I healed up from the attack, Brady and Sol took turns teaching me self-defense. Luckily that summer I grew six inches, and then another five the year after. And I hit the weights."

It had done a body good . . .

"It wasn't about vanity," he said, reading her mind with his usual ease. "It was about survival. I did what I had to in order to survive, and so have you. But you already know that . . ."

Reno bumped his big head to Dell's chest.

Dell made a soft clicking sound with his mouth and the huge horse bumped him again, knocking him back a step, making him laugh softly.

Reno snickered in response, almost as if he was trying to imitate Dell's laugh.

Dell ruffled the horse's ears and gave him a smacking kiss right between the eyes, then turned to Jade, eyes serious. "You're only as strong as your biggest weakness."

"Is that right? What's your biggest weakness?"

"Back then, it was trying to be something I wasn't."

"And now?" she asked.

His mouth quirked. "Apparently, it's my fiancée."

She froze. "So you did hear."

When he just looked at her, she sucked her lower lip between her teeth. "It was for you, you know. A favor."

"Yeah? How do you figure?"

"I saved you from having to worry about Leanne. Hell, I saved you from messy emotional problems with *any* woman. You're saved from having to deal with real love and genuine passion. You are welcome."

He went brows up. "So I should be thanking you, then."

"I . . ." She let out a breath. "Okay, not exactly."

"You know that news travels fast out here. People'll have us married with children in no time."

"Oh God."

Because she looked much as he imagined he'd looked earlier with Adam, he could laugh. "It wouldn't be that bad."

She shrugged but looked unconvinced. And he realized he really had no idea what her hopes and dreams were for herself. None. "You don't see yourself married? A mom?"

"I try not to look that far ahead."

"And they call *me* tight-lipped," he said. "Come on, Jade. Tell me about you."

"What do you want to know?"

"More than you get a hard-on for organizing things."

"Like?"

"Like . . . why you come all photo ready to a job you're obviously overqualified for, wearing designer clothes when you're going to get dog and kitten hair all over you."

She shrugged. "I know how to run a washing machine."

"Okay, so why don't you date? You're sexy, smart as hell, and know your way around a good conversation. Yet whenever a guy approaches you, you use cynicism and sarcasm to scare him off."

"Not my fault if a guy's scared off by a little attitude."

She was throwing off some good 'tude right now. "Tell me what scared you so bad you ran from Chicago," he said. "Don't you think it's time?"

She stiffened and turned away. "What it's time for is to get back to work."

Eight

The next morning, Jade arrived at Belle Haven before dawn's first light for their biweekly vaccine clinic. She sat in her car, eyeing the walk to the front door.

Another vet clinic had been hit in Coeur d'Alene the night before, and it was all over the news. Dell had upgraded the security system, adding cameras at the front and back doors and several panic buttons throughout the clinic with a direct line to emergency dispatch.

His cool, calm, almost ruthless efficiency told her that he was very serious about this. And if Dell was serious, it meant he had a good reason. Dell had a lot of really great qualities, but allowing others to see his weaknesses wasn't one of them. This place, and the people and animals in it, were his. No sharing. The protective, possessive side of his nature should have threatened her peace of mind but at the moment she was glad for it.

Still, she had to make the walk from her car to the door. "Going to need reinforcements for this," she told Beans and put in her iPod earphones. She hit shuffle and Eminem came on.

Eminem was an ass kicker.

Still, she kept the volume down so she could hear what was going on around her. Normally she liked to get in a half hour before anyone else to set up, but nerves jittered through her stomach as she headed across the lot.

Inside, past the alarm and behind the locked door, she started breathing again. She let Beans loose, uncovered Peanut, and began to get ready for the mob scene that always occurred on free clinic days.

Because she couldn't deny the slight nerves still jangling, she cranked the volume on Pink and was singing along, trying to enjoy the solitude and quiet. After a few minutes she felt herself begin to relax at the regular, familiar routine of turning on the equipment, checking the supplies, organizing the files for the day. She walked past the drug cabinet, as always automatically reaching out to make sure it was locked.

It was. It was always locked, but to make sure was a comfort. She went still when the hair at the nape of her neck rose, then tore out her earphones in time to catch a whisper of sound, the soft brush of a man's footstep. And then another, telling her that there were two of them behind her.

"Do as I say, bitch, and I won't hurt you. Yet."

Dark fear as he emphasized the words with the cold muzzle of the gun thrust under her jaw.

Frozen with fear, she tried to turn her head to look at him, but he ran the tip of the gun from her jaw down her throat and over her collarbone to skim her breast. "Let's go," came the low, rough voice. "Unless you want to spend some time out here with me first . . ."

She felt the hand on her arm and heard her own whimper.

"Jade. Jade, it's just me—"

"Man, she's too far gone to hear you."

"I know. Fuck—"

Jade felt herself being picked up. She struggled automatically, panic welling, blocking her throat so that all that escaped was another pathetic whimper.

"You're okay. Jade, can you hear me?" A hand rough with calluses stroked gently down her hair. "You're safe."

Just a flashback. That's all. A flashback triggered by the Halloween mask from two nights before, not to mention hours of tossing and turning, culminating in having the bad timing of being nearly scared out of her own skin in front of the drug cabinet.

Which is where she'd faced her own nightmare once before.

"Here," Adam said to Dell, dragging a chair over. "Sit with her here, I'll get her some water."

Her brain didn't seem to want to connect with reality, and she couldn't draw air into her lungs. Embarrassed, she buried her face into the crook of Dell's neck and tried to breathe him in instead.

"Jade. Jade, listen to me." Dell, speaking in that quiet calm voice of his, the one that made her struggle to settle just so she could hear more of it. "You're safe. I've got you."

She nodded, hoping she looked like she was back in control of herself. But she figured she must have failed because he ran his hands slowly up and down her back, soothing her, whispering softly to her, words she couldn't quite catch but it didn't matter. His voice was heaven. If he kept talking, just like that, she thought maybe she could even start breathing again.

Adam came back with a glass of water. "She okay?"

"Yes." Dell cupped her face in his big hands, his own face so close to hers. "She's okay."

Jade nodded, even though she had a grip on his shirt, tight enough to hurt her own fingers. But she didn't let go as she drew in a desperate gulp of air and let it out.

"She's hyperventilating," Adam said quietly.

"No, she's got this. You've got this, Jade," Dell assured her and took the water from Adam to hand to her.

"Slow sips," Adam said, hunkering down at her side, his eyes on her face.

"I'm fine," Jade said, and gulped down the water, relieving her parched throat. Apparently freak-outs made one thirsty. Who knew?

Adam took the glass from her and that's when she realized . . . she was in Dell's lap.

"Careful," Adam said when she stood up. "You don't have your sea legs back yet."

"I'm fine," she said. A broken record. It didn't escape her notice that Dell made sure to be very close to her, close enough to grab her if she started to lose it again.

But she wouldn't. Hell no. She was overcoming.

Dammit.

"I'm sorry," she said.

Adam and Dell exchanged a long look and she grimaced. "Okay, so I'm working on it."

Dell's eyes never left hers. "What's setting you off?"

She shook her head. Not going down that road. Luckily for her the phones were starting to ring, and that was her cue. "Nothing. It's nothing. Got to get the phones."

"Jade—"

But she was already scrambling out of there for the sanctuary of her front desk.

Dell's last few appointments of the day were worming puppies—always fun—and examining a twelve-year-old German shepherd suffering from pneumonia. The owner was Gil Roberto, the local mechanic. He and Max had been together for all twelve years. Gil was sitting on the floor with Max's head in his lap, looking like he was about to face the firing squad. But Dell drained Max's lungs in a quick procedure, and Gil was able to take Max home.

It was a good end to a rough day. Dell had kept his eye on Jade, but she'd played things close to the vest. Still, there was no doubt she was working hard at keeping it together, but whatever the other night had dragged back up for her, it had shaken her to the core.

Tired and dirty, Dell showered in the bathroom attached to his office. When he came out, he found Adam in his office chair, feet up, leaning back, messing around on Dell's laptop. "You'd better not be looking at porn," Dell said. "You crashed the entire system last time."

Adam didn't bother to acknowledge his brother's presence.

"Don't you have your own office right down the hall?"

"It's your turn to buy dinner," Adam said, still staring at the laptop screen. "I'm thinking pizza."

"Yeah. Sure."

Adam looked up and eyeballed him. "You figure out what's up with our fearless girl?"

"No."

"She's still not sharing?"

"Would you?"

"Something bad happened to her," Adam said.

"I know."

"You going to ask?"

"No," Dell said.

"Why not?"

Dell slid his brother a long look. "Did pushing ever help you?"

A ghost of a smile crossed Adam's mouth. "No."

Dell shoved Adam's feet off his desk, and that's when he realized . . . the office was clutter-free. He had two filing cabinets—usually fully loaded with stacks of shit on top—and then a credenza, as well as a set of chairs used as crap collectors. But everything was completely cleaned off. "Holy shit."

Ever alert, Adam looked around. "What?"

"The entire room is clean."

"Yeah, I assumed you finally shoved the entire mess into the trash to start over."

Dell hauled Adam out of the chair, then sank into it himself, whipped around, and opened the drawers of the credenza.

Organized and neat as a pin.

"You get some sort of extreme makeover TV crew in here when I wasn't looking?" Adam asked.

"Jade," Dell said.

"Jade what?"

"She did this."

"Actually," Jade said from the doorway. "I brought in a hazmat team to handle it."

Adam flashed her a rare smile.

"Wow," Jade said, smiling back. "You ought to do that more often. Oh, and line one. It's Holly for you."

Adam's smile faded.

Holly was the daughter of Donald Reid, an extremely wealthy businessman who'd bought up a bunch of failing ranches and had somehow turned them around in a bad economy. His daughter Holly had recently joined him from New York. She was some big financial wizard and the bane of Adam's existence. Donald was rich, but also a big old softie, and often fostered young search-and-rescue puppies for Adam until they were old enough to be trained and adopted. The problem was, Donald had been spending a lot of time up north helping upgrade his sister's ranch.

This left Holly handling the entire Reid empire, puppies included. She and Adam were oil and water, which was hugely amusing because it was nice to see the infallible Adam messed with for a change.

"I'm busy," Adam said to Jade calmly, also amusing. The calmer Adam appeared, the more rattled he was.

"Already told her you were in," Jade said. "Sorry."

Adam's left eye twitched.

Jade nodded. "And yeah, you should be afraid. Very afraid. That woman is one pissed-off client."

Dell snorted, taking care to step out of the way before Adam could smack him upside the head.

"Why is she mad?" Adam asked Jade.

"Because you're breathing," Dell said. "She's always mad at you. Question is, why? What did you do to piss her off this time?"

Adam's expression was one hundred percent impassive. A battle-ready soldier. One who was staring at the phone like it was a spitting cobra. "I dropped off her father's new puppy yesterday," he said.

"Donald out of town again?"

"Yep."

"Well, pick up the phone," Jade said. "You can't just leave her on hold."

Dell leaned in and hit Speaker on the phone.

Adam flipped him off, but with a resigned expression, he said, "Connelly."

"*You*," came Holly's voice, crystal clear, and so cold icicles nearly formed in the air. "You did this to me on purpose, didn't you? What was it, some kind of sick revenge?"

Jade looked at Dell but Dell shrugged. Hell, he had no idea. If Jade played things close to the vest, Adam was the master.

"Revenge?" Adam repeated as if discussing the weather. "For what?"

"You know damn well for what."

"I'm in the middle of a meeting, Holly," Adam said. "You'll have to get to the point."

"Okay, the point. The point is you're an ass—"

Adam scooped up the phone, taking her off the speaker. "Calling me names isn't going to encourage me to come rescue you. Again." Adam paused, the picture of polite listening. "Is that even anatomically possible?" He listened some more. "Only if you ask me real nice—" He winced and set the phone back into its cradle. "She had to go."

Jade shook her head. "It's really such a surprise that you're not married."

When she was gone, Adam looked at Dell. "Pizza."

"If you tell me what Holly said."

"She said that if she ever got ahold of me, she was going to do to me what the puppy did to her Prada pumps."

"Ouch."

"Yeah. And she was pretty specific about where she planned on shoving the shoe remains."

Dell winced. "So maybe we should go get the puppy and rescue Holly before we eat?"

"Hell, no. I'm going to bring her two more puppies later on tonight."

Dell stared at him. "You're insane."

Unconcerned, Adam shrugged.

"She's going to kill you."

"She can try."

Adam wasn't playful much these days; in fact, he hadn't been since he'd left the National Guard after a rescue had gone bad a few years back where half his team had been killed. In the time since, he'd been dancing around a boatload of guilt and a dash of PTSD for good measure.

But he was definitely showing signs of playfulness now. Or so Dell hoped. "Or you could stop baiting her and try something else."

"Like?"

"Like sleeping with her."

Adam slid him a look.

Now it was Dell who shrugged. "Or hey, go on living like a monk, driving the rest of us out of our fucking minds. Your choice, man."

"Not all of us feel the need to sleep with anything in a skirt."

"You used to," Dell pointed out.

"Things change."

Dell shook his head and left his office. Jade was standing at her desk pulling on a long, fuzzy angora sweater that Dell happened to know would cling to her every curve.

"Adam and I are getting dinner," he said. "Come with us."

She slapped a couple of disks into his hand.

"What's this?" he asked.

"Your backups."

"I like my clean office," Dell said.

"You mean you like having furniture that's furniture instead of crap collectors?"

"It wasn't that bad."

"No, it was worse."

Adam was grinning as he joined them. "Aw. Your first fight as an engaged couple."

Jade ignored this. "I've laid out the payables that need attention and brought up all the outstanding receivables that I could find, though it'd be more accurate if you finished entering your accounting for this month."

They'd all been running like crazy for most of the day. How had she managed to do all this as well?

"And with another few hours I could probably get your checking account reconciled." She gave him a look of reproach. "You're three months behind."

"I'm getting to it."

"If you do it in the first week of the new month, you can close that month out and your accounting system takes you all the way to the financial statements. Assuming you finish entering your receivables."

Dell blinked. "For eighteen months you've been answering my phones and setting up my schedule and bringing my patients back to me like you were born to be a receptionist. You never once mentioned all these other talents."

She grabbed Beans's carrier and her purse and headed for the door. "My talents are on a need-to-know basis."

Adam raised a brow.

Yeah. She was definitely feeling better. But then he saw it, her slight hesitation at the door.

She didn't want to go to the parking lot.

"Adam," Dell said. "I'll meet you at Risolli's."

Adam never took his eyes off Jade, frozen in clear agonizing indecision. Nodding, he shifted around her, gently squeezing her arm before slipping out the door.

Jade mentally put on her big-girl panties and strode out the door the same way Adam had. Of course it was much easier to face her demons with one hundred and eighty pounds of solid muscle at her back, and Dell *was* at her back. He followed her to her car, waiting silently while she set Beans in the back and buckled her in. A breeze blew across the lot, and a branch cracked. She stiffened, but Dell's hand slid to her lower back, warm and sure. Steadying. She closed her eyes. "I'm just thinking about where I want to go for dinner," she whispered.

"Risolli's. Risolli's is where you want to go for dinner."

"Risolli's is a heart attack in the making," she said automatically.

"They have salads. Just think about it. And while you're thinking . . ." He wrapped his arms around her, all the way around her from behind. "Think about this," he said.

The hold was almost an exact replication of how she'd been grabbed that night and she froze.

"Where are your keys to the meds lockup, bitch?"

"I don't have keys," she said.

"Wrong answer."

She heard the pathetic little ragtag whimper drag up from her throat. "Dell."

"I know," Dell murmured very softly. "It's an aggressive move, and your heart's pounding and you're probably hardly able to hear me over the roar of the blood in your ears but listen to me, Jade. It's just me, and you have nothing to be afraid of with me. Break free."

"I can't."

"Goddess Jade doesn't know the meaning of the word. Fight, Jade. Do whatever you have to do to get loose. You don't have to be a victim."

A moment ago she'd been happy to have him at her back but now that he was using it on her it was a different story entirely. She could feel the strength in his arms, the heat of him behind her and could hardly breathe.

He didn't rush her, just gave her that same, steady patience he gave his animals. But she wasn't an animal, and she couldn't turn off her brain. This wasn't going to work. "Dell," she said hoarsely, the panic choking her. "Please—"

"First rule of self-defense. Stay calm and think as the situation develops."

Calm was out of the question. Not with flashbacks making her vision blurry. Or maybe that was the lack of air since she was holding her breath.

"Second rule, show no fear or hesitation."

Right. She'd get right on that.

"Breathe, Jade." He brushed his jaw to hers. "Come on, tough girl," he murmured softly, in direct opposition to the tight, unforgiving hold he had on her. "You can do this. There are many ways, but we'll take it one at a time. I'm a bad guy. How do you get away from me?"

"I don't know!" she cried, her hands coming up to grip his arm around her waist. But all that did was remind her of just how strong he was.

"The human skull is a powerful weapon all on its own," he said. "Don't waste your time trying to step on my toes or elbowing me in the ribs. None of those moves will do anything but piss someone off. Bash my face with the back of your head."

"What?"

"Connect once, maybe twice with your attacker's face or collarbone and you'll deliver some serious damage, trust me. Do it."

"Do it, give me your keys. Now."

She shook her head, and another guy in a mask moved into her line of sight, roughly pushing someone.

Karen, a floor nurse.

Jade gasped when the second masked guy casually set the muzzle of his gun to Karen's temple. "Bet you can find the keys now," he said.

He was right. Jade pulled the keys out and threw them at him. He snagged them out of midair and, with a smile that still haunted her dreams, dragged her along with him to the drug storage.

"Jade." Dell was saying her name, quietly but firmly, in a voice that demanded she pay attention. "Jade, you can do this. As soon as the adrenaline kicks in, everything will seem to happen in slow motion. If you stay calm, your mind will process thoughts so rapidly that it will even seem like you've got hours to make a decision on how to react."

She closed her eyes and tried to fall into her adrenaline instead of fighting it. She didn't manage until he tightened his grip. Then she drew in a breath and snapped her head back.

Dell dodged to the side, but she still managed to hit him on the cheekbone, and he immediately dropped his hold on her.

Spinning around, she stared at him, horrified.

But when he straightened, he was smiling. "Nice." He lifted his hand to touch his cheekbone, already reddened.

"Oh my God. I hurt you."

"That's the point," he reassured her, looking proud. "It works, Jade. Every time. I was only able to dodge it because I knew you were going to do it. With the element of surprise, you'll break anyone's hold on you."

"Anyone's?"

"You have to be confident. You have to picture it. You have to believe it. But yeah. Anyone's. Now can we get some pizza? Adam's a fucking diva when he's hungry."

She let out a breath, marveling over what she'd just done, more than a little desperate to believe. It had been a long time since she hadn't worried about the shadows and the boogeyman. She thought she was good at hiding it but apparently not. She'd seen the look Adam and Dell had exchanged. It wasn't a new look, she saw it every time they dealt with a hurt or abused animal. It was their protect-the-innocent-animal look.

She hated that she was the hurt animal. Hated.

At least they hadn't pressed her to talk about it, hadn't called her out on her undeniably odd and peculiar behavior—at least not really—and for that, she'd been eternally grateful.

But she was pretty sure her pass was over.

"There are more moves, Jade," Dell said. "I can show you how to break the hold if you're grabbed from the front, too, and lots of other self-defense tactics."

The power of that surged through her and overcame her embarrassment and shame. "Really?"

"Sure. After a couple of months of practice, you'll be in lean, mean, fighting-machine shape."

A couple of months . . . "Dell. I've told you, I'm leaving at the end of the month."

His expression didn't change. "You've said that before and not gone back."

Oh God. Is that what he believed? That she wasn't leaving? "This time I am. I have to."

A muscle ticked in his jaw. "Fine. You still have a month." His face was still calm. Controlled. "We'll make it work."

Nine

Once again Dell rolled out of bed before dawn. He showered and headed out. Way out, passing through Sunshine, past Belle Haven and into the hills.

She was leaving. By the time the first snow hit, Jade would be gone. He felt more for her than he wanted, way more, so it was just as well that she was leaving.

Shaking his head at that ridiculous logic, he kept driving. Forty-five minutes later and light-years away from anything remotely resembling a town, he pulled to a stop. He got out of his truck, waving some of the dust away from his face. The road out here was always a dust storm, every single time. Grabbing his bag, he headed toward the double-wide.

The trailer had been here for as long as he could remember, sitting square on thirty acres of absolutely nothing.

He came every week. Nila didn't ask him to. She wouldn't.

But he came, anyway.

He couldn't explain why. Adam thought he was crazy, but he never said a word about it.

He didn't have to. Dell already knew it was stupid and pathetic.

But still he came. As he reached out to knock on the door, it opened and she stood there in ragged jeans, an old sweatshirt, and no shoes. Her long black hair was streaked with gray now and plaited in a single braid down her back. Her eyes were black and gave little away.

Dell got his eyes from her.

She didn't smile, she never did, but he could tell she was relieved to see him as she stepped aside to make room for him.

Waiting there, lined up on the narrow orange and brown trailer couch, were others: two women, an old man, a teenager, and two younger children—all with an animal at their feet or in their laps.

Dr. Doolittle time.

Nila handed Dell a cup of coffee, not meeting his eyes. She never did. He accepted the coffee and moved to the small Formica table, opening his bag, pulling out his laptop. This was an unofficial visit, it always was, but he still kept records as well as he could. "Who's first?"

The youngest, a girl who couldn't be more than five, stood up, a tiny kitten clutched in her hands as bedraggled as the little girl.

And Dell's day began.

Two nights later, Jade walked up to the front door of Dell's house, not quite sure if she was excited or nervous.

Both, she decided.

Definitely both.

The other evening, when he'd grabbed her from behind . . . she'd thought she'd expire on the spot from fear and panic. But then he'd shown her how to break free of the hold.

She went to the occasional yoga and Pilates classes, but that was about it for her. She'd never done martial arts or self-defense, but Dell was a big guy and she'd broken free from him.

Crazy as it seemed, it had given her hope. And she'd followed the scent of that hope all the way here.

She'd been to Dell's house before. They all played poker every few weeks, usually in his dining room. But she'd never come alone, and she might not have now either but he'd been asking for two days and . . .

And she was curious. And afraid. And . . . and he opened the door wearing black workout shorts and a T-shirt that was wet and clinging to his torso.

And then she forgot to think at all.

His hair was damp, and he was rubbing a towel over his face, breathing hard, looking like he'd been enjoying whatever he'd been doing. "You came," he said.

He'd thought she wouldn't. She did her best to roll her tongue back into her mouth. "You look busy."

"Nope. Just kicking Adam's ass."

Dressed similarly, Adam came into view behind him and snorted. "Not even on a good day, man. Though I'll give it to you that you're better these days." He nodded to Jade. "You should have seen us when we were kids. He was so uncoordinated, he couldn't walk across a room without falling over his own scrawny legs. At least he outgrew his glasses. Christ, was he ugly. It took him years to grow into his current look."

"Hey," Dell said. "You do realize you look just like me."

"No, *you* look like *me*."

Jade followed them both into the kitchen, marveling at how they seemed to take perverse pleasure in making fun of each other's vulnerabilities at every turn. And yet the connection between them was unmistakable.

She shrugged it off to the mystery of the male psyche, watching as Dell grabbed two bottles of water, tossed one at Adam, then downed his in long, greedy gulps while Jade stood there looking at two of the finest male specimens she'd ever seen.

Adam tossed his empty bottle into a recycling bin and nodded to Dell. "Be sure to thank Jade for saving your hide. Five more minutes and I'd have been wiping the floor with you."

Dell grinned. "Whatever you have to tell yourself to sleep at night."

Adam shook his head, like he couldn't believe how lame his own brother was. Moving to the door, he slowed in front of Jade and lightly tugged on a strand of her hair. "I'm better than he is," he said with a head jerk in Dell's direction. "When you're done pounding him into the mat, I'll be happy to step in."

"Yeah, yeah." Dell shoved him out, then turned to Jade. "Want something to drink first?"

"Only if you think a tequila shot before learning how to kick ass is a good idea."

He smiled. "You're nervous."

That was putting it mildly. She'd been thinking about this for two days now, in between fielding calls from everyone in town about her supposed engagement to Dell. Knowing that if *she* was getting cornered, he had to be getting it way worse, she'd called Leanne and told her that the engagement was off.

Now the story running through town was that Dell had dumped Jade because he was a tragic alpha hero, wounded and terrified of love.

Dell had laughed it off, assuring her he couldn't give a shit what people made up about them. And she knew he was being honest—he definitely didn't worry about what others thought. He was classic alpha that way.

But she'd wondered . . . how much of the whispers were really made up? He'd been very careful in his life in regard to the chosen few whom he trusted. She hadn't worked for him for eighteen months and not understood that much of that easygoing and laid-back nature was only skin-deep, that no matter what he showed the general public he was actually intensely private and quite closed off.

She figured the mock engagement, and then the supposed cancellation of said engagement—leaving him "wounded" and needing some alone time—worked for him.

"Come on," he said, leading her down a set of stairs to a basement. "We'd better start before you change your mind and run out on me."

She was already beginning to sweat. "I don't run." *Liar, liar.* "But I could use that tequila shot now."

"Be good," he said, "and I'll get you something after. Sol used to serve us tea when he was kicking our butts."

"Tea's only good if it comes with cookies."

He laughed. "Tea's good never."

"Sounds like Sol was a sweet man."

"He was two hundred and fifty pounds, and six feet four inches of solid muscle. He was also ex-marine, and didn't know a smile from his own ass. He wasn't sweet, but he was . . . everything else. At least to us."

The basement was completely finished and had been turned into a gym. Equipment was lined on one wall, a treadmill, elliptical trainer, a selection of machines with a large maximum-load capacity, and free weights were in front of a bank of mirrors. Along one side, across from the riders, was a large padded mat area, as well as a huge flat-screen TV and entertainment center mounted on a wall. Music was blasting out of it. "The man cave," she said. Feeling a little intimidated, she pulled off her sweatshirt. She hadn't been sure what to wear but had settled on yoga pants and a tank top.

Dell aimed the remote at the entertainment system and the music cut. He tossed the remote aside and took her to the mats in front of the mirrors. "Anyone can learn this, I promise."

She nodded, hoping that was true. "Like you learned it."

"There's something about getting your ass handed to you daily that motivates you."

She looked around, curious. "How many women have you brought down here to . . . help train?"

She expected him to laugh, or at least give off a wicked smile, but he slowly shook his head, his warm brown eyes even on hers. "None."

"Come on. The way you date?"

"I've never brought a woman to my house."

"Ever?"

"Ever. And you're stalling. Step onto the mat."

She touched it with her toe. "Usually a guy buys me dinner first."

He held out his hand for hers, eyes steady. Calm. "Come on now, tough girl," he said in the same tone she'd heard him use on a wild stallion just before horse-whispering the thing into a puddle of goo.

She wasn't a puddle of goo *yet*, but she followed his soft command and reached for his hand. "Where do we start?" Her voice didn't sound as confident as she'd have liked. Being in Dell's very nice arms to be kissed was one thing. And a very nice thing. Being there to try to escape wasn't nearly so nice. It was claustrophobic and terrifying. He was big, bigger than either of the two men who'd held her that long-ago night.

"Let's finish teaching you how to break out of a hold from behind," he said, going directly to the source of her anxiety without passing Go.

She nodded and he moved behind her, and this time when his arms came around her, she was prepared.

Or so she told herself.

But he was built like a wall of granite, and her breath hitched. "I know," he said. "But remember. Let the adrenaline work in your favor." His voice was low and steady, and she nodded.

But this hold was different. He had one forearm banded tight around her waist like before, but the other was at her throat and she didn't have the mobility to get him with a head butt.

Plus there was the added rush of it being Dell, not a bad guy. Dell, with his familiar scent and voice . . . and confusing emotions, battered her.

Fear.

Excitement.

Panic.

Arousal.

"Turn your chin toward my elbow," he said. "Force it down to relieve the pressure against the side of your neck so that you don't go unconscious if the pressure increases. Then you stomp the shit out of his insole with your heel. If you can, reach over your shoulder and poke out his eyes. Or, if your arms are pinned too low, like I've got you now, grab and twist his nuts."

"What?"

"Trust me, that's the most effective tool in your arsenal. He'll drop like a stone."

"Have you thought about any possible future children you're risking?"

"Well, maybe you could skip the twist part." He tightened his grip, signaling that he wasn't going to let her slip into brevity. "You want to make it so that they can't see, can't breathe, and hopefully can't run after you."

"Dell." She gripped his forearm, the one over her throat, her legs trembling.

"I've got you, Jade. I promise. Nothing bad is going to happen to you here. Ever."

"I'm sorry. I don't know why I'm shaking."

"Don't be sorry. You know I'll stop if that's what you want."

She closed her eyes and tried to collect herself.

"Jade?"

"No. Don't stop." She drew a deep breath. "Do you really want me to stomp on your foot and attempt to poke your eyes out?"

"Yes."

She closed her eyes again, drew in yet another bolstering breath, and stomped the shit out of his foot. When his arms fell away from her, she whirled and took a step back.

But he didn't drop like a stone. He came at her and grabbed her again, from the front this time. Suddenly she was up against him in a tight embrace, her chest, belly, and thighs pressed to his. Completely overwhelmed, she gasped.

"Backing away was good," he said. "But you stopped. Never stop. Because once you do, you have to be prepared to fight, in which case you need to be either two arm lengths away from him—outside of his kicking range—or all the way in tight against him. Anything in between is leaving yourself too open. If you can, run. Fucking run for the hills and scream for help while you're at it. You okay?"

She nodded, all she could manage.

"Good," he said. "Couple of ways to get out of this. A knee to the groin works. Move fast and hard. Follow it up with a kick to the guy's knee or lower abs if you can reach them. Kick straight ahead using the bottom of your foot like you'd kick in a door. If he somehow manages to come at you again, use your elbow and smash him in the face, throat, or neck. Then back to your standby option—run like hell."

She was doing her best to stand there flat up against him and be casual, but she was so incredibly aware of every inch of him that she couldn't find an ounce of casual. "Dell," she whispered, and dropped her head to his chest.

"Okay, it's okay," he said, mistaking her distress. His warm exhale tickled her ear as his arms loosened. "Breathe, Jade. Then think. What's your first move?"

She breathed as ordered, then came up with her knee.

He deflected enough that she grazed his thigh, but he still went down to his knees.

It worked. Holy shit, it really worked. Shocked, she covered her mouth and stared down at him.

As he had earlier, he lifted his head and flashed her a grin. "Nice. Except you forgot to scream and run like hell."

Before she could move, he'd grabbed her and tugged her down to the mat, pinning her beneath him. Taking her hands in his, he yanked them over her head and peered into her eyes. "First," he said. "Remember. It's just me. Second . . ."

She came up with her knee.

"Yes!" he said, deftly rolling aside and coming up on an elbow with another dazzling smile, by which time she'd run across the room, away from him. "See? You're a natural."

He spent the next two hours putting her through the paces. And that night, she slept like the living dead, with only the weight of Beans on her chest instead of the usual ball of anxiety.

* * *

By the end of the next day, they'd seen forty patients, among them seven-week-old Rhodesian ridgeback puppies, a four-year-old shih tzu with colitis, a basset hound with OCD, and a bunny who had nothing wrong with him other than he was owned by Mrs. Wycoff, who was old and very lonely.

Dell healed them all with equal ease.

Oh, to wield that power, Jade thought. Good thing he had no idea exactly how much power he had. She began to close up. "Peanut want a cracker?" she asked the parrot.

She'd been trying to teach Peanut to say the sentence "Peanut want a cracker" to distract the parrot from saying "boner" at inopportune times. But Peanut was pretending to be mute today.

Jade was just about ready to switch to the phone service for the night when the phone rang, so she grabbed it.

"Hello, Jade. It's Melinda. Is Dell in?"

Melinda ran a thirty-thousand-acre ranch up north. It was one of the ranching accounts Dell had added now that Brady had fixed up their Bell 47 chopper to fly to farther locations. Dell went to Melinda's ranch one Saturday a month, where he tended to her animals' care.

And, according to the rumor mill, he attended to Melinda's care as well.

Dell was in his office with Brady, and his office phone line was lit. "He's on the other line," Jade said.

"No problem, I'll call him on his cell later tonight. Let him know I'm ready for him tomorrow."

"Sure." And if Melinda could say "ready" with more sex in her voice, that would be just freaking fantastic. "Will do." Jade forced herself to hang up calmly. "I'm ready for him tomorrow," she mocked in a sex kitten voice.

"Ah. Melinda."

Jade nearly fell out of her chair and Bessie the cleaning lady cackled good and hard over that. "She does seem to have her hooks out for him, doesn't she?"

"I . . . I didn't notice."

Bessie cackled again. "And I hardly noticed that lovely shade of green on you, dear."

"I'm not jealous."

"Of course not." Bessie looked pointedly at the message Jade had written and crumpled. "Don't worry. Your secret crush on the doc is safe with me."

"Crush on the doc," Peanut said.

Jade glared at the parrot. "What?"

"Boner."

Jade stood up and pointed at her. "You can't say 'Peanut wants a cracker,' but you can say 'crush on the doc' and 'boner'? Are you kidding me?"

"Crush on the doc! Crush on the doc!"

Bessie laughed so hard that Jade thought she'd cough up a lung right there, but she went back to sweeping. Jade narrowed her eyes at Peanut.

"Pretty Peanut," Peanut whispered.

Jade sighed and went to work, fantasizing about her next self-defense session and kicking Dell's very fine ass. She was halfway there, picturing taking him to the floor and . . . and what? She had lots of options, as he'd taught her.

Kicking.

Hitting.

Jabbing.

But there was something wrong with her brain. It wouldn't go there. Instead, she imagined dropping him to the mat and . . .

Stripping him. Stretching out over the top of him and . . .

Eating him up like a hot buttered biscuit.

Dammit. Now she was heated up herself and having a hot flash to boot. She fanned the air in front of her face, which didn't help.

"So . . ." Lilah said at her side, making Jade jump. "What's got you all hot and bothered?"

Bessie came through with her broom again. "Ask Peanut."

"Crush on the doc," Peanut said.

Jade closed her eyes.

"Fascinating," Lilah said. "*That* I have to learn from a parrot? You've been holding out on me."

"Don't be ridiculous. Peanut has no idea what she's saying."

"Boner," Peanut said.

Lilah grinned. "Okay," she said to Jade. "Start at the beginning and leave nothing out. Tell me what's up."

"The temperature, dammit. Too many bodies in here."

Lilah's gaze slid across the room to where Dell and Brady had come out from the back. Dell's gaze tracked directly to Jade.

"Uh-huh," Lilah said.

"I know what you're thinking," Jade whispered. "But stop it. So there's a little sexual tension in the room between Dell and me, it's nothing. *Nothing.* In fact, picturing him as old and flabby right now. Flatulent. And see? I'm cooler already."

"I was going to suggest turning down the thermostat."

"Or that," Jade muttered to Lilah's laugh.

The next day, Jade got an e-mail attachment from Dell—a spreadsheet to-do list with only one thing on it.

Training session #2 tonight. My house, seven o'clock.

There was a code, too. The key code to his front door, she realized. She wouldn't have to knock, she could go right in.

Which is why he'd given it to her, of course, so she wouldn't get there and while standing on his porch waiting to be let in, change her mind.

But she couldn't just let herself in. Could she? Besides, he'd been gone all day, up north at Melinda's.

He wasn't spending the night up there?

She showed up at his house exactly on time and after some hesitation, entered the code and let herself in.

Dell was in his kitchen, staring into his refrigerator, which had not magically filled itself. It'd been a hell of a long day at Melinda's ranch, and he was dead on his feet.

Normally he spent the night up north. Usually with Melinda. She was smart, funny, and beautiful, and with two ex-husbands, she wasn't looking for anything more than a good time. No harm, no foul.

But last month he'd had Brady fly him home the same day as well.

He'd repeated the pattern today, marking two full months of dateless Saturday nights for him.

A first.

He heard his front door open and Jade's footsteps coming through the living room. He knew without looking that she was wearing her Nikes, which she wore only for him. For the rest of the world she wore designer heels or boots.

He liked her stripped down to casual. To what he thought was the real Jade beneath the glamorous veneer. He liked that he alone saw her this way. Not that he could explain to himself why.

"Thought you had a date tonight," she said, appearing in his doorway.

"My date's you." He shut the refrigerator. "I can make you dinner after you finish wiping the mat with me."

He added her quick smile to the list of things that he liked, though he had no idea if her grin was because he hadn't stayed at Melinda's or the idea of wiping the mat with him. He suspected the latter.

The list of things he liked about Jade was very long and growing, he thought as they went downstairs and she pulled off her sweatshirt. He liked how she threw herself into any task with everything she had, including this one—which she wasn't altogether comfortable with yet. He liked the way her skin glowed. He liked the way she shoved her hair back from her face to stall before getting on the mat, and he *really* liked the way her nipples hardened and pressed against her T-shirt.

Yeah, that was his favorite. "Ready?" he asked.

"I was born ready."

Not for me, though he suddenly wished otherwise. They worked for a half hour before she asked for a water break. As she tipped her head back and drank from a bottle he handed her, his gaze drifted up the length of her body where she was draped over a weight machine trying to catch her breath. Her T-shirt was sticking to her, and it made her look tough, like maybe she could kick some serious butt. It also emphasized her curves, making his mouth water.

Her hair had dared to disobey and was coming out of her fancy twist but he could still see the nape of her neck. The creamy pale skin there was driving him insane. It was the vulnerability of that one little spot, the way a few strands of red silk curled damply to it.

He wanted his mouth there. Of course he was shit out of luck on that particular fantasy, which could get in line behind all the other fantasies he had filed in his brain under Goddess Jade.

"Dell?"

She'd finished her water and was facing him, expression determined.

He was so going down.

And not ten minutes later she went for the slam dunk and he was on his knees on the mat, hands holding his junk, gasping for breath and trying not to throw up.

Yeah, she was not nearly as soft and vulnerable as he'd thought.

"Oh God. Oh God, Dell, I'm sorry! You said jam my knee up and—"

"It's okay," he croaked, and slowly fell over. "I'm okay." Or as okay as he could be with his nuts in his throat. Hell, he wasn't ready to have children, anyway. He felt her crawl close and put her hand on his lower abs. "Back up, I don't want to throw up on your pretty Nikes."

She didn't back up, she leaned over him, her fingers drifting lower to cover the hand he was using to cup himself. He knew why *he* was doing it, he was holding on to the goods to make sure they were still there. But she . . . "Jade—"

"Did I hurt it?"

"It" twitched. "No," Dell said, both to her and to his dick's unspoken and hopeful question of getting lucky.

"Are you sure? Maybe I should . . . look."

He opened his eyes and met her worried ones.

"I worked at a medical center for eight years, remember?"

Because he wasn't ready to move—or let her look, *Jesus*—he said, "Tell me about the job."

"I was in charge of . . . everything."

He choked out a laugh. "So what's so different from now?"

That earned him a small smile and she wrapped her fingers around his wrist and tried to lift his hand off his groin. Her fingers brushed against him and in spite of the fact that he was still hurting, he got hard. Perfect. "Jade—"

"If you're bruising up, we need to ice—"

"I'm not bruising."

She pulled his hand away and stared down at the crotch of his basketball shorts.

He lifted his head and looked, too, the both of them taking in the very obvious bulge between his legs. "I think I'm going to live," he said wryly.

She swallowed hard and wet her lips.

Groaning, he thunked his head back on the floor. "Not helping."

Her gaze met his, and that's when they heard it. The front door slamming shut. And then Adam's boots on the cellar steps.

Jade leapt to her feet and practically ran for her sweatshirt, which she was just pulling over her head when Adam appeared. Jade sent his brother a weak smile. "He might not be in fighting condition at the moment."

And then she was gone.

Adam looked at Dell prone on the mat. "She flatten you?"

"Yeah."

Adam just shook his head. "Food?" Then he went back upstairs, apparently in search of said food.

Dell rolled to his knees, disgusted with himself. *Great way to make her feel comfortable and safe.* He scrubbed a hand over his face feeling . . . discombobulated. It took him a minute to realize that was because she'd walked. Usually he did the walking. That's how it always worked. "I guess not this time," he said to Gertie, who'd lumbered down the stairs to investigate. Gertie snuffled and plopped down at his feet. She might not have a graceful bone in her body, but she wouldn't walk away. At least not unless someone bribed her with food . . .

Ten

Dell spent Sunday deep in the Bitterroot Mountains with Brady and Adam, working volunteer S&R. Late that night they'd located the lost hiker and flown back to Sunshine.

Brady went home to Lilah. Adam had a class to give.

So Dell was on his own, and he crashed early in his own bed. Not that being exhausted helped him sleep. He woke up several times, the latest at dawn when Gertie leapt on his bed and slobbered on his face.

Her version of the good-morning kiss.

He shoved her off him and got into the shower. At Belle Haven he rode Kiwi, then let himself into the office just as Jade arrived. He'd called her several times since Saturday night, all of which she'd ignored.

Which made sense. He'd invited her over for self-defense training, promising to teach her moves to make her feel safe. And then he'd turned into a fifteen-year-old boy and gotten hard in class. "Jade."

She had the phone headset on. She raised a finger to indicate she needed a minute. He could see now that she was accessing the center's messages from their service, typing them into the spreadsheet that she had up on her screen. She was crazy about her spreadsheets. She'd uncovered Peanut, and the parrot was preening and humming to herself. Beans was watching Peanut with avid, narrow-eyed interest.

Gertie had found the sole sunny spot in the room and was already snoring.

Jade's fingers were a whirl on her keyboard. She worked hard here, and she was his responsibility, as much as any of the animals were. He took that very seriously.

He wanted her to be able to count on him.

Always.

Which meant he needed to work on the self-control. The only thing that kept him coming back to the straight-and-narrow was that clearly she'd been hurt. Some fucker had put his hands on her and terrorized her, and seeing her suffer the aftereffects killed him.

That was not to say that having her sweet, curvy body so intimate with his wasn't having a toll.

It was.

And that toll had kept him up at night. Hell, last night he'd had to get up at two in the morning to abuse himself in the shower.

He probably should have abused himself again this morning just to cover his bases.

Jade's fingers were a blur on her keyboard, but then suddenly she stopped and pulled off her headset. "Twenty-five messages today. Must be Monday."

"Jade, about Saturday night—"

"I never thanked you."

This derailed him. "What?"

She lifted her head and met his gaze. "For spending so much time with me."

"Sure, but I wanted to apologize for—"

"Nothing," she said, shaking her head. "You have nothing to apologize for. It was my fault. I, um, put my hand . . . there, and then it—"

She broke off suddenly, eyes locked on something over his shoulder.

Dell turned around to find Adam standing there, brows up.

"Don't stop on my account," Adam said. "It's just getting good."

Dell blew out a breath and considered killing him but he had patients arriving. "Go away." He turned back to Jade, but she was gone, heels churning up the big reception area as she went to the wall of files and began pulling down the day's scheduled patients.

"So," Adam said, "she put her hand where?"

Two days later, Jade was sitting in Lilah's kennels. They were in Lilah's office, surrounded by Abigail the duck, Lulu the lamb, and several dogs, all snoozing.

It was naptime in Lilah's world.

Lilah and Jade were munching on deli sandwiches, which Jade had brought over to spend her lunch hour with some female company.

"He's going to be back any minute," Lilah was saying as she decimated a pickle, talking about her favorite subject.

Brady, of course.

Dell had been gone all morning with Brady, out on a ranch about a hundred miles east where Brady had flown him, taking care of a difficult high-end breeding mare's birth.

"It didn't go well," Lilah said, patting one of the dogs who lifted its head and sniffed. Twinkles belonged to Brady, but Lilah considered him hers. She handed him a piece of turkey from her sandwich. "In fact, it went awful."

"What do you mean?" Jade asked.

"They lost the mare. She'd stroked out and Dell had to put her down."

"Oh no," Jade breathed.

"The owners were so distraught they couldn't sit with the horse during the euthanization."

"They let her die alone?"

"No." Lilah shook her head and Jade knew. Dell. Dell had stayed with the horse. Jade's throat ached for him because she knew him. He'd have sat on the straw-covered barn floor with the horse's head in his lap, stroking her face and talking to her until she closed her eyes for the last time. It was who he was. "Damn."

Lilah nodded. "Been a long week. How are you doing?"

Jade sipped her iced tea. "Good."

"Good as in 'I don't want to talk about it' or good as in 'good.'"

Jade looked at her.

Lilah looked right back, innocent-faced.

Jade had no idea how Lilah could have heard about her kissing Dell. But she planned to play it cool just in case. "Maybe we should save some time and you should just skip to the part where you tell me exactly what you want to know."

"Okay, well something scared you last week in the parking lot and you've been jumpy ever since."

Not where Jade expected this conversation to go. "Who told you that?"

"Hell, honey, this is Sunshine."

Right.

"And Dell's been teaching you self-defense, and now you're talking about going back to Chicago—which you left to come here because, as you told us, you wanted better skiing in the winter. Now I'm thinking that's not true." She paused, brows up. "How am I doing so far?"

Jade stared down at her turkey on multigrain. "It's . . . complicated."

"Are you okay?"

"I'm working on it."

"Is there anything I can do?"

Again, Jade's throat tightened. She'd lied, omitted, kept a good part of herself closed off, and Lilah didn't care about any of that, all she wanted to know was if Jade was okay. "You're already doing it."

Lilah smiled and offered her some chips. "He's a good man, you know."

"Who?"

"You know who."

Yeah. She did.

"A *really* good man."

Jade nodded. "I know."

"Do you?"

Jade looked at Lilah.

Lilah smiled sweetly. Expectantly.

And Jade had to laugh. "You're fishing."

"Yes," Lilah admitted without shame. "I'm totally fishing."

"Why?"

"Why?" Lilah just shook her head. "You know how insatiably nosy we all are. Something's going on. We just don't know what, and it's killing us."

"There's nothing—"

"Oh, please. If there's nothing going on with you two, I'll eat Abigail."

Abigail the duck lifted her head and looked reproachfully at Lilah.

"Seriously," Lilah said to Jade while patting Abigail on the head. "There's no way it's nothing."

"Based on what?" Jade asked.

"Based on the fact that whenever you and Dell are in the same room, all these little flames flicker between you."

"Flames."

"It's a metaphor," Lilah said.

"For?"

"Sexual tension."

Jade stared at her, then laughed.

"And Adam told Brady he interrupted the two of you in Dell's gym."

"What, is this high school?"

Lilah grinned. "Well, we've all been together that long, so yeah, in emotional years, we're still in high school. You two doing it or what?"

"Okay, wow." Jade shook her head. "We are so *not* going there."

"Please! Oh, please, let's go there!"

"I didn't ask you about your . . . *flames* when you first started circling Brady," Jade said.

"Aha!" Lilah jabbed a finger in Jade's direction, triumphant. "You are! You're circling Dell."

Jade sighed. "Okay, maybe I'll cop to the circling. But that's no secret. We've always circled each other."

"But something's different," Lilah insisted. "I can feel it."

Was it? All her life Jade had been the master at compartmentalizing the people in her life. She'd put Dell in the slot for boss and left him there for eighteen months. She'd been okay with adding him to the friend slot as well, but that had taken him a good long time to earn.

And he *had* earned it.

He was a friend, a good one. She knew he'd give her the shirt off his back without a moment's hesitation. That had made it easier to feel safe in Sunshine, she'd be the first to admit. And she loved Lilah. She loved Adam and the others, too, but Dell . . . From the start he'd been different. Somehow he'd burrowed deeper, gotten past her walls though she couldn't have said how.

Or why.

But Lilah was right—something *was* happening between them. She didn't know what exactly but whenever he was close, her senses went on high alert and she strained to get even closer. When he touched her, her entire body tingled.

She wanted him.

She, who hadn't had sex in over a year and a half, wanted the guy who'd probably had sex last weekend.

It made no sense but in her mind he was changing, becoming something other than just her boss and her friend, something that was both safer and far less safe at the same time.

"Maybe you two can fall in love and get married, like me and Brady."

"Lilah. You know I'm going back to Chicago."

"So? We have the chopper. You'll commute."

Jade stood. "Would you look at the time? I've got to get back to work now."

"Oh, come on, just give me a hint."

"You want a hint?"

"Yes!"

"Abigail just pooped on your shoe."

Lilah was still swearing when Jade made her escape.

The next night, Jade let herself in to Dell's house again. He'd left her an e-mail about another training session and she'd dropped everything to be here.

Everything being season one of *My So-Called Life* on DVD . . .

She found him in the gym, already stripped down to black basketball shorts and a black T-shirt, and she stared at him because he didn't look like her boss. Or her friend.

He looked . . . hot.

He turned and their eyes met. Yearning flowed through her, yearning for a man. This man. She felt silly for staring, but he was staring, too.

"I'm wearing a cup," he said, and she laughed. Tension broken, as she knew he'd intended.

But she still wanted him.

For two hours he reviewed joint manipulation and using an attacker's own weight and momentum to bring him down. It was fascinating but involved close hand-to-hand contact.

Body-to-body contact.

In short, he was all over her, his hands on her body, maneuvering her into place and positions as he worked her hard, harder than she'd thought he would.

Finally she flopped to the mat flat on her back, gasping for air and sweating. "I can't feel my legs."

He crouched at her side, not breathing hard at all, the bastard.

"The least you can do," she said, between gasps, "is pretend to be winded."

"There's no pretending between us, tough girl. If you want to be as good as me, you have to work for it."

She laughed. "Conceited much?"

"No. Just good. Thanks to Brady."

"Did he beat you up until you cried, too?"

"More than once. But you're not crying. Get up. One more time."

She wanted to whimper and curl into a ball. Instead she rolled to her feet.

"I'm going to come after you, right at you," he said, warning her but not babying her. "You know what to do."

She inhaled, accessed all the knowledge he'd given her, and let her brain select one of the judo moves he'd taught her. It was a lot like taking on a charging bull, but she managed to catch him when his weight shifted off his leading foot.

His momentum should have taken him down hard, but he was still better than her, and at the last second he brought her with him.

She landed on her back, with him on top. He lay along the entire length of her, his hands holding her wrists to the mat. Lifting his head, he looked down at her. The raw intensity of his dark gaze spoke to the woman inside of her. The sound of his deep voice was like a caress of warmth against her chilled skin. "Your move," he said.

Thanks to his careful tutoring, she did have moves. She could pick one and be efficient because she wasn't panicked.

Nope. She was something else entirely.

But he was braced, ready for her, and aroused as hell or not, she intended to win today. Hell, every time. So she picked an option that she knew he didn't expect. Using her newfound confidence, she looked into his dark eyes and let all the yearning and heat that had been gathering for months now show in her eyes.

He immediately relaxed, his own eyes softening. "Jade."

It was inevitable, really. They'd been in close quarters, touching and grappling and grabbing. Sweating. It didn't get more personal than that, and another man might have taken advantage of it.

But he'd been careful not to. And he didn't now, either. She waited until he rose lithely to his feet and reached down to pull her to hers. She gripped his hand hard with hers . . . and fell back, into a roll.

Surprised, Dell followed her completely over, and while he was still in motion, she dropped on him and set her elbow to his windpipe.

There was a long beat of silence and then Dell laughed. Jade was still enjoying the sound of that laugh when he abruptly switched their positions, rolling on top of her, once again pinned her down, his face hovering an inch from hers. "Who taught you to fight dirty?"

"You."

He laughed again, kissed her on the tip of her nose, and sprang up gracefully in one smooth motion, pulling her with him. "Just remember that all fights are dirty." He tossed her a bottle of water and grabbed one for himself. "You did great tonight."

"Yeah?" His praise washed through her, warming her from the inside out.

"Oh, yeah." His eyes met and held hers. "I think you're amazing, Jade."

She started to look away but found she couldn't.

"Amazing," he repeated softly, simply, as he moved closer. "Strong as hell. Smart. Brave. Resilient."

She opened her mouth to thank him, but her throat was too tight to speak. Once upon a time her family's approval had meant everything to her, but though they'd always meant well, she'd arrived in Sunshine with no sense of self.

Over the last year and a half she'd started to find herself. The real Jade, and that real Jade wanted to be those very things that Dell had just said: strong, smart, brave, resilient. He didn't use empty platitudes or pretty words, ever. He didn't have to. So when he said something, he meant them.

And damned if she didn't like looking at herself the way he saw her. Damned if she didn't want to be *that* woman. No, he hadn't taken advantage of their closeness. So she would. "Dell?"

"Yeah?"

She tossed her water aside and put her hands on his chest, running them northbound, winding her arms around his neck.

He went stock-still. Well, except for closing his eyes and a sexy muscle in his jaw that bunched tight. "Jade—"

"Shh," she said, watching his lips quirk as she animal-whispered *him* for a change. "Just stay calm, Dell. And keep breathing. This won't hurt, I promise."

He let out a rough exhale that turned into a groan when she brushed her lips against his, once.

Twice.

His eyes opened, dark and intense.

Hot.

One big hand ran down her spine to rest at the small of her back; the other gripped her hip. They were inches apart from each other, sharing air.

One inch one way, Jade thought. One more inch would change everything.

Everything.

She gave a brief thought to stepping back, but it was too late.

Far too late.

So she closed the gap, absorbing the heat of him and the fact that he was so big. And hard.

Everywhere.

She let out a little hum of pleasure at that as she slid her fingers into his hair and drew his mouth back to hers.

Eleven

Dell was lost in the kiss before Jade tightened her grip on him and made a soft, sexy whimper, but when her tongue touched his, desire exploded as the kiss deepened into a hot, intense connection that blew the circuits in his brain.

She moaned and melted into his body, her fingers tightening painfully in his hair. Hell, she could make him bald if she wanted, he didn't care, just as long as she kept on kissing him just . . . like . . . that . . . *God.*

"Dell—"

"I know." He dipped his head and dragged his mouth down her throat, one hand fitting low on her back, the other sliding down her leg, lifting it to his hip so he could grind against her. The insanity continued when she clutched at him and arched closer, as if she couldn't get enough. Her hands were everywhere, running her fingers through his hair, stroking them down his neck, giving him a shiver all the way to his toes. Then she worked her way beneath his damp T-shirt and dug into the muscles there. He was already granite hard when she rocked herself against him. This was because he had no blood left in his head. He sucked in a breath and once again took her mouth with his.

Like a match on dry timber.

Her arms wound around his neck as she went up on tiptoe, molding her body to his. Yeah, God yeah. Her lips immediately parted and her tongue slid to his, hot and wet, and he groaned into her mouth as he stroked up her ribs, his thumbs lightly brushing the underside of her breasts.

Making a low purring noise, she tried to climb up his body. "Dell—"

His answer was to press her up against the wall, dragging his mouth down her throat to taste the pulse racing at the base of her neck.

She moaned and held his mouth to her skin with a hand on the back of his head, again rocking the apex of her thighs into him. He wanted to take her right there against the wall, he wanted that more than he'd ever wanted anything in his life. He sucked in a breath and reached for the hem of her T-shirt to rip it off when he heard someone clear their throat behind them.

Jade went stock-still, and Dell pulled his mouth away and rested his forehead against hers.

"Huh," Adam said behind them. "The hand thing makes a lot more sense now."

Jade tore free of Dell. Putting her hand to her lips, she stared up at Adam, her chest rising and falling like she'd just run a mile. "We—we were training."

The corners of Adam's mouth quirked as he rubbed his jaw, doing his best to hide his amusement. He failed. "Yeah? You could make a million bucks off a DVD of that kind of training."

Dell gave him a shut-the-fuck-up look. Jade moved past them both and grabbed her purse.

"Jade—"

"Sorry, it's late. I didn't realize how late. I've gotta go, I have a thing . . ."

"Jade."

But she was gone and two seconds later the front door shut somewhere above them.

"You are such an asshole," Dell said to Adam, and shoved past him, heading for the stairs.

"Really? Because I'm not the one kissing my receptionist, the receptionist who's clearly battling some demons."

Dell turned around on the stairs and nearly plowed Adam over. Adam arched a brow, silent.

Dell blew out a breath. "You're an asshole."

"Repeating yourself. It's the first sign of guilt, man."

"She's not just a receptionist. She's . . ." More. She was much more to Belle Haven, and it was to his own shame that he'd only begun to realize it as she'd effortlessly taken over the dreaded bookkeeping with seamless ease, freeing up hours a day for him. "And I told you we were training tonight."

"Yeah. You were training real hard." He shook his head. "Do you have any idea what you're doing?"

Dell shoved his hands in his hair. "Does it look like it?"

"You could hurt her." Adam paused. "Don't."

"I—"

"Don't."

"You really think I'd hurt her?"

Adam just looked at him.

Okay, so he didn't have a good track record. Who did?

"Just slow down," Adam suggested.

Slow down? He and Jade had been co-workers and friends for a year and a half already. She was leaving in a matter of weeks. How much slower could they go? He pushed free and took a shower and a drive, and look at that, he ended up at Jade's place. As he got out, he knew that for once Adam's radar was off. It wasn't Jade in danger of getting hurt.

It was him.

An hour later Jade was on her couch. She'd checked her locks, engaged her alarm, fed Beans, and had her *Oceans 11* DVD in and playing. Some people knitted when stressed out over things like kissing their boss. Some people ate potato chips.

Jade watched movies with Matt Damon in them. With the movie playing in the background, she was working her way through her things-to-do-in-her-spare-time spreadsheet. This meant she was painting her toenails, reading the stack of *People* magazines she hadn't yet gotten to, and catching up online with her financial obligations.

All while trying to not think about the fact that she'd thrown herself at Dell.

Because she had.

Thrown herself.

With a remembered groan and a hot blush, she covered her cheeks and closed her eyes. "This is bad," she whispered to Beans.

"Mew."

"I was hoping you'd disagree. Although . . ." She blew out a breath and leaned back. It had felt good to have his hands on her. Really good. And his mouth.

God, his mouth.

It had been too long for her, way too long. Her own doing, of course. For a long time after the attack, she hadn't wanted to be touched. Even though she hadn't been raped, she'd felt a disconnect from others and hadn't wanted physical contact.

Seemed that was changing.

On the coffee table, her cell vibrated an incoming call.

"Darling," her mother said. "You missed your weekly check-in, I was worried."

When Jade had left Chicago, her family had threatened to come after her and drag her back. Lovingly, of course. They had only her best interests at heart, and she'd scared them.

She'd scared herself.

But she'd needed the space and the time, and they'd finally come to an agreement. She would call and check in once a week, and in return, they'd let her be. She called them every Wednesday evening. "*American Idol* isn't over yet. I didn't want to interrupt."

"I don't like the new judges," her mother said. "You need anything?"

This was always the first question asked. Followed quickly by the second: "And are you okay?"

Jade shook her head and pinched the bridge of her nose. "I'm fine, Mom. Really."

"You don't sound it. You sound nasally. Are you sick? If you catch a late-night flight, we could have you taken care of by morning—"

"Not necessary. How's Dad?"

Her mother sighed. "Okay, the same as always, I expect. Stubborn and working himself into the ground, of course. Which means he's overworking himself running the show. And we all know that only speeds up the symptoms of his Parkinson's."

"He's not listening to his doctors?"

"Your father? Hello, have you met him? He knows it all, remember? And we both know there was ever only one thing that kept him home, happy in the knowledge that he didn't have to work every day, and that was you being in the office instead of him. Baby, you know I don't want to rush you . . ."

Jade kept her unladylike snort to herself.

"But you're really coming home?"

Jade closed her eyes. "Yes."

"Have you given notice there then? At your little dog place?"

Jade rubbed her forehead and stared down at her toes. She'd done a damn good job with them if she said so herself, though they needed another coat. "It's an animal center, Mom. We see all animals, not just dogs."

"And you . . . enjoy it. Checking in dogs."

"I know you don't get it, but I've been very happy here."

"In Idaho."

In Jade's mother's opinion, the entire country consisted of three cities. Los Angeles, New York, and Chicago. Anything in between belonged in some alternate universe, Idaho included.

"Idaho is very nice," Jade said.

"So you've said. Why don't I come visit?"

"No!" Jade lowered her voice with effort. "Like I said, I'm coming home."

"Before November first."

"Yes."

"I could help you pack."

Aka call a moving company. "I don't have much to pack."

And she didn't want any visitors here. So far she'd managed to avoid a family invasion by going home to Chicago on the occasional holiday. The last thing she wanted was for them to show up en masse and see her life here. Not that she was ashamed of it. She wasn't at all. But neither was she ready to share this world she'd found for herself.

Still, her mother meant well and missed her, so Jade made nice for a few more minutes, then hung up, feeling the usual guilt wash over her. She put a second coat of nail polish on her toenails and didn't think of Dell or how she'd nearly inhaled him whole.

Much.

And in any case, it was hardly her fault. He'd more than met her halfway, and good Lord Almighty, he was no slouch in the kissing department. She'd nearly gone up in flames for him right there on the mats. One more minute of his amazing mouth on hers and she'd have stripped off her own clothes to get his hands on her.

Except that Adam had shown up.

Again.

She was suspecting a conspiracy but really he'd done her a favor because she had no business starting anything with Dell.

None.

They'd had all this time and hadn't acted on their attraction. And now she was leaving. Getting involved with Dell was out of the question.

Not going to happen. And anyway, it had been nothing but sheer hormones. That's all. And pheromones. And good God, sheer testosterone, the stuff came off him in waves when she wrestled around with him on those damn mats.

"This is why normal people have regular sex," she told Beans. "Keeps them sane. Sane by orgasms."

Beans didn't seem impressed by this kernel of knowledge.

"Okay, so I'm low on self-control," she admitted. "Sue me. But it's his fault—you should have seen him in those shorts, all hot and sweaty and . . ." *Gorgeous.* "Look, all I need to do is . . . not look at him." Ever.

She'd have sworn that Beans rolled her eyes on that one before she leapt to the back of the couch and began to wash her face. "Oh, please. If you'd been standing in front of him, all hot and intent and protective and . . . *hot*, you'd have jumped him, too."

Beans finished her face and went to work behind her ears.

Jade shook her head and set down the bottle of nail polish. She'd had a glass of wine, but she was still unnerved, quivering with tension and unused adrenaline. If Adam hadn't interrupted them, what would she be doing right this very minute? She was picturing it when the knock came at the door; she jumped and knocked over the nail polish. She righted the bottle, attempted to keep her heart in her chest by pressing hard between her breasts, and did the duckwalk to the door so that she didn't smear her toes. She looked through the peephole, then went still.

Dell. He'd showered, put on jeans and a long-sleeved graphic henley that emphasized the chest and arms she'd had her hands all over earlier.

He looked . . . perfect.

She looked down at herself. She wore the oversized Harvard sweatshirt she'd pilfered from Sam years ago, *Toy Story*–themed pajama bottoms. At least she didn't have on her donkey slippers; they were by the couch waiting for her toenails to dry.

Yeah, she was a catch.

When she opened the door, Dell wore a solemn expression—until he took in her pj's.

At that, a small smile crossed his mouth.

She tried to remember if she'd put mascara back on after her shower. She hadn't.

When it became clear she wasn't going to invite him in, Dell simply stepped into her. And dammit if she didn't back up, and then she was watching his very fine ass as it moved into her place.

He stood in the center of her living room and turned to face her. "We have unfinished business."

Twelve

They had unfinished business?

Assuming he meant their near physical miss, Jade hesitated.

With another small smile, Dell shook his head. "I meant your training. You left early."

"Figured we were done."

"Yeah. That got a little out of hand." He paused, but she shook her head.

"If you're going to try to apologize again, don't."

He just looked at her with those dark eyes, and she let out a breath. "Look," she said. "We both know the truth is that I kissed you, so if anyone should be apologizing—"

"I'm not apologizing for the kiss."

"Oh." She blinked. "Then . . . ?"

Instead of answering, he sat on her couch in the same place she'd just vacated and took in the movie playing on the TV, the spread of fingernail polish, the half-eaten bowl of popcorn, the opened laptop.

Too late she realized what she had up on the screen.

He smiled, then laughed out loud, his amusement eradicating the lines of tension in his beautiful face. He leaned forward to read more.

"Hey," she complained. "That's private." She moved toward him to shut the laptop, but he held her off, easily grabbing both her hands in one of his wrists and tugging her down beside him.

"Watch the freshly done toenails!"

He grinned and did just that, taking in the pale blue polish. "Pretty." Then he went back to her screen, reading her things-to-do-in-her-spare-time spreadsheet:

1. Organize junk drawer.
2. Clean hairbrushes.
3. Relax.
4. Don't think about Dell.

Dell slid her a look but didn't point out the obvious, that she wasn't doing anything on her list.

"Cute pictures," he said of the piglet and calf pictures on the other half of her screen. Both were close-ups of two adorably earnest but wary faces. "Friends of yours?"

She sighed. "Yes." When he only looked at her, brows up, she shrugged. "I've adopted them from Adopt a Farm Animal." She tugged her hands free of his and refilled her wineglass.

"You adopted a pig and a calf?"

"It's the late-night commercials. They play sad music and show pictures of abused, neglected animals."

His smile widened.

"They look *right* at you! Oliver, the calf—" She pointed at the picture. "He'd been abandoned and had nearly *starved to death* before he was rescued. And Miss Piggy was heading to the bacon factory. Now I write a check for fifteen bucks a month and they live happily ever after. What's the big deal?"

"Christ, you're cute."

"I—" She narrowed her eyes at him. Cute? "You take that back."

"Okay, you're not cute. You're . . . sexy as hell."

They both looked at her attire and he laughed when she winced. "You are," he maintained.

"You're a very nice man to lie like that." She grabbed the laptop from him, shutting the screen. "And now you'll forget about the fact that I'm so pathetic that I watch DVDs on Friday and Saturday nights instead of going out."

He looked at her for a long moment and she groaned and covered her face. "Don't tell me that's why you're here, that you thought I was feeling . . . vulnerable." She dropped her hands and glared at him. "Because if you say that, I'm going to kick your ass, Dell, I mean it."

Reaching for her wine, he helped himself.

"Say something," she demanded.

"Are you kidding? I don't want to get my ass kicked. And you could do it now, too." He flashed a grin but she just stared at him, deadpan.

He sighed. "I'm not here because I thought you were vulnerable. I'm here because you ran off rather than face the fact that we—"

"Hey. I didn't run off."

"Jade, you left smoke in your wake."

Okay, so she'd run off. Bad habit. "It was just a kiss."

He slid her a look.

"Okay, it was an unexpectedly great kiss."

He nodded. "Yeah." His voice was low and a little rough, and she felt her nipples harden at the sound of it. "Each time gets even greater."

Oh so true. "But we'd be stupid to keep doing it."

"Right." He looked at her. "Why's that?"

"Because . . ." God, his eyes. And that gorgeous mocha skin, sun-burnished and so smooth, except for a five o'clock shadow across his jaw after a long day. She already knew how it felt beneath her fingers, which were itching for another touch. "Because we work together. Because you date like other men change socks. Because I'm leaving soon. Pick one."

"Right," he said, nodding agreeably. "I almost forgot about all that."

She nodded.

He reached out and ran a finger along her temple, making her . . . yearn. She leaned into him and closed her eyes.

"And we're more than co-workers," he said quietly.

"We're friends."

He didn't say anything and she opened her eyes.

"Yeah," he said. "We're friends."

"Friends don't kiss like we did without becoming . . . naked friends."

"And?"

"And you have a no-relationship decree in place. You've told me so yourself. And even if you hadn't, your actions speak louder than words."

"What does a relationship have to do with becoming naked friends?"

Okay, he had her there. There was a silence, and she waited for him to push the issue, but he just started eating her popcorn. Then he took another drink of her wine. "I thought maybe you were upset about something else," he finally said.

"Like what?"

"I thought maybe me touching you brought up some bad memories." His eyes never wavered from hers so when she grimaced, she knew he saw it.

"I . . . No. Not like you're thinking." She looked down at her hands, which twisted together until her knuckles turned white. She hadn't talked about this. She didn't want to talk about this. But she could admit he deserved a few answers. "I wasn't raped."

He covered her hands with one of his as he let out a low breath that had a lot of relief in the sound. "I'm glad. But something happened to you."

"Yes." His skin was warm on her suddenly chilly fingers and she found herself turning her hand palm up so she could hold on. "A long time ago."

"Eighteen months."

She stared down at their entwined fingers. "Eighteen months." She shook her head. "But I'm fine now and getting more fine all the time. I don't need a babysitter, Dell. Or a shoulder to cry on."

"Well, that's a relief. I never know what to do with tears."

Not true. Just this morning she'd seen him holding forty-eight-year-old Missy Robinson, who'd fallen apart in the exam room when he'd had to tell her that her Alaskan husky had cancer. He'd held her for as long as she'd needed, looking devastated for her but perfectly at ease in the role of comforter. "With all those women you date, I'd think you'd have a lot of practice at tears."

She had no idea why she said that. His dating, or not dating, wasn't her concern.

Dell grabbed the bowl of popcorn and the remote and leaned back. "Maybe I'm not quite the hotshot you think I am."

She stared at him. He was good at letting people come to their own conclusions, and he'd certainly never tried to be anything he wasn't. His eyes met hers, clear and warm and open. "What are we doing, Dell?"

"Well, I'm hoping to watch a movie and eat the rest of your popcorn."

"Because . . . ?"

"Because I like this movie and I love popcorn. And because Adam's at my house barbecuing chicken and vegetables. *Vegetables*." He shuddered again.

After *Oceans 11*, they switched to *SNL*. "I bet this isn't how most of your dates end," she said.

He was quiet a moment. "Was this a date?"

She met his gaze. "If it was, it'd be my first since—" She paused. "A really long time."

"How long?"

"Eighteen months."

"How does it feel?"

She thought about it. "Good," she said honestly. "But what about you—"

He put his finger on her mouth. "I'm good, too, Jade. More than good. Don't worry about me." He ran his hand up and down her back until she relaxed again. At some point she realized her eyes were closed and she lifted her head in shock.

She was curled up against Dell's side. He was asleep on his back, one arm around her, his torso rising and falling with his slow, steady breaths, even with Beans sitting on his chest.

"Hey," she said, sitting up and poking Dell in the side.

He mumbled something beneath his breath and didn't budge.

Jade scooped the kitten off of him, set her on the floor, and poked Dell again. "Wake up."

Both arms came around her, snuggling her in close as he pressed his face into her hair. "Mmm. You smell good."

"Dell, wake up!"

His mouth was on her neck now. "I'm awake," he said, and licked the spot he'd just kissed. "You taste as good as you smell, did you know that?"

Then he cupped the back of her head in one big hand and kissed her again, her mouth this time, and she gave herself up to it, to the heat of him, his taste. Their bodies were plastered together and he was rock solid against her, his arms flexed tight around her. "Are you really awake?"

In answer, he tugged her even closer and deepened their kiss, taking his time about it, too, moving slow and almost unbearably erotic against her, his hands sliding under her shirt, his fingertips resting just beneath her breasts. She wasn't wearing a bra, and when he discovered that he lifted his head and looked at her, his gaze sleepy and heavy-lidded, pulling her in, making her want to fall into him and drown.

"Dell." She sucked in an uneven breath, shockingly turned on. "Are you up?"

"Yeah," he said, and pulled her over the top of him so that she could feel exactly how "up" he was. His chest was hard, his abs were hard, his thighs were hard.

Everything was hard.

Her eyes must have gone wide because a low chuckle accompanied the slow rock of his hips to hers. A tug of her hair brought her line of vision up to meet his once more. She quivered and he urged her down to him, and then somehow she was kissing him again. God, she could kiss him forever.

Beneath her shirt, his fingers stroked her skin and she thought, *Up an inch!*, and then in the next beat he'd done exactly that and the desire exploded.

When she came up for air, Dell had one hand palming her breast, his thumb gliding back and forth over her nipple, making her squirm with pleasure. Or maybe that was his other hand, inside the back of her pajama bottoms, gripping a butt cheek, his fingers gliding over the silk of her bikini panties.

She was no better. She had both hands under his shirt, low on his abs, her fingers playing with the loose waistband of his jeans. She lifted her head and looked at him. "There's this thing about sleeping with someone. It creates a false sense of intimacy and leads to . . . things."

"Things?"

"Sleepy sex. It leads to sleepy sex. You know, the kind of sex you wouldn't have if you were all the way awake."

He laughed softly, his eyes black with desire. His hands gripped her hips with a familiar possessiveness that maybe should have turned her off but instead turned her on. From his intense expression she knew that even though he hadn't come here for this, it was certainly what he was going to do. "I don't know about you," he said. "But I don't do a lot of sleepovers period. So this . . . sleepy sex is new for me." His eyes lit. "Be gentle."

His hands went to her hips as he slowly arched into her, making her realize he was still incredibly aroused. "Dell—"

He put a finger over her lips. "We're done denying, Jade." A statement not a question. He let his words hang between them for a long beat, then gently nudged her off of him. He rose and headed to the door.

She stared at him. "Wait—" What? That was it? Dammit! He couldn't leave now, not when she was all hot and bothered! To cover that, she sat up and pulled on her donkey slippers. She needed the armor. "No good-bye?"

Dell was looking hot and bothered, too. And . . . yum. He checked the lock on her door and came back, standing over her. "There's not going to be a good-bye," he said. He pulled off his shirt and dropped it to the floor. Then he covered her body with his, pressing a muscled thigh between hers to spread them, making room for himself. "Not until dawn. Hell, maybe not even then because my first appointment tomorrow isn't until nine."

Oh. *Oh.* She was surrounded by him, a bicep on either side of her face. She could turn her head and press her lips to his flesh and at just the thought she experienced a wave of desire that swamped her. "I have to be at work at seven thirty," she said. "My boss is a real hard-ass."

He smiled. "I could make you forget him."

She nearly climaxed at just the sound of his voice rumbling in her ear. He could make her forget everything, including how he never kept the women he slept with. "Kiss me."

He gave her one last long look before lust completely consumed him and his mouth came down on hers. He devoured her. There was no other word for it. He stripped her out of her sweatshirt and pulled off her donkey slippers one at a time, and she would have sworn he was laughing as he tossed them over her shoulder. But then she slid her hands down his chest, over hard abs and then lower, cupping him.

He stopped laughing.

She outlined him with her fingers, impressed and also a little worried. It'd been a long time, a really long time, and he seemed . . .

Big.

She must have let some of her worry show because he cupped her face and kissed her deep, angling his head to get more of her until she was clutching at him in desperation. Shifting lower, he kissed her jaw, her throat, her shoulder, moving to the swell of her breast.

A slow, warm heat began to fill her, building as he sucked her nipple into his mouth, rolling it between his tongue and the roof of his mouth. Gasping, she arched her back, lifting herself to him.

He smiled as if he'd won a prize and then went back to his diabolical torture, leaving trails of fire on her skin everywhere he touched or kissed.

Which was everywhere.

Her breath was catching with each new caress as she lay writhing beneath him. She needed . . . God, she wasn't even sure, she couldn't think, she couldn't form words, she certainly couldn't stop herself from making sounds she'd never heard herself make before.

But Dell didn't appear to need words or direction. After all, the man made his living reading the body language of animals, and he was reading hers with shocking ease. His hands were on the move southward, caressing her stomach, her thighs, until her pj bottoms got in his way and he tugged them off. Now she was beneath him in just her panties, which he seemed to like because with a hand on each inner thigh, he took a good long look and growled deep in his throat. His fingers played with her through the silk and came away wet, making him groan. The sexiest sound she'd ever heard. The desire she was feeling was bordering on untenable, stronger than anything she'd ever experienced. "Dell—"

"I know." His hands slid down her hips, catching the tiger silk along the way and pulling them down her legs. "Christ, Jade. You're beautiful." He stroked a finger over her, then inside her, and it was all she could do not to levitate off the couch. At that moment she was so far gone he could have done anything, asked anything of her.

But he didn't.

He wasn't taking, he was giving, shifting down her body to do so, pressing his mouth to her hot center, teasing, reducing her to nothing more than a quivering, panting, begging boneless mass. Yes, begging. He had her begging, adrift in the sensations of the rough demands of his tongue, teeth, and hands, which were sending shock waves down her body until she felt her toes curl, until she burst.

Shattered, actually. Breathing like a lunatic, hot, sweaty, desperate, she surged up and undid his jeans and shoved them down to his thighs and found him as impressive as she'd imagined.

They put on the condom together. Or rather, he worked at rolling on the condom while she attempted to help but really was just using the opportunity to stroke and caress him.

He didn't seem to mind, but she wasn't nearly done teasing him the way he'd teased her so mercilessly when he apparently decided the hell with playing and slid into her in one smooth, hard thrust.

The air left her body as she rose to meet him, pulling him closer, digging her fingers into his flesh as he began to move. Mindless, she rocked up into him, the pleasure was so intense, she cried out with it.

How had she not missed this?

But she knew. It was him making her feel like this. No one else but Dell could do it, the way he moved inside her, his muscles hot and tense beneath her fingers, his eyes dark and fiercely intense on hers.

Just looking at him, something in her chest cracked and opened.

Her heart.

It shattered right along with her body as she pulsed and throbbed, tightening around him. He was filling more than just her body and she knew it. God, she knew.

He sped up his pace and she met every thrust with her own startling level of passion. She could hear his ragged breathing in her ear, feel his heart pounding against her chest.

Or was that her breathing, her heart . . . she didn't know. "Dell."

His hands tangled in her hair, pulling her head to meet his mouth. This kiss was rough, demanding everything of her and she willingly gave it. Her hands traveled everywhere on his body that she could reach and it still wasn't enough. She planted her feet on the couch and lifted her hips, pushing into him, doing some demanding of her own.

His control snapped and he thrust into her one last time, taking her right off the edge with him.

When she came back to herself, her heart felt as full and achy as her body. She didn't know what she expected to happen next. She never knew with him. But he stayed deep inside her, holding her tight, his breath warm against her temple. Snuggling in, she let her eyes drift shut as her heart pounded against his.

After a few minutes, he stirred. "You okay?"

"Mmm." It was all she had.

But it was apparently all he needed, because he grabbed the throw blanket from the back of the couch and covered them, then settled them more comfortably and kissed her. "I've wanted to do that for a long time."

"How long?"

"Long."

All the yearning and wanting in the world wasn't going to change anything between them but in that moment, with him holding her close, obviously content to stay here, right here, it was enough.

It had to be enough.

She woke up the next morning from a really great dream and stared into Bean's green eyes.

"Mew," she said. The cat was sharing Jade's pillow.

It was the same story every morning. But unlike every other morning, Jade was wrapped up in another body. A big, warm, mocha-colored hunk of tough muscle that was still deeply asleep.

He'd expelled a lot of energy last night. All night . . .

There was stubble on his square jaw, and his lashes were jet black and sinfully thick.

Definitely not a dream, she thought, and though she had to get up, she took a long moment to just look at him, knowing if she didn't move fast, get out of his arms instead of remaining snuggled in all perfect like she was made for him, it was going to be hard to ignore what had happened here last night.

Real hard.

Thirteen

One minute Dell was deep in the land of the living dead, the kind of sleep that comes after great sex, and then in the next, he was blinking at the sudden light.

"It's time to get up."

He squinted blearily at the woman wrapped in a sheet at the side of the bed.

Jade. Mmm, Jade. She looked good in nothing but a sheet but he knew how she looked even better.

Reaching out, he took a hold of a corner of the sheet and tugged.

There was a female squeak, then the flash of bare ass as she ran for the bathroom.

Grinning he rolled out of bed and followed, but she'd locked him out. "Hey."

"Just because we slept together does *not* mean we're going to share a bathroom," she said through the door. "Go away."

"Jade, I've seen every inch of you. Hell, I've had my mouth on every inch of you. Let me in, I have to—"

She opened the door and came out wrapped in a robe. She looked him over and her gaze softened.

Yeah, now that was more like it. With a smile, he stepped into her, the part of him happiest to see her arriving first, bumping into her belly.

"Oh, no," she said, slapping a hand on his chest. Her other went to his mouth. "No. Don't say or do anything more until I've inhaled some caffeine. I need caffeine." She closed her eyes when he slid a hand down her back to grip her sweet ass. "Dell, help me here. I can't be strong and make the right decision without caffeine."

He sucked on the tip of her pointer finger. "Decision?"

Her fingers began making their way slowly down his chest. "Yeah. The age-old question—round two or the walk of shame?"

He had both hands on her arms now, one working southward to get beneath the robe. "I vote for round two."

"We have work."

"I can hurry." Hell, if her fingers kept on their current southern trajectory, this whole conversation was going to be a moot point.

"I don't know," she said. "You weren't very good at hurrying last night. You took your sweet time, kissing and licking and touching . . . everything." She was a little breathless now.

He liked her breathless, a lot, and with a flick of his fingers, he tugged open the loose knot on the front of her robe. God, there was nothing as perfect as a woman all soft and warm in the morning. Pushing her robe off her shoulders to the floor, he kissed her hard.

"Dell—"

"Your way," he said against her mouth. "Whatever you want, Jade. Take it."

She took the suggestion with a seriousness that made him want to smile. "My way," she repeated, and nipped his earlobe between her teeth before pushing him up against the wall.

"I think I'm going to like your way," he managed as she dropped to her knees.

"That's a safe bet," she murmured.

After Dell left, Jade got into the shower and told herself that what had happened last night—and this morning, good Lord, this morning!—was nothing more than an expression of pent-up lust.

And now that they'd given in to it, it was over and done.

Pent-up lust quenched.

She had no idea what Dell was telling himself, he tended to keep his own council. Although holy sweet Moses, he'd looked knee-knockingly fine in her small shower, bumping those long legs and arms on the tile every time he'd moved. He'd used her soap and shampoo, and now he was going to smell like her all day.

The big Dell Connelly, smelling like peaches and cream.

She dressed and moved through her living room, stopping to stare at the couch. None of the cushions were in the right place. One of the three was on the floor, another upright on the arm, and the third lying haphazardly in the center of the room. The memory of what they'd done there made her flush, and not with embarrassment. She righted the cushions, found a condom wrapper on the floor and then caught sight of herself in the bathroom mirror when she went to throw it away.

Her eyes were bright, her cheeks flushed. Her nipples visibly hard. There were invisible reactions going on, too, and she rubbed her thighs together, feeling that she was damp from just thinking about Dell. *You need to get a grip,* she told herself sternly, and left for work.

Dell's first appointment of the day was with Lilah, who'd brought in a new rescue, a two-week-old kitten. Dell gave the little thing the once-over and pronounced her in decent health for being undernourished and abandoned.

Lilah nodded with relief and hugged the kitten close. "She's so little and yet so tough. It makes me want to keep her."

Dell's eyes drifted out the open exam room door to the front desk, where Jade sat running his world. She stopped typing to gently admonish Beans, who'd just taken a swipe at Gertie's face, then went back to her computer. He wondered if she was making one of her spreadsheets.

And if he was on it. She'd certainly had some Things To Do to him earlier, and though they'd "hurried," he'd still nearly been late.

But not too late for her to stop him as he was leaving and look solemnly into his face. "What just happened between us doesn't change anything."

Actually, it changed everything. "Like?"

"Like no preferential treatment at work from you. And in return, I won't be looking for a ring and a white picket fence."

"Well, that's a relief. I don't like white fences."

"Dell."

She'd been serious, and he could admit a huge relief that she felt so strongly about not getting attached. Getting attached to him was never a good idea. He hurt people that way because he didn't get attached back.

Ever.

He was pretty sure he was missing the attachment gene. Then he realized Lilah had said something to him several times and he'd missed it all. She was now staring at him with open amusement.

"I said," she repeated patiently, "like someone else we know."

"Huh?"

She patted him on the shoulder. "I said Beans is coming along nicely, too. Like someone else we both know." She paused. "She looks good today. Happy."

"Beans?"

"Don't be stupid, Dell."

Right. He busied himself with the chart, knowing *exactly* why Jade was happy. It was called multiple orgasms.

"Probably you never even looked in a mirror this morning," Lilah said, running her fingers through his hair fondly, then giving up when she couldn't get it in any sort of order that pleased her. "But you're wearing a matching expression."

"I'm always happy."

"Not always," she said. "Let's talk about it."

"Let's not."

"Oh, come on! Obviously something's up."

"Your hormone levels. You should have them checked."

She rolled her eyes, then her smile faded. "Seriously, Dell."

"Oh Christ, Lilah. You have a fiancé now. Bug him with this emotional shit."

"You know Jade's leaving." Lilah's eyes held worry, for the both of them. "What's going to happen then?"

"Nothing."

She stared at him. "Nothing? What do you mean, nothing?"

She was the closest thing he had to a sister. Which probably explained the urge to wrap his fingers around her neck. "Does Brady realize how annoying you are?"

"Yes, and he loves me, anyway. Dell, we have to do something."

"We?"

"Yes. Clearly you need my help."

"No, I don't."

"Oh, for chrissake." She clapped a hand to either side of his face and made him look at her. "You get that this isn't just about Jade's issues, right? That your abandonment issues are coming into play here, too?"

He stepped back from her. "What? I don't have—"

"Hello! You were abandoned by your mother, your father, then a handful of idiotic foster care providers, Sol, and every single bonehead bimbo you've ever dated, and now Jade if she really leaves as planned. So yeah. You do, Dell. You have abandonment issues."

Dell looked out the door. No one was paying them any attention but he shut it anyway. "Okay, first of all, my dad *died*. Sol *died*. They didn't leave me on purpose."

"It's still abandonment."

"Lilah," he said, shaking his head. "You're wrong. And I have people. I have Adam and Brady."

"Because they're the same as you, you're just all so frigging stubborn, you stick together like glue."

Okay, *that* might be true. "The women," he said, continuing his defense. "I've always been the one to walk away from any woman in my life."

"Yes. You've made sure of it. Walking the walk, talking the talk, but keeping it all deceptively shallow and casual so that you're alone. You've made sure of it. Because then you aren't going to get hurt."

He stared at her. "If I'm so busy being alone, why are you still in my life?"

"Because I'm a bully." She smiled and hugged him. "Oh, Dell. You've always been there for me, you've helped me so much. I love you, you know."

He sighed. "I love you, too."

"Then, for once, let me help you."

It would be easier to just bash his head in.

She pulled back and looked into his eyes. "Let her in."

He'd deny that as a possibility but there was a problem with that. Because he was pretty sure Jade was already in. All the way in.

In general, Dell was excellent at compartmentalizing, and he could reason and logic away most problems with little trouble. So it was frustrating that he found himself unable to do that with Jade, especially after Lilah's visit earlier. His day ran long. He lost track of how many dogs, kittens, and various other creatures he saw.

Let her in . . .

Dell trusted Lilah, but he wasn't altogether sure she knew what she was talking about this time. Both Keith and Mike had left when Jade appeared in his office doorway. "I need you a sec."

He followed her down the hall to . . . the supply cabinets?

She touched the drug lockup. "I just checked to make sure it was locked up for the night," she said quietly, turning her back to him to stare at the cabinet. "And it made me wonder if I'm better." She put her hands on the locked door and bowed her head slightly. "Do it," she whispered. "Attack me again."

Again? "Jade." Her name felt like it was torn from his throat. "I—"

"Do it!"

There was a terrible pause where he'd have sworn he heard her heart pounding from where he stood. With a sick feeling deep in his gut, he came up behind her just as Adam came into the room.

Jade froze. Dell felt the change in her instantly and glanced at Adam, who stopped where he was.

Jade's breath hitched.

"It's just me," Dell said quietly to her. "You can do this. Remember how I showed you in my gym." He stepped closer, into her space now. A strand of her hair stuck to the stubble on his jaw and then she trembled, killing him. "Jade—"

"Shh." Dropping her head to the cabinet, she spoke to herself. "It's easier in the gym. It's less real."

"We don't have to do this—"

"Yes, we do. Someone's still hitting vet clinics."

At the realization that she didn't feel safe here in his place, a helpless fury rushed him. "Jade—"

"Please, Dell? I want to do this here, in the real world, until I don't want to throw up at the thought."

No one understood that better than him. He wasn't sure exactly what had happened to her, but he was good at guessing. She hadn't fought back and that haunted her. She wanted to be strong. He understood that, too, the need, the passion driving her to make sure she was strong no matter what. So he tightened his arms on her and pressed her up against the cabinet.

She stomped on his foot, plowed her elbow into his belly, and when he bent with an "oomph," she whirled, a pen in her hand, ready to poke him in the eye.

Which, thankfully, she didn't. She dropped it to the floor and stopped short, breathing hard. "Oh God."

"Nice," Adam said, nodding. "Follow up?"

"A knee to the family jewels." She swiped her forehead with her arm. "Drop him like a stone."

"Sounds good," his brother said. "I wouldn't have minded seeing that."

Dell slid his brother a long look and received a rare but genuine laugh. Adam humor.

"I could use a pizza now," Jade said.

Still smiling, Adam raised his hand. "My treat," he said. "Promise to do that again tomorrow and I'll spring for the beer, too."

Two days later Dell was sitting in his office staring at the files on his desk. He needed to work, but he hadn't written a word in ten minutes. For the millionth time, his gaze landed on Jade out in the front room.

He'd thought that her request and his promise to treat her the same at work was just the usual womanspeak for we are now sleeping together so I own you.

But she'd meant it. She hadn't tried to discuss their night or, to his chagrin, repeat it.

She was closing up for the night; straightening the chairs along the wall, talking to Gertie who was padding along after her, then laughing at something the silly parrot repeated as she wiped down the front reception counter with her special antiseptic wipes.

He loved to watch her.

It wasn't just the clothes, he decided, taking in her black pencil skirt and kick-ass heels, the ones that had little bows at her ankles. It was the way Gertie loved her. The way she'd taken on Beans. The way both of them, dog and kitten, followed her around like she was the Pied Piper.

It was . . . well, fucking adorable, for one thing. And for another, he found it hot. Her loving his animals was hot.

She moved back to the computer and sat, staring at the screen, fingers whirling on the keyboard. Her hair was carefully contained and controlled

in some complicated twist up on her head, and her white blouse . . . Christ, had it been unbuttoned that far when she'd first come in this morning? Because damned if she didn't look like every man's secretary fantasy. In fact, just like that, it started to play in his mind.

Slowly she rose to her feet. Licked her lips as she reached up and undid her hair, shaking her head, causing the soft, silky waves to tumble to her shoulders.

Oh yeah.

Nice.

Her fingers began working the buttons on her snug white blouse, revealing a black lace bra beneath which barely covered her nipples and—

"Jesus, where the hell are you, Disneyland?"

Dell blinked at Adam, who'd come and perched a hip on the desk. He stared at Dell with a straight face, but he knew his brother better than anyone on earth.

Adam was laughing his ass off on the inside, the fucker. "Not Disneyland."

More like *Penthouse Forum* . . .

Adam gave a purposeful, knowing look in the direction where Dell's gaze had been fixated.

Jade. Not giving him a naughty secretary striptease . . .

Dell kicked his office door shut.

Adam's mouth twitched and he leaned forward, opening the door again.

Jade glanced over, saw them, and gave a quizzical look.

Adam waved at her.

Jade paused, narrowed her eyes, then went back to her work.

Adam turned to Dell. "This is new, you doing all the mooning. Usually it's the women showing up or calling incessantly. But now it's you. You're the one mooning now." He shook his head. "Poor dumb bastard."

Dell shoved Adam off his desk. "Don't you have something to do to earn your keep?"

Adam smiled. He knew damn well that his business, the classes, the training, the breeding . . . all brought good money into their pockets. "You're pissy. You know what that means? That I'm right."

"Really? You want to go there? Maybe I should get Holly on the line for you. Then we'll talk pissy."

"Hey, at least I'm not changing my MO midgame," Adam pointed out.

"Huh?"

"You let Jade come to your house," Adam explained.

"Yeah. To train her. You'd have done the same thing."

"No, I'd have brought her to the gym in town. But you. You took her home."

"So?"

So they both knew that Jade was the first woman Dell had ever had out there.

"Next thing," Adam said, "you'll start thinking about giving her the key code."

The guilt must have shown on Dell's face because Adam tipped his head back and laughed. He was still laughing when Dell, not liking where this was going, turned back to his work. "Why are you here, anyway?"

"Training."

"I mean why are you *here*, in my office, bugging the shit out of me?"

"Other than it's fun to fuck with you?" Adam shrugged. "Thought we'd get something to eat." He took another peek at Jade. "You figure you know what you're doing? Because both Brady and I have our doubts."

He had no clue. "You and Brady should fuck off."

Adam took one look at his face and shook his head, still amused. "Good to see this on the other foot for a change."

"Shut up."

"I'd be worried about Jade, but you know what? Even with whatever's clearly bothering her, she's still going to eat you up and spit you out."

Dell could get on board with the eating him up part. "What the hell does that mean?"

"Hey, if you don't know, I can't help you." He tapped Dell on the head with his knuckles. "Yeah, still hard as wood. You always did have to learn the hard way." He headed to the door. "My money's on you, though."

Fourteen

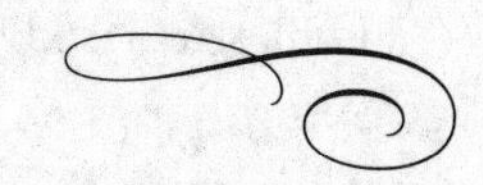

Late the next afternoon, Jade signed in the last patient of the day—Lulu the lamb was by turns sweet, curious, and holy hell on wheels.

Keith had brought Mrs. Robertson and Lulu to an exam room. Jade was at her desk doing the whole wind down for the day when she heard Mrs. Robertson and Dell laughing.

Two minutes later, Mrs. Robertson and Lulu checked out with Jade and left.

Jade turned to her last chore, Dell's laptop. The other day on the helicopter back from a S&R training, he'd made a bunch of notes for her to add to patient files. She'd been asking him to e-mail them to her, but he hadn't, so she'd confiscated the laptop to do it herself.

That's when she found the patient files she'd never seen before, a whole set of them that had never been entered on the books. Frowning, she scrolled through them. Well-puppy and -kitten checks, simple surgeries like neuters and spays, dentistry, vaccinations . . . Confused, Jade searched, but though she found names, dates, and detailed services provided, there was no billing information.

Because he hadn't billed, she realized. Not for any of it.

She went deeper and found that these services occurred approximately once a month and went back years. Thoroughly baffled, Jade went into the back and found Dell in front of the x-ray machine, laughing with Mike, who was cleaning up the equipment.

"What's wrong with Lulu?" Jade asked.

"She ate Mrs. Robertson's birth control pills," Mike said.

"That's not dangerous for her?"

"Not the pills," Dell told her. "But the case is . . . problematic."

Jade stared at Dell. "She ate the case, too?"

Dell smiled. "Yeah but no worries. The x-ray shows she broke up the case pretty good, though. It's going to all come out okay in the end."

Both men cracked up at this. When they'd composed themselves, Mike said good-bye for the night.

Dell surprised Jade by snagging her hips and drawing her in close, gripping her with a protective, possessive familiarity that should have pissed her off.

Instead, her heart stuttered to a stop. She looked down at his hands on her, at his fingers, the ones she'd had on her body all night long three nights ago now, tender. Rough.

Demanding . . .

Tilting her head up, she looked into his face. "What are you doing?"

"Breaking my promise. I'm gonna kiss you, Jade." He flashed her a wicked smile that blew a few brain cells. "Want a breakdown of what happens next?"

"I—" It shouldn't be so sexy when he spoke in that low alpha voice. She lost her train of thought when his hands ran up and down her sides, dangerously close to the swells of her breasts.

"God, I love this top," he murmured, dipping his head to kiss her neck. "And you smell good enough to eat."

"Dell, we're at work."

"When we're not at work, you ignore me."

"That's . . . that's not true." Was it? "You didn't come by or call, either."

He went still and stared at her, looking genuinely flummoxed, as if he was so used to women coming to him that he'd not even thought of it. "You are so spoiled," she said. "And—" Her phone was vibrating in her pocket. She pulled it out, saw that it was her mother, and put it back into her front pocket.

Dell's brows went up.

"It's nothing." But the phone kept vibrating insistently.

Dell slid his hand into her pocket, taking his sweet-ass time pulling out the phone, making sure his fingers brushed against her hip bone, letting his thumb slip beneath the waistband of her skirt to touch bare skin as he looked at the ID screen. "It says *Mom*," he said. "Jade, you can't ignore your mom." Before she could say a word to that, he hit Answer and said "Jade Bennett's phone, how can I help you?"

Jade tried to snatch the phone back, but Dell used his superior height

against her. "Yes," he said very sweetly into the phone. As if he were ever *sweet*. "As a matter of fact, Jade is right here. Hold on a moment."

She snatched the phone. "Mom, is everything all right?"

"Of course, darling."

"Okay . . . but I'm at work, you know that, right?"

"I know." Her mother's voice was clear enough for Dell to hear. "So who was that lovely young man?"

Dell preened.

"Was that your secretary?" her mother asked.

Jade smirked at Dell. "Not quite. Mom, you know that I'm the secretary here."

"Actually," Dell said. "You're more than—"

Jade slapped her hand over his mouth. "Can I call you back after work?"

"Oh, there's no need. Just wanted you to know that I went by your town house today and aired it out for you. I was thinking a fresh paint job."

It was difficult to concentrate with one hundred eighty pounds of solid muscle and testosterone pressing into her. "I just painted it."

"Eighteen months ago. And how about some new furniture? Just yesterday I found this adorable King James end table—"

"Mom—"

Dell made the most of their close proximity and sank his teeth lightly into the lobe of her ear. Desire rolled through her and she barely managed to swallow her moan. Shoving at him, she said, "I don't need new paint or new furniture, but thank you."

"Plants, then. How about a few plants, something to make it homey for your arrival."

"No plants," Jade said firmly, giving up trying to push Dell away as he kissed his way down her throat, his hands gliding up to cover her breasts. Damn. He was good . . .

Her mother gave a long-suffering sigh. "Okay, but new bedding and towels. I'm going to insist, Jade. It'll be a welcome-home present."

"I know you're trying to help," Jade murmured, her head thunking back on the wall when Dell's thumbs rasped back and forth over her nipples. "But . . ."

But she'd lost track of the conversation since only half of her was half paying attention; the other half was now quivering with anticipation of where Dell's mouth and hands would go next. "I don't need a welcome-home present." She felt Dell's reaction to that in the slight tensing of his muscles. "I've got to go, Mom," she said, and slid the phone back into her pocket. "And *that's* why I don't answer my cell when I'm on the job," she said, trying for glib.

He didn't play. In fact, his face was carefully cleared of all emotion. "You wanted to go over something with me," he said.

It took her a moment to change gears—he was much better at it than she was. "I got the files off your laptop." She handed over the computer. "And while I was there, some other files popped out at me. Services you've provided but not charged for."

His gaze flickered, but he said nothing as he took the laptop.

"Do you need help with the accounting?" she asked as Adam came into the back.

"There is no bookkeeping for these accounts," Dell said.

"Pro bono work?" Jade asked.

Dell flicked a glance at his brother, then back to Jade. "Yes. I go out to the Tall Rocks area once a month and give a clinic for the people out there who can't afford vet care for their pets."

"On the Indian reservation there?"

He looked surprised that she knew. "No, just off the reservation."

"If you put it on your books, it's a write-off."

"I don't want the write-off," he said.

"But—"

"No," he said, and walked away.

"Confused?" Adam asked her.

"Yes."

Adam nodded. "It's because you asked him the wrong question."

"What's the right question?"

"Why does he do it?"

Jade looked into the dark eyes so like Dell's. "Okay, why does he do it?"

"Because no matter what he wants us all to believe, he cares for people as much as he cares about animals. It's a pack leader thing. He won't let himself turn his back on anyone in his pack, like it or not."

"But why can't he take the write-off?"

"Not can't. Won't."

"Why?"

"Now that's a far more complicated question," Adam said.

After what had happened against the x-ray machine, and what hadn't happened, Dell made himself scarce the next day. Not hard to do with the schedule they had all morning, which had been double booked because he spent the afternoon out west making ranch rounds. From there he was called to an emergency at Melinda's, which Brady flew him to. When Jade had locked up for the day, it was Adam to walk her out to her car, standing there big and protective, making sure she got off okay. "You have a training session tonight," Adam reminded her.

"Still?" Jade asked. "But isn't Dell—"

"Still."

She went home first and changed. "Men are stupid," she said to Beans.

"Mew."

She sighed. What had she expected? That Dell would stop being Dell? That they were in a relationship?

Of course they weren't in a relationship. She'd made it perfectly clear that she was leaving, and he didn't do relationships, anyway.

Which disturbed her more than it should. But regardless, she drove to his house for her scheduled self-defense session. She walked up to his door and stared at the keypad in indecision. She ran a hand over her clothes. Tucked a strand of hair in place.

Chewed on her lower lip.

She was nervous, which she hadn't been since their first session. But things were different now. They'd slept together for one thing. Before, using the key code to let herself into his house had been . . . a friend move, not a lover move. God, no. He'd never even had a lover here to his house.

And now . . . now she wasn't sure what they were.

The door opened unexpectedly, and she hurriedly pasted a smile on her face.

It was Adam. He stood back and let her in.

"Oh," she said in surprise. "Where's Dell?"

"I'm your stand-in tonight."

She ignored the ping of loss. "You should have told me. You don't have to—"

"Want to," he said. "And don't worry. I'm better than he is."

She smiled, thinking this would be far easier with Adam than Dell, but her nerves only increased as they moved down to the gym.

After her attack, she hadn't wanted to be touched. Dell had broken through that barrier, but that was Dell.

Adam was . . . not Dell.

Okay, so it didn't make any sense, but all she knew was that her feet didn't want to take her to the mats.

Adam stood stretching while she made a big production out of setting down her purse and removing her sweatshirt.

And then another long production of making sure her shoes were both tied tight.

And then double-tied.

One could never be too careful . . .

"Jade." Adam's voice was always low and measured. He never wasted a single word. If Dell was the laid-back, easygoing one of the family, Adam was his virtual opposite. Quiet. Guarded. Stoic. His version of the Connelly Self-Protection Plan.

She sighed. "Yeah?"

Looking at her with steady patience, he gestured to the mat.

She walked onto it.

"You look like you're going to the guillotine," he said, sounding a little amused.

"No, really. I'm fine. Really."

"That was one too many *really*s."

She grimaced and he shook his head. "How about we work on something not physical?"

She let out the breath she hadn't realized she was holding. "Like?"

"Weapons."

She laughed, the tension loosening a little. "Weapons aren't physical?"

"Not like hand to hand is, no. If you have a weapon, you're far less likely to ever be a victim."

"I'm not comfortable carrying a weapon," she told him.

"You don't have to. You can have something that can be *used* as a weapon, something easily and quickly accessible. Get your purse."

She grabbed it and hugged it to her chest.

He gave a little smile. "Don't worry, I have no desire to ever comb the mysterious depths of a woman's purse. Pull something out from there quick, just the first thing your fingers grab."

She pulled out a compact-sized can of hair spray.

"Perfect. If someone surprises you in a parking lot—"

She winced, and he continued on, more gently now. "If someone does, you'll spray him directly in the face. Best if you can get it right in his eyes."

She'd actually done that to herself once by accident and it had hurt like a bitch. But . . . that long-ago night, she'd had her purse and the spray wouldn't have helped her. "If he's got a gun," she said softly with a remembered shiver.

"Then you bide your time to make your move. It's actually hard for an attacker to keep track of everything; the job, the gun, the hostage. When he takes his eyes off you for even one second, you smash the heel of the can into his nose, throat, or against his temple. Whatever's exposed. If you're already down on the ground, go for his foot or kneecap. Groin, if you can reach. Hit hard and don't hesitate. Women hesitate."

She nodded. "No hesitating. Got it."

"Now grab something else out of your purse."

"You don't want to test me with the can?" she asked, surprised. "Dell always makes me try everything on him."

He shook his head and muttered something beneath his breath about his brother being both a softie *and* a sucker. "Hell no, I don't want to test your smashing me in the face with that can. I've seen you beating up the copier. I know what you can do. Pull something else out of your purse."

She stuck her hand back in and this time latched onto a pen. She shrugged in apology.

"No, that's good," he said. "It's pointy."

She stared at the pen. "Yeah. So?"

"So all you have to do is remember that pointy things are more effective on something *soft*. Like the throat, the eyes, abs, groin."

She felt a little sick at the thought of using the pen on a man. "You guys sure are obsessed with your . . . groin area."

"No doubt," he said, sounding amused again. "But you have to be careful. If you use something like a pen to strike at a hard point—a kneecap, for example—chances are that your weapon of choice will just bounce off without doing any real damage, and then you'll have just pissed him off. That won't be good."

When the moment had come for her, she hadn't done anything to protect herself. She'd been too scared, and that was her secret shame—she'd *let* herself be a victim.

Adam's expression softened. "Just remember, something hard like the can goes to bone, pointy goes to soft tissue. It's really as simple as that, Jade. The next time you're walking from point A to point B, just make sure you're holding your keys or a pen or a can of hair spray. Hell, it can be a fucking can of vegetables, it doesn't matter. As long as you're thinking ahead, staying calm, keeping your head up, and being vigilant, you'll never be a helpless victim again."

At the *again* her head came up, but he was moving away, toward the refrigerator to get them each a bottle of water. Grateful he wasn't going to push or ask, she let him talk her into giving the mats a try. They went over some of the other techniques that Dell had been working on with her, but they cut it short because her shoelaces were bothering her.

Aka she wasn't ready to wrestle with anyone other than Dell. Rather than face that, she made an excuse about being tired, and Adam walked her out to her car.

"So," she said, casually as she could, "where's Dell tonight? Still at Melinda's ranch?" Because everyone knew what Melinda and Dell did after a long day on the ranch, and it didn't involve work.

Hypocrite, she told herself. *He and I have the same relationship.* Or they had, for one night . . .

Adam shook his head.

"Is that no, you don't want to tell me?" she asked. "Or no, you don't know?"

He actually gave her a rare smile. "You're too smart for him, you know that?"

"He's on a date," she said flatly, not willing to be distracted, even if he had a pretty great smile.

"Listen, I'm not sure what happened between you two, but—"

"I reminded him that I'm leaving soon," she said.

"Ah," Adam said, nodding. "Well, that'll do it."

"Do what?"

"You're leaving," he said, as if it was the most obvious thing in the world. "Dell doesn't 'do' leaving. At least not anymore. He leaves first. Always."

Fifteen

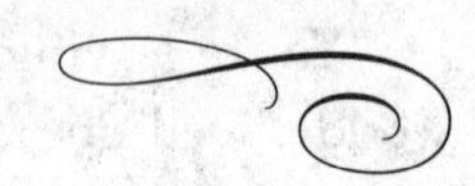

Dell was already back in Sunshine, a hundred miles away from Melinda's ranch. At the bakery, to be exact, eating a half-dozen donuts, because for the third time in a row he hadn't stayed for a date with Melinda.

Although he should make a date—with a shrink.

He wondered what Adam was teaching Jade right this very minute. And if she was wearing that look of intense concentration she got when he was showing her a new move, the one that said she was earnest and serious and focused on kicking ass.

God, he loved that expression.

Adam appeared at his side and plopped into the other chair at Dell's little table. "You're an idiot."

"Aw, thanks."

Adam reached out and snatched an old-fashioned glazed donut.

"Hey."

Taking a huge bite out of it, Adam leaned back. "Don't you want to know *what* makes you a fucking idiot?"

"No."

"It didn't go so well with Jade tonight."

Dell straightened. "What do you mean? What happened?"

"She was nervous about tangling with me on the mat."

"She tell you that?"

"No, she told me that she was exhausted, so we had to stop."

Dell blew out a breath. "I don't get it, she's been doing so well."

"Yes, and this is where the fucking idiot part comes in. She's good with *you* touching her. She feels safe with *you*. What the hell is going on with you two?"

"Nothing. She's leaving."

"Yeah," Adam said. "I got that. But she's not gone yet. You're just backing out of her life?"

"What part of *leaving* don't you understand?" Dell asked.

"If it were me, I'd take every last second I had."

"Yes, well, I always was smarter than you."

"Come on," Adam said, shaking his head. "If this were any other woman, you wouldn't give a shit that she was leaving. It wouldn't matter."

"We work together."

Adam waved this away as inconsequential. "You know what my point is."

"Not really." But Dell did. Christ, he did.

"You going to tell her how you feel about her before she goes, or are you going to be a total pussy about it?"

Telling Jade that his feelings for her had changed, deepened, felt like the dumbest of all the dumbass moves he'd ever made. He didn't want Jade to consider him as her . . .

What?

Christ. "I have to go."

"Shock."

"What does that mean?"

"You're so smart," Adam said, stealing the very last donut as he rose. "You figure it out."

Jade went to the animal center instead of home. She'd been running some accounting reports and wanted to check on them.

Or . . . she wanted to keep herself busy.

She decoded the alarm, flipped on the lights, and sat at her desk, immediately losing herself in the comfort and stability of accounting. Accounting didn't require much. The numbers either added up or they didn't, and the predictability of the work was soothing all in itself.

After an hour, she got thirsty and headed into the staff room for a bottle of water. She stepped into the room and as her hand reached out to flip the light switch on the wall, she heard it.

A loud exhale.

Male.

Panic. Her hand flailed and instead of getting the light switch, she hit the counter. Her fingers wrapped around something and without thinking, she held it out in front of her as a weapon just as a large shadow surged upright at the table in front of her.

"Holy shit," she gasped.

"Holy shit," someone else gasped, and then there was a beam of light that blinded her.

Jade stepped backward, out of the room, then whirled and ran down the hall to the front desk, where she groped for the panic button, which she hit five hundred times in a row.

"Jade?"

She was still hitting the button as she looked up. Keith stood in the doorway wearing nothing but his long hair standing straight up on one side and a pair of Big Dog flannel boxers that said BLOW THIS down the fly. She was so shocked, she just stood there, her finger still on the button.

"Dude," Keith said, scrubbing his hands over his face. "You scared the shit out of me."

Knees wobbling, Jade sank to her chair. "What are you doing here?"

"My roommate got lucky tonight and he made me leave so he could have the place to himself."

"So you were sleeping here?"

He gave her a reproachful look. "*Was* sleeping. Jesus, you are one noisy chick. What were you going to do with that?"

Jade looked down and realized that she was gripping a plastic fork. It had been what she'd grabbed off the counter. "I . . . I think I was going to stab you with it."

"Dude." He scratched his chest. "Gotta piss." He vanished in the back.

The front door crashed open and Dell burst in. Jade stared at him. He stared right back, concern and anger and fear all over his face as he came to her. "Jade." He sounded horrified as he reached her, hauling her up out of her chair and wrapping his arms around her tight. "You hit the alarm? What happened, are you hurt?"

"No, I—"

There was a scuffle of feet in the doorway to the back rooms, and in the same instant Dell whipped Jade behind him. There was a gun in his hand.

A gun.

Keith was in the doorway again, still in his BLOW THIS boxers, holding an opened soda. His eyes went wide at the sight of Dell standing there, gun drawn. "Holy shit," he said in a repeat of what he'd said to Jade, jerking, spilling his soda down his bare chest. "Am I dreaming?"

"I came into work because I knew I wouldn't be able to sleep," Jade started.

"Unlike some of us," Keith muttered.

"And I came in on Keith sleeping in the back room, but before I realized it was him, I'd hit the alarm. I'm sorry, Dell."

He swore and tucked the gun into his jeans waistband at the small of his back. Then turned and hugged Jade in close. "Don't be sorry. You did the right thing."

"It's my fault," she whispered, pressing her face into his chest. His *bare* chest because he was in jeans and an unzipped sweatshirt with nothing beneath it. His athletic shoes were unlaced and he didn't appear to be wearing socks.

He'd been in bed.

Beneath her cheek she could feel his heart pounding hard and fast. She'd wondered what it would take to ruffle the unflappable Dr. Dell Connelly.

She'd found it.

Her.

Her safety. "You have a gun?"

"I get notified at the same time as the police when the alarm goes off. I saw your car in the lot. I thought—"

He'd thought she was in danger.

Still holding her against him, Dell reached into his pocket. "Need to call this in and tell them it's a false alarm—"

Before he could finish that sentence, several squad cars came flying into the lot, lights flashing.

"Dude," Keith said on a sigh.

The next morning, Jade was at her desk staring down at the newspaper. There were two stories of interest. The first one was front page. The guys robbing the vet clinics in the state had been caught in Boise when they'd tried to hit a twenty-four-hour emergency pet hospital. No one had been injured.

The other story was on page three.

> Dr. Dell Connelly's ex-fiancée and receptionist at Belle Haven catches their animal tech Keith Roberts In the Act. Of Sleeping.

Sighing, Jade tossed the paper aside. The police had been quite understanding of the mishap. Keith got over himself. Dell swore he wasn't upset with her, but something had happened.

He'd pulled back. She didn't know why.

After morning rounds, he'd gone into surgery and Jade spent the time reorganizing files and updating inventory. Dell was gone for a few hours, seeing pets at a vet hospital about an hour away. When he called her from there about some records he needed, he sounded perfectly pleasant.

And perfectly not himself.

"Dell," she said after she'd told him where to find the records. "Are you okay?"

"Of course," he said, then paused. "And you?"

An odd longing filled her. A longing for him, which was unsettling. She wanted . . . well, she didn't exactly know.

And wasn't that the problem.

"I'm peachy," she said, and when he'd hung up she smacked herself in the forehead with her phone, castigating herself aloud. "Peachy? You're *peachy*?"

"I think pineapple works better," Adam said, walking through the reception area. "It's prickly." He flashed her a quick grin, making her laugh and shake her head.

"You on for tonight?" he asked.

Tonight was poker night. Dell, Brady, Adam, and Lilah were religious about the twice-monthly get-togethers. Dell hosted them at his place and these guys took their poker very seriously. "Yes," she said. "I'll be there."

"Bring your cash and valuables," he said.

Two weeks ago Jade had cleaned Adam out. He wanted his revenge. "There's going to be an ass-whooping tonight."

"Hmm," she said. "I'll bring my can of hair spray, too, in case it gets ugly."

He reached into the candy jar on the counter that Jade used to bribe little children into behaving. "You can't scare me like you do Dell."

She went still. "Is that what I do, scare him?"

Adam flashed her a look of sympathy that she didn't want. "Jade—"

"No, never mind." Standing, she nudged him clear of her area. "Okay, out you. I have to close up."

He managed to grab a handful of candy before she pushed him away. When she was alone, she looked at Gertie. "Men are annoying."

Gertie cocked her head in agreement, but Jade let out a low laugh. "Oh, who are you trying to kid? The minute he shows his face, you'll drop everything for him. Face it, Gert. You're a Dell 'ho."

Gertie grinned and drooled.

Jade sighed. She was a Dell 'ho, too. She finished closing up and got Beans into the carrier, surprised when she straightened to find Adam back in her space. "You didn't have to wait for me. The bad guys have been caught."

He shrugged. "Humor me." He paused. "And about Dell. He—"

"You don't have to explain him to me." She pointed to a stack of phone messages from the day, which she'd already entered onto a spreadsheet and sent to Dell's e-mail.

Adam picked up the messages and flipped through them. "Okay, Tina's his housekeeper. Shelly's a good friend of mine. She called me, too, wanting to know what to get the man of mystery for his birthday next month. I told her a kick in the ass. Amanda . . ." He lifted a shoulder and stared at that message. "Okay, that's a new one," he admitted, rubbing his jaw. "And probably not worth remembering."

Jade sighed. "She's a drug rep."

"And you think Dell's into her?"

"No," she admitted. "He took her to lunch last week when she drove in from Boise, and since then she's called twenty times, but he hasn't gotten back to her."

"And how many times has Melinda called?"

"Four, and there's two hang-ups, which thanks to the magic of caller ID, are also hers."

Adam just shook his head. "Christ, you two are a pair."

Dell was slumped in his dining room chair as he gathered his cards in. He'd lost.

To Jade.

Fitting, he thought. Since he'd already lost her—a fact that had been slammed home to him last night. Only a few weeks ago, what had happened in the clinic last night would have paralyzed her with fear and insecurity. But the self-defense he'd taught her had bolstered her confidence and given her some belief in herself.

And now she was going to use that newfound strength to leave here.

Great job, Connelly. Well done.

Jade was smiling as she gathered all his nickels and dimes in close, making careful, perfect stacks.

"So you have what," Lilah said to Jade. "A few weeks left?"

Jade didn't look up from her winnings. "About."

"Wish you wouldn't go," Lilah said. "We're going to miss you."

"You're the only one who can keep the knucklehead in line," Adam said in agreement.

The "knucklehead" didn't speak because if he did, it would be to utter the two words that had been stuck in his throat for so long he was choking on them.

Don't go.

"This was always a temporary situation," Jade reminded them softly. "But I'll miss you guys."

"Me too," Lilah said, and pulled Jade in for a tight hug, the full-body kind that only women could pull off. "You're leaving me here with all this testosterone, it's not fair."

"I'll visit," Jade said.

"Promise?"

"Promise."

Lilah sniffed and nodded and then composed herself. Jade did the same. And just like that, it was over and the two of them were smiling again.

Not Dell. He couldn't have smiled to save his life. His throat burned. Fucking burned.

Lilah filled the silence, talking about flying to Chicago to visit Jade and shop, flirting with her husband-to-be, making fun of Adam for losing when he wanted to win so bad.

Brady was just sitting there, clearly enjoying Lilah's antics. Adam was quiet, probably calculating his revenge hand.

"Love how you always kick their asses," Lilah said to Jade. "Promise me you'll fly in for our poker nights once you go home. Brady can get you in the chopper."

Brady nodded his agreement of that and Adam said something about how he'd have to start saving up for that since she kept killing him, but Dell couldn't joke about it. Hell, he could hardly fucking breathe.

And how the hell *she* could, he had no idea.

Two weeks . . .

"My deal." Jade took the cards, shuffling like a pro. "Five-card stud. Deuces wild." She dealt, then surveyed her cards with that same little smile she always gave her hand.

She had a helluva poker face.

And if she'd looked like a naughty secretary yesterday, tonight she looked like a gambler's wet dream. Snug, silky, long-sleeved T-shirt with an equally snug vest that tied up the center into a bow between her breasts.

He wanted to tug on that tie with his teeth.

Her jeans were cut low, and when she leaned forward to collect her winnings or to toss her cards, her shirt rose a little, revealing a mind-melting strip of smooth, creamy skin.

And just the very tiniest hint of twin dimples above the best ass he'd ever seen.

Christ, she was killing him.

He drew two cards and came up with three tens and a deuce. He went all in.

Brady shook his head and folded. "Sucker."

Adam looked pained and also folded.

Lilah grinned but joined Adam and Brady in folding.

Jade pushed her money to the center of the table. She was in.

Dell looked into her eyes, and it might have been just the two of them—except for their audience, of course. The Three Stooges, watching them like a prime-time sitcom.

"You packing any heat?" Jade asked, studying his face.

"A little late to ask," he said. "You're all in."

"In more ways than one," she murmured. "Going to show me what you've got?"

In more ways than one? What did that mean? He revealed his cards. "Three of a kind."

Jade's brows went up. "Nice," she said, but stopped him when he leaned forward to collect the pile.

"Not so fast." She laid her hand out.

Full house.

Brady and Adam grimaced in tandem. Lilah chortled with glee.

Jade smiled and gathered the booty toward her. "You lost, Dr. Connelly. All of it."

Yeah. A feeling he was getting far too used to.

Much later, Dell was alone on his couch. He had his remote in hand, and Gertie doing her best imitation of a lap dog, leaving a good amount of slobber on his thigh.

A knock sounded at his door.

Not Adam or Brady. They'd left an hour ago, and besides, they both had keys and absolutely no care for Dell's privacy whatsoever. They'd just barge in.

Dell glanced at his watch. Two in the morning. Frowning, he shoved Gertie off him and headed to the door, glancing out his living room window as he did.

Jade's car was in the driveway.

What the hell? Gertie peeked, too, and gave a bark of wild enthusiasm.

Speeding up his pace Dell pulled open the door, reaching down to grab Gertie's collar just before she could launch herself at Jade.

"Gak," Gertie said, back paws on the ground, front paws in the air as Dell held her back.

"Were you sleeping?" Jade asked, her hands tightly clasped together. She sent a quick look over her shoulder as if the dark night was unnerving her. "You were totally sleeping, right? Never mind." She started to turn away, but Dell used his free hand to snare his second female of the night, catching Jade in the back of her jacket and reeling her to him. Because it was cold, he pulled both woman and dog into his house and shut the door.

Gertie shoved her face into Jade's palm, blithely demanding a rubdown, which Jade granted. Everyone seemed happy with the momentary distraction, especially Gert. After a moment, the dog shuffled back off to her spot on the couch.

"I—" Jade let out a breath. "I'm sorry if I woke you."

"I wasn't sleeping. I was just sitting here thinking of how broke I am."

She smiled, and he felt the usual reaction in his chest. And south. "Not that I'm complaining," he said. "But what are you doing back here?"

She hesitated. "Remember how when you were a kid and you knew something was a really bad idea, but you wanted to do it anyway, even when everyone from your nanny to your best friend told you it was stupid?"

He'd been moved around too much for best friends. Adam had fit the bill, but if Dell had gone to do something stupid, Adam had most likely been the ringleader. "Never had a nanny."

She nodded with a little grimace. "I knew that. I didn't mean . . . I just . . . The stupid thing. I'm trying to tell you about the stupid thing I want to do."

"The thing your nanny and best friend would try to talk you out of."

"Yes. But they're not here. And you . . ." She shook her head and walked into his living room and looked around.

"Forget something?"

"No, I was just sort of hoping to find your Adopt-a-Farm-Animal type of secret thing you do when you're alone."

"Guys have . . . different alone-time activities than women. Very different."

She laughed and dropped her coat to his couch. Okay, that meant she was staying, for at least a few minutes.

Or maybe not.

He'd long ago given up trying to read her mind. She'd changed out of her gambler's wet dream outfit and was now in a snug black sweat suit. The bottoms were contoured to her body. The hoodie was unzipped to just beneath her breasts and beneath was a lacy white number that fucked with his head. She entwined her fingers and looked at him.

He looked back.

With a sigh, she sank to his couch and patted the spot next to her.

He joined her, trying not to notice that she smelled like heaven on earth or that he managed to sit as close as he could without actually sitting on her. Which made him no better than his own damn dog.

"You haven't been yourself," she said softly. "You know, since we . . ."

Actually, to be technical, it had nothing to do with their night and everything to do with the fact that she was leaving Sunshine. But he had just enough pride to keep his mouth shut.

Barely.

Because if he opened it he'd do it. He'd say it.

Don't go.

So instead he did something even more dumb. He dragged her up against him and kissed her, because he remembered how good she tasted, remembered that soft, sexy as hell little sound she made when he touched his tongue to hers. Remembered what it had been like to be inside her, how she'd felt all silky soft and naked in his arms.

She kissed him back until he was hard with hunger and need, but even he knew it wasn't all physical. There was a deep and overwhelming longing within him, one he'd successfully buried for a long time but he was having trouble putting it away again.

"Dell?"

No. No talking, because he knew damn well the wrong thing would come out.

The begging.

Because God, really? What the fuck did he know about keeping a woman in his life? Not nearly enough to keep Jade with him, that was for damn sure.

Which didn't stop him from pushing her down to the cushions and covering her body with his to kiss her again.

"Aren't you going to ask me what stupid thing I wanted to do?" she whispered.

"Please, God," he breathed against her neck. "Say me."

She bit her lower lip but burst out laughing, anyway. "Dell." She dropped her head to his chest. "This is all your fault. I just keep thinking about our night. I know it was a onetime thing, it *has* to be a onetime thing. I'm leaving, and you don't do more than one night things, and . . ." She lifted her head and looked at him beseechingly. "Can you help me out here? Be the voice of reason?"

"What do you expect me to say, *don't* want me? Are you kidding?"

"Tell me it was bad," she said. "Like . . . *bad* bad. So bad that we don't need to repeat it because it was so *bad*."

Letting out a breath, he opened his mouth.

She nodded, eager to hear what he might say.

"Jade."

"Say it."

"It was bad. So bad we should repeat it to learn from it."

She went still, then snorted. "Way to be strong."

He knew every bit as much as she that this shouldn't happen. It was risking too much. Someone was going to get hurt.

Too late for that . . .

And in any case, he couldn't let her go. In fact, his arms came around her and held on. "Jade, what the hell am I going to do with you?"

"Are you as scared as I am?"

"Terrified," he said. "Hold me."

She laughed but did just that. "You know," she said, mouth against his ear. "Someone once told me that when I'm in an unsure situation, calm assertive dominance is best."

He stroked a finger over her jaw, tucking a strand of hair behind her ear. "You want me to assert some calm dominance now? Over you?"

She shivered and her eyes darkened. "Maybe just this once . . ."

As he went from zero to sixty in less than a second, rising with her in his arms to head for his bed, he had to wonder just who was the one in control.

Sixteen

The next morning Jade slumped at her desk and eyed the clock as she yawned widely. It was only eight o'clock.

She'd gotten maybe three minutes of sleep the night before, and so had Dell. He had to be dragging every bit as much as her.

Bringing up the day's to-do list, she added, *Get a nap.*

Dell came in wearing work boots, low-slung jeans, a hoodie, and an opened down jacket, looking far more like a Hollywood version of the mountain vet than the real thing.

Except the dirt on his boots and the straw on his shoulder and back were real, and so were the shadows beneath his eyes.

Yep, he was dragging as much as she. Only he looked much better while doing it.

He pushed his sunglasses to the top of his head and looked at her, his cheeks ruddy from the cold air, a day's growth on his square jaw.

He'd been riding. She'd seen him out the window tearing across the meadow on Kiwi's back, the man and the horse beautiful in the weak sun that was trying to burn through the fog.

She looked around her for a distraction, but everything was in place. Her pencils perfectly lined up. The files were pulled. Peanut was on top of Jade's printer. Beans was curled up on Jade's lap. Gertie lay at her feet, staring up at her with love and adoration.

None of them needing a damn thing from her, for once.

"You were gone when I got up," he said.

"Had things to do," she said. "The boss is real demanding. I left you a note."

"Yes, thanking me for last night." His gaze held hers. "You sneaked out."

"Don't be ridiculous," she said.

"You *sneaked.*"

Okay, she had. She'd held her breath and slipped out of his warm, strong arms, grabbing her clothes off his floor and dressing on her way to the front door. "Fine!" She stood up and tossed her hands high. "I sneaked out. Are you telling me no woman's ever sneaked out on you before?"

The look on his face answered her question, and with a sigh of disgust, she started to turn away, but he took her by the arms and lifted her up so they were nose to nose.

She wasn't sure where he was going with this, but by the sparks in his eyes she was going to guess maybe some more calm, assertive dominance . . .

Suddenly the door opened and in came Keith, with Mike right behind him. And then Adam. All three stopped short and stared at the two of them.

Dell set Jade back down and she backed away from him, attempting a smile. "Morning," she said, and turned to her workstation. She felt Dell looking down at her but she didn't meet his gaze.

"Is everything okay?" Mike asked.

"Yes," Jade said, and felt Dell move off. She let out a low breath and watched him go, then turned and nearly ran smack into Adam.

He picked up the schedule she'd printed out for him, and studied it. "Going to be a long day," he said.

He wasn't kidding.

At lunch Jade locked the front door after Dell and Adam left for their usual cholesterol overload. She looked around at the empty place and tried to rub the matching ache between her breasts.

She couldn't.

She and Dell had spoken several times since their . . . what had it been, a fight? Not exactly. There'd been no raised voices, no slammed doors, no pouting or brooding.

But things were off. He hadn't laughed when Peanut had announced to a room full of waiting patients that she had a "crush on doc."

He hadn't teased her when she'd brought him the lab reports to go over. He hadn't let his eyes warm when he looked at her. Actually, he hadn't looked at her.

With a sigh, she put in her earphones, cranked her iPod, and turned to the accounting.

Her version of relaxing.

Now that she finally had all the accounts entered, it was sheer joy to balance the numbers out every day, and she watched with great satisfaction as reports ran down her screen.

Pink came on, her voice a gorgeous low, husky rock-and-roll rasp. Jade loved Pink. Pink was strong. Invincible. "You're fucking perfect," Jade sang along with the song, standing up to put more paper in her printer. Fucking perfect . . .

Dell. Dell was fucking perfect.

She couldn't help it, then, the song demanded it. She was already standing so her body moved with the music. It was her line dancing teacher's fault, she used this song sometimes, the PG-rated version, of course. With a little shimmy, Jade whirled and—dammit!—came face-to-face with Dell and Adam.

With a surprised yelp, she yanked out her earplugs and searched for her dignity.

There was none to be found.

"Do you think she was singing to you or me?" Dell asked Adam.

"Me," Adam said. "You're nowhere close to fucking perfect."

Oh God. Jade put her hands to her very hot cheeks.

"You might want to try a dance class," Bessie said, coming through with her push broom. "You're stiff as my broom."

"I'm in a dance class," Jade said.

"Maybe you should get a refund."

"I thought she moved pretty good," Dell said.

Jade would have shot him a shut-up-and-die look, but she was too embarrassed to meet anyone's gaze directly.

"I could teach you some moves," Bessie said, planting her broom right in the middle of the room and giving a little hip shaking boogey that had some parts of her jiggling more than others. Since Bessie was five foot two, both vertically *and* horizontally, she nearly gave herself a black eye, but she looked pleased with herself. "Yeah," she said. "I still got it. I'd show you my never-fail-to-get-me-some move, but the last time I tried it out for Mr. Southwick, I pulled something in my hindquarters. Had to go to the doctor and everything."

Dell grinned.

Even Adam was smiling.

Jade sank to her chair and stared at the phone. Why did it never ring when she needed it to? She did her best to look busy. Busy while sweaty and out of breath. She heard footsteps move away from her and she sighed in relief.

They'd left her alone.

"I like your moves," came Dell's low voice near her ear, making her jump. He put his hands on the armrests of her chair and whipped her around to face him.

"Everyone should dance on their lunch break."

She tried to glare at him but he wasn't laughing at her. His eyes were dark. And warm. "Don't be mad. Seeing you so comfortable here is the sexiest thing I've ever seen."

She gave him a push but she might as well have tried to move a brick wall. "You think everything's sexy."

He shook his head. "I'm pretty sure it's just you."

She hesitated. "Dell, are we okay?"

"You mean because of this morning?"

"Yeah."

"I don't know. Why did you leave like that, like I was your dirty little secret?"

There was something in his voice now. Same tone, but there was definitely something new. Temper, she realized. He was always so careful to show the world nothing but easygoing and laid-back no matter what the circumstances. For some crazy reason, seeing the extra depth went a long way toward defusing her.

Maybe because she knew that if he was showing her his feelings, she meant something to him. "I had to get to work," she said. "That's all."

"Or . . ."

"There's no 'or,'" she said, not sounding nearly as calm as him. She was good at hiding in a very different way than he was.

"There's definitely an 'or,'" he said. "You didn't trust yourself with me."

Okay, now that was annoying. Mostly because it was true. "I stayed all night. I trusted you right through what, a half box of condoms?"

He nodded agreeably, but she had his number now. He was feeling anything but agreeable. "So this is just sex," he said.

She stared at him, unable to believe that this had gotten so off track. "Is it ever anything else for you?"

For a moment there was a sort of horrible beat of weighted, awkward silence, and she'd have given just about anything to take back the words, but Dell let out a mirthless laugh. "Okay, let me get this straight," he said. "You tiptoeing off in the middle of the night is my fault?"

"It was dawn, Dell."

"Fuck, Jade." He pressed the heels of his hands to his eyes. "Uncle. I give up. I can't guess anymore. You're going to have to come right out and tell me."

"Tell you what?" She knew what, she knew exactly what, but she needed to buy herself a second. Or a bunch of seconds.

He dropped his hands to his sides. "What the hell I have to do so that you'll feel safe with me."

"I do!"

"With your body, maybe." He gave a slow shake of his head. "When I'm buried deep inside you and you're panting out my name, wrapped tight around me . . . yeah, you know you're safe with me, then, that I'll take you where you want to go. But any other time it's like pulling teeth to get you to tell me things about you."

Panic licked at her. "You know me."

"Some things, like you snub your nose at almost all crap food—except ice cream. Ice cream you hoard like it's your crack. You like your clothes and yet you don't mind getting animal hair on them. You have to have things in careful order because it makes you feel in control, and yet there's one area you like to be just a little bit messy and unorganized."

"Uh—"

"In bed," he said bluntly. "In bed you don't mind giving up control."

She blushed. "See that? You do know me."

He was already shaking his head. "It's not enough."

"What could you possibly want to know that you think you don't?" she asked.

"Why you're really here. What your life was like in Chicago. What happened to you to make you leave. Why you slowly came to life here, and yet you're still going back."

The little ball of anxiety in her chest, the one that had been there since she'd slept with him and then done something even worse, started to fall for him, grew and spread so that she couldn't breathe. "You say that like you're an open book," she managed.

His eyes never left hers. "I am an open book, Jade. For you. I may be a little slow on the uptake in the emotion department, but you can ask me anything and I'll answer."

Would he? His expression was intent. Focused.

And wrenchingly, bluntly open.

He meant it. She could ask him anything. Like . . . was he falling, too?

Except . . .

Except she wasn't ready for the answer.

"Only you won't ask me anything, will you, Jade? Because you're good with this, just as it is. And hell, why not? It's all I ever do, right?"

"Dell," she said softly in regret. She'd hurt him. She'd never even known she could.

"Give me a few minutes before you let Keith bring any patients back," he said, and vanished into his office.

There was little that got to Dell. Abuse or neglect of any kind. Someone fucking with someone he cared about.

But a woman? A woman hadn't gotten to him in a long time, if ever.

Which was what made the way he felt about Jade so difficult. He'd been waiting for her to make the next move. He'd been waiting for a week now, and he wasn't good with waiting. In fact, he sucked at it, mostly because he'd never done it before.

Adam thought he was an idiot. Dell was leaning toward agreeing with him.

Brady thought he should cut his losses and forget it. After all, she was leaving.

But Dell couldn't fold, not yet. He wanted . . . Christ. He wanted so much it hurt.

And yet it had to be *her* move . . .

It was the end of a very long day. Still in scrubs, he stood at the window watching a storm move in—not nearly as nice a view as the one from his desk if he leaned forward just so to catch a glimpse of Jade—but definitely safer.

Besides, he'd watched her enough today. Just a few minutes ago she'd been checking out Ashes, an Australian blue heeler, who'd managed to stab herself on a low-lying branch in the woods. The branch had caused considerable damage to Ashes, requiring surgery, a drain, and multiple visits. Nick, Ashes's owner, was an out-of-work construction worker who faithfully paid cash for each visit. He'd been standing there meticulously counting out money from his wallet and must have fallen short because Jade covered his hand and shook her head, sending him on his way.

Once Nick had left, she'd gotten up and added three twenties to the cash box.

From her own purse.

Behind Dell, he heard the click click clicking of heels coming down the hall toward him. Jade, of course. And given the attitude in every step she made, she'd discovered what he'd done and they were heading for their second fight in three, two, one . . .

She stalked into his office and stopped, hands on hips, giving him that teacher to errant pupil look that always made him so hot.

She didn't speak.

He could appreciate the tactic but he wasn't in the mood. Besides, there was little he could do to get on her good side now. And it wasn't as if she cared about getting on *his* good side. "Problem?" he asked calmly.

"You know there is."

Her legs looked ten miles long in the skirt she was wearing today, and her cute little boots had given him dirty thoughts all day long. He really liked watching what he'd come to think of as the Jade show. Today, for instance, after getting caught dancing—Christ, he'd loved that—she'd sat at her desk, doing that little OCD thing she did with her pencils, lining them up perfectly, making her lists.

And she was leaving . . .

She ran his office, she managed his life, she made things . . . easy for him. Easy and good.

And in return he'd thought he was giving her something. Stability. Comfort. Safety.

When he pictured his world without her in it, something funny happened inside him.

He went cold.

She held up her paycheck. "This, Dell. This is the problem. My paycheck. It isn't right."

"No?"

"You know it isn't." She set it on his desk, then stabbed at it with her finger, pushing it across the wood surface toward him. "You seem to have given me a raise."

"Are you objecting?"

"Hell no. I've earned it. But double? You nearly doubled my salary?"

She was wearing peach gloss today, and he gave brief thought to yanking her onto his lap and settling this pent-up anger between them in the age-old way of the Neanderthal caveman dwellers.

He wasn't sure why he was giving her this big push now. It felt an awful lot like desperation, a last-ditch effort to see if she'd stay.

"Dell."

"You're doing the work of office manager and full-charge bookkeeper," he said. "I'm just giving you the money that goes with it. You're getting what's fair."

"This is hardly fair."

"No? Okay, how much more do you think—"

"Oh my God, you are the most stubborn-ass, confusing, arrogant man on the planet!"

"So I take it that you're not going to thank me for the raise by having your way with me then?"

She smacked him upside the back of the head with the envelope. Figuring that fighting back was fair, he went with the caveman urge and yanked her into his lap. He slid one hand to the nape of her neck, the other to her waist and leaned in, pressing his forehead to hers. "To first blood or the death?"

"I feel like we've already drawn blood." But she melted into him a little, his favorite ice princess, and for a long beat they just breathed each other's air.

"I know what you're doing," she finally whispered.

"Do you?"

"Yes." She cupped his face. "You're woman-whispering me with the alpha-dog move, touching my neck, pretending to be trying to get lucky to throw me off, but you're really doing the whole calm, assertive domination thing."

"No, the domination thing would be stripping you naked and sprawling you out on my desk so I could—"

"Dell." She shook her head but gave herself away by biting her lower lip and glancing at his desktop. "I can't take the raise or the job."

"You already have the job, Jade."

"But—"

"You're leaving," he said. "Yeah. Believe me, I know."

"Do you? Do you really? Then why haven't you put out an ad for my replacement? I could train them."

Fuck, how he hated that idea.

She sighed and dropped her head to his shoulder. With a sigh of his own, Dell slid his hand down her back for the sheer pleasure of touching her. "Just tell me this. *Why* are you going back? Is it for duty or because you miss your life there?"

"What's the difference?"

"Missing your life is one thing. And a good reason to go. You tell me it's because you miss your life and I'll step back and be happy for you."

"And if it's duty?"

He gave a slow shake of his head. "I don't see how that can be a good enough reason to give up your life."

"And I don't see how that's your call," said a male voice from the doorway.

The guy was thirtyish, leanly muscled, and dressed like he was heading to an A-list event. And he was apparently familiar to Jade because she leapt out of Dell's arms with a surprised gasp.

"The front door was unlocked," the guy said. "But the front desk was deserted, so . . ."

"You're . . . here," Jade said, and walked into his arms.

Dell couldn't see Jade's face, but he could see the guy's as he squeezed Jade, his expression a grimace of relief and love, his hands fisting on her sweater as if he couldn't get enough. Jade appeared to be doing the same and Dell stood, fighting an entirely different Neanderthal caveman dweller urge now.

Jade finally pulled back from the warm hug and smacked the man hard in the chest. "I told you not to come here," she said.

"And I listened. For a year and a half." He tugged on a strand of Jade's hair. "Now introduce me to the man who just had his hands on you and is looking like maybe he wants to kill me."

Jade looked back at Dell, not giving much away. "Dell, this is my cousin Dr. Sam Bennett. Sam, this is Dr. Dell Connelly, my . . . boss."

At the slight hesitation, Sam's mouth twisted into a wry smile. "Interesting inner-office policies," he said directly to Dell, eyes cool in a way they hadn't been with Jade.

"Sam," Jade admonished, and pushed him toward the door. "Wait for me by the front desk." She added a second shove, then when Sam was gone, turned back to Dell. "Sorry about that. He's a little protective."

Dell just looked at her, willing her to talk to him without him having to give her the inquisition, but this was Jade. The Queen of Emotional Fortress.

"I'll see you tomorrow," she said. "Okay? We'll discuss this"—she pointed to her paycheck—"further."

"That's not first on my list," he said.

Her eyes met his and something happened. The air condensed and a fierce hunger gutted him.

Her expression mirrored what he felt and it was staggering. "I won't be here tomorrow," he reminded her. "I'm flying up north for the next few days to cover the ranches I'm under contract with."

"That's right." She nodded. "Monday, then." She started to leave the room, but paused and moved toward him instead. "Dell, I—"

He had no idea what she meant to say. He didn't care. His circuits had crossed and rather than go back to his desk, he reached for her.

She met him halfway and slid her hands into his hair as he hauled her up against him. Their mouths collided in a hard, deep kiss. No tenderness, not an ounce. In its place was a boatload of frustration and aggression, which was working for him until she abruptly pulled away and, with one last look, left him. Dell told himself to get used to it.

But he was starting to think that wasn't going to happen.

Seventeen

Jade cooked Sam dinner that night. She waited until her second glass of wine kicked in to ask. "Why are you really here?"

He smiled at her, as always utterly at ease in his skin. Which, given how handsome he was, couldn't have been too difficult. "Thought maybe you missed me," he said.

"Hard to, when you call me every day."

"Every two days, tops."

She shook her head, having to admit it was good to see him. "You know I'm coming back. You didn't have to show up."

"Sandy crashed the computer system."

"You flew here to tell me that? Aren't you busy? Don't you have any patients to see? Who's in charge?"

"See? We need you." He smiled. "Had frequent-flier mileage and a day off."

"We both know that Sandy's actually more qualified than me," Jade said. "She's a CPA." Sandy had been promoted from accounts manager, where she'd worked only part-time because she liked being home with her kids.

Everyone was happy with her work performance, though Jade's family complained that she had the personality of a pencil. "There's no way she crashed the computer system."

"Okay, she didn't," Sam admitted. "But she did leave coffee rings on your desk. Your pencils are homeless. And she doesn't use spreadsheets. She scribbles her notes on sticky pads and slaps them everywhere. It's raining yellow sticky notes."

Jade opened her mouth, then shut it again. "Some people don't find spreadsheets all that effective."

There was a beat of disbelieving silence from Sam on this. "Okay, who are you and what have you done with my favorite cousin?"

"Your only cousin."

"Jade."

"Sam."

"I mean you didn't even comment about the pencils. The pencils, Jade, are all over your desk every night. There's no organization. And she's not filing daily either, she's—"

Jade tried to ignore the pencils, but it took an embarrassing amount of effort. "I *am* coming back, Sam. By the first, as I promised you."

He was quiet a minute, his gaze reflective as he looked around at her loft. "But you're happy here."

She paused. "I am."

"You look it. You look good, Jade. Not like your old-self good but different good. Maybe even better good."

She didn't know what to do with that so she picked up the wine bottle and refilled both their glasses.

"You going to ever tell me about him?" Sam asked quietly.

"Who?"

Sam gave her an impressive eye roll. "The guy who had his hands all over you who."

"He . . . I . . ." She blew out a breath and shook her head. "No." Dell was hers, and maybe she'd blown it with him in more ways than one, but if nothing else she'd forever have the memory of how he'd given her life back to her.

"He means something to you," Sam said.

He meant everything to her. "How do you know he's not just a wild fling?"

"You don't do wild flings. You don't do anything without your entire heart and soul."

"Yeah, well," she said, "do me a favor and don't let that secret out of the bag."

Sympathy and worry filled his eyes now, and he opened his mouth, but she jabbed a finger in his direction. "Don't do that. Don't suddenly start feeling bad for badgering me to come back."

"If I badgered—"

"If?"

"Okay, *when* I badgered, it was because I thought you were alone. I didn't want you to be alone."

She sighed. "It's a done deal. I've given notice to my landlord."

"And your boss?"

"And my boss," she said as evenly as she could, ignoring the little pang to her heart at the thought of leaving Dell. "But this was always a temp position. A service will fill it for him with no problem."

"But—"

"No. No buts. And no second-guessing or regrets. If there's one thing I've learned, it's that neither of those things does anyone any good."

On Sunday, Jade took Sam to the airport and went into work. She did that sometimes, went into the office to catch up on paperwork or clean up. She couldn't help herself. She went straight to her desk, pulled up her to-do-at-work list and got to it.

One of the things she wanted to do before she left Sunshine was upgrade Dell's computer system, so that things would run smoothly when she was gone. It was a perfect day for it, so she called Dell's cell just to make sure he wasn't going to be trying to access the system remotely.

When he answered, he sounded breathless and in a hurry, and then she remembered: he was still up north.

Melinda's ranch was up north.

"Connelly," he said again.

Clearly he hadn't looked at the caller ID. Jade paused, thinking about all the reasons why he'd be breathless and too harried to look at the screen. The number one item was because he was in Melinda's bed.

In Melinda.

God. A root canal without drugs would be preferable to this, and her thumb hovered over the End button.

"Hello?" There was some rustling noise, then, "Jade?"

Great. *Now* he looks at the ID screen.

"Jade, you there?"

"Yes." She winced. "Listen, sorry to interrupt. Forget I called." She disconnected and tossed her phone into her purse. From the depths, it began to vibrate so she grabbed her entire purse and shoved it into a drawer where she couldn't hear it anymore.

* * *

That night, Dell and Adam were sparring in Dell's basement gym. They were going at each other street style, no rules, fighting dirty.

It suited Dell's mood. He'd been gone for three days, attending to his ranch accounts, working around the clock. He'd been getting in the chopper with Brady when Jade had called and then hung up on him. There'd been something in her voice that he hadn't liked, but she'd ignored his subsequent calls. By the time he'd gotten back to Sunshine, she was nowhere to be found. He'd tried the office, her place, Lilah's . . .

Finally, he'd left her a "Jade, call me now" message, born out of sheer frustration.

She hadn't called.

He and Adam were pretty evenly matched until the sound of soft footsteps coming down the stairs caught Dell's attention. He turned his head to see Jade in a fuzzy sweater, gauzy short skirt, and those boots of hers that always corroded all common sense. He opened his mouth to greet her and found himself eating the mat. When he could gasp some air into his lungs, he rolled to his back.

Adam was gone.

Jade was on her knees at his side. Actually, there were two Jades.

No, three. Dell closed his eyes. "Where did he go?"

"Home. Said he didn't want to embarrass you when you tried to retaliate and got your ass kicked for the second time."

Jesus. "I'll kill him later." With care, he got to his knees and then stood up, pulling her with him. No way in hell was she getting away. "Want to tell me what that was about earlier?"

"No. I want you to show me that move. The one Adam just flattened you with."

"Well, I wouldn't say flatten exactly. I—"

"Show me."

"It's a rough one—"

"Show me."

He showed her. He had to do it several times, it was a complicated move. Each time she hit the mat and was slower to get up. "Jade—"

"Again."

Determination and grit blared from her every pore. No fear, no hesitation, just as he'd taught her himself. So damn if he'd tell her she'd had enough. They went over it again.

And again she landed on her back. But this time she stayed down, eyes closed, face pale and damp.

Goddammit. Dell swore and dropped to his knees at her side, planting a hand on either side of her hips. "Jade. Jade, talk to me, are you—"

With both hands she pushed hard, right into the crook of his elbows.

With a surprised "oomph" his arms collapsed and he fell over the top of her. "Christ, Jade. I'm sorry, I—"

She brought her knee up. Not hard or fast enough to hurt him but only because she held back. Purposely. Protecting the goods, he pressed her flat, holding her there with his body and regarded her warily. "You're mad at me."

"Well, give the doctor an A plus."

Yeah, she was right. It had taken him long enough. Slowly, aware that she could absolutely unman him if she wanted, he pulled back and sat up. "What did I do?"

"You're breathing, aren't you?"

He paused. "Is this about the other day at the center? Because you're the one who said that this was just sex," he reminded her grimly.

She narrowed her eyes.

No, not about that. Apparently he was the only one brooding about that. Pretty fucking pathetic given that the just sex thing had always been his own MO.

"This isn't about the other day."

He mentally hit rewind on the past few days. He'd flown up north. Worked his ass off. Stayed in a hotel with Brady, which had pissed off Melinda, but he hadn't wanted to be with her. Not that he could explain why when she'd asked. Hell, he couldn't even explain it to himself. Being with Melinda had always been great. Fun. Easy. No strings attached—his favorite way to have sex.

But when she'd leaned in to kiss him, he'd yearned for a different set of arms and a touch that turned on his mind as well as his body. "Jade, you're going to have to give me a hint."

"Okay, you're spoiled and egotistical and annoying." She fisted her hands in his shirt. He figured she was going to shove him farther away but she hauled him back down over her. "And you're an orgasm hog."

He choked. "What—"

"Yeah. And I really, really, really want to hate you, but I-can't. I'm going to settle for intense dislike."

He shook his head, trying to loosen some reason, because either he'd had his clock more royally cleaned by Adam than he'd thought, or she'd gone off the deep end. "I'll cop to the spoiled, egotistical, annoying accusations. But back to that orgasm thing—"

"God, you are such a . . . *guy*! That's all you heard, right? Orgasm? I mean you *just* slept with Melinda and you still—"

"Okay, whoa." He shook his head and laughed. In hindsight, that might have been a mistake because Jade turned wildcat beneath him. He actually nearly lost his grip on her because she and that damn effective knee nearly took out his entire future line of Connellys. "What the fuck, Jade."

"You're the one who keeps telling me to hit the groin area. I've never had angry sex, but I want to have it now."

He shook his head, trying to both focus and hold her down at the same time. Not easy. Good to know he'd been successful at teaching her to fight. He might have taken pride in that except he was very busy trying to protect himself and not hurt her in the process. He shoved a leg between hers and she countered by wrapping one of hers around his waist to try to roll him. He could feel every inch of her plastered up against him. If he wasn't so confused, he'd be turned on as hell.

No, scratch that. Even with the confusion, he *was* turned on as hell. "You think I slept with Melinda . . ."

"I don't care." She was breathing heavy, still struggling beneath him. "You don't do relationships, so why should I care?" She nipped his jaw with her teeth, eyes hot and clearly pissed off, which for some sick reason really worked for him. "Jade—"

"Don't talk. There's no talking in angry sex."

Right. Because angry or not, this was just sex. But then she squeezed his ass at the same time she bit his lower lip, and his dick bypassed his brain, going instantly hard as a rock. "Jade, I'm all sweaty."

"Don't care about that, either."

He felt like he'd been clubbed over the head. Everything about her said Furious-but-Aroused Female and while he stared at her, suddenly so turned on himself he could hardly breathe, she hauled him down to her and kissed him, shutting down the rest of his remaining operating brain cells.

Eighteen

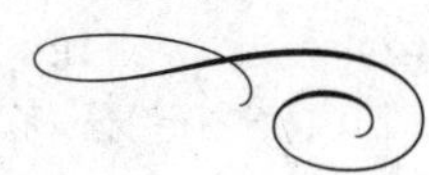

Jade hadn't come here for this, for Dell's amazing mouth on hers, his hands on her body, the rough rumble of a very sexy, very turned-on man as he tried to eat her alive.

Oh, wait. She totally had.

Maybe after three long days of stewing about some of the things they'd said, on top of months and months of denying her feelings for him, all while pretending that what was happening between them wasn't really happening, her body had taken over her brain.

And though she'd been the one to instigate the kiss, Dell had certainly taken over, capturing her lips in a long, deep sensual kiss that had melted all her bones. She was still flat on her back on the mat with him holding her down when she heard herself moan. He straightened his arms, pulling back an inch to stare at her.

She wasn't sure what he was looking for, but evidently he found it in her expression because then he was kissing her again; hot openmouthed kisses along her jaw to her neck.

She moaned again and gripped him tighter, shifting her head to the side to give him better access, which he took, nibbling at the base of her throat before sucking the skin there into his mouth. It was as if he'd pulled a cord weaved through her very center and her hips thrust against his.

"Not here," he said, voice rough, his mouth never pausing in its quest, moving along her collarbone now. "Not on the mats. I need a shower, and we're going to take our time. *Not* here," he repeated.

"*Here.*" Her fingers slid into his hair to direct his face back to hers. "Now. Right now, you . . . you—"

"Orgasm hog?" he offered.

"Why are you still talking?" she asked, tearing at his shirt. She could hear the need in her own voice and didn't care, didn't care about anything other than getting him inside of her.

He made a noise deep in his throat and came up on his knees to yank his shirt over his head, tossing it aside.

God, he had a beautiful body. While she was admiring it, he shoved her skirt up.

"My boots," she said.

"The boots stay." Still on his knees, he tugged the straps of her bra to her elbows and watched as her breasts popped out the top of her demi-bra. "You are the most beautiful thing I've ever seen," he murmured hoarsely, taking her in from messed-up hair to boot-covered feet.

The words shouldn't have moved her. This was nothing more than a mutual satisfying of needs. Not emotion-based. *Need*-based. But she shivered with desire. "Why are you still talking?"

"I can multitask." He stroked a finger over her lace panties. "So demanding on the outside, so tough." He slid his finger beneath the lace, unerringly finding the exact spot to have her writhing beneath him. "So soft and creamy on the inside."

She made a sound that revealed her desperation, and he lifted his intense gaze from what he was doing to look at her. "Be sure, Jade. Because once we get on this train, we're riding it home."

"Do I feel like I'm not sure?"

"Fuck, no. You feel ready for me. You feel amazing." Leaning over her, he kissed her hard and deep, then pulled back to look at her sprawled out beneath him, then swore reverently beneath his breath. His body was hard all over and she wanted him. Tired of thinking, she planted her feet on the floor, knees bent, and grinded shamelessly against him, drawing a groan from him.

Good. Rearing up, she licked her way over a pec, flicked at his nipple, and headed downward, nibbling at his six-pack abs. Loving how unsteadily he was breathing, she pulled at the drawstring of his shorts and dipped her hand inside.

She didn't have to reach very far to wrap her fingers around his silky hard length.

He groaned and she watched the muscles of his abs contract as she tightened her grip and stroked. Then she tugged the shorts to his thighs and leaned in to tease him with her tongue.

"Oh Christ," he gasped. "That's good." His hands went to her hair and tightened for a minute, his head falling back on his shoulders.

But then he pulled free.

In one smooth motion, he rose fluidly to his feet and grabbed her up in his arms.

She wrapped her legs around his waist and lifted her head for a kiss. Holding her up with a hand on her ass, the other still in her hair, he started moving.

Up the basement steps.

Through the kitchen.

Up another set of stairs.

Into a dark room and then . . .

A bathroom.

"Condoms," he said, and plopped her on the counter. He yanked open a drawer and then another, swearing as he rifled through them.

"Why aren't they by your bed?"

He glanced at her. "I told you, I don't bring women here. And while we're talking again, I didn't sleep with Melinda. Haven't in months. Haven't slept with anyone but you. So really, if anyone's been an orgasm hog, it's you. If you go by sheer ratio, anyway . . ."

She stared at his broad back as he tried his last drawer, swearing roughly as he emptied it out on the counter. Comb, deodorant, new toothpaste . . .

Box of condoms, unopened.

"Thank Christ," he said fervently and tore the box open. Grabbing one, he turned to her, reaching out as if to pick her up again, probably to take her to his bed.

She didn't want that. That would be personal. That would be lovemaking, and she'd come for sex.

Angry sex. Because she'd been so angry. Or hurt. Actually it was some terrible combination, but he kept defusing her without even trying. Dammit. Dammit, how was she supposed to hold on to her temper with him? And she *needed* to hold on to it, needed that badly because with angry sex, she couldn't mistake this for anything else. Or so she hoped. So she snatched the condom from him. Hands freed, he used them on her, gliding them up her torso to her breasts. Her nipples were still peeking out of the demi-bra, and he bent and kissed her right nipple, then drew it into his mouth, sucking until she clutched at him.

He kissed his way to her other breast.

Her head fell back against the mirror, her body humming with need. "Dell," she said, her boots clunking against the cabinet below.

He ran a hand down her leg to her ankle, lifting it so that the bottom of her boot rested on the countertop, effectively opening her to his gaze.

Stepping back, he looked his fill and groaned again, then grabbed her hips and rocked into her. At her needy whimper, he slid a hand across her belly and then beneath her panties, expertly stroking her with the callused pad of his fingers before moving one into her. She heard herself cry out and bit her lip.

"No," he said. "I want to hear you." He scraped the lace to the side to watch as he teased her slippery folds until she writhed and cried out again.

"Yeah," he said. "Like that. More, Jade."

"In," she gasped. This wasn't like her. She didn't sit naked except for boots on counters with her legs spread, she didn't demand sex, she didn't talk dirty, but she couldn't stop herself. Not with Dell. "I need you inside me," she said. "I need you in me now."

But he wasn't done with her yet because first he drew the agonizing torture out until her toes curled, until sensations were flowing through her hot, heavy body, until she was an inch from bursting. Then he replaced his fingers with a most impressive erection, pushing into her body inch by delicious inch. When he finally began to move, she gave herself over to the pleasure.

God, the pleasure. "*Please.*"

"Anything, Jade. Anything you want."

"You." It was all she could manage as he changed the angle of his penetration, making her gasp and clutch at him. "Just you."

He began to move, one hand gripping her bottom, the other sliding between them, using his thumb to apply exquisite pressure on her swollen flesh.

It sent her skittering right off the edge, crying out his name, barely conscious of the fact that he followed her over, gripping her in his big hands as he came hard, grinding his hips to hers to savor the last of the pleasure.

When she came back to herself, she realized she'd snuggled into his arms, her face pressed to his throat. He was nuzzling her hair, his breathing as ragged as hers. "You okay?" he murmured.

Still unable to speak, she settled for nodding. But her head was spinning. Because that? That had been a hell of a lot more than angry sex. "I need some room."

"Why?"

"Because I'm still mad at you."

"You're still mad at me?" he repeated, clearly baffled by this.

She sighed. "You didn't sleep with Melinda," she explained.

Dell lifted his head and blinked once, slow as an owl. "So you were mad when you thought I slept with Melinda, and now you're mad because . . . I didn't?"

She hopped off the counter. "I have to go." She adjusted her bra and panties and looked around for her clothes, remembering she'd left them in the basement.

Great.

"Jade." He blocked her exit. "What the hell are we doing? Tell me what's going on."

Admit that she'd done the unforgettable and fallen for him? No thank you. "Move, please."

"No."

Fine. He wasn't going to let this go so she searched her brain for a plausible lie. "I wanted to give you your messages."

He looked at her. "Try that again, your left eye twitched."

"So?"

"It always twitches when you lie."

Dammit. She put her finger to her eye.

"Jade."

She blew out a breath. "You already know."

"Tell me, anyway."

"Fine, but it's not pretty. I thought you were having sex with Melinda. And . . . I turned a ridiculous, ugly shade of green."

He went brows up.

She tossed up her hands. "And even though I told myself that was great, that you could do whoever you wanted, I kept picturing it . . ." She closed her eyes. "And I got . . . I don't know."

"Green."

"Yeah." She covered her face. "Maybe."

He pulled her hands down. "Green looks good on you."

A terrible confusing combination of annoyed and amused, Jade walked out of the bathroom, cursing herself for having to make the walk of shame through his entire house for her clothes. She couldn't find her shirt fast enough, so she grabbed his.

"You don't have to go," he said as she shimmied back into her skirt.

"Yes, I do."

Because it was getting harder and harder to hold her heart from him. In fact, if she kept this up, she knew she wouldn't be able to do it at all.

"Jade."

Throat tight, eyes burning, she turned back, then gasped softly as he cupped her face and kissed her. If he'd kissed her long and deep, she might have been able to resist, but he was far more devious than that. His mouth was devastatingly gentle. Tender. A sweet good-night kiss.

But not a good-bye kiss.

Oh, damn, she thought when he pulled away and walked her out to her car. Damn. She was in big trouble.

The next day Jade got out of bed before dawn. Actually, to be exact, it was four thirty A.M. It wasn't a time she'd seen often and she yawned more than once on the drive.

She'd watched the calendar and told herself she was merely indulging her curiosity, but she knew it was more than that.

Much more.

She pulled back onto Dell's street less than seven hours after she'd left and saw that his truck was still there. Finding it unlocked, she sighed in relief and climbed in to wait. Ten minutes later his front door opened. It was still dark, but she could see his outline as he headed for his truck carrying what looked like grocery bags and his medical bag.

He stopped short, presumably at the sight of her car. Then he turned to his truck. She gave him a little wave.

He walked through the dark, foggy, chilly morning, stowed his stuff behind his seat, and angled in behind the wheel. "You didn't want to stay last night, so what's this?"

"You said I could ask you anything, that you're an open book."

"Yes," he said, with a great deal of wariness.

"Where are you going?"

He paused. "If you're asking, you must already know."

"All I know is that every Monday, you start about a half hour late. And until I got my hands on your laptop, I had no idea why. But you're going somewhere and providing your services to someone, a bunch of someones, who clearly mean a lot to you. I figure it can't be too close or you'd just have them come to Belle Haven. So I got here extra early just in case."

"Jade, why does this matter to you?"

Because you matter . . . "You said you wanted to get to know me. Maybe I feel the same."

He studied her a long moment, then shook his head but started his truck.

They drove for an hour straight out into the middle of nowhere before Dell turned off at some invisible landmark, because Jade sure as hell didn't see a sign. Or even a road. He switched into four-wheel drive and kept going.

"Getting nervous?" he asked when she white-knuckled the dash over a particular bad rut.

"It has occurred to me that out here would be a great dump site for my body." The next rut nearly rattled her teeth right out of her head. "Probably I should stop watching *Criminal Minds* before bed, it makes me see a serial killer in everyone."

"I know something else you could do before bed . . ."

Yeah, yeah.

He flashed a grin in the rising dawn. "You know, you hopped into my truck. I didn't coerce you."

"My mistake."

After another ten minutes, they began to pass some signs of civilization. Mobile homes and trailers, each more run down than the last. He parked in front of a double-wide with bars on the windows and turned to her, smile gone. "You can wait here if you want."

"Are you going to tell me what this is about?"

"I told you. Pro bono work for people who can't afford pet care."

She knew there was more, it was in every line of his body, but he said nothing more, just grabbed his black medical bag and got out. He waited for her, and together they walked to the trailer.

It was that brief beat of time between dark and dawn. Purple and pink light hovered in the air, made evanescent by a low-lying fog.

The door to the trailer opened before Dell could knock, revealing a woman somewhere in her fifties. She had dark skin, dark eyes, and dark hair streaked through with silver. She took a look at Dell, then Jade, and arched a brow.

The movement, the subtle, almost wry surprise, was so instantly recognizable to Jade that she almost gasped.

The woman was clearly related to Dell.

Stepping back, she allowed them access without a word.

Dell set his hand on the small of Jade's back and urged her into the trailer. He didn't introduce her to the woman. In fact, he pretty much dismissed both of them and walked through to the small living area.

There, lining a bench, sat a small crowd, each person with an animal.

Dell sat at a nearby table, opened his bag, and pulled out his laptop. This he thrust at Jade. Apparently, she was going to make herself useful.

The first patient was held by a ten-year-old girl with jet black hair and matching eyes. Clutched in her hands was a skinny, scrawny cat, both looking terrified.

The woman who'd answered the door smiled at the little girl, nodding encouragingly.

The girl shuffled closer.

"Hi, Lakota," Dell said to her. "How's Duncan doing?"

Lakota didn't speak, she just nodded. Dell gently took Duncan from her and gave him an exam. "He's asthmatic," Dell said in a low voice to Jade, gesturing that she needed to take notes. "Lakota found him a few months back. Note that there's still no weight gain. Heart rate, one eighty; respiratory rate, forty-eight breaths a minute. No heart murmurs and his abdomen palpates normally, but he's dehydrated." He looked at Lakota. "He needs to have more water. You need to make sure it's always available to him. You've been giving him his meds?"

When Lakota nodded, Dell rummaged through his bag and brought out a small pill bottle. "Here's what he'll need until next time."

"Dell," Jade said softly. He couldn't give a minor meds like that, he . . .

Once again the older woman stepped forward and put her hands on the girl's shoulders. And that's when Jade saw another resemblance—they were mother and daughter. Jade glanced at Dell, who was looking at her, eyes as dark and silent as his family's. Jade sat back, sorry she'd started to speak, even sorrier that she'd doubted him. Bowing over the laptop, she went back to note taking.

Two hours later, Dell had seen the last of the people waiting and he was stuffing his instruments back into his black bag.

Jade shut the laptop and stood. On the walk outside to the truck, Dell shook his head. "I can't believe you Dell'd me."

She had. She totally had. "I'm sorry."

He shook his head. "Don't be. I'd give these people whatever they needed, legal or not."

She stared at him. He was utterly serious. Before she could ask him why, the door of the trailer opened behind them.

The woman, whom Jade now knew was named Nila, came out.

Nila's gaze met Jade's. "Thank you," she said.

Jade stopped, surprised. She glanced at Dell, who was still walking. He hadn't stopped. "For what?" she asked the woman.

"For coming out here, for giving back to people that most others have forgotten about."

Jade looked at Dell, who was at the truck now, then back to the woman. "I didn't do much. It's all Dr. Connelly's doing."

"Yes." The woman nodded, without looking at him. "But he won't take my thanks."

Jade nodded at her and got into the truck. They had an hour before their first patients at Belle Haven would arrive, and she figured they'd just make it. "You were amazing back there."

Dell put the truck into gear and began the considerably rough drive back without a word.

"That woman . . ." Jade turned in her seat to watch Dell's reaction. "Nila. She's related to you."

They hit a rut and she nearly kissed the windshield. Dell stopped the truck and turned to her, tightening her seat belt.

They were on the move again before he answered. "Yes."

Jade drew a breath. "She's your mother."

"Birth mother."

Jade nodded. There was a difference, of course. A birth mother was exactly that. The giver of life but not necessarily the caregiver. "Why did you bring me?"

A very small smile came into his eyes. "You hijacked my truck."

"You could have told me to get out."

"Jade, has anyone ever successfully told you what to do?"

"No," she admitted.

They were quiet a long moment, then Dell let out a long breath. "You wanted to know me. I'm not sure why that means something to me, but it does. So I brought you." He glanced over at her. "I can count on one finger the number of people outside of Brady, Adam, and Lilah who have been inside my home, who have unlimited access to my computer, who know what I do every Monday morning for a woman I shouldn't give a shit about."

Her breath caught. "Me."

"You." The sun slanted in, blinding them. He put on his sunglasses. "You're in. As in as you can possibly be. Your turn, Jade."

Nineteen

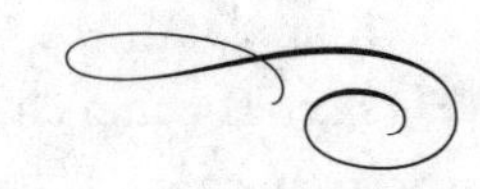

Two days later, Jade had lunch with Lilah in town at the bakery, where they stuffed themselves with turkey and cheese croissants. Lilah was entertaining herself by turning her ring finger to and fro so that the sun coming in through the window hit the diamond just right and glared into Jade's eyes. "How do you get any work done if you're staring at that thing all day?" she asked, slipping on her sunglasses to keep from being blinded.

"It takes concentration, believe me." Lilah grinned. "Hard to believe, right? That Brady and I live together now—*and* I still love him."

Jade tried to fathom it. Living with a man. Letting him see the morning routine. Having to share closet space. Needing to consult someone when she ran out at midnight because she had to have ice cream.

"You ever done it?"

"Live with a man?" Jade shook her head. "Nope."

"Is there someone back home, waiting on you?"

"After a year and a half," Jade said lightly, "I'd have mentioned it, don't you think?"

Lilah shrugged. "You're pretty tight-lipped."

"There's no one."

Lilah tilted her head. "So you and Dell . . . ?"

"How did we get on this subject?" Jade asked. "We're talking about you, sharing your space with a man. And how does that even work, anyway? What happens if he leaves the toilet seat up? Drops his tighty-whities on the floor? Eats your emergency stash of ice cream?"

"Brady doesn't wear tighty-whities. Sometimes he doesn't wear any underwear at all."

There was a beat of silence as they both contemplated that image for a moment.

"And if he eats my ice cream—and he does—he buys more."

"Are you telling me he has no bad habits that drive you nuts?"

Lilah laughed. "Well, he's a man, isn't he? Of course he drives me nuts. He's stubborn as a damn mule, he thinks he's always right, and he hogs the remote."

"So how are you going to live with that for the next sixty years?"

"Buy another TV."

Jade stared at Lilah. "I'm serious."

"So am I," Lilah said.

Jade must have looked confused because Lilah patted her hand. "You do realize that none of those things are deal breakers, right?"

"How do you know?" Jade asked. "Maybe a year from now, you'll—"

"What? Get tired of the way he looks at me as if I'm his entire life? Get over the fact that for the first time ever, someone wants me for me? That the man somehow actually enjoys making me happy?"

Jade stared at her. "The ice cream . . ."

"I'll buy a lifetime supply of ice cream. Hell, I'll even pretend he's right some of the time . . . it's worth it. He's worth it. And you know what? So am I." Lilah popped her last bite into her mouth and pointed at Jade. "And so are you." She pointed to Jade's plate, and the half of her croissant still sitting there. "Now see, that's why you look so hot in all those pretty clothes of yours. You have self-control. Too much even."

"I'm taking a line-dancing class. If you think I have too much control, you ought to see me on Wednesday nights."

"Yeah? Any cute guys in it?"

"Not that kind of lack of control. I didn't know how to dance before. So I'm pretty much winging it."

Lilah was looking at her with approval. "You're trying to learn how to have fun."

"Yes."

"Maybe you should take Dell with you."

"Dell doesn't need to learn how to have fun. He invented the word."

Lilah gave her a little smile. "You of all people shouldn't let his protective shell fool you. You're smarter than that."

Jade let out a breath. "You know he does pro bono vet work every Monday?"

"Yes, and I know he didn't tell you that. He doesn't tell anyone."

"I went with him."

Lilah's brows shot up so far they vanished into her hair. "You went with him?"

"I just showed up at his house in the morning and got into his truck. He had no choice."

Lilah laughed at that. "Honey, that man has all the choices in the world, and all the brawn. Believe me, if he didn't want you to go, you wouldn't have. He must have needed you there."

Now it was Jade's turn to laugh. "Need? Dell doesn't need anyone."

Lilah was shaking her head. "He might like to think it—all three of them do. But it's not true. Brady realized it with me. And someday Adam and Dell will know it."

"Know what?"

"That needing someone isn't the same as being weak. That they can still be big and bad and strong and still lean on someone. You're that someone for Dell."

Jade's heart stopped. "Lilah, I—"

"I know." Lilah covered Jade's hand with her own. "You're leaving. I don't want you to. I've been trying not to say that because you have to go back, I get it. But I'm sick over it, and if I feel that way, I can only imagine how Dell feels."

"I've got a temp service on standby and the front desk running like a charm. Anyone can take over, they'll be fine."

"You know damn well that's not what I'm talking about."

Brady walked through the door juggling two hot dogs and a large soda from the convenience store up the street, tailed by Dell and Adam. Dell was also armed with crap food, but Adam strode directly to the bakery's front counter.

Adam was the only one of the three who cared in the slightest about what he put into his body.

"He's going to order tea," Lilah murmured. "That man is hot, but he doesn't know much about how to eat."

Brady's gaze went directly to Lilah, and he gave her one of those smiles that told the whole world they'd very recently been naked together and were planning on getting that way again as soon as possible.

Dell was on his phone, but his eyes tracked to Jade in a way not all that different from Brady, and her pulse kicked up. Brady had already dragged a chair to the table and was kissing Lilah hello when Dell kicked another chair over. He glanced at Brady and Lilah kissing like their mouths were fused and something flickered in his gaze.

Jade wasn't sure what he was thinking, but she knew what she was thinking. That the intimacy between Brady and Lilah was so easy and real. Which stirred up a surprising twinge of envy.

A woman came into the bakery and saw Dell. "Finally," she said. "I catch up with you."

He looked up and gave her an easy smile. "Stacy."

Stacy was a petite, curvy brunette in jeans, boots, and a broad smile. "I wanted to tell you that Trickster's feeling so much better. We appreciate your house call the other night. I'm just sorry you had to leave so fast. Was everything okay with the emergency call?"

Brady and Lilah were preoccupied with something on Brady's iPhone. Jade tried to busy herself with her own cell phone, but her ears weren't on board with that plan and she eavesdropped shamelessly.

"Yes," Dell said. "It's handled."

"I was thinking maybe you could come back out tonight," Stacy said, hunkering at his side, giving him a nice view down her top. "My kitty needs a checkup."

Jade, who'd just taken an ill-timed drink of her water, choked.

Dell slid her a glance and she went back to studying her cell phone, like *look at me, I'm just sitting here working . . .*

"Tonight's not great," Dell said to Stacy.

"Oh. You working?"

"Teaching a self-defense class, actually," he replied, and this time didn't look at Jade at all.

"After, then."

Dell didn't say anything. Clearly taking that as agreement, Stacy leaned in even closer and whispered something in Dell's ear, and though Jade nearly fell out of her chair to try to catch it, she couldn't. Whatever it was, he had no reaction at all as Stacy sashayed out of the place, taking one last look over her shoulder at him.

Jade rolled her eyes and stuffed the rest of her croissant into her mouth in three bites, not even tasting it. Which meant that on top of being inexplicably irritated, she was also going to have to work out to lose the extra million calories she'd just consumed.

Lilah was helping herself to Brady's soda. "Was Lulu delivered to the kennels while I was gone?"

"Yes, and Dell had just come by to get me. She was very happy to see him, so happy that she ate one of his socks."

Dell pulled up the leg of his jeans. He had only one sock on.

"Sounds like she thinks she's a goat."

Brady leaned back in his chair, tilting it so that he was leaning against the wall as he grinned. "Turns out lambs don't recognize calm assertive. All they want is something to eat." He tugged a strand of Lilah's hair fondly. "Saw that new puppy you rescued. Cute little guy."

"Yeah, but I think I've given everyone in town a puppy by now. Not sure who I can get to take him."

"You've never given Jade a puppy," Brady said.

"That's because Dell's her puppy."

Brady cracked up. Dell kicked the leg of Brady's chair, almost toppling him over.

Brady dropped his chair back down and looked at the soda, which had spilled on his chest. "You do know I can still kick your ass, right?"

Dell leaned close to Jade, slipping his arm around her. "I have a kick-ass partner now. You can't take us both."

"I knew it!" Lilah grinned, pointing at them. "You're an 'us'!"

"Hey, man, this was a clean shirt," Brady grumbled, swiping his chest with napkins.

Lilah smacked him. "Did you not hear?"

Brady lifted his head. "Hear what?"

Lilah ignored him, looking between Dell and Jade. "So what is this? What does this mean?"

"It means that I can finally kick Brady's ass," Dell said. "With Jade helping me."

"And . . . ?"

"And we'll take Adam, too. Just on principle."

Lilah sighed. "One of these days you'll admit it."

Jade didn't look at Dell, because she knew better. She knew that while sometimes she and Dell were indeed an "us"—like when they were working or possibly naked—most of the time there was no "us."

They both wanted it that way.

Besides, Dell wasn't interested in an "us" and even if he was . . .

You're leaving . . .

She kept forgetting that one pesky little thing. And maybe she kept forgetting because at some point she'd started thinking about not leaving . . .

Twenty

At ten o'clock that night, Jade answered her door to Dell. She had *The Notebook* on pause on the TV and a half-empty box of tissues on the coffee table. "Dell?"

He narrowed his eyes. "What's the matter?"

"Nothing."

He pushed past her and entered her place. "Well, come right on in," she murmured.

He turned back to face her. "I thought you'd come over for some gym time but you didn't show. And you've been crying."

"I'm watching *The Notebook.*"

He looked confused so she filled him in. "A go-to sob movie."

"Why would you have a go-to sob movie?"

Clearly the man had never felt the need to just cry. "Never mind. And I didn't come over because I thought you'd be with Kalie."

He looked even more confused than before. "Who?"

"Kalie, Cara . . . whatever her face, from the bakery earlier."

He pinched the bridge of his nose and studied his shoes for a long moment but apparently no wisdom was forthcoming on how to deal with Crazy Females. "I'm not sleeping with Melinda."

"You've said."

"And I'm certainly not sleeping with Stacy. There's only one woman in my bed." He stalked toward her and hauled her in against him so hard the air escaped her lungs. "Her name is Goddess Jade, and she's got my full attention."

Her heart stuttered in her chest and her hands slid up his chest.

"So now if we're clear on that," he said, forehead to hers, "let's move on to the next portion of the meeting."

Her heart, her traitorous heart, took a hard leap thinking maybe he was going to say that he'd changed his mind about relationships and he wanted one. With her. "Which is?"

"Your to-do list." He lifted her off her feet and started toward her bed. "I know I'm on it, I put myself there. Now I'm adding you—" He broke off because his phone was vibrating between them. With a low oath he stopped, read the text, then swore again. "It's Adam. One of his clients has a dog in labor. She's in trouble and on the way to the clinic. Adam's two hours out."

"So more angry sex is off the table?"

"I wasn't angry," he said.

"Then what kind of sex were you hoping for?" she asked, grabbing her coat and purse as they moved in tandem to the door.

"I was wide open," he said as they made their way down the stairs and into the night. "Maybe boss-and-naughty-secretary sex?"

"Seriously?"

Unembarrassed, he shrugged.

She was quiet a moment, considering as they walked to his truck. "There's always doctor and nurse," she heard herself say.

He slid her a wicked bad boy smile as he opened his passenger's door for her. "You want to play nurse?"

"Oh no. I get to be the doctor. *You'd* be the nurse."

He tipped his head back and laughed, and she found herself grinning. *Grinning.* "So that works for you?" she asked. "Being the nurse?"

"For you, Jade, I'd be anything you want."

If only that were true . . .

An hour later, Dell was sitting on the floor in the surgery suite next to a large open box. Inside was Rose, the laboring golden Lab with the bad timing. Adam was on his way in, but for now Dell's only assistant was Jade.

She sat on the other side of the box, stroking Rose's face.

Rose lay quiet, her sides rising and falling quickly with her restless panting, eyes closed. She was clearly having contractions, readying her body for the pushing. Dell was waiting for her to start licking herself, a sign that birth was imminent.

Rose's owner was Michelle Eisenburg—the woman whose son had inadvertently caused Jade's parking lot breakdown all those weeks ago now. Dell had promised he'd take care of Rose as if she were his own, and sent her home to relieve the babysitter.

"You know," Jade said. "I've been here a year and a half and I've never seen puppies delivered." She shook her head in the quiet room. "I've never even had a puppy."

"Ever?" Dell asked.

"My mother's allergic. I sneaked a puppy in once, kept her for a week before my nanny ratted me out. I was grounded for a month."

Dell ran his hand down Rose's side, gauging her breathing, her contractions, as always fascinated by these little peeks into Jade's childhood, which were like fairy tales compared to his growing-up years.

"What about you?" she asked. "Tell me about your first dog."

"Bear." He closed his eyes, remembering. "Adam and I found him when he was nothing but a few days old, blind, starving." Just a tiny handful of skin and bones, he'd been filthy and mewling. Dell had taken one look at the newborn puppy and had one thought, that it was even more pathetic than him. "We were living with our dad, then," he said. "My dad said the thing would die that night, but it didn't." Bear hadn't died the next night, either. Dell had nursed him back to health. "He grew into this huge mutt who took up more of my bed than I did."

"Aw. You saved his life."

"Yes. And then he saved mine several times over, so we were quite the pair."

"He saved your life?"

Dell gave a mirthless smile. "I was a sickly, skinny ten-year-old, and far too dark-skinned for the very white neighborhood we lived in. Bear proclaimed himself a brother-in-arms. He once scared off three kids who tried to drag me into an alley."

She was smiling. "Good. Did Bear live to a ripe old age?"

Dell bent over Rose. "I don't know. We had to give him away when we went to the first foster home."

"Oh," she breathed with a world of empathy in her voice. She slid a hand to his back, and then she set her head on his shoulder. "I hate how bad things were for you, Dell. I hate how hard your life was."

"It's not hard now."

He felt her smile against him and wanted to turn and pull her in close.

"Dell?"

"Yeah?"

"Do you ever think about what would happen if I stayed?"

He went still, something kicking in his gut hard. And if he was being honest with himself, it was both hope and fear. "I didn't know that was an option."

She shrugged but was just as still as him, as if she was waiting for a certain reaction from him.

But which reaction exactly, he wasn't sure.

Then Rose whined and began to rustle frantically around, staring wide-eyed and terrified up at Dell. He rubbed her sides. "First one's coming."

Jade straightened but kept her face averted. Still, it didn't take a genius to tell that his nonreaction had been the wrong one. "How can you tell?" she asked.

Rose grunted, and the first puppy slid out.

"Well, that's a clue," she said.

Dell waited to see if Rose would lick and tear the amniotic sack off, but she seemed confused and unsure so Dell gently tore the membrane and allowed the fluid to be released. Rose dutifully took over bathing the newborn with her tongue while Dell tied off the cord and made sure the puppy was breathing.

Things moved quickly after that. Three more healthy puppies in a row, and then one that wasn't moving. Dell wrapped the puppy in a small warmed towel and dried it aggressively, trying to stimulate it so it would cry. Crying was the natural way to clear the mouth and trachea of amniotic fluid.

But the puppy didn't draw air.

"Oh no," Jade breathed, leaning over him. "Is she going to make it?"

Dell worked the puppy for over a half hour, but it was no good. There was no heartbeat. And when Rose started to push again, he set the wrapped stillborn down to help her.

Twenty minutes later, Dell had helped extract all the stragglers. One by one he and Jade dried the pups with sterile towels, cleared their mouths, and set them back next to Rose to keep them warm. When Rose was alert and starting to nurse, Dell went to his office to call Michelle and fill her in.

By the time he finished and went back to check on Rose, it was nearly four in the morning. Not sure where Jade was, he picked up the stillborn and moved out the back door to sit on the top step with her, staring out into the black sky.

Adam showed up with a quiet greeting for Jade as he leaned over her and looked into the box. The corners of his mouth quirked at the blind, soggy puppies nuzzled up against Rose. His sharp, dark eyes counted them up. "Six."

"Seven. We lost one."

Adam let out a breath, barely discernible, but she was learning to read him now. Grief for the one they'd lost.

"Where's Dell?" he asked.

"He went to call Michelle."

Adam was quiet a moment, stroking Rose. "He takes it hard. Losing them. Always did."

"He feels things," Jade said. "Deeply."

"Deeper than the rest of us. Always did that, too. Along with the whole saying good-bye issue."

Jade met his gaze. "Good-bye issue?"

"Doesn't like 'em. In fact, he'll go out of his way to avoid them."

"Meaning?"

"Love isn't real, at least not the kind you get from people. Never get too close, leave 'em smiling . . ."

She inhaled. "But leave 'em."

He nodded. "So you do understand him."

All too well. But there was something in Adam's voice she'd never heard before.

Protectiveness.

Dell might be a grown man, but Adam was the older brother, if only by two years. "He has seen more than his fair share of good-byes," she said softly. He and Adam both had.

"And he makes sure to say them first if he can," Adam said. "But the animals are different. He'd never leave an animal first, never."

"He doesn't blame himself, does he?"

"Not for the animals, no."

Jade stood up and brushed off, wanting to go find him. "Are you saying he blames himself for all the human good-byes in his life? None of them were his fault."

Adam lifted a shoulder. "You know that self-blame isn't logical."

Yes, she knew. She knew exactly. She'd been blaming herself for a year and a half for the attack that hadn't been her fault.

"Our dad died in a car accident on the way to a job he hated with a passion but kept to provide a roof over our heads. Sol died while riding broncos on a day that Dell had missed his competition. Then I left him to go off to the National Guard because there was nothing other than jail in my future if I stayed. And you—"

"That's all ridiculous," she said. "Not a single one of those things were his fault. And me . . ." She wasn't sure she'd ever heard Adam string so many words together at once, but when he did, he packed a punch. "What about me?"

Adam didn't answer.

"He's not blaming himself for me leaving," she said slowly. "I was always going to go."

Adam just looked at her from those dark, dark eyes.

She stared at him some more, feeling her heart quicken as she took in everything that he wasn't putting to words. "I'm not abandoning him. We're not . . . He and I . . ."

One of the puppies mewled and Adam stroked a finger over the tiny body, whispering something softly to it until it stilled.

"I mean, it's not like we're . . ." Jade broke off.

"You're smart," Adam said in the same soothing voice he'd just used on the puppy. It was shockingly effective. "You'll catch up eventually."

Oh God. She was pretty sure she'd done that now. Just because she and Dell had never put a label on their relationship didn't mean that it didn't exist. Of course it did. True, it was different from any other relationship she'd ever had. It was also true that there'd never been a man in her life who could drive her crazy in one moment and then make her tremble in the next like he could. He was her best friend. Her lover.

And she was desperately afraid he had become much more than that.

But just because *she* understood that didn't mean he did. "He doesn't do relationships," she said. "You know that." And she was discovering something that she hadn't known about herself—she liked him too much to do anything less. Too bad she had no idea what to do with that.

"So you really are going."

"I always was." What she didn't say was that her own reservations about leaving were keeping her up at night. But given Dell's reaction—or lack of—to her trying to talk to him about it, it didn't matter all that much. "It's not like I'm suddenly abandoning him because we didn't work out. We did work out, as much as he allowed us to. We both knew this was coming." She stood up. "I'm going to go find him."

He wasn't in his office or anywhere that she could see, but the back door was ajar. She found Dell on the top step in the dark night, his big body hunched protectively over a small, still bundle in his hands.

Heart squeezing, she sat at his side. "Hey." She nudged him gently with her shoulder, and he nudged back but said nothing.

"Rose is okay," she said quietly.

"Good."

"And now I'm wondering about you. Are you okay, too?"

"I just always take a minute with them. Afterward." His voice low and a little raspy, like it hurt him physically to lose any animal, no matter how short a time he'd known them.

He hadn't taken his hands or his eyes off the carefully wrapped puppy, and Jade couldn't take her eyes off of him. Without being consciously aware of moving, she scooted closer, setting her head on his shoulder.

For a moment he didn't move, then slowly he shifted and leaned into her. She slipped her arm around his waist and he shifted even more, turning into her, pressing his face to the crook of her neck.

She went still as her heart squeezed. Always it'd been him offering her comfort, safety, whatever she needed, but now for the first time he was taking those things from her.

She didn't dare move, not even when her toes and fingers and nose and nipples got so cold she could no longer feel them. In fact, she wanted to never move again. She wanted to preserve this quiet closeness between them that felt almost more intimate than when they'd been naked.

But Dell pulled back and straightened. "You're frozen. Get back inside."

He was already regretting the brief moment of weakness. If she wasn't still so touched that he'd trusted her enough to see it, she'd have rolled her eyes at the utter manness of the move. "Dell—"

"I've just got to take care of her first, then I'll be right behind you." He stood and pulled her up.

"Need help?" she asked, knowing what he'd say even before he shook his head with a quiet thanks and vanished.

She went back inside, looking around at the animal center that was as much a part of him as any of his long, perfect limbs. It was a visceral reminder how much more than a good-time, funny, charming guy he was. He had this huge capacity to care, and something else, too.

He hadn't just picked a job for himself the way most people did. The way she had. He hadn't let other people's wants and goals guide him.

The way she had.

No, not Dell. He'd instead chosen a life that suited him to the core. One that gave him pleasure and was an innate part of him.

She hadn't done that. Not until she'd come here, to Sunshine. To Belle Haven. She went to her desk thinking she was here, she might as well get something done. She'd barely booted up in the semidark front room when Dell came back through.

"You're not working," he said.

"Well, I—"

He pulled her out of her chair. "You're going home to bed."

Back to being the alpha pack leader. "I'm okay, Dell. What we haven't established is if you're okay."

He didn't move but she felt him draw in a deep breath. "Why wouldn't I be?"

She wanted to say because he acted like he was all alone in charge of everyone and everything, when in reality, the people he had in his life wanted to take care of him every bit as much as he took care of them. She wanted to say how sorry she was for how he'd grown up, but that would go over about as well as hugging him right now would.

Screw it, she thought, and ran a hand up his arm, over his broad shoulder, over his throat to his jaw, which she brushed with her fingers.

Reaching up, he took her hand in his and squeezed her fingers gently, then brought them to his mouth and lightly brushed his lips over her palm. "I'm okay, Jade. I'm always okay. You don't have to worry about me."

She stepped into him, her breasts brushing his chest, their thighs touching. "Did you always know?" she asked quietly. "That you were meant for this?"

Bending his head, he lightly rubbed his lips to hers. "Kissing you?"

"Yes," she murmured. "No." She let out a low laugh and stepped back. "*No.*" God, he was good, too good, at distracting her. "At this. Your job. Being a vet."

"Actually, for most of my growing-up years, I was pretty sure I was meant for nothing good."

She opened her mouth to vehemently oppose that but he kissed her again. "I'm lucky, Jade," he said against her mouth, his hands going to her hips to hold her against him. "I didn't get screwed up, at least not too bad. I might be commitment shy and not big on traditional relationships, but thanks to Sol, I got into college and figured my shit out and ended up with a skill that works for me."

"And it's a bonus that you love what you do."

"Yeah. A lot. I highly recommend it."

"Working with animals?"

"Loving what you do."

She lifted her head and looked at him as he stroked his fingers over her jaw and into her hair, which he tugged lightly so that she couldn't pull away. "You ever going to try it?" he asked, his mouth whispering over hers.

"Maybe I already have." She gripped him tight as her body reacted to his with hopeful little tremors. "How about you? Maybe it's time for you to try something new, too."

"Like?" he asked.

"Like . . ." She nipped at his lower lip, giving it a little tug until he hissed in a breath. Then she soothed the sting with a kiss. "Like . . ." *Needing me . . .*

Adam stuck his head in from the back. "Michelle just called, she's on her way in to pick up Rose and the puppies. There's also a message on the phone from the Anderson ranch that they need you out there pronto."

Dell stayed still against Jade for one beat, and she thought maybe he'd ask Adam to handle something. Or let her help in some way.

But Dell never passed off responsibilities, and as he'd proven over and over, he sure as hell didn't need anyone to step in for him. He pulled away from Jade and looked at Adam. "I'll call Brady and have him get the Bell ready for flight. On your way into town to get your things, drop off Jade. I'll handle Rose and the Anderson ranch."

He was standing right there in front of Jade, right there, close enough to still touch, yet he was a thousand miles away on his own island. Dell Connelly Island. Where no one and nothing could touch him.

Twenty-one

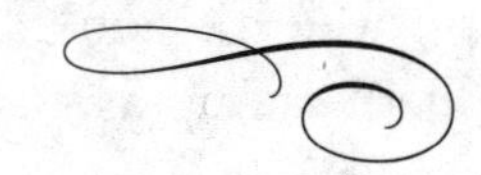

Because she was a glutton for punishment, on Monday morning Jade was leaning against Dell's truck at four thirty A.M. when he came out of his house carrying two bags of what she now knew would be groceries and his medical bag slung over his shoulder.

This time he didn't look surprised to see her. He just shook his head, shrugged out of his jacket, and tossed it to her. "Are you nuts?" he asked. "It's forty degrees and you're in just a sweatshirt."

"I got hot in that trailer last time." But she gratefully slid into his jacket, inhaling his scent and greedily wrapping herself into it, trapping his body heat for herself. "And it's thirty-two."

"Winter's coming."

She nodded as he started the truck and shoved it into gear, taking them to the highway. He drove like he did everything else in his life, with apparent effortless ease. Without his jacket, he wore only a light blue button-down shirt, untucked over faded jeans that made his legs seem like they were a mile long. His sleeves were shoved up, revealing forearms corded with strength. He had one big hand on the wheel, the other shoving his still damp hair out of his face. The Dell version of hair combing.

"The next time I drive out here, you'll be gone," he said.

This was true.

"Friday's it, right?" he asked.

Next Monday was the first. In order to fulfill her promise to Sam and her parents, she'd have to start driving back to Chicago by Friday.

Four days. "Thursday," she whispered.

Silence greeted this.

"You won't hardly even miss me," she said. "I've taught Keith enough to maintain the front until you get a replacement. And the temp agency is on notice, by the way. I wish you'd let them send someone out this week, but either way you're going to be fine. You don't need me." She held her breath, hoping against hope that he would say that he *did* need her.

In some aspect of his life. In any aspect of his life.

But he didn't. He said nothing at all. And she wasn't going to bang her head up against the wall seeking something that hadn't been given to her freely.

Nila was waiting on them. Unlike her son, she looked very surprised to see Jade again. "Are you Dell's woman?"

"I'm my own woman."

There was a slight spark of what might have been humor in Nila's eyes. "You know what I'm asking."

Jade looked at Dell, who was suddenly engrossed in unpacking his bag. Gee, wasn't he a help. She was tempted to give his mother the same line she'd once given Leanne and tell her that they were engaged just to see him swallow his own tongue. "I'm just helping."

"Why?"

"Because I like to help."

Nila looked at Dell. Dell looked right back at her, not explaining himself. He wouldn't.

Even if Jade wished that for once he would.

They turned to their waiting patients. There was a cat in labor, another who needed dental work, and two dogs who'd been in a vicious fight and needed cleaning and stitching up, all of which Dell took care of with relative ease.

The last patient was a little girl sitting next to Lakota.

The little girl was clutching a dead rabbit. "You fix," she told Dell, and set the rabbit on the exam table.

Dell's gaze met Jade's and she gave a slight shake of her head, utterly unable to imagine how he was going to handle this one. He very sweetly and gently wrapped the rabbit up and took both girls outside. Jade watched through the window as they walked out into the open land until they were nothing but three tiny pinpricks on the horizon.

"He'll help them bury the rabbit and say good-bye."

Jade turned and faced Nila, who stood there, eyes dark and solemn, long braid hanging over her shoulder. "He doesn't like good-byes."

"And you think that's my fault."

Jade didn't want to go there. "It's not my place to judge."

Nila turned and poured two cups of coffee, handing one to Jade. "You're polite. Too polite to tell me what you really think. But it's true. I was a terrible mother for him and Adam. My only defense is that I was young. Too young."

As far as defenses went, it was a good one.

"He turned out to be a good man, in spite of me," Nila said quietly. "You make him happy."

"Oh. We're not—"

Nila shook her head. "I don't need your words to tell me what I can see with my own eyes. You're the first one in all this time to hold his heart. I hope you manage to take better care of it than I ever did."

In the pit of her stomach, Jade knew otherwise. That regardless of whether or not she held a special place in Dell's heart, she wasn't going to be the keeper of it.

He didn't want her to be.

Behind her, the trailer door slammed open with enough force that Jade nearly jumped out of her skin. A young man stood there, eyes narrow, teeth bared. He was in his late teens and built like a linebacker. He was obviously Native American, and spitting fury. "You told on me?" he grated out. "You told my parole officer that I cut classes?"

"Because you did," Nila said.

"You have to take it back!"

"I'm your teacher, Robby. You know I won't lie for you." Nila set her coffee into the sink and closed her fingers around a paring knife there, her gaze meeting Jade's with a clear message. Be aware.

Jade's heart leapt into her throat. With a growl, Robby pushed forward and crowded both Jade and Nila in the kitchen up against the sink. "Tell him you were lying," he said through his teeth, his face close. Too close. "If you don't, he's going to send me back to juvie."

"All you have to do is show up for classes," Nila said. "All of them, including your anger management class."

With a yell of frustration, Robby threw out another arm, this time swiping everything from the counter in one fell swoop, sending it all flying. A set of keys hit Jade in the face. Nila was sprayed with hot coffee from one of the mugs, but she still gripped the paring knife from the sink. "Stop. Robby, stop."

Robby grabbed Nila's arm and twisted.

With a cry of pain, Nila dropped the knife and scrambled back against the counter, bumping into Jade, who was doing her best to be invisible.

Robby picked up the knife and stared at it as if transfixed before lifting his gaze to Nila.

Both Nila and Jade shrank back and down, hunkered together against the laminate wood behind them. Jade could feel something warm trickling down her temple and she swiped at it.

Blood.

She'd been cut by the keys. Nila was pulling her shirt away from her body, and Jade hoped that the coffee hadn't burned her too badly.

"You've ruined my life," Robby yelled. "Because of you, they'll try to make me go back. I won't go. I won't." He jabbed the knife in their direction for emphasis.

Jade's hand found Nila's, and they gripped each other for all they were worth, staring in horror up at the teen.

"This isn't going to help your cause," Nila told him, her voice admirably even. Dell had gotten that from her, his nerves of steel.

Jade wasn't feeling nerves of steel. She had nerves of Jell-O and they were jumbling around in her stomach.

You don't have to be a victim.

Dell's words. But Dell was outside, possibly out of screaming range. No one was going to get them out of this, they were on their own. Her purse had been on the counter but had hit the floor with everything else on the counter. It was right behind her, and gazing still warily on Robby, she slowly slid her hand into it, wrapping her fingers around the first thing she could.

A tampon.

That wasn't going to help.

She fumbled a bit and found what she'd hoped for. Her compact can of hair spray. God bless Adam and the hair spray lesson.

Robby was gripping the knife tight, looking beyond reason with some wild eyes and a menacing stance that did not bode well. "J-just put the knife down," Jade said softly.

Could she pull the can out fast enough to spray him in the eyes? And what then? She and Nila had to get to the door, which Robby was blocking.

Robby's eyes slid from Nila to her. They were black, his pupils fully dilated. He was sweating, panting with exertion.

He was on something. "There's no way out for me," he said solemnly.

"There is. There always is," Nila said.

Jade hadn't breathed in far too long. Panic had long ago blocked her throat. If Dell and those two little girls walked back into the trailer right now and startled Robby, it would go all bad. That terror outweighed the terror of taking action. "If you stop now and just leave," she said, "nothing terrible has happened. You don't have to take this any further."

"I have no way out," he said again, and lifting the knife, reached for Nila.

Dell had been right when he'd told Jade that adrenaline would kick in and everything would happen in slow motion. She pulled her hand out of her purse, hair spray in hand, and nailed Robby right in the eyes.

In slow motion.

Stopping short, Robby bellowed with rage, his hands going up to his face.

That's when Jade kicked him. She was lower than him, still crouched next to Nila so that her leverage was bad, but she got him. She got him right between the legs and he dropped like a stone.

Nila scrambled up, grabbed Jade by the hand, and had them stumbling out of the trailer in the bright morning sun where they gulped air like they'd been running a marathon.

"Nice shot," Nila breathed, bent at the waist, hands on her thighs. "Good aim."

"I was aiming for his knee," Jade said. "I didn't mean to get him . . . there."

Dell and the two little girls came around the corner of the trailer, holding hands. Nila rushed toward Dell. "Need your phone," she gasped.

Dell pulled out his phone. "What's the matter?" His gaze was on Jade, and it narrowed in concern. "What happened?"

"Your woman-who-isn't-your-woman is one tough girl," Nila said, and called 911.

Twenty-two

When they got back to Sunshine, Dell pulled up to his house, where Jade's car was. He'd wanted her to take the rest of the day off but she wasn't having any of it.

"You have two stitches over your eye," he said, trying to reason with her, but really, he should have known better. There was no reasoning with a woman.

She wanted to work.

"Two stitches is nothing," she said. "The doctor said I wasn't concussed."

"He also said you were damn lucky."

"So were you. I was so afraid you were going to come back into the trailer and startle him and that he'd cut you and those little girls."

He stared at her. "So you were trying to protect me?"

"Well . . . yeah. And you should have seen me trying to do it with a tampon."

"What?"

"It's the first thing I grabbed in my purse."

He chuckled, even as his own ego bumped up against the pride he felt for what she'd done. But every single time he looked at the bandage above her eye he flashed back to her and his mother stumbling out of the trailer like two drunken sailors, both looking like they'd just been in a bar brawl.

The reality of what had happened had been worse, though not nearly as bad as it could have been.

But she'd handled herself.

At the very small smile that crossed his lips, Jade cocked her head. "What?"

"You kicked his ass."

A small smile of her own crossed her lips. "Well, not quite his ass."

Dell let out a low laugh. "You did what you had to do."

"I did, didn't I?" She shook her head. "It seems like a dream now. I was terrified at the time. And pissed off. So pissed off. I mean if he'd waited a few minutes before he'd come in, you could have done all the ass kicking."

Reaching across the console, he stroked a finger above the bandage. "I'm proud of you, Jade."

Her eyes went a little shiny, and she took a moment to answer. When she did, her voice was soft and husky, telling him how much his words meant. "I'm a little proud of me, too. I faced my biggest nightmare and beat it down."

"You ever going to tell me about that nightmare?" he asked, tucking a strand of her hair behind her ear, ducking down a little to maintain eye contact when she tried to look away.

"It's over and done," she said. "It's all in the past."

"Not when you're still letting it affect you here and now, it's not."

She stared stubbornly out the window, the set of her jaw telling him she was done talking.

"Jade—"

"It doesn't matter now."

"Because you're leaving?"

That startled her into looking at him. "No." When he lifted a brow, she sighed. "Maybe I'm just tired of it having such power over me."

"Then stop giving it that power," he said. "You've never told anyone about it. You're hoarding it, storing it up, letting it eat at you."

"Not today. Today I made Robby eat it."

"Yeah, and you did great. But—"

"Dell." She rubbed her temples. "I don't want to do this."

With him. Right. He nodded, trying not to react to that even though he felt kicked in the teeth. "Okay, let's get you back to your loft so you can rest, then." He unhooked his seat belt and got out of the truck, moving around to physically extract her from the car if he had to.

Adam came out of the house but Dell shook his head and Adam stopped on the porch. Dell opened the passenger door for Jade, reaching down to help her.

"I'm *fine*."

"I need you to cooperate on this," he said.

"You *need* me to cooperate? Dell, you never need anything, and you don't need this. I'm *fine*."

He drew a deep breath. She wasn't going to do as he asked. Of course not. Because if he looked her up in the dictionary, she'd be there under STUBBORN.

And he'd be right next to her. "I need you to rest. The doctor said—"

"Wow." She leaned back against his truck and crossed her arms. "Look at you throwing around that *need* word. The next thing you know, you'll be telling me how you *feel*."

He stared at her incredulously. "You think I don't feel?"

"Dell, the only time I have even an inkling of what you're feeling is if your tongue is down my throat."

"What? That's crazy."

"Oh, really. It's crazy." She tossed up her hands. "Then tell me. Tell me right now. How do you feel?"

"About what?"

"Anything. You pick."

He narrowed his eyes. "Is this a trick?"

"Not even a little bit."

"Okay." He searched his brain. "I feel . . . angry over what happened to you. I should have been there, right there. I brought you and put you in danger—"

"We both know I pretty much forced you to bring me," she said dryly. "And please. Alpha male aside, I know damn well you must have other feelings than anger."

"Okay . . ." He tried to access one. "I'm hungry."

"You're what?"

"Hungry. I haven't eaten since last night and—"

Jade pushed off his truck and headed to her car.

Confused, he followed her, ignoring Adam's smirk. "See, it *was* a trap. You're mad because I didn't come up with whatever it is you wanted to hear."

Jade tossed her purse into the car before straightening and facing Dell. "Tell me one thing, Dell. The women you've dated. What's their biggest complaint about you?"

"That I don't . . ." He broke off.

She lifted a brow.

"Engage. I don't engage my emotions with them." He grimaced. "You wanted to know how I feel about you."

She didn't answer and he sighed. "Jade, I'm not good at this. It's why I don't do relationships."

"Getting that. Gotta go," she repeated.

Her eyes, Christ. They were suspiciously bright. The pulse at the base of her neck beat as frantic as a hummingbird. "I'm driving you," he said.

"Not necessary." She flashed him a forced smile, slid behind the wheel, and pulled out.

Adam came up to Dell. "She okay to drive?"

"Yes," Dell said, and it was true. She was okay. Much more okay than him.

Her car vanished down the street before Adam spoke again. "So you let her get attacked by some punk-ass with a knife? How the fuck did that happen?"

Dell shook his head. "Mom had the knife. The punk-ass took it from her."

"And Nila?" Adam didn't like to call Nila "Mom." He didn't like to call her anything. But he betrayed his concern when he asked, "She get hurt?"

"There was a scuffle. She got hit with a mug of hot coffee and suffered some second-degree burns on her stomach and chest, but she's okay."

"Jesus," Adam said.

"Yeah." Dell turned toward the truck, made a detour, and punched the closest tree.

Pain sang up his hand, wrist, and arm.

"Well, that was stupid," Adam said. "You break it?"

"No." Dell opened and closed his hand carefully, and winced. Probably not, anyway . . .

"Feel better?" Adam asked.

"No."

"So she really schooled you on that feeling thing, huh?" Adam said.

Dell wished he hadn't punched the tree so he could punch Adam. "Shut up."

"Why? Because you know she's right?"

"Right about *what*?"

"That you don't do need. And you don't feel."

Fuck the fact that his hand hurt like a son of a bitch, he was going to hit Adam, anyway. "You know that's not true."

Adam nodded. "Yeah. But I'm just your sorry-ass brother. I don't give a shit if you show your feelings or not. She's the one who needs to know."

Dell stared at him. "What, are you Dr. Phil all of a sudden? You, who haven't looked at a woman since you got back from your last mission? What the fuck, man? Why don't you worry about your own love life, or lack thereof?"

Adam shrugged. "Fucking with you is more fun."

Dell stalked to his truck, shoulder-checking Adam hard as he did.

Adam let that go, which was just as well.

Because yeah, Dell had been schooled. Not only that, he was one hypocritical son of a bitch. All this time, all these months, he'd been so proud of himself for helping her. For giving her a job. For being there for her. For boosting the confidence that had grown inside her. For showing her how to face her demons and keeping her safe.

He'd actually thought that *he'd* been saving *her*.

Instead, he'd had it all ass-backward. *She'd* been there for *him*. She'd supported him, she'd made him look at himself differently, changing what he'd thought he'd wanted out of life. It used to be enough for him to have Belle Haven, to have just Adam, and Brady and Lilah. He didn't need more.

But that was no longer the case. Now when he went to sleep at night, he lay there wondering what Jade was doing and why she wasn't in his bed.

He didn't want to be alone anymore.

"Man, you're going to have to get over yourself," Adam said.

"You get over yourself."

Adam snorted. "That the best you've got? Why don't you just go after her, dumbass?"

"Thursday is her last day."

Adam rubbed a hand over his jaw. "Well, damned if that didn't sneak up on us."

Dell looked down the road where Jade's car had vanished. "Yeah."

* * *

That night on the drive home from work, Jade quickly realized the weather had taken a left turn directly into winter. She hadn't turned the heat on high enough and the loft had a chill when she entered. She fed Beans and went directly to her laptop and her things-to-do-when-upset list.

Bath.

Candles.

Ice cream.

She combined all three, stripping and sliding into the water.

Beans sat on the mat, well out of the reach of any possible stray water drops, cleaning behind her ears.

Jade was halfway through the ice cream when her cell phone rang.

Jade set her bowl on the edge of the tub and gingerly leaned over to the sink counter where her phone sat. It was Lilah. "Hey," she said. "I'm in the bath so—"

"You okay?"

Jade eyed the phone warily. "Why?"

"Just wondering."

Jade sighed. "Dell or Adam called and asked you to check up on me."

There was a guilty pause followed by a guilty laugh. "I know you said no good-bye party, but how about we go out for a drink?"

"Already there," Jade said. She'd added a glass of wine to her pity party and it was nearly gone. Someone knocked at her door and she went still. "Wait—are you here?"

"No, but I can be."

"Lilah, I'm fine." She stood in the tub and accidentally splashed Beans, who sent her a reproachful look. "Which of them called you, Lilah?"

"Oh God. Don't make me tell you that."

"I just want to know who's knocking at my door at"—she looked at her watch, also on the counter—"ten o'clock at night."

"Honey, you don't need me to tell you who's on your doorstep."

Jade's stomach clenched. Too much ice cream. "It could be Adam."

Lilah laughed. "And the Tooth Fairy is coming by later, too. Look, we both know who's at the door. Answer it. Talk to him. He's worried about you."

"I'm in the bath."

"Naked?"

"Well, that is my usual preference for bathing."

"One of us has to see you tonight, Jade," Lilah said. "It might as well be the one of us who's falling in love with you."

Jade went still, then jerked at the second knock on her front door. More water splashed over the sides of the tub and Beans trotted out of the room in self-defense this time.

"Jade?" Lilah asked. "You still there?"

"Dell's not falling for anyone, Lilah. He's a serial dater and doesn't believe in relationships."

"He hasn't had a real date in months. And don't look now, but he's got plenty of relationships in his life. Adam, Brady, me, his mother—though he'd deny that to his dying day, the stubborn ass—and . . . you."

There was a third knock, not nearly as patient as the first two. "Dammit, I gotta go. I'll deal with you later." Still dripping wet, she wrapped herself up in her bathrobe and gave herself the quick once-over in the mirror. No makeup, hair a mess—hell, who was she kidding? Her entire being was a mess. With a sigh, she moved through the loft to the door. Maybe he'd left, maybe . . .

"Jade, open up."

"I'm fine. I told you I was fine."

"Okay. Great. I'm not."

Letting out a breath, she undid the security chain, unbolted the door, then pulled it open.

Dell's hands were braced high on the doorjamb. His head was bowed, and when he lifted it, his eyes trailed up from her bare feet and legs to the robe that clung to her, heating her skin inch by slow inch. By the time his gaze met hers, his eyes were dark, filled with an emotion somewhere between possession, protection, and lust. "Invite me in, Jade."

He wasn't even going to try to sweet-talk his way in. He wanted her to invite him.

And that wasn't all he wanted. He wanted some answers, too. She knew this. Just as she knew she hadn't been able to give anyone those answers in all this time. But maybe . . . maybe that was the problem. God knew, keeping it in wasn't working for her.

Maybe it *was* time to try something new.

So she drew in some air and stepped back. He didn't move, just stayed in that position, arms up, eyes stark, expression bare.

Waiting.

"I want you to come in," she said.

He dropped his arms and ignored the space she'd made, stepping into her, pushing them both into her place and shutting the door behind him.

Twenty-three

Dell followed Jade into her kitchen, trying like hell not to notice that her white fluffy robe was sticking to her obviously wet body. Water dripped from her hair and her legs, and her feet squeaked on the tile floor. He was here for a reason, but that reason was fuzzy now that he had her in sight, all dewy fresh, no makeup, smelling like some complicated mix of sweet, sexy woman. "Jade."

She turned back with a bottle of wine, which she poured into a glass before handing over to him.

"I've already had mine," she said. "You might want to catch up."

She didn't look completely toasted so he tossed back some wine.

"You want to talk," she said.

Actually, he wanted to strip off that robe and lift her up to the counter so he could have his merry way with her. But first things first. "I want *you* to talk."

"About?"

"Come on now, Jade. This has gone on too long. It's time."

She played with the tie of her robe a moment before lifting her gaze to his. "As you know, before I came here, I ran a large medical center." She paused. "One night we were held up in the Urgent Care for drugs. I was the one who let the intruders into the lockup to get those drugs."

Dell set down his wine, thinking he probably needed something stronger for this, much stronger.

"The following week," she went on, "against my family's and doctor's wishes, I got into my car and drove west for a few days and ended up in Sunshine."

Dell took a careful breath but otherwise didn't react. He didn't want her to stop talking. "Doctor?"

"I needed something to eat," she said. "So I went into the bakery on Main and heard the woman behind the counter talking to another woman about Belle Haven. It was Lilah, and she was saying how the animal center needed a receptionist to man the desk and answer the phones because your old receptionist had left to have a baby and you guys were trying to do it on your own. I didn't need a job, but I *needed* a job, you know?"

No. No he didn't know. "Jade, the robbery. Previously, you'd said you were attacked. How badly were you—"

"After Lilah paid and left, I asked the lady behind the counter how to find the animal center. And then I drove out there. Got lost twice. Adam found me in the middle of the road trying to get my GPS to work, and he led me to Belle Haven. You were sitting in the middle of the waiting room floor wearing scrubs and a doctor's coat, playing with Mrs. Nelson's eight-week-old pug puppies. They were climbing all over you, and the phone was ringing and your computer was frozen, and you were just sitting there, calm as can be. Laughing. You were laughing at the puppy trying to climb up your chest to lick your face."

Dell remembered that. Adam had opened the door for her and she'd walked in, eyes hidden behind her big mirrored sunglasses, wearing white jeans and an aneurysm-inducing pink fuzzy sweater that somehow went with her red hair, looking as if she'd walked off a movie set.

He'd been a little dazzled.

And more than a little head over heels in lust.

But then she'd dropped to her knees and had loved up one of the puppies, letting it crawl all over her fancy clothes, not caring about hair or slobber.

She'd wanted to sit behind his desk and answer his phones, and he'd had to change gears because he'd needed someone to do those things. He'd conducted a real interview, and they'd hit their first problem—in spite of the intelligence and wit blaring from those green eyes, she couldn't provide references. Or proof she could indeed handle the job.

He'd known she wasn't from Sunshine, or anywhere close. That was obvious. Everything about her, from her clothes to her speech to her mannerisms, spoke of a big city and big money.

"Belle Haven was so . . ." Jade searched for the words. "Warm. Open. Inviting. Not at all like the uptight medical center I'd come from. There was no tension, no angry, sick, frustrated people waiting for hours, no harried office staff fighting insurance companies for approval. Just you. And you looked so easygoing," she said softly. "So . . . laid-back. Fun. I wanted to work for you."

"So you did," he said. "And it's been great. But Jade, you've got to tell me. Tell me what happened to you."

"It was late." She let out a long breath. "I'd stayed because it was month's end and the accounts payable and receivable clerks had gotten behind, not sending me their reports until the very end of the day. We were closed and I was just leaving, walking through the parking lot when someone ran at me. It looked like a teenager in a hoodie, so I stopped. I thought he was hurt, but"—here she squeezed her eyes shut—"he lifted his head and straightened. He wasn't a teen. He was a full-grown man, wearing a Halloween mask."

Dell heard the sound escape him, a low murmur of regret and horror for her, remembering how she'd fallen apart in the parking lot at Belle Haven when she'd faced yet another Halloween mask.

"Before I could react," she went on, "he'd shoved me and I fell to the asphalt. And then . . ." She cut herself off and shook her head.

"Jade." Dell pulled her close and wrapped her arms around him. "Stay with me."

"I am." But she burrowed in, pressing her face into his neck. "He had a gun. He pulled me up and yanked me close, holding his arm over my windpipe so I couldn't breathe. I could feel blood running down from my hands and knees where I'd gotten scraped, and he kept tightening his grip and . . . and I couldn't breathe."

With another low sound of empathy and fury mixed, Dell pulled her in even tighter, as if he could fight her eighteen-month-old demons for her.

"He made me unlock the front door and dragged me through the reception area, demanding to know where the meds were kept. He wanted OxyContin, Vicodin, morphine, whatever we had. He needed a fix, he was shaking bad. I should have—I should have . . ."

"You did what you had to," Dell said, stroking a hand up and down her back to remind her that she was here, safe. "And you survived." Her robe and body were damp, and she was trembling. He tried to wrap himself around her to give her his body heat. "That's all that matters now."

Face still pressed to his throat, she shook her head. "That's just it, I didn't do all I could. I did nothing."

"Jade—"

"No, it's true. When I was on the ground, I could have kicked at him standing over me. I could have tried to fight back and I didn't."

"He had a fucking gun," Dell said, hating that she'd ever felt so helpless. "You didn't have the tools to fight back. It wasn't your fault."

"But what happened next was." She gulped in more air. "I wouldn't tell him where the meds were, so he dragged me through to the back. Karen was still there, one of our nurses. She was working late, too, cleaning up. She came out of the small kitchen area and he—"

Dell was already hating this story. Hating it with everything he had. "He what, Jade?"

"He pointed the gun at her and said if I didn't tell him where the meds were, he'd shoot her."

Dell closed his eyes and rested his cheek on the top of her head, wishing he could take it all away.

"I told him," Jade said. "I told him what he wanted to know, but he hit her, anyway, in the face with his gun. He made me tie her up to a chair and then dragged me down the hall. I fell and nearly took him down with me, which really pissed him off. He kicked me in the ribs and I couldn't breathe again. I still couldn't breathe when we got to lockup. Corey was in the room, we surprised him."

"Corey?"

"A lab tech. He was studying for his exams. We startled him. When he saw me, all the blood startled him. I looked much worse than I was."

"Jade." Dell could barely speak. "God, Jade."

"Corey jumped up and . . ." She tightened her grip on him, both hands at his chest, grabbing his shirt and a few chest hairs to boot. "He shot him," she whispered. "In the thigh. I screamed, and he shoved me up against the meds lockup and demanded the key or he was going to shoot Corey again. But the key wasn't on my ring, I didn't have it there because it's too dangerous. But when I refused to get it, he—"

God, he didn't want to hear this. "Jade."

"He touched me. With his gun. He rubbed it over my breast and when my nipple got hard, he laughed and said we were going to have fun after. Corey yelled at him from the floor where he was bleeding like crazy, told him to leave me alone, and I could hear Karen screaming for help from the kitchen . . . and you know what I did?"

Dell shook his head.

"Nothing. I did nothing."

"You were scared, Jade."

"I was useless."

"You were in shock."

"So was Corey," she said. "So was Karen. They were both hurt—"

"So were you."

"Not like them."

She blamed herself, he realized, for not suffering as much as they had.

"I wasn't hurt like they were," she said again. "And yet they never stopped fighting. I never started." Galvanized into action by her own words, she shoved him away and grabbed the wine, tossing back a healthy long pull right from the bottle. Gently he took it from her.

"I let him into the meds lockup," she said, not looking at him, swiping her mouth with her arm. "I let him take whatever he wanted as I begged him not to hurt me." She looked away. "After . . . I figured there had to be something fundamentally wrong with me that I hadn't been strong and brave."

"No," he said fiercely. "There's nothing wrong with you. Jade, tell me he didn't hurt you."

"The police came. Someone in the next building over heard Karen screaming. The guy who had me, he had an accomplice. He was in the getaway car, but he came in to shut Karen up. The police burst in just in time. We were saved. No thanks to me."

"You weren't . . ."

"No. He intended to rape me, he told me several times." She shuddered. "In graphic detail. But he didn't get to it." She closed her eyes. "I grew up hearing how strong I was. How I was meant for big things, how I could do anything I wanted. That I'd been born for running the family show, so to speak. But I wasn't strong. I was weak."

What she'd been raised hearing from her family sounded more like a major contradiction to him—do what you want, but make damn sure that what you want is to do our bidding . . . "You're human, Jade. That doesn't mean you're weak."

She turned from him and shrugged. "Everything I knew about myself was wrong. Nothing felt right. I couldn't find my footing."

"Anyone would have felt that way."

"It was my own doing."

"The holdup wasn't your fault."

She rolled her head on her neck, like her muscles hurt. Since she was tense enough to shatter, it was no wonder. He put his hands on her shoulders. Her muscles were bunched and tight as rocks. He dug his fingers in a little and she exhaled, dropped her head back to his chest.

"When I left Chicago," she murmured, "I wanted to find myself again, but I couldn't. I think it's because I was trying to be someone who no longer existed."

He dug in on a particularly tightly knotted muscle and she hissed in a breath. "God, that feels good." She tilted her head to give him more room to work. "I think working at Belle Haven was supposed to be a statement, like look at me further sabotaging myself . . . but the joke ended up on me. I like it here. I like who I became here. And I liked to think I brought some things to the job that no one else has before."

"Hell yeah, you did," he said. "And you became an important, integral part of the place." He turned her to face him. "You know that, right?"

She gave a little smile. "Turns out I have mad skills no matter what type of an office it is."

"Turns out," he said, smiling back. God. She looked so beautiful bare of makeup, bare of the clothes, of any of her usual shields. Just Jade. "But that's just the job," he said. "Did you figure out who you are outside of work?"

"Not a line dancer."

He smiled. "Okay. Anything else?" When she didn't say anything, he did. "You're a good friend."

She choked out a half laugh, and then another. And then as if her legs were weak, she slid down until she was sitting on the floor, her back to the cabinet. "Dell, I was here for a year and a half before I even let any of you come over here. Lilah—"

"Loves you. Adam loves you." He hunkered beside her. "We all—"

She covered his mouth with her hand. He gently kissed her palm and pulled it away. "You give something to each of us. Hell, you give something to perfect strangers, like when you paid the rest of Nick's bill from your own money."

"You saw that?"

"I see lots of things." He kissed her palm again, and held it in his. "I see the real you, Jade."

She stared at him. "Do you think you can tell me who that is?"

He dropped all the way to the floor next to her and hauled her into his lap. "The real you is the woman who gets to work early to make my day easier because she cares. The real you is the woman who goes to lunch with Lilah even though for the fifth time that week she's going to ask you if Lulu should be allowed at the reception, and even though you likely want to strangle her, you still smile and suggest that probably it's not a good idea to allow lambs at the wedding reception. The real you is the woman who can make both of my big, badass ex–military brothers smile." He lowered his voice and put his mouth to her ear. "The real you is the woman who, when you're naked in my arms, gives me absolutely everything you have."

She closed her eyes. "How do you know?"

"Because I've never seen you give anything less, in everything you do."

"You helped me."

Maybe. She'd come to Sunshine seeking confidence and inner strength, looking to find herself. He'd done his best to give her whatever she needed but in the process he'd helped her become strong enough to go back. "So why are you going back now?"

"My dad's ill. He has Parkinson's and hasn't been able to run the business for a long time. I was doing it for him, and when I left, they temporarily promoted a family friend to my position. Sandy's good, really good actually, but . . ."

"But she's not you?"

A small smile crossed her lips. "She doesn't want the job long-term. She wants to get back to part-time so she can spend more time with her young kids."

"They could promote someone else."

"I promised. And I always did really mean to go back. I love my job with you and love the friends I've made . . . I'll never forget any of it. But I pretty much ran away from home, you know? I can't just . . . keep running. Without a compelling reason to stay, it's time for me to go."

He looked into her eyes and saw regret, and he wondered if it was as painful as the regret swelling in his chest cavity. "So stay for a compelling reason."

What might have been a brief flash of humor came and went in her eyes. "Like more naked-friends sex?"

He nearly said, *Stay and you can have any kind of sex you want, as long as it's only from me,* but that would sound an awful lot like begging. "As hot as naked-friends sex would be," he said slowly, "you need to know, this isn't anywhere near as casual as that. Not for me."

"But . . . but casual is your thing. It's your signature. It's what you do."

"No, actually," he said. "My usual thing is even less than casual. But that went out the window with you eighteen months ago."

She shook her head. "Don't do this to me," she whispered.

"Do what? Tell you how I feel? You asked, remember? And yeah, you're leaving. I've heard the news flash. But we can . . . visit."

"Visit."

"Yes," he said firmly. It would suck but it was better than nothing. "The occasional holiday, weekends, whatever."

She stared at him as if he'd lost his mind. "Dell, it's seventeen hundred miles. We can't casually date from seventeen hundred miles away."

"It's a flight." He shrugged casually, even as his heart was pounding, pounding, pounding.

Her eyes hadn't left his. "I didn't know you'd want that."

Okay, that hurt more than it probably should. "Even casual friends would visit, Jade. And as we've already established, we're more than that."

"I'd have to think about that," she said very softly, cutting out his heart. "Keeping this up once I leave."

Because he didn't trust his voice, he nodded. He had not seen that one coming. He started to get up, but she grabbed his wrist and he looked down at her hand on his arm. Pale. Small. Deceptively fragile-looking.

"I'd have to think about it," she repeated. "Because I don't know about my ability to keep this up with someone I care so much about *and* keep it as light as our distance will dictate."

Dell wanted to point out that the distance part was her own doing, but she moved into him, pressing that warm, curvy body against him until his ability to talk, much less think, became impaired.

She brushed her mouth to his ear. "Dell?"

He let out a shaky breath. "Yeah?"

"Ever had good-bye sex?"

He made the fatal mistake of meeting her gaze. Her eyes were soft, solemn, as she rose up on her knees and gently touched her lips to his. "Jade—" He gripped her hips as his entire body reacted to that slight, almost chaste kiss. "I—"

She outlined his lips with her tongue and he groaned, sucking it into his mouth. God, he loved the taste of her, the feel of her. He couldn't seem to get enough. He was starting to wonder if he'd ever get enough when her hands slid under the hem of his shirt and over his abs.

"Mmm," she said in response to the feel of him, like maybe she couldn't get enough of him, either. "Off." Then she shoved the shirt up. When he took over the task, pulling it off, she straddled him, a knee on either side of his hips. Bending low, she licked his nipple.

He sucked in a breath, which made him realize his mouth was open to speak, but whatever he'd been about to say was gone since all the blood had drained out of his now poor, dehydrated, useless brain.

"I want you," she said against his lips, pinning him to the cabinet at his back. "God, I want you. Please, Dell."

He made a noise deep in his throat and kissed her long and deep. Not enough, not nearly enough, he thought. He had to touch her. "Stand up."

"What?"

He went for the belt of her robe. "What do you have on under here?"

"Um. Me."

He groaned again and tugged it open. She was right, nothing but warm, damp, sexy, curvy woman. His hands looked so dark against her pale skin and turned him on even more than he already was. "Stand up," he said again, then without waiting for her, lifted her by the hips so that she was standing, still straddling him.

Perfect.

Leaning in, he nuzzled at her belly button, then lower. Then lower still. Above him she made a low sound of hunger that went straight through him, then repeated it when he slid his hands up the backs of her legs and grabbed her ass, urging her a little closer so that she had no choice but to lean over him and slap her hands on the kitchen counter.

"I've been *aching* to do this," he said, and gently ran his thumb over her glistening folds, opening her before leaning in to stroke her with his tongue, sampling different spots, loving her reaction to each. A murmur, a gasp. His name torn from her throat. She was quivering in minutes, her breath choppy, her hips rocking into him, and he couldn't get enough. "You taste good, Jade."

"Oh God. Oh God, *there*—"

If he hadn't already known exactly her "oh God, there" spot, the way her fingers tightened in his hair would have been a big clue. Loving the sexy sounds being ripped from her throat, and the way she looked above him, damp and trembling and gorgeous, he gave her exactly what she wanted, building her orgasm until she shattered.

Her knees collapsed and she slumped against his chest. Stroking a hand down her back, he pulled her close and kissed her neck.

"Please tell me you have a condom," she said.

In his wallet, which contrary to what she probably thought, he'd put in there with her in mind. "Jade—"

She clapped a hand on either side of his face. "Yes or no."

"Yes, but—"

"Get it. For the love of God get it now."

He reached into his back pocket for his wallet, not easy with her straddling his lap and very busy with her own agenda—unzipping his jeans. She freed him, then she tore the packet open with her teeth, laughing when she spit out the corner of the wrapper over her shoulder. "Always wanted to do that," she murmured, and sheathed him, leaving him panting and sweating by the time she was done.

"Now," she whispered, demanding, sure of herself, the sexiest thing he'd ever seen. She wrapped her hand around him, lifted herself up a little, and took him deep.

"Oh, fuck," he managed.

"Yes, please."

He choked out a laugh and closed his eyes, thunking his head back against the cabinet, hissing in a breath when she bent over him and nipped at his exposed throat. Banding his arms tight around her, he opened his eyes and met hers as they began to move in tandem. Faster. Harder. She was moaning and whimpering for more, and he gave it, feeling . . . so much, lost, found . . . completely undone.

When she sucked his earlobe into her mouth and flicked it with her tongue, he knew he was an inch from losing it. "Jesus," he breathed, trying to slow her down. "Jesus, Jade. Wait—"

No good, she was too far gone, grinding on him, making those sweet noises that told him how good he was making her feel, that she was as gone as him, and he nearly went off on that knowledge alone.

"I need you, Dell," she murmured softly, her hands in his hair, her eyes on his. "Need me back."

"I do."

"No. No, I mean—"

He stroked a hand up her thigh, rasping his thumb over ground zero, and she sobbed out his name and arched into him. "Come," he urged her, wanting to watch her fly before he did. "Come for me, Jade."

And with a soft cry, she did.

He joined her, a kaleidoscope of colors bursting behind his eyes. For a moment he actually thought he was having a stroke, but it couldn't possibly feel this good to stroke out.

From the dim recesses of his mind he realized that there was an odd ache in his chest that both hurt and felt right at the same time. He knew the reason, but it could wait until she was gone. Until he was alone again. Alone, which had always worked out so well for him.

Too bad he suddenly—or maybe not so suddenly at all—no longer really believed that.

Twenty-four

Jade opened her eyes some time later. Dell had moved them to her bed and they'd fallen asleep. He was warm and she snuggled closer, kissing his shoulder, wishing . . .

That this was real. That she could figure out a way to make it real that worked for everyone.

Dell's breathing changed, and she knew he was awake. "Hey," he murmured, voice low and sleep rough. "What's wrong?" When she said nothing, he ran his fingers over her skin, and finally she sighed. "I had a dream. About my family."

"About going back?"

He never said home. Sunshine was home. For him, Sunshine had been the first place to ever feel like home. So she nodded again.

Brushing his mouth over her temple, he skimmed his way to her jaw. "You're conflicted."

It wasn't a question, but she answered anyway. "Yes."

"You have choices, Jade. You always have choices." His mouth moved along her throat, making her shiver.

"Like?" she asked, clutching at him.

"Like staying."

Her heart took a hard, hopeful leap. "If I took you up on that, you'd regret it," she said, a little breathless. She needed to drop this conversation now, while she still could.

"You don't know what I want."

A truer statement had never been uttered. "So tell me."

His tongue teased her skin, and she began to lose grip of her thoughts. "You," he said. "I want you."

Want, not need. She arched up against him as his hands ran over her body. "You have me, Dell." Wrapping her legs around his hips, she pulled him to her, locking eyes with him. "All of me."

"For now," he said.

Confused, she opened her mouth, but he used that to his advantage, kissing her hungrily, pushing closer, his body covering hers. The sheet tangled between them, not hiding a thing, not that he was big and hard. *Very* hard.

Dell yanked the sheet away and then he was on her, warm skin in place of the cool cotton.

Her eyes slid shut as his lips moved over hers. She'd learned he loved to kiss, to explore, and she loved to let him. It made her feel . . . wanted. Cherished. Sexy. He'd seen it all before, of course, every inch of her, and yet each time he kissed the small scar on her knee from a long-ago childhood mishap, or ran his tongue over the curve of her breast or the length of her hip with such appreciation, it sent tingles through her. Like now. Her fingers tightened in his hair and brought his mouth back to hers. "Again?"

"Yes," he breathed against her lips. "And then again. Because as it turns out, I don't think I can get enough of you."

"I have no self-discipline when it comes to you," Jade said much later.

Dell didn't open his eyes, but he did let out a low, rough-sounding laugh.

"I'm not sure how that's funny," she said.

Dell lifted his head, his hair tousled from her fingers, his expression one hundred percent pure sated male. "You expect to be disciplined during sex?"

"I—"

He laughed again and she elbowed him.

Ignoring that, he reached for her, but she shoved him. "No. Oh no. We've had enough."

He was still laughing when he easily pulled her in close and nuzzled his face in her hair. "Speak for yourself. I'm not sure I could ever get enough."

Running her hand down his beautiful back, she closed her eyes and wished she were brave enough to believe it.

* * *

When she woke up, Dell was gone. She ignored the little ping of disappointment and glanced at Beans.

"Mew," Beans said, a knowing look in her sharp eyes.

"No, I am *not* wishing he was still here. Sheesh, what do you take me for, a sex addict?"

"Mew."

With a sigh, Jade showered, dressed, and grabbed Beans and got to the office at the same time as usual, but unlike the usual, she wasn't the first one in.

On her desk sat a hot coffee and a bag from the bakery. An egg and turkey bacon croissant, which she dove into as if she'd spent all night running a marathon.

Or being made love to for hours on end . . .

The croissant was so good she moaned as she ate it. Forget having sex all night long. She wanted to have this croissant all night long.

"Mmm," came Dell's low, sexy voice in her ear as his arms encircled her from behind. He nipped at the side of her throat. "That sound you make. It drives me crazy, especially when I'm buried in you and—"

Her cell phone rang.

Drawing a shaky breath, she pushed Dell away and grabbed it.

"The first is Monday," Sam said. "You on track to be here?"

Jade's gaze met Dell's. She knew he could hear Sam. "Yes. I'm leaving in two days."

Sam's relieved expulsion of air sounded in her ear. "I'll fly out and drive back with you."

"No. No, I want to do it alone," she said, still holding Dell's unwavering stare. "I'll be okay."

She hung up and sighed. "Dell—"

"I know. You . . . promised."

He understood promises, he understood loyalty, and he was very good at hiding his thoughts when he wanted to. For a long moment, he continued to look at her as if he wanted to say something, but he didn't. He simply nodded. "Do you need any help?"

She felt her heart crack right up the center. No matter what she needed, he was there for her, sometimes even before she knew what that might be. Yes, he was obstinate, way too sure of himself, couldn't put real words to an emotion to save his life, and yet . . . and yet he had her back in a way no one ever had before. "I really wanted to train someone for you."

"I'm not replacing you, Jade. No one could."

"Dell—"

"I'm going to be fine. Don't worry about me." And then he was gone, the door to his office shutting quietly.

Okay. Good. He was going to be fine. And if he wasn't . . . well, no one would ever know because that's how he operated.

That's how they both operated.

On Jade's last day, Belle Haven had a record number of patients. This was due more to people wanting to see Jade before she left than any of Dell's skills, and he knew it.

But he couldn't blame anyone. He felt the same. He wanted as many last looks at her as he could get.

They met at Crystal's that night, he, Adam, Brady, Lilah.

And Jade.

They shared two pitchers of beer and stories. Lilah brought a cake. "Not homemade," she said. "Because we all know I can't cook worth shit." She hugged Jade hard. "Dammit, I'm testing this waterproof mascara tonight." She sniffed. "I'm really going to miss watching you keep Dell off balance."

Dell would have argued, but it was hard to argue the truth. Jade had been keeping him on his toes since the day she'd walked into his life.

They all walked out to the parking lot together and Lilah hugged her again. And then again, until Brady pried her loose. "She's coming back to visit," he assured Lilah, and looked at Jade. "Right?"

Jade, eyes shimmering brilliantly with unshed tears, nodded. Brady pulled her in close, whispered something Dell couldn't catch, and when he pulled back, Adam moved in. He didn't speak, just hugged her, then tugged lightly on her hair, his eyes solemn but affectionate.

Dell waited until everyone pulled out and it was just him and Jade in the parking lot.

"It's late," she said, voice thick. "And I want to leave before dawn."

He nodded. She didn't want him to follow her home. Message received. "Jade—"

"I don't know how to do this," she whispered. "I don't know how to say good-bye to you."

"So don't."

"Dell—"

He put a finger to her lips. "I just mean that I'll come see you."

She closed her eyes, then nodded. Then she stepped into him and hugged him hard, eyes fierce. "Make sure that you do."

He stood in the lot and watched her drive away. He got into his truck and turned toward home.

Except he went right instead of left, and let his heart steer him to where it thought home was.

Jade's.

She opened the door, eyes and nose red. "This is a bad idea," she said shakily.

"Spectacularly," he agreed, and shut the door behind him. Then he found himself pushed up against it and she kissed him, all hot, confusing desperation, which unleashed his own.

"We shouldn't do this," she said against his mouth when they came up for air.

"No." Look at him, all agreeable, as if his heart weren't breaking in fucking two. Her body heat was seeping into him, warming the core of him with the very essence of her. Then she made a sound in the back of her throat and cuddled in, soft and pliant and willing. God, so willing.

They dove at each other. Apparently, they were doing this.

Lacing his fingers into her hair, Dell took her mouth in a drugging kiss, holding her face in one hand, sliding his other down her back to cup her ass, squeezing until she moaned. He worked his way down her body, divesting her of clothing as he went. She moaned again when he flicked his tongue over her puckered nipple and arched into him with a gasp when he dropped to his knees, pinned her hips to the door and kissed his way lower. By the time he made his way to her center she was writhing beneath his hands, the little whimpers coming from her the sexiest sounds he'd ever heard.

"Dell," she panted. "Now. God, please. Now."

Her face was upturned, lips parted, her eyes closed, her fingers digging into his shoulders. He'd never seen anything hotter. "Come first," he said. "I love to watch you come."

"Oh God. I . . . Don't stop. Don't ever stop."

She came on his fingers, and then on his tongue, and then again when he surged upright, magically produced a condom and entered her right there, taking her against the door.

"Oh," she cried, her fingers digging into his back. "We need to—"

"Yes." They needed to do this. Now. He did his best to move slow, to build up the pressure for her, trying to show her a patience he didn't feel. But she bit his neck and then sucked a patch of skin into her mouth, flicking her tongue over it, and slow went out the window. "Jade—" He wanted to tell her to relax, that this was it, their final time and he wanted—*needed*—to make it last.

But she wasn't feeling the same need. She grinded against him and he closed his eyes. No, that made it even worse.

Or better . . .

Her hands were everywhere, grasping ahold of anything she could brace herself with, and though he tried to keep the pace steady, she wasn't helping, moaning his name, arching against him, trying to climb inside his body. He felt her body tighten around him as she burst and he opened his eyes to watch, but that proved to be his undoing and he came with her, hard. When his knees gave out, he slid to the floor, barely managing to keep a grip on her. Not that she noticed. She was limp, content, and clearly sated, and for once he felt the same. Breathing hard, he braced them against the wall and held her close.

"Gonna miss that," she said hoarsely against his chest.

Yeah. Big-time.

"Are we going to get up?"

No. He wanted to stay here, right here, still inside her body, in her life. "I'm not ready to let go of you."

With a soft little hum of agreement, she cuddled in tight.

Twenty-five

Nearly a week later, Dell shut himself in his office after a long day and sank exhausted to his chair. He'd caved and called the temp agency (emphasis on *temp*) on the second day. He'd told Jade he wasn't going to replace her and he wasn't. The agency had sent a perfectly nice twenty-two-year-old receptionist from Boise, who was interested in wintering in Sunshine to ski on the weekends.

That was the same excuse Jade had given him when she'd come to Sunshine and it hadn't escaped him, and as he thought of her, as he had for five straight days now, he felt a stab of pain in his chest.

Of course that might just be the fresh scratch from pec to pec, courtesy of one pissed-off feline from an earlier patient visit.

His day had sucked.

His life sucked.

Leaning back in his chair, he closed his eyes, wanting to snap at whoever had just opened his door and let themselves in. "It's called a knock."

Ignoring his scowl, Lilah sat on the corner of his desk. "You okay?"

As if he were too busy to talk, he stared at his computer—which wasn't even booted up. "Yeah."

"You working?"

"Yep," he said, without taking his eyes off his blank screen.

She came around the desk and stood behind him, staring at the blank screen along with him. "Dell—"

"Look," he said. "I know you think you're trying to help with the phone calls, the texts, the lunches you keep bringing by, but I want to be left alone."

"Really? Because when *I* was hurting, you never left me alone. You badgered, bullied, and pretty much shoved me back to the life of the living."

"I'm not you," he said, closing his eyes.

The next sound he heard was that of his office door shutting quietly. He dropped his head to his desk, pounding it a few times because he was a complete asshole.

When the door opened again, he didn't lift his head. "I'm sorry. I just want to be alone."

"Got that loud and clear. And nice job on kicking the puppy, you asshole."

Adam. He sighed. "I meant for you *all* to go away."

"Aw, and here I wanted to join your pity party."

"Fuck you."

Adam came around Dell's desk and kicked Dell's chair back from it. "You sent her away and now you're punishing everyone that's left. What the hell's that?"

"I didn't send her away. She left all on her own."

"So ask her to come back."

Dell shoved Adam away and stood up, stalking to the window.

"It's unlike you to hole up and hide out."

"I'm not."

"Bullshit you're not. How many women have you dated this year?"

Dell craned his neck and narrowed his eyes at his brother.

"Yeah," Adam said. "I can't count, either. You've never even looked back. But you're looking back now. Why don't you just man up, tell her how you feel, and work it out?"

"We're *not* talking about this."

"Okay. Except we are." Adam took the desk chair and made himself comfortable, leaning back, folding his fingers together over his abs. "Because I've been voted to kick your ass into gear."

"Look, she was needed back at home, so she went. It's not that far. We're going to visit."

Adam nodded.

"And anyway, I should be relieved. It's a forced slowing-down period, right? Things . . . they were getting a little out of hand."

"Out of hand?" Adam repeated. "Is that what you kids call falling in love these days?"

Dell turned to face Adam, his ass resting against the windowsill because his legs felt a little wobbly. "Who said anything about love?"

"Oh, that's right. You only love four-legged furry creatures."

"Fuck you."

"Aw, you're repeating yourself again." Adam stood. "Listen. What happened to us when we were kids, that was . . . fucked up."

Not wanting to hear this, or anything else for that matter, Dell gave Adam a push toward the door.

Adam took a step back but held his ground. "But we still managed to make something of ourselves."

"Adam—"

"That was all you, man. Brady and I kept our heads on straight because we had you to look after. And then later on when the both of us lost it, *you* kept your head on straight. You give everything you have to us, to this place, to the animals that come to you in it. So why can't you give everything you have to the one woman who's ever made you happy?"

"Look, I told you, we'll be okay. I'll see her whenever I'm in Chicago, and—"

"You're in Chicago never."

Dell gave Adam another push to the door.

"Good talk," Adam said, just before Dell slammed the door in his face.

It took three days for Jade to get back to Chicago. The drive was easy enough, smooth weather, no car problems. Her phone rang steadily. Lilah, checking in with traffic reports, wanting Jade to know about the cow reportedly on the highway in Wyoming, and the detour in Nebraska, and that Lilah had already planned a Chicago trip.

Jade had hung up each time smiling.

Then tearing up.

She missed Lilah already.

Brady called, letting her know he'd changed her oil the night before she'd left and also put on new windshield wipers.

Adam called several times as well, asking about work and scheduling. Things they both knew that he already knew.

No pressure to come back, not from any of them. They wanted what was best for her.

They wanted her to be happy . . .

Dell didn't call. She didn't expect him to. But she picked up her phone often and thumbed to his contact info, then set her phone down.

Back in Chicago, she went straight to her town house. There were no surprises. Well, except that when she set Beans's carrier down and opened the door, the cat didn't want to come out.

Jade coaxed her with some treats, but after she ate them she went right back into her carrier with a low growl that Jade would have sworn said, *This is not home.*

Jade's mother had sent people in to clean periodically and Sam had long ago adopted her few plants, so she shouldn't have been surprised to find everything in order and in its place, smelling slightly of lemon cleaner.

It was bigger than she remembered. More open.

More empty.

She'd spent her first day alone, not having told anyone she was back, but by day two Sam had sniffed her out.

He let himself in with his key and called to her from the front door. "Jade?" Before she could blink, he'd crossed the living room, hauled her off the couch, and was hugging her. "Jesus, are you a sight for sore eyes." Pulling back, he stared down into her face and smiled.

When she didn't return it, his slowly faded. "You okay?"

"Of course," she said. "Just tired from the drive."

"How tired? Because your mother's expecting you for dinner."

"I know. I'll go get that over with and then come back here and crash, I think. Catch up on some sleep. Three solid days of driving is pretty exhausting."

"Is that all it is?" Sam asked quietly, still holding on to her. "Trip exhaustion?"

Pulling free, she moved around, running a finger on some of the pictures on the walls, pictures of her and her family over the years.

Friends.

Old friends that had easily vanished from her life when she'd left here. There'd been a few token efforts to keep up, from both sides, but that had petered out with shocking ease.

Now she looked at the pictures and realized her real friends were seventeen hundred miles away in Sunshine, Idaho.

And possibly her heart.

"Jade?"

Throat burning, she turned to face Sam, forcing a smile that totally crumpled when he just looked at her and said her name.

"I'm just really tired," she whispered, and swiped angrily at the sole tear that escaped. "That's all."

And utterly belying these words, she burst into tears.

His face softened and he gathered her in, stroking her hair. "Oh, Jade. It's going to be okay."

She nodded and tried not to snot on his shirt, hoping he was right. That somehow it was going to be okay.

Sam drove to Jade's parents' house, which worked for Jade. She was too nervous. Unsettled.

Heartsick.

She stirred when Sam got off the freeway two exits early.

"What are you doing?" Jade asked.

"Need to go by the center and pick up some files to read tonight."

Panic slithered through Jade. "No."

Sam slid a look at her, then did a double take, his easy smile fading into worry. "Jade."

"I'm not doing this now."

"They're expecting you tomorrow, you know that, right? I thought it'd be easier for you if we went there now, tonight. When there's no one there. You can walk through, get your bearings."

Her pulse was up to stroke level and her palms were sweating. "I'm not going back for the first time at night."

Again Sam sent her a questing, concerned look but he didn't press. He simply executed a U-turn and got back on the freeway without another word.

"Thanks," she said quietly.

"I just got you back." He reached for her hand to give it a gentle squeeze. "I'm sure as hell not risking chasing you out of here."

Ten minutes later, they pulled up to her family home, which was a large Colonial with a circular driveway lined with oak trees and strategically placed flowerpots to give a sedate but elegant glow of color.

Growing up, she'd run across the grass, picked flowers for the neighbors, and climbed the trees. Despite the place's sophistication, it had been a warm, family home.

There were cars in the driveway, too many, which made her stomach jangle uncomfortably. Never in her life had a crowd bothered her, certainly not a crowd of what was sure to be people she knew and knew well, but as they got out of Sam's car, she held on to the door a little too long.

Sam came around for her and took her hand. "Ready?"

"As I'll ever be." But at the front door she hesitated again. It hadn't been that long, she'd flown home for a long weekend for her father's birthday. And then over Memorial Day for another quick trip when her cousin had had a baby.

"Jade," Sam said softly.

"Give me a minute." Or another year and a half.

But then the matter was taken out of her hands when the door whipped open and her mother stood there.

"Well goodness, darling. You're standing out there like a delivery person waiting for a tip." Lucinda Bennett had given up practicing medicine five years ago now to dedicate her time to Jade's father, but she hadn't given up a single concession to looking good. She was in a black Prada cocktail dress, her carefully maintained red hair twisted up out of her face. She was as beautiful as ever as she gestured for Sam to come in, giving him a hug that she had to reach up for since Sam was a foot taller than her.

Sam dutifully bent and kissed his aunt on the cheek, gently squeezed Jade's shoulder, and moved into the house out of sight.

Lucinda took Jade's hands into her own and held tight. "So you don't escape."

"Mom."

"What, you ran off once. I am not risking it again." She looked Jade over. "Your hair's getting long."

"Yes." Jade resisted patting at it self-consciously. "Mom, I—"

"And you haven't been wearing sunscreen religiously like I taught you—you have a tan. Darling, your skin is your age meter."

Jade let out a low laugh. "I know, Mom."

"And what is that you're wearing . . . *jeans?*"

"Yes."

Her mother's eyes lifted to Jade's and filled. "And the cashmere sweater I sent you for your birthday." She tightened her grip on Jade's hands. "Oh, baby. Are you really here?"

"Yeah, I'm really here."

Lucinda pulled her in for a warm hug, then stepped back, searching her pockets for a tissue, which she used to dab precisely at her eyes. There was never an excuse for running mascara.

"Where's Dad?" Jade asked.

"Right here, pumpkin." William Bennett rolled into the foyer. Even in his motorized wheelchair, he still cut an imposing figure. He had straight shoulders and thick gray hair that gave an impression of great knowledge and power. He held out his arms and Jade crouched at his side and hugged him.

"Thought I was going to have to come get you myself," he said with affection in his voice.

"I promised, didn't I?" Jade said, some of her joy at seeing him diminished by the feel of him in her arms. Thinner. He'd lost weight.

A line appeared between his brows. "Honey, I don't give a fig about a promise. I thought you were back because you wanted to be."

"Of course she wants to be," Lucinda said. "Chicago's her home, we're her family."

William cupped Jade's face and looked into her eyes. "You're really okay?"

"I'm okay." When he didn't relax, just kept looking at her, into her, she sighed. "Do you want me to promise?"

"No more promises," he said softly, for her ears alone. "Family isn't solely about obligation."

Jade didn't have words for that, so she hugged him again.

"Stop making me cry," Lucinda said behind them. "I don't want to be blotchy for pictures."

Jade's stomach shifted. "Pictures?"

"We're having a welcome-home party."

"Now?"

"Well, when else?" Her mom pulled Jade through the foyer toward the grand living room. "I sent Sam for you to make sure you showed up."

Oh, for the love of—

"Surprise!" yelled a bunch of voices as people popped up from the furniture and out of the woodwork—friends and family she hadn't seen in far too long.

Jade's gaze sought out a guilty-looking Sam's.

Sorry, he mouthed. But before she could do anything—and killing him seemed to top her personal wish list—she was surrounded.

Twenty-six

Dell was as good at denial as the next guy, but even he was going to need some good distractions to get through Jade's being gone.

Turned out, he got plenty of distractions.

He was called into Belle Haven at five A.M. A five-month-old golden retriever had consumed a kitchen towel and gotten deathly ill.

Dell met them at the center and confirmed his suspicions—the dog's intestines were blocked by towel shreds. He operated and was back in his office by seven, leaning back in his chair studying the ceiling.

His eyes felt gritty. He was exhausted, but every time he closed his eyes he saw Jade. He could feel her touch, hear her laugh, taste her tears in their last kiss.

Closing his eyes, he took a deep breath. He'd been such a cocky son of a bitch. He'd actually convinced himself that Jade being the one to walk away was a good thing. He wouldn't have to break her heart.

And then he'd gotten his broken. He had definitely not seen that one coming . . .

His door opened. "Mrs. Mason's Chinese Shar-Pei puppy is in exam one," Keith said. "Star was wounded in a scuffle with a housemate."

The twelve-week-old Star weighed all of ten pounds dripping wet. Her "housemate" was a twenty-pound Siamese cat with the disposition of Scrooge. Shit. Well, he'd needed more distractions . . .

It was easy enough to busy himself. He'd already fucked up his neat, organized office. That had happened the day Jade had left. He was back to his old ways. If she wanted to fix it, she'd have to get her sweet ass back here.

Only that wasn't going to happen.

If he wanted her sweet ass back here, he was going to have to go get it. He was going to have to figure his shit out, figure out how to give her what she wanted and get what he wanted at the same time.

The next day Jade got up, showered, dressed, and drove into work. She parked in the lot, grabbed her purse, and reached into the backseat for Beans's carrier.

Which wasn't there, of course.

Jade had left the cat in the town house. The medical center was no place for her.

Beans had taken this as the final insult. After a three-day drive and being thrust into yet another new environment, she'd revolted, retreating to beneath Jade's bed, and no coaxing or bribing could get her to come out.

Jade had been forced to leave her there or be late for work, but she felt like shit, like she'd let down the one friend she had in the same state as her. She locked her car and hurried out of the lot into the biting November cold. Her hand was in her purse, fingers wrapped around her can of hair spray.

Adam would be proud, she thought, not allowing herself to think of Dell because thinking of Dell brought a rush of emotions that made her knees weak and threatened her mascara.

And everyone knew, a Bennett never let her mascara run.

It was bright daylight and there was no danger now, not like there'd been that night, but unreasonable fears always trumped logic. She practically ran up the steps and then stopped, hand on the door.

The point of no return. Sandy was supposedly perfectly happy with going back to managing the Urgent Care Department of the center, but still, Jade didn't like the idea of pushing her out.

Jade, Jade, Jade. What you don't like is the idea of being back . . .

She took her hand off the door handle. A woman and a man walked up the steps behind her. The woman smiled politely and said, "Excuse me," gesturing that Jade was in her way.

Jade backed up. The building was a large glass and concrete beauty, surrounded by other equally impressive buildings. Her father loved architecture.

Belle Haven wasn't an architectural marvel, but the country exterior surrounded by the majestic, rustic Bitterroot Mountains had felt infinitely more warm and accepting and inviting.

Home . . .

She shook her head. The parking lot behind her was as busy as the streets, and so was the front door. People were entering and exiting around her. Between each, Jade stared at the door but never quite managed to walk through it. After a few minutes, the door opened and Sam came out. He was in a doctor's coat with a stethoscope around his neck, his badge pinned to a pec pocket: DR. SAM BENNETT.

Clearly he'd been working but had either looked out one of the windows or been alerted to her presence. Who knew what she'd drawn him away from. "I'm sorry, Sam."

"Jade—" He put his hands on her arms. "You're shaking. Come inside, we'll get some coffee and—"

"No." She pulled free, taking one of his hands in hers and staring up into his handsome, caring face. "Sam, listen to me."

"I'm all ears for you. You know that. Talk to me."

"You remember how this used to be so exciting that we'd show up for work early? That everything we accomplished here was a thrill?" She could see in his eyes he knew exactly what she meant, that he still felt that way. She swallowed the lump in her throat. "I don't feel that way anymore."

He shook his head but she squeezed his hand. She needed to say this. He needed to hear it. "Being here isn't the same for me. The very things that fueled me, working with people, living in a big city—it all paralyzes me now."

"Jade," he said, sounding raw and devastated. "You can talk to someone about that—"

"It's not the attack." She pressed the heels of her hands to her eyes, then dropped them. "Okay, that's what started it. But that's not what it is now. I'm not afraid, I just don't want to be here. I've changed, Sam. This place isn't for me anymore. And to be honest, I don't think it ever really was."

"What are you talking about? All your life you were groomed for this."

"Exactly. I was groomed. I never made the choice. I'll take responsibility for that, but it's time, past time, for me to do what's right for me."

Going up on tiptoe, she brushed a kiss to his jaw. "I love you. Please believe me when I tell you that I wanted to do this for you, for all of you. But I can't." She hugged him and felt the vibration of his cell phone furiously going off in his pocket. "You're needed inside."

He squeezed her hard. "You're going back."

Yeah. She was going back. She knew it as she crossed the lot and got into her car. She didn't want to run a big empire. She wanted to sit at the front desk of Belle Haven and run that world. She wanted to see friendly faces, she wanted to play poker with her friends, she wanted to listen to Lilah wax poetic about Brady, she wanted to watch Adam play his tough guy while melting over the puppies he bred.

She wanted . . . Dell.

No, he hadn't asked her to stay. He wouldn't. It had been her decision to make and he'd trusted and expected her to make the right decision for herself.

She'd screwed up there.

She'd screwed up a lot. But she was hoping she was smart enough to learn from her mistakes.

Back at her town house, she stuck her key in the lock, figuring she'd pull Beans out from beneath the bed and load her things, which she'd never unpacked.

That should have been a sign.

She had no idea exactly what the plan was. Just get in her car and drive? Show up in Sunshine and hope that the relationships she'd forged there were as real as they felt?

Count on Dell being happy to see her?

But all those thoughts were derailed when she realized her alarm was decoded. Her dad was in his chair in her living room, Beans in his lap, eyes closed in bliss, purring.

Jade stared at her. "Are you kidding me?"

Her dad smiled. "She's a sweet thing."

Hmmm. Jade gave Beans a long look, then crouched at her father's side. "Sam called you."

He nodded. "Sam called me. I had my driver bring me here, I hope you don't mind." His tremors were slight but more noticeable than the last time she'd seen him. "He's waiting outside for me."

"Dad." She had to find a way to explain it all to him, why she couldn't do this, why she couldn't stay, how she never meant to hurt him, but she had to do this for herself. "Dad, I—"

He covered her hand with his, and when she looked up and met his gaze, his eyes were full of something she hadn't expected.

Understanding. "It's okay, Jade," he said. "Whatever it is, just tell me."

"You always said I could do whatever I wanted," she said softly, and her voice caught. Dammit. Dammit, she was already too close to tears.

"Yes," he said. "Whatever suited you."

"The thing is, I never really knew what that was."

He ran a thumb over her knuckles. "Now, see, I was under the impression you did."

"I wanted to make you happy," she said.

"Oh, Jade." He closed his eyes, then opened them, a world of emotion there. "You've always made me happy."

"Because I lived here and ran your medical center. I was your Jade."

"You're still my Jade."

She shook her head. "No, I'm—"

"You're also your own version of Jade. That's new," he said, his voice carrying a tremor, too, she realized.

Her eyes filled. "Yes. Dad, I'm not . . . I can't . . ."

"You aren't staying," he said.

God. God, this was hard. "No, I'm not staying. I'm so sorry."

"Oh, honey. Don't ever be sorry for being who you are. Most of us go our whole lives not really getting it right, just settling." He tugged a strand of her hair. "Do you have any idea the strength it takes to *not* settle? To keep pushing and seeking for what works?"

It was like a huge weight lifted off her chest. She could breathe again, and when her dad was gone, Jade looked for Beans.

Who was once again beneath the bed. "We're going back," she told the cat, bending low to look into her eyes. "Home."

Beans just stared at her.

"To Sunshine."

Beans paused, just long enough to make it clear that this was Beans's decision and no one else's, and then she walked out from beneath the bed, head high.

They were going back. Not running from something this time. But running to . . .

An hour later, Jade was staring at her spreadsheets. She was leaving tomorrow and she'd made a list of lists to keep organized. She had a things-to-do-before-selling-the-condo list. And a buy-for-the-trip list. A who-to-call list. And she was working on a places-not-to-stop-at list, which would include that rest stop in Nebraska that never had toilet paper. Her tummy rumbled, reminding her she hadn't eaten since . . . She couldn't remember. She scoured the kitchen and came up with a box of graham crackers, a candy bar, and a bag of marshmallows.

S'mores supplies from two years ago when she'd had a party. She eyeballed Beans. "Dinner's on me tonight." She stepped onto her front porch and looked at the small little hibachi barbecue that also hadn't been used in far too long. There was frost on it.

She went back inside and searched for something for kindling. The only thing she could come up with was her business cards. She put on a wool coat, hat and gloves, and using her business cards, built a very nice little bonfire, if she said so herself.

She figured she had maybe half an hour before someone reported her to the association and they complained. They could all take a flying leap, she was out of here in the morning.

She was putting the finishing touches on her first s'more when a car drove up. Damn, that was fast. She peeked, then went still, certain her eyes were deceiving her.

Because it was a cab, and she recognized the dark silhouette getting out of it. Dell, with a duffel bag slung over his shoulder.

Her mouth fell open.

It stayed open as he paid the cab and headed up the walk toward her.

His eyes tracked to hers and locked on, and she felt a surge of warmth spread through her. God, he was a sight for sore eyes in jeans and a down jacket, hair tousled, eyes tired—though they sparked at the sight of her.

She sparked, too. In her good parts, certainly, but most of all in her heart.

He'd come here.

All the way here.

Why?

He took the steps two at a time with his long legs, and then he was standing right in front of her. "Hey."

She tilted her head back and tried for cool but couldn't access any cool. "Hey," she whispered.

He dropped the duffel bag and hunkered at her side. "You did say we could have the occasional weekend. Too soon?"

The lump in her throat was back, but she swallowed it and smiled, so damn happy to see him she could hardly put words together. "So you flew out here to go on a date?"

His lips curved, and something happened inside her chest. It filled with . . . hunger. Longing.

Need.

"A date sounds good," he said. "We never really did much of that, did we?"

"No." She crumpled up a few more spreadsheets and tossed them into the dying flames. "But that was okay with me. You didn't keep any of the women you dated. And even if you had, I didn't want to be one of your . . . gaggle." She handed him a stick and a marshmallow. "S'more?"

"Gaggle?"

"A family of noisy geese. Or in your case, all the single women in all the land."

His smiled widened, but he took the stick and snatched three additional marshmallows. "You aren't part of my gaggle, Jade. You never were." He eyed the small stack of business cards she had left but was smart enough not to mention them. Instead, he concentrated on carefully constructing a s'more with the same precision he used in surgery.

Jade could hardly believe he was here. She wanted to throw herself at him. Instead, she stuffed her face with her own delicious s'more, then licked chocolate off her fingers. "I'm surprised to see you," she said as casually as she could. "Given your whole no-relationship decree."

He took his time creating another s'more. "If you think about it," he finally said, "we already have a relationship."

This admission caught her by surprise. She'd known. She just hadn't realized he had as well.

"It sort of sneaked up on me," he said softly, reaching past her for more chocolate. "Tripped me up some, I'll give you that. But it's true. We're friends. Maybe even best friends. Unfortunately, it's not enough for me."

She stopped breathing.

"Is it enough for you, Jade?"

She opened her mouth, but before she could answer he hedged his bet by lowering his head and gently kissing her. "You asked why I'm here," he said against her lips. "It's because you're a part of my life, you're a part of *me*, Jade, the most important part, actually, and have been since the day you walked into Sunshine."

She stared at him while her heart slowly rolled over in her chest and exposed its tender, vulnerable belly.

He stood, tugging her up with him and wrapping his arms around her. "You should know that my office is a mess. I fucked up the computer system. And the printer won't work."

"Hmm." She hung on, snaking her hands beneath his jacket and shirt just to touch his warm, smooth skin. "It's only been five days."

He tightened his grip on her. "Five and a half."

Her hands settled on his chest, where she could feel his heart beating under her fingers. Strong and steady. Sure. "Dell."

"Yeah?"

"I've missed you, too."

"Good." He lowered his head and kissed her, his lips promising everything his words never did.

Twenty-seven

Somehow they moved inside, mouths still fused. From a distance, Jade could hear ringing, but she didn't want to take her mouth off of Dell's to figure it out. If she stopped kissing him, it might turn out to be a dream.

"Your phone," he said against her lips, then pulled reluctantly back.

She walked into her den, which she'd always used as an office. It was her fax machine, and as the papers started to spit out, she smiled, knowing she'd made the right decision.

Dell had followed her in, removing his jacket. "What?" he asked.

She held up the list of painters her mother had sent over. "I'm going to put this place up for sale."

He went still, his eyes guarded, so carefully guarded they pierced her heart. "What does that mean?"

"It means," she said, "that the next time you want to pick me up for a date, it'll take you a whole hell of a lot less time to get me."

He didn't smile. He took the fax out of her hand and set it on the desk. He pulled her to him and looked into her eyes, his own expression dialed to his surgery face, the one that gave nothing away. He looked utterly impenetrable, but she knew him now, and she knew that he was at his most vulnerable when he felt he had to hide his thoughts. She knew that her leaving Sunshine must have brought some of his deep-seated abandonment issues to the surface, yet he'd done his best to deal with that while still stepping back and letting her make her own decisions. Bringing her hands up, she cupped his face. "You remember what I told you about my grandmother?"

He didn't blink at the subject change. "Yes. You were named for her."

"Yes, so I'd have her strength. I never even questioned it. I willingly followed the path she'd started. I let myself be an empty mold. No one meant to hurt me, but all my life I allowed others to make my path for me. After the attack, I lost that path. I lost me. Do you know how I found myself?"

He gave a slow shake of his head.

"It was you, Dell. Your belief in me, to make me strong enough to say good-bye to a life I wasn't really living, to get my own life, to choose who I am, to build that person. To be strong. Like you."

"Jade." His voice was thick. Clearly he was stunned and deeply affected to hear that he'd so impacted her life. "It was all you."

"I know what you did that day you first had me organize your desk and then let me look at your accounting. And then again when you showed me how to break out of that hold. If it wasn't for you, I'd never have discovered who I really was. Or the fact that I am not defined by the worst day of my life."

His eyes softened. "I just wanted you to never be afraid again. To believe in yourself. And then, when that started happening, when you started gaining confidence, I realized the truth. It was happening, exactly what I wanted—you were learning to live without fear and getting strong . . . so that you could leave. I was helping you leave." Letting out a low laugh, he pressed his forehead to hers. "Christ, that sucked." He tilted his head and kissed her gently, eyes open, locked on hers. "I love you," he breathed. "I love you so goddamn much it hurts."

Her heart swelled. A single moment of terror had led to her running from everyone and everything she'd ever known, but she could no longer regret or resent it.

Not when it had all led to this, to the best moment of her life.

She pressed her hand to his chest. "I love you, too, Dell. With all my heart. And I want my job back."

The corners of his mouth tilted up in a slow, intimate smile. "I was hoping you would."

"You should know, I gave up my lease on that loft in Sunshine. I'll have to find something else."

"I know a place."

"Yeah?"

"Yeah," he said. "It's not too far from work."

"Tell me about it."

"It's a house. Airy rooms, wide-open space. There's ice cream in the freezer at all times. Pizza on speed-dial. Cats are welcome. And there's a gym. Comes with a personal trainer. Interested?"

Her heart caught. He'd been serial dating for years and had never even brought a woman home with him. Not once.

Until her. "More than you can imagine."

"Good." He kissed her, not gently this time. "There's only one thing left, then."

"What's that?"

"The terms."

She turned, and he unzipped her dress so that the bodice fell from her breasts to the crook of her arms. Stepping close, he pressed himself against her. She could feel him hard against the cleft of her buttocks as he dipped his head and nipped at the nape of her neck. "T-terms?" she managed.

"Are you a bed hog?"

"I—" One of his hands slid up to cup her breast, his fingers teasing her nipple until she moaned and ground into him. "You already know that I am."

"That'll have to go on the spreadsheet." He ran his lips down her throat to her shoulder. Her knees buckled, but he had her.

"S-spreadsheet?" She sounded like Peanut.

"Yes. We'll need a spreadsheet to keep track of things. We don't want any hard or hurt feelings. I'm a hot-water hog. That'll go in my column. I'll have to make retribution for that . . ." He pushed her dress over her hips so that it dropped to the floor, leaving her in her lace bra and matching thong, which pulled a rough groan from deep in his throat as he stroked the curve of her breast.

A rush seared through her so strong it was almost painful. She held her breath and waited, for it to relent, for it to lessen into a normal level of desire, but there was nothing normal here, nothing in her realm of understanding.

She'd never felt like this with anyone else before. "Will we share the cooking?"

"Or dialing for takeout."

She started to laugh but choked on it when he pressed a hand low on her spine, urging her to bend over the desk slightly. "I dreamed about you last night," he said, voice rough.

"You did?" She flattened her hands on the wood as he slid a hand up her thigh and let his fingers brush the front of her lace thong. "You dreamed about doing this, here, with me?"

"Yes." His tongue traced the shell of her ear. "I dreamed of you, like this." He thrust two fingers into her in one long, smooth movement. She gasped. With no effort, and without relenting the rhythm of his fingers, he rearranged her to suit him, spreading her legs a little, bending her over more so that he could continue to drive her mad.

Or make her beg.

"What else?" she whispered. "What else was in your dream?"

He produced a condom and protected them both. "Taking you like this."

Wriggling back against him, she reached back and grasped his thigh. He ran a finger down her ass and she wriggled some more. "Please," she murmured.

"Yes. But this first." He whipped her around and set her on the desk. "I want to see you. Watch you as you come, my name on your lips." Her thong vanished, and a second later he was poised at her entrance.

Teasing.

"Dell." He was there, right there and every part of her body was trembling, on fire, so ready that each breath brought a new wave of desire and need for him. She lifted her hips, hoping to tempt him as she tried to angle herself but he held her still.

She moaned and arched against him, her breasts pressing into his chest. He slid into her in one thrust, filling her, somehow touching every part of her, giving her the connection she'd been craving, needing. She let her head fall back on her shoulders and closed her eyes. "What else? What else did you dream?"

"Open your eyes," he said, voice rough as he thrust again, deeper.

Farther.

Filling her more than she'd thought possible.

She struggled to open her eyes, and found his hot and intense on her. "This, Jade. I dreamed of this. The way you're looking at me, how you feel beneath me, all of it. Every night. Every minute." His hand slid between them, unerringly finding her so that she arched into him, meeting his thrusts, clinging to him as the sensations swept over her body, building, heating, until she exploded. Somehow she managed to keep her eyes open, letting him watch as everything within her tightened and burst.

That was all it took. His control snapped, and he thrust into her hard, fast, and then stilled, groaning her name as he came.

It took her a while to come down, and even then the tremors still spiraled through her, giving her little aftershocks. "Jesus," Dell breathed, shaking his head like he was dazed.

"How is that even possible?" she asked. "How come that's still so . . . amazing, every single time?"

He was still inside her, and getting hard again. "Animal attraction."

"So you're saying . . ."

"It's not going away."

"That's what I was afraid of." But she wasn't afraid. Not of this, not of him. She was exhilarated.

Bending low, he breathed the words against her mouth. "I'll never get enough of you, Jade. Never. Now kiss me. Kiss me and seal our deal."

And that's just what she did.

One

Kate Evans would've sold her soul for a stress-free morning, but either her soul wasn't worth much or whoever was in charge of granting wishes was taking a nap. With her phone vibrating from incoming texts—which she was doing her best to ignore—she shoved her car into park and ran across the lot and into the convenience store. "Duct tape?" she called out to Meg, the clerk behind the counter.

Meg had pink and purple tie-dyed hair, had enough piercings to ensure certain drowning if she ever went swimming, and was in the middle of a heated debate on the latest *The Voice* knockout rounds with another customer. But she stabbed a finger in the direction of aisle three.

Kate snatched a roll of duct tape, some twine, and then, because she was also weak, a rack of chocolate mini donuts for later. Halfway to the checkout, a bin of fruit tugged at her good sense so she grabbed an apple. Dumping everything on the counter, she fumbled through her pockets for cash.

Meg rang her up and bagged her order. "You're not going to murder someone, are you?"

Kate choked out a laugh. "What?"

"Well . . ." Meg took in Kate's appearance. "Librarian outfit. Duct tape. Twine. I know you're the math whiz around here, but it all adds up to a *Criminal Minds* episode to me."

Kate was wearing a cardigan, skirt, leggings, and—because she'd been in a hurry and they'd been by the front door—snow boots. She supposed with her glasses and hair piled up on her head she might resemble the second-grade teacher that she was, and okay, maybe the snow boots in May were a little suspect. "You watch too much TV," Kate said. "It's going to fry your brain."

"You know what fries your brain? Not enough sex." Meg pointed to her phone. "Got that little tidbit right off the Internet on my last break."

"Well, then it must be true," Kate said.

Meg laughed. "That's all I'm saying."

Kate laughed along with her, grabbed her change and her bag, and hurried to the door. She was late. As the grease that ran her family's wheel, she needed to get to her dad's house to help get her little brother, Tommy, ready for school and then to coax the Evil Teen into even going to school. The duct tape run wasn't to facilitate that, or to kill anyone, but to make a camel, of all things, for an afterschool drama project Tommy had forgotten to mention was due today.

Kate stepped outside and got slapped around by the wind. The month of May had burst onto the scene like a PMSing Mother Nature, leaving the beautiful, rugged Bitterroot Mountains, which loomed high overhead, dusted with last week's surprise snow.

Spring in Sunshine, Idaho, was MIA.

Watching her step on the wet, slippery asphalt, she pulled out her once again vibrating phone just to make sure no one was dying. It was a text from her dad and read: Hurry, it's awake.

It being her sister. The other texts were from Ashley herself. She was upset because she couldn't find her cheerleading top, and also, did Kate know that Tommy was talking to his invisible friend in the bathroom again?

Kate sighed and closed her eyes for a brief second, which was all it took for her snow boots to slip. She went down like a sack of cement, her phone flying one way, her bag the other as she hit the ground butt first with teeth-jarring impact.

"Dammit!" She took a second for inventory—no massive injuries. That this was in thanks to not having lost those five pounds of winter brownie blues didn't make her feel any better. The cold seeped through her tights and the sidewalk abraded the bare skin of her palms. Rolling to her hands and knees, she reached for her keys just as a set of denim-clad legs came into her field of vision.

The owner of the legs crouched down, easily balancing on the balls of his feet. A hand appeared, her keys centered in the big palm. Tilting her head up, she froze.

Her polite stranger wore a baseball cap low over his eyes, shadowing most of his face and dark hair, but she'd know those gunmetal gray eyes anywhere. And then there was the rest of him. Six foot two and built for trouble in army camo cargoes, a black sweatshirt, and his usual badass attitude, the one that tended to have men backing off and women checking for drool; there was no mistaking Griffin Reid, the first guy she'd ever fallen for. Of course she'd been ten at the time . . .

"That was a pretty spectacular fall," he said, blocking her from standing up. "Make sure you're okay."

Keep your cool, she told herself. *Don't speak, just nod.* But her mouth didn't get the memo. "No worries, a man's forty-seven percent more likely to die from a fall than a woman." The minute the words escaped, she bit her tongue, but of course it was too late. When she got nervous, she spouted inane science facts.

And Griffin Reid made her very nervous.

"I'm going to ask you again," he said, moving his tall, linebacker body nary an inch as he pinned her in place with nothing more than his steady gaze. "Are you okay?"

Actually, no, she wasn't. Not even close. Her pride was cracked, and quite possibly her butt as well, but that wasn't what had her kneeling there on the ground in stunned shock. "You're . . . home."

He smiled grimly. "I was ordered back by threat of bodily harm if I was late to the wedding."

He was kidding. No one ordered the tough, stoic badass Griffin to do anything, except maybe Uncle Sam since he was some secret army demolitions expert who'd been in Afghanistan for three straight tours. But his sister, Holly, was getting married this weekend. And if there was anyone more bossy or determined than Griffin, it was his baby sister. Only Holly could get her reticent brother halfway around the world for her vows.

Kate had told herself that as Holly's best friend and maid of honor, she would absolutely not drool over Griffin if he showed up. And she would especially not make a fool of herself.

Too late, on both counts.

Again she attempted to get up, but Griffin put a big, tanned, work-roughened hand on her thigh, and she felt herself tingle.

Well, damn. Meg was right—too little sex fried the brain.

Clearly misunderstanding her body's response, Griffin squeezed gently as if trying to soothe, which of course had the opposite effect, making things worse. Embarrassed, she tried to pull free, but still effortlessly holding her, Griffin's steely gray eyes remained steady on hers.

"Take stock first," he said, voice low but commanding. "What hurts? Let me see."

Since the only thing that hurt besides her pride was a part of her anatomy that she considered No Man's Land, hell would freeze over before she'd "let him see." "I'm fine. Really," she added.

Griffin took her hand and easily hoisted her up, studying her in that assessing way of his. Then he started to turn her around, presumably to get a three-hundred-and-sixty degree view, but she stood firm. "Seriously," she said, backing away, "I'm good." And if she weren't, if she'd actually broken her butt, she'd die before admitting it, so it didn't matter. Bending to gather up her belongings, she carefully sucked in her grimace of pain.

"I've got it," Griffin said, and scooped up the duct tape and donuts. He looked like maybe he was going to say something about the donuts, but at the odd vibrating noise behind them, he turned. "Your phone's having a seizure," he said.

Panicked siblings, no doubt. After all, there was a camel to create out of thin air and a cheerleading top to locate, and God only knew what disaster her father was coming up with for breakfast.

Griffin offered the cell phone, and Kate stared down at it thinking how much easier her day would go if it had smashed to pieces when it hit the ground.

"Want me to step on it a few times?" he asked, sounding amused. "Kick it around?"

Startled that he'd read her so easily, she snatched the phone. When her fingers brushed his, an electric current sang up her arms and went straight to her happy spots without passing Go. Ignoring them, she turned to her fallen purse. Of course the contents had scattered. And of course the things that had fallen out were a tampon and condom.

It was how her day was going.

She began cramming things back into the purse, the phone, the donuts, the duct tape, the condom, and the tampon.

The condom fell back out.

"I've got it." Griffin's mouth twitched as he tossed it into her purse for her. "Duct tape and a Trojan," he said. "Big plans for the day?"

"The Trojans built protective walls around their city," she said. "Like condoms. That's where the name *Trojan* comes from."

His mouth twitched. "Gotta love those Trojans. Do you carry the condom around just to give people a history lesson?"

"No. I—" He was laughing at her. Why was she acting like such an idiot? She was a teacher, a good one, who bossed around seven- and eight-year-olds all day long. She was in charge, and she ran her entire world with happy confidence.

Except for this with Griffin. Except for anything with Griffin.

"Look at you," he said. "Little Katie Evans, all grown up and carrying condoms."

"One," she said. "Only one condom." It was her emergency, wishful-thinking condom. "And I go by Kate now."

He knew damn well she went by Kate and had ever since she'd hit her teens. He just enjoyed saying "Little Katie Evans" like it was all one word, as if she were still that silly girl who'd tattled on him for putting the frogs in the pond at one of his mom's elegant luncheons, getting him grounded for a month.

Or the girl who, along with his nosy sister, Holly, had found his porn stash under his bed at the ranch house and gotten him grounded for two months.

"Kate," he said as if testing it out on his tongue, and she had no business melting at his voice. None. Her only excuse was that she hadn't seen him much in the past few years. There'd been a few short visits, a little Facebook interaction, and the occasional Skype conversation if she happened to be with Holly when he called home. Those had always been with him in uniform on Holly's computer, looking big, bad, and distracted.

He wasn't in uniform now, but she could check off the big, bad, and distracted. The early gray dawn wasn't doing her any favors, but he could look good under any circumstances. Even with his baseball hat, she could see that his dark hair was growing out, emphasizing his stone eyes and hard jaw covered with a five-o'clock shadow. To say that he looked good was like saying the sun might be a tad bit warm on its surface. How she'd forgotten the physical impact he exuded in person was beyond her. He was solid, sexy male to the core.

His gaze took her in as well, her now windblown hair and mud-spattered leggings stuffed into snow boots—she wasn't exactly at her best this morning. When he stepped back to go, embarrassment squeezed deep in her gut. "Yeah," she said, gesturing over her shoulder in the vague direction of her car. "I've gotta go, too—"

But Grif wasn't leaving; he was bending over and picking up some change. "From your purse," he said, and dropped it into her hand.

She looked down at the two quarters and a dime, and then into his face. She'd dreamed of that face. Fantasized about it. "There are two hundred ninety-three ways to make change for a dollar," she said before she could bite her tongue. Dammit. She collected bachelor of science degrees. She was smart. She was good at her job. She was happy.

And ridiculously male challenged . . .

Griffin gave a playful tug on an escaped strand of her hair. "You never disappoint," he said. "Good to see you again."

And then he was gone.

Two

Five minutes later Kate pulled up to her dad's place. One glance in the rearview mirror at her still flushed cheeks and bright eyes told her that she hadn't gotten over her tumble in the parking lot.

Or the run-in with Griffin.

"You're ridiculous," she told her reflection. "You are not still crushing on him."

But she so was.

With a sigh, she reached for the weekly stack of casserole dishes she'd made to get her family through the week without anyone having to actually be in charge. She got out of her car, leaving the keys in it for Ashley, who'd drive it to her private high school just outside of town.

Tommy stood in the doorway waiting. He wore a green hoodie and had a fake bow and arrow set slung over his chest and shoulder.

"Why are you all red in the face?" he asked. "Are you sick?"

She touched her still burning cheeks. The Griffin Reid Effect, she supposed. "It's cold out here this morning."

The seven-year-old accepted this without question. "Did you get the tape?"

"I did," she said. "Tommy—"

"I'm not Tommy. I'm the Green Arrow."

She nodded. "Green Arrow. Yes, I got the tape, Green Arrow."

"I still don't see how duct tape is going to help us make a camel," he said, trailing her into the mudroom.

She refrained from telling him the biggest aid in making a camel for the school play would've been to give her more warning than a panicked five A.M. phone call. Instead she set down the casserole dishes on the bench to shrug out of her sweater as she eyed him. She could tell he'd done as she'd asked and taken a shower, because his dark hair was wet and flattened to his head, emphasizing his huge brown eyes and pale face. "Did you use soap and shampoo?"

He grimaced and turned to presumably rectify the situation, dragging his feet like she'd sent him to the guillotine.

Kate caught him by the back of his sweatshirt. "Tonight'll do," she said, picking back up the casseroles and stepping into the living room.

Evidence of the second-grade boy and the high school–junior girl living here was all over the place. Abandoned shoes were scattered on the floor; sweatshirts and books and various sporting equipment lay on furniture.

Her dad was in the midst of the chaos, sitting on the couch squinting at his laptop. Eddie Evans was rumpled, his glasses perched on top of his head. His khakis were worn and frayed at the edges. His feet were bare. He looked like Harry Potter at age fifty. "Stock's down again," he said, and sighed.

Since he said the same thing every morning, Kate moved into the kitchen. No breakfast. She went straight to the coffeemaker and got that going. Ten minutes later her dad wandered in. "You hid them again," he said.

She handed him a cup of coffee and a plate of scrambled egg whites and wheat toast before going back to wielding the duct tape to create the damn camel. "You know what the doctor said. You can't have them."

His mouth tightened. "I need them."

"Dad, I know it's hard," she said softly, "but you've been so strong. And we need you around here for a long time to come yet."

He shoved his fingers through his hair, which only succeeded in making it stand up on end. "You've got that backward, don't you?"

"Aw. Now you're just kissing up." She hugged him. "You're doing great, you know. The doc said your cholesterol's coming down already, and you've only been off potato chips for a month."

He muttered something about where his cholesterol could shove it, but he sat down to eat his eggs. "What is that?" he asked, gesturing to the lump on the table in front of him.

"A camel." It had taken her two pillows, a brown faux pashmina and a couple of stuffed animals tied together with twine, but she actually had what she thought was a passable camel-shaped lump.

"All I'm saying," he said, "is that you should stop treading water and try for some fun. Live a little."

"You think I have no life."

Ryan blew out a sigh. They'd been down this road before. "You know what I think. I think you do everything for everyone except yourself. Look at your track record. You've had exactly one boyfriend in five years, and you're still making him coffee every morning."

"And you're still driving me to work so I can fill you in on the school gossip without you having to actually pay attention in the staff room," Kate said more mildly than she felt. Maybe because she heard the underlying worry in Ryan's voice, and she didn't want anyone to worry about her. She was fine. She was great. "We use each other. And we're both fine with that."

Ryan reached over and pulled out the fancy, thick white envelope with the gold embossing sticking out of her purse. "Fourteen more days."

"Hey," she said, trying to grab it back.

He waved it under her nose. "Treading water, Kate. And the proof's right here. Just like it was at this same time last year. And the year before that."

Again she tried to grab back the envelope.

"Why do you carry the offer around with you when you know damn well you aren't going to go?"

She wanted to go. But . . . "It means a whole year away from here."

"And?"

She blew out a breath.

"It's a dream come true for you," he said quietly.

It was. Being offered a full scholarship to the graduate program for science education at the University of San Diego—a world away from Sunshine, Idaho—was her dream. It would take a year to complete, ar entire, glorious, science-filled year. With the degree—and the grant th Ryan promised to get her if she finished—she could bring a new exciting science program to the county's school district. It was somet she'd wanted for a long time. Some women wanted a spa week wanted to go dissect animals and work with scientists whose wo admired for a long time. Yes, it would be great for the school truth was that Kate wanted it for herself.

Badly.

Ashley burst into the kitchen wearing a way-too-short skirt, a skimpy camisole top, and enough makeup to qualify for pole dancing. In direct opposition to this image, she was sweetly carrying Channing Tatum, the bedraggled black-and-white stray kitty she'd recently adopted from the animal center where she volunteered after school. Contradiction, meet thy queen.

Channing took one look at the "camel" and hissed.

"What the hell is that?" Ashley asked of the makeshift prop, looking horrified as she cuddled Channing.

"Don't swear," Kate said. "And it's a camel. And also, you're going out in that outfit over my dead body."

Ashley looked down at herself. "What's wrong with it?"

"First of all, you'll get hypothermia. And second of all, no way in hell."

Ashley narrowed her overdone eyes. "Why do you get to swear and I don't?"

"Because I earned the right with age and wisdom."

"You're twenty-eight," Ashley said, and shrugged. "Yeah, you're right. You're old. Did you find my cheerleading top?"

Kate tossed it to her.

Ashley turned up her nose at the scrambled eggs, though she fed Channing a piece of turkey bacon before thrusting a piece of paper at Kate. "You can sign it or I can forge dad's signature."

"Hey," Eddie said from the table. He pushed his glasses farther up on his nose. "I'm right here."

Kate grabbed the paper from Ashley and skimmed it. Permission slip to . . . skip state testing. "No." Skipping testing was the last thing the too-smart, underachieving, overly dramatic teen needed to do.

"Dad," Ashley said, going for an appeal.

"Whatever Kate says," Eddie said.

"You can't skip testing," Kate said. "Consider it practice for your SATs for college. You want to get the heck out of here and far away from all of us, right? This is step one."

Ashley rolled her eyes so hard that Kate was surprised they didn't roll right out of her head.

Tommy bounced into the room. He took one look at the camel and hugged it close. "It's perfect," he declared. Then he promptly inhaled up every crumb on his plate. He smiled at Kate as he pushed his little black-rimmed glasses farther up on his nose, looking so much like a younger, happier version of their dad that it tightened her throat.

A car horn sounded from out front. Kate glanced at the clock and rushed Tommy and Ashley out the door. Ashley got into Kate's car and turned left, heading toward her high school. Tommy and Kate got into the waiting car, which turned right to head to the elementary school.

Their driver was Ryan Stafford, Kate's second-best friend and the principal of the elementary school.

And her ex.

He must have had a district meeting scheduled because he was in a suit today, complete with tie, which she knew he hated. With his dark blond hair, dark brown eyes, and lingering tan from his last fishing getaway, he looked like Barbie's Ken, the boardroom version. He watched as Kate got herself situated and handed him a to-go mug of coffee.

"What?" she said when he just continued to look at her.

"You know what." He gestured a chin toward the cup she'd handed him. "You're adding me to your little kingdom again."

"My kingdom? You wish. And the coffee's a 'thanks for the ride,' not an 'I don't think you can take care of yourself,'" she said.

Ryan glanced at Tommy in the rearview mirror. "Hey, Green Arrow. Seat belt on, right?"

"Right," Tommy said, and put on his headphones. He was listening to an Avengers audiobook for what had to be the hundredth time, his lips moving along with the narrator.

Ryan looked at Kate. "Thought you were going to talk to him."

She and Ryan had once dated for four months, during which time they'd decided that if they didn't go back to being just friends, they'd have to kill each other. Since Kate was opposed to wearing an orange jumpsuit, this arrangement had suited her. "I did talk to him," she said. "I told him reading was a good thing."

"How about talking to himself and dressing like superheroes?"

Kate looked at Tommy. He was slouched in the seat, still mouthing along to his book, paying them no mind whatsoever. "He's fine." She took back Ryan's coffee, unscrewed the top on the mug, blew away the escaping steam, and handed it back to him.

"You going to drink it for me, too?" he asked. He laughed. "Just admit it. You can't help yourself."

"Maybe I like taking care of all of you. You ever think of that?"

"Tell me this, then—when was the last time you did something for yourself, something entirely selfish?"

"Ryan, I barely have time to go to the bathroom by myself."

"Exactly," he said.

"Exactly what?"

Now she laughed. Ryan shook his head and kept driving. They passed the lake just before the bridge into town. The water was still and flat in the low light. On the far side was the dam that held back the snowmelt, controlling the volume feeding into the river so that Sunshine didn't flood. Along the very top of the dam was a trail, which Kate sometimes ran on the days that she wanted to be able to fit into her skinny jeans. Up there, at the highest pool was an old fallen Jeffrey Pine. On its side, battered smooth by the elements, it made a perfect bench.

It was her spot.

She went there to think or when she needed a time-out from the rest of the world, which happened a lot.

"You get a date for the wedding yet?" Ryan asked.

No. She'd put that particular task off, and now, with the wedding only two days away, there was only one man who'd made her even think about dating. But tall, dark, and far-too-hot Griffin Reid was way out of her league. In fact, he was so far out of her league, she couldn't even see the league. "Working on it."

Ryan made a sound of annoyance. "You've been saying that for months." He glanced at her over the top of his sunglasses. "Tell me it's not going to be me."

"Hey, I'm not that bad of a date."

He slid her another look. "You going to put out afterward?"

Kate whipped around to look at Tommy, but the kid was still listening intently to his book. "No," she hissed, and smacked him. "You know I'm not going to put out. We didn't . . . suit that way."

"Well, I'm hoping to . . . 'suit' with one of the bridesmaids." He glanced at her again. "You ought to try it."

"Sorry. The bridesmaids don't do it for me."

He smiled.

"Stop picturing it!"

Ryan's smile widened, the big male jerk, and she smacked him again.

"I was thinking maybe I'd accept and go this time," she said.

"But?" he asked.

"But," she said. "Next year is crucial for Ashley. We have colleges to decide upon . . ."

"Uh-huh," Ryan said. "And last year it was Tommy's health."

"He had pneumonia." Snatching back the envelope, she shoved it in her purse.

And they didn't speak again for the rest of the ride.

Photo by ZRstudios.com

New York Times bestselling author Jill Shalvis lives in a small town in the Sierras full of quirky characters. Any resemblance to the quirky characters in her books is, um, mostly coincidental. Look for Jill's bestselling, award-winning novels wherever books are sold and visit her website, jillshalvis.com, for a complete book list and blog detailing her city-girl-living-in-the-mountains adventures.